FEATHERS ON THE WINGS OF LOVE AND HATE:

Let the Gun Speak

Volume 1 in the series, second edition 2011

BY

John Grit

To all those who have fought oppression and injustice throughout history. If you love people, you want them to be free.

DE OPPRESSO LIBER

Chapter 1

The sixteen-year-old boy ran from death and toward life.

The killers who hunted him were from the city. He designed to draw them into his world far from concrete and wheels where they must put their feet down, into the same mud he must, and every bush is a hiding place, every trail a kill zone.

He ran. Above him, towering pines and wide oaks draped with Spanish moss, below, knee, waist, and chest-high saw-toothed palmetto stem and green frond, fringed with brown. And at his ankles, turkey oak and blades of grass in the sun-freckled places that he skirted, both small and wide glades. Then, back under the shadow of subtropical forest canopy he ran.

His feet tread on layers of moldering leaves and he sunk into the mud of Adam. Down into slough, across creek, and deep into swamp, he ran.

The unmarked, timeless footpaths he knew so well were those of primordial ancestors who too fought for freedom, killed for family, and died for life. Each step took him deeper into the primitive. The wall of green that opened five, ten yards before him and closed in behind as he ran beckoned him into the emerald obscurity of forest and swamp. Deeper into the anachronistic places he raced, far from modernity and the government's advantages. The last remnants of places still in a timeless struggle to outlast eternity. Just north of where Acuera once endured the death hunt and fought the first enslavers, distant brother to Osceola, another patriot of his people and land. His feet tread where Osceola fought Andrew Jackson and his soldiers, until he was lured to a "peace council" and arrested. He died in prison, undefeated in battle, but felled by the treachery of enslavers.

On this day, killers sent by new slave masters hunted the boy who ran not from the fight, but to, not out of fear, but rage.

Body unloosed, every cell of each muscle willing ever more speed. The body's pain be damned. Wails and screams of pain were unheard, their protestations voided, drowned out by a deeper pain that knew no bottom, no height, no breadth, such a pain that could not be measured by any yardstick of dimensions.

The heart beseeched the mind. The mind commanded the body, made accusations of weakness. The body obeyed and would obey beyond all imaginable human limits of endurance. Muscle, tendon, cartilage, and bone strained for hours. Still, the heart beseeched. The mind commanded. The body obeyed.

Thus far, his body had been left unscathed by his enemies, but his heart wounded. Such a wound he knew could never heal. What Timucua saw, he would never forget.

A hollow empty ache seeped into his gut, the second the rage started to ebb. And what frightened him, the only thing that did, was the ache threatened to have no horizon, no mercy, and no reprieve.

As he ran from early dawn into late morning, he began to welcome the searing pain deep in his lungs. His muscles had long since stopped their screaming, given up on begging for mercy. The pain in his lungs distracted him from his deeper pain of loss.

His mind raced. No government has the right, and no government should be allowed the power to deny God-given human rights. His thoughts screamed and echoed in his skull. *It was murder! Senseless. Sadistic. Insane.*

All his life he had feared the abstract danger of the national police. Like death, it was something to keep pushing ahead of your life. As if it could forever be kept in the future by pretending the storm clouds were not getting closer. His life was rained on today, and his heart struck by a bolt from the darkest cloud in human history.

The farther he ran, the more he began to love a concept born of the human heart. A dream called freedom, born in the fourth decade of the third millennium, as anachronistic as the woods around him. If you love people, you want them to be free. His painful lesson of this day is that freedom is the catalyst for human rights and dignity. To value such things is not enough. One must be willing and able to fight, kill, suffer, and die for such a treasure, or someone will take it from you.

Freedom should be a gift passed down, unencumbered by liens of debt but that is not the way of the world. The debt is never paid in full, and it is paid forward, not back. He thought of these things as he ran.

He vowed to himself, and the souls of those murdered, to make the dream of freedom born on this day the driving force of his life. A grand, if not grandiose, pure, innocent, childlike dream, born of the spirit of a child turned man, that he hoped would outlive the boy and then the man, perhaps in the end living on beyond all reasonable hope, even if held together by little more than scar tissue and iron will. Above all, let it live on.

This day came sooner than he had wanted, but desires, intentions, plans, and dreams are impotent against the heavy-booted march of time. Death of life and other things often come out of season. He had always known this in the back of his young mind. This day had to come. He could do nothing to stop it. Its progression had been fate-driven, deliberate, and inescapable for sixteen years now, his life's omnipresent shadow. A boy cannot outrun his shadow. He knew better than to even think of it.

However, why could not this day have come next fall or next year? No matter, it is here. He was born with a wild heart. There are enemies of wildness, too chaotic they say; sooner or later, the small remnants of surviving freedom lovers had to be hunted down. It would be foolish to try to tame such a wild heart. Just kill him.

For now, speed became the center of his world. His hungry legs ate up yardage upon yardage. The equation of time and distance must be transformed, conquered. It was his first task. They will use machines, dogs, and two and a half centuries of military and law enforcement training and unlimited resources. He had only his legs and his mind.

His eyes carried the look of a pursued animal as he ran through the woods with an expression of half terror and half-unstoppable determination, cutting a hard edge to his face that belied his youth. Iron will was being forged in a furnace of hate, hammered by pain, pain not evident on the surface, but ever present within. Boy became man, man became freedom lover, and freedom lover became freedom fighter. His enemies gave death to freedom. His dream was to give it new life. With each powerful stride, he sloughed off his boyhood as a growing snake sloughs off its too-small skin.

He pushed through the brush at top speed. Branches clawed at his olive drab cotton jacket and pants. His boonie hat of like material and coloration was pulled low to give some small protection to his eyes, as brush whipped at his red-welted, bleeding face. Branches snapped as he bulled between closely standing trees, weaving around what he could not penetrate, pushing through what he could. Six-inch deep, standing swamp water exploded under his homemade boots of leather soles and welters with canvas twelve-inch high uppers. He was wet and muddy to his knees. His jacket and the T-shirt under it, were soaked with sweat under his arms and halfway down his back. White salt ringed the dark wet areas.

The contents of his military surplus backpack weighed thirty pounds. However, gravity it seemed, had lost partial control of it, and now it streamed along behind him as a pursuing bird of prey, bouncing so much it was riding on air more than on his back. He had left his former life behind, now even the pack could not keep up, tethered by its shoulder straps only. At this moment, it contained nearly all of his worldly possessions. Enough to keep him on the run for a few days.

In his hands, he held an eight-decade-old relic of the Korean War known as the M1 Garand rifle, a gift from his grandfather who had purchased it from a gunsmith that specialized in rebuilding M1s. The rifle was in as new condition when purchased. This was years before all firearms were banned. He just used it to kill two murderers who were exactly six hundred yards from the muzzle when he pulled the trigger. It was designed as an implement of war that freedom might be purchased with blood, a tool useful a century ago, still useful today.

Now a team of trained killers hunted him. If they caught him here, he might get to kill one or two, before they took his young life. He found such a possibility abhorrent, and the thought brought his cold rage back to a boil. He would not sell his life so cheaply. He had just begun to show them, to show them his family's blood is not free. Before he dies, he will have them staggering under the weight of the price they will have to pay.

The wages of revenge are unmercifully small and bitter. He knew this because he had been nurtured to listen to the better qualities of his heart. However, his heart was itself bitter, as it pounded in his chest, pumping a deep hunger for bitter revenge throughout his soul, a hunger he knew would demand a long walk through hell before it was satiated.

In the back of his mind, he knew there had to be more than revenge. Was there no reason or purpose for his birth, his family's years of diligent sacrifice and tutoring? Thus far, he had done little with it. He was just a farm boy. The waste of a life: the greatest of all sins. He now understood why his mother and grandfather had worked tirelessly to teach him, demanding he learn all he could. In him, they saw the embodiment of all their hopes. One last chance their lives would produce something that endured and endured. One shining example of what they could have been and done with a little more freedom. The essence of two souls, two lives, mingled with what the long-dead father and his genes contributed. All the generations since Geneses, distilled into one boy.

No!

They would not kill him.

Not on this day, or the next, or the next. He will demand the very last payment, the last pound of flesh. He was young, but not naïve. He knew what he was also demanding of himself. Every pound of flesh he took from them, would require some of his own. Every misery inflicted upon his enemies, would be inflicted upon him. All debts are paid. If not by the borrower, then by the lender. *Any price!* His heart was screaming at his mind. *Any price!*

He had much work to do. If need be, he will become death to give life, dark to give light. He was born into the miasma of a people chained by tyranny. He will show them the chain is made of links of people. Break the people and you break the chain. Machines of tyranny do not bleed, but the pawns of tyrants do. Bleed them white. Break the people, break the chain.

He had never run this fast for so long before, and the boy was learning just how much unmerciful punishment his body could take. Pushing his heart rate into the danger zone even for a healthy teenager, he felt the blood-pumping organ pound in his chest. His lungs burned as every muscle in his body screamed for more oxygen. He ignored it all.

Still he ran.

His war was only hours old. Already, the sun shined on a face soldiers would recognize, but not his mother. They have seen such faces throughout the ages, and in the mirror of their mind. The more delicate facets of his character were forced to yield to unity of purpose. What was left was the cold steel of a man; a soul so distilled and condensed, little of the warm human was left. He refused to allow himself to be frightened by what he was becoming. It was part of the price. *Any price,* he reminded himself.

Urgent murmurings echoed in far-off trees, catching him by the ear and bringing him to a stop just on the far side of an ancient oak tree. Its four-foot thick trunk offered protection from any rifle bullet.

He forced himself to stop gulping humidity-drenched air long enough to listen. From deep within a stand of pines, up on the higher ground from whence he came, his hand-cupped ear aimed for best effect, came hysteria-filled frantic, full-throat caterwauling, rising as he listened, the full volume spent by distance.

The effect the sound had on the boy was palpable. At least three dogs were hot on a trail.

He had purposely sought out the wet, and the wet trail had slowed their nose, but not their legs. Hungry with vicious hate, they were relentless. Though so far off he could barely hear them between his own gasps for air, he knew by their "music" they were not on a leash. Knowing no man can keep up with a free-running dog, he was sure those who hunted him were some distance behind.

He wondered just how far behind, as he checked a compass hanging from his neck, and then stuffed it back under his shirt so it would not be flopping around and catching on brush. Earlier in the day, heading east, the sun was his guide, but now it was too high in the sky.

Running again, full speed. His body screamed resurging protestations. He ignored it as he had for hours now. The gloom of his immediate environing world did not care enough to take notice. He felt not worthy of the company of even disinterested spectators for some small measure of moral support. His struggle was his and his alone. A flash in his mind, living and dying in a millisecond, gave birth to a mere reflection: perhaps God…No. Why would God care?

The cry of the dogs made it clear to him he was being hunted like an animal. Somehow, he found it both terrifying and demeaning at the same time. Fear and rage formed an alliance and filled him with deadly resolve.

He knew what he was going to do. It was in the back of his mind all morning long, but now it was a dead certainty.

Running through the woods, his legs surged him forward, seeking out the wet, carrying him farther down into the lower lands. The last quarter mile took him over the threshold of physical endurance and into weariness, he never knew existed. Though his mind took no more notice than the emotionless woods environing his heart, soul, and body, his flesh was screaming, "Six hours! Six hours! No more!"

He found what he was looking for and turned north to follow a creek upstream. There was only one place for miles that a man could cross without sinking up to his armpits in swamp sludge. He may just be far enough ahead of the dogs.

The boy was tired, but he did not know how close he was on the verge of killing himself before his enemies had a chance. He feared they might have used the steel of a helicopter to eat up miles in minutes, that the flesh and bone of his legs had spent hours conquering. His tenacity denied the futility of pitting flesh against modern technology.

The boy must run two miles upstream before he could cross over. He knew these woods, this swamp. There was one place where the creek bottom was solidified by an Indian mound of freshwater snail shells, left hundreds of years ago by a murdered tribe, the Timucua. A people misnamed by their Spanish enslavers who could not pronounce their word for terrible enemy. Hundreds of flooding hurricanes had washed it out and spread shells across the bottom of the creek.

Several dogs cried out.

They sound so damn close.

He waded across, knee-deep, watching his step. The tea-colored water was warm. Then he ran back downstream on the other side. He must endure two more miles to earn his respite from this self-inflicted torture.

There is only a small window of time left.

With no reserve of strength to call on, the boy found he was running on legs that refused to obey his will, and he caught himself running slower than he would normally walk. Falling to his knees, he cursed his very soul for such a shameful display of weakness. It seemed to him the worst sin he had ever committed.

So close!

He cursed himself once again and found to his amazement he was either lifting his body from the muddy ground, or pushing the earth several feet lower. At the moment, his pounding head would not allow him to ponder such mysteries. He wondered where the drums were. He could not think for the war drums pounding, drowning out all thoughts. With each rapid beat, blood pulsed in his head.

Only God knows what price to place on my life, and God just upped the ante.

He found himself replacing his empty reserves of strength with one last measure of will.

He had paid the price of tuition, a lesson learned, engraved in his heart, and cached in his mind forever. Never give up! Make them pay. Your life is the only thing you ever really own and then only if you do not give it away. Make them pay.

Will, hardheaded will, the only force strong enough to bear the weight of fatigue now bearing down on his resolve, kept him going long enough to make it to the kill zone he had decided on. By the time the dogs swim the creek, he will be waiting. Courage, will, resolve, all mental muscles of the human spirit that must be exercised to be conditioned to a high level. Another lesson learned, cached in his mind, and burned into his heart.

This time the fight will be on his terms. This time *he* has chosen the kill zone, and *he* will draw first blood.

On the east side of a wet glade, in what was otherwise thick brush, the boy found bullet-stopping cover and concealment. Behind to the east, there was plenty more to make possible a hasty retreat. In the brush to the west, there were narrow firing lanes allowing him to get a shot at anyone on the other side of the creek seventy yards away.

The foundation of the ambush site was the creek, itself a veritable moat offering hindrance to his enemies, giving the gift of time, time enough to put a bullet into them. Anyone who tried to cross would be mired in mud. They will believe he had just crossed there and will try to follow. They will learn too late that they did not chase him here; he had led them here.

While waiting, he took his first drink in hours. His throat had turned into rough-sanded leather, that now felt the delight of the tepid liquid. He kept his thirst under control and drank in measured haste, to avoid vomiting it back up.

He rested his canteen on his knee and peered over a three-foot-high windfall, an ancient oak. His mind raced faster as his pounding heart began to slow. He chastised himself under his breath. "Damn it, think! You will only get one chance at this."

He was betting on the long chase, causing some of his pursuers to be left behind by the more fit. He hoped he would not be forced to take them all on at once. At the farm, he counted ten and killed two. Since he believed they had been close on his heels all morning, he thought they must have started out after him within minutes after he fled. Perhaps more men had been flown in by helicopter, but he had not heard any aircraft all morning.

He spoke softly to himself. It helped him think. "They probably left one, maybe two, behind to guard the APC. That leaves six or seven coming at me as I sit here."

The boy shook his head. Worry creased his young face making him appear much older. "God, I hope they left a couple of the fat-asses behind."

For the first time in hours, he felt his heart slowing down to a more normal number of beats per minute, and his chest was not heaving as deeply and rapidly. However, he still had a throbbing headache, and every muscle in his body screamed to be put out of its misery.

He spoke softly to no one but himself. "I hope they make it here before the dogs get downstream on this side. The last thing I need is for the dogs to reveal my location just as the murdering bastards get to the kill zone."

He shook his head. "I can go crazy thinking about everything that can go wrong. After all, only my life depends on me not screwing up."

After some moments of confusion among the dogs where the boy had crossed the creek, they found the scent trail again and were on their way. To the boy, their foreboding, swelling voices echoing among the trees seemed primal. Wails from specters of long ago could not have been better soothsayers, carrying chilling communications from the dead.

The dogs did not sound like any hounds he had heard before. This made him wonder what breed they were. There was no hysterical agitation in their voices now, only determined rage. The dogs had a fresh scent trail again, and their full cry could be heard no more than half a mile away. They sounded like roaring lions.

As the boy kept careful watch, using the far extreme of his eyes' ability to see through the brush, like looking through a picket fence, he kept track of the dogs with his ears. "Sounds like they are heading east, following that quarter mile dogleg bend in the creek. They will be here soon."

The time window was getting smaller.

"Guess I'm going to see the elephant, as Grandpa used to say."

Both hands tightened suddenly on the rifle's stock. Eyes sharpened to a fine edge. The cold harshness of his intent was mellowed only by the sun's freckling of the woodland floor and his body, dispersing the edges of his form, hiding from all eyes that death awaits here at this very spot in the woods and no other. He felt the immersion of his body between nature's debris-littered swamp floor and the towering green gloom of his environing kill zone. He sunk himself into oblivious obscurity, an insignificant nothingness of freckles, of dispersed multicolored light and degrees of shade. The woods became his appendages, his body lucent; only he knew where his body ended and the woods began. Conversely, a new form from within solidified, self-birthing, drawing first breath, but no infant, bloodied by the kills of countless death hunts with a hundred generations of warrior blood surging hot through his veins.

Careful not to move anything but his eyes, he pulled the rifle butt tighter against his right shoulder and pushed the safety off with the back of his trigger finger. He rested his left hand on the windfall, holding the rifle loosely. The back of his hand felt many sharp edges of the bark probing his flesh. He looked over the sights to focus his attention on a small area in the shadows, just behind an eight-foot tall cabbage palm.

His eyes had seen something catch a freckle of light, as it rained down in a streaming slant after managing to penetrate the swamp's canopy of treetops fifty feet above. Whatever it was, it had slid once again into the shadows just out of sight. It seemed too tall to be a deer or any other wild creature.

He knew the only thing he should move until the first shot was his trigger finger. As long as he remained perfectly still, even binoculars would not be enough to betray him. He relied on nature's toolbox of camouflage. His lucent form remained absorbed by the emerald and brown, and dark and light of the menacing jungle. He must let them come to him. Motion and sound will betray them. They will make the first mistake.

Chapter 2

The boy swore he could hear the clock of eternity ticking as he waited for whatever was behind that palm tree to move.

Something crashed wildly in the brush off to the left and farther back from the creek.

That's two.

It was too far into the weeds for him to see, so there was no need to take his eyes off the shadow. His ears tracked the sound while his eyes waited.

He moved only his eyes, slowly, methodically searching.

Let them make the first mistake. The one who does will be the first to die. I can't give away my position until at least one of them is dead. I've set the trap. Now wait for the moment to trigger it.

Still another something moved closer, from farther downstream.

That's three. How many more?

His eyes darted in a panic, from dark spot, to shaded area, to bush, to tree.

Stop it you fool. Slow down. You can't see anything like that.

He began to slowly, systematically sweep the area on the other side of the creek, searching for movement, penetrating the subtropical jungle.

His breathing became erratic, catching, snagging, as on the sharp teeth of a coarse file, tension rasped into raw nerves.

Someone coughed, telling him there was a fourth man closer than the others were, not far from the shadow he watched.

The woods are getting crowded.

His mouth became bone-dry, and had the taste of bile. He wanted a drink of water. Now that he had rested enough, he felt he could go on, he wondered why he ever stopped running.

This is crazy! I'm just a farm boy who never killed anyone until six hours ago. They do this crap for a living.

He inhaled deeply. Once. Twice.

Stop it.

In an effort to buttress his resolve, he purposely thought of his family. In his mind's eye, he watched national police beat down and then kick his mother and grandfather. For the hundredth time, he saw the impact of bullets and spray of blood. Flaming heat seared his heart, burning away every emotion but seething rage. The heat of hate: a fire they started.

Instinctively, he understood the necessity of keeping that fire under control. He must use his head. Blind rage was as dangerous as the trained killers who hunted him, but its caustic acid could be used to erode away all hesitation to kill.

The boy heard his grandfather talking to him, echoes from many years gone by.

"Just sit back motionless and read the woods like a book. Remember, you can almost always hear farther than you can see in thick woods, and don't ever forget that works both ways. Don't just look. You got to learn to see in thick woods. It doesn't come natural. You got to teach yourself to catch movement and faint flickers of light, anything that don't look quite right, like it don't belong there. Learn to separate the fauna from the flora. Movement boy. That's what will betray your enemy. Movement in the woods, especially on a windless day."

His imaginary patriarch sat beside him and whispered in his ear.

"Every time you go into the woods, you should learn something and add to your skills. That's why I don't mind you spending so much time in the woods. It's an important part of your education. It may save your life someday. Remember what I said about shooting? Every called shot is a learning experience. Fail to call the shot, and you're just wasting ammo. It's the same when learning how to hunt or to be hunted. Don't waste your time out here playing, learn."

Sometimes, the most unexpected of events happen slowly. From out of the shadows came the one most dangerous. Little by little, he flowed like molasses on a cold morning into a small dappling of sunlight. His image slowly materialized as pieces of a mosaic. Never more than a six-inch patch of him could be seen at any one time, but the boy knew he was there. That made all the difference. The fatal difference.

With little wind to mask any unnatural sounds, the boy's ears would have heard it, if there had been anything to hear.

This one is quiet in the woods. He knows how to hunt. I have to kill him first.

Predator hunts predator. One honed by training, experience, and the lessons of a path of choice. The other newly forged in a white-hot furnace of pain-fueled hate and the blows of a hammer yielded by circumstance out of his control.

The killer, who had years before chosen to throw away all principles of conscience as part of a contract with the Unity Party, just took his last full step on earth. In return for being allowed to exist, if not actually live, he had murdered, terrorized, imprisoned, and tortured.

The boy, who until six hours ago simply desired to be left alone to live in peace with his grandfather and mother on a backwoods Southern farm, was about to take his third human life. The lifeblood of that peaceful desire had spilled out in ropes of crimson. The image of the murder of his family, permanently etched in his memory, was playing over and over in his mind.

"Hey, Simmons!" A disembodied voice called out from deep in the brush. "I told you not to get too far ahead. I'm the one with the RF receiver."

The dangerous one turned his head and took only a half step to his right. In that second before the shot, he threw a look of disgust in the direction the voice came from. His anger over the man's stupidity showed visibly, but the boy could not see.

The boy would never see the paid killer's face. Only an eight-inch diameter area of the government agent's right chest was visible to his young eyes. He made that his target while looking through the rear peep sight. Holding his breath, he slowly increased pressure on the trigger. Before his finger overcame the last ounce of trigger pull, he refocused his eye on the top edge of the front sight. In a millisecond, the hunted became the hunter, and a small piece of copper-coated lead exploded into a killer's right lung, giving him an agonizing, suffocating death.

Before the rifle's bark finished thundering across the landscape and echoing among the treetops, a heavy crash could be heard as the man fell in some brush, then a long haunting moan.

The boy had already lain on the ground behind the windfall and was crawling closer to the other end where there was more foliage to hide him, but he might see just well enough to get one more shot.

Another moan came from the thrashing brush, every decibel dripping with pain.

The boy tried to ignore it. Still, it grated at him just enough that he wanted to yell out, "Payback's a bitch isn't it?"

He took no pleasure in the man's agony, but he would be damned before he let it bother him. After all, did he not want to cry out in pain all morning long and at this moment. Besides, the man's moaning might attract more targets.

Then...

Silence.

Not yet gone, but no longer able to make a sound, his lung partially collapsed and fast filling with blood, the agent was helpless, waiting for death to end his suffering. Stupidity of his own team members and a boy with an obsolete rifle had laid him low.

Now with his strength ebbing, all his body could give him were shallow rapid breaths. His eyes rolled back in their sockets.

The right shoulder blade had been shattered. Bone splintered and produced secondary projectiles as they followed the bullet out, ripping a gaping exit wound. Frothy, pink, oxygen-rich blood bubbled out the small entrance wound in an expanding puddle upon his shirt. A century-plus old technology just proved it is still capable of producing the stuff of nightmares. As he lay there in the swamp mud, all the advantages, the training and experience, he had over the boy had been for naught. He was just dead.

Clumsily, the one who had called out to Simmons, crashed through the woods, running toward the edge of the creek, carbine swinging wildly in both hands. His protruding belly was hanging jellified, inches beyond his pistol belt. His shirt soaked with sweat, face streaming, and eyes frantic. He stopped and fell to one knee, concealed only to his waist by a clump of straw-colored wiregrass and a small yellow-green turkey oak.

His face was rigid with tension. He shouldered his carbine and swung the barrel. He aimed at nothing in particular, while he emptied a magazine on full automatic into the surrounding flora. A sweeping spray of bullets across his vision.

After he inserted a fresh magazine, the woods became quiet again. Terror showed in the man's eyes. He had just earned a high score at the department's shooting range, but paper targets do not shoot back from concealment. His eyes darted from nothing to nothing, not giving his mind time to register what his eyes might see. The wall of green was before him in every direction. Every tree, log, or bush could conceal death.

It began to all seem so natural to the boy. If he had time to think about it, he would have been shocked by his lack of repulsion and remorse. A strange feeling took hold of him. He felt, sometime in a previous life perhaps, he had killed here before. The scene looked so familiar, like the chance meeting of an old friend not seen in years and presumed long-since dead. Something told him that everything in his life had led him to this. The boy now understood the meaning of the shadow he could not outrun.

A slight thrashing in the brush, where the wounded man was, interrupted the silence. His final death throes? No. A third man was checking on the dead man.

The one who had just shot yelled out, "Where are you Simmons?"

If Simmons could answer, his voice would have been drowned out by the bark of the boy's M1 rifle. No matter. The one speaking to Simmons lost most of his upper head and nearly all of his brain. The man's carbine was catapulted six feet into the air by a powerful paroxysm of his arms, as the bullet short-circuited his nervous system. It landed with a splash in a shallow puddle of muddy water twelve feet in front of where the dead man fell. A spreading circle of crimson around his head stained the black swamp water that he now lay in.

Again, the boy crawled closer to what had been the tree's top. Dead branches supported vines and other vegetation that had grown up through them after the tree had fallen. The spade-shaped, saw-tooth-edged vine leaves danced and fluttered ever so slightly in the rising breeze, mottling the form of anything immersed within.

Here the boy waited.

Seconds ticked away and turned into minutes.

Instantly alarmed, the boy turned to the sound of the rapid patter and splash of something not human running through shallow water. He was just barely aware of heavy breathing. Then a blur of dark fur came running from behind a cypress tree.

An inkling of fear surged in his nerves, sending rapid-fire impulses from his brain. Muscles obeyed their orders, though lagging behind time, it seemed to his mind, now willing more speed of action. He twisted his upper body and fired from the waist. The rifle muzzle was only inches from the dog's chest. There had been no time to aim. The bullet traversed the entire length of the body to exit through the spine near the root of the tail.

The force of the charge lived after the dog's death. Its heavy body landed on the boy's chest, slamming him against the windfall with enough force to hammer the breath from his lungs.

Before he knew it, the other two dogs were on him, charging in with mouth wide open. The ferocity of one was thwarted at the last moment by a blow from the steel butt of his rifle.

The third dog rushed in with head held low, teeth exposed, and a low rumble of a growl. Its powerful jaws, clamped on his left forearm when he used it to shield her actual target: his throat.

The animal was more powerful than he could believe possible. It yanked him from where he sat and began to drag the entire weight of his body as it rapidly jerked its head from side to side, massive jaws pressing with a viselike grip, a deep rumbling growl emanating from her throat. Teeth ripped at his flesh and dug into bone.

There was no way he could get the rifle pointed at his attacker, so he released it from his grasp and pulled his grandfather's .45 caliber pistol. He shot the animal through its left eye and out the back of her head.

He swung the pistol to shoot the last animal, but it was already on the attack, coming in to rush for the throat. By accident, he slammed the pistol hard against the face of the oncoming beast, breaking its jaw as flesh and bone clashed with steel.

Only slightly stunned, the animal's resolve undiminished, it rushed in again to press home the killing bite with jaws wide open. A .45 caliber bullet crashed through the roof of its mouth and out the top of its head.

He rolled over to his rifle. Just twelve inches above him, tree bark flew off the windfall. Bullets chewed at the wood.

Well, I guess one of them finally found me.

Strangely, he was more embarrassed by his mistake of forgetting about the dogs than worried about being shot. Perhaps because there was three feet of oak wood between him and the bullets.

Damn! They were trained to stop barking when they got close. And they were trained to kill.

He looked over at the one whose jaw he broke. There were stainless steel canine implants in its oddly gaping mouth. They were unnaturally long and sharp. There was a collar device with a short antenna around its neck. He now understood what the "RF receiver" was for. The animals themselves were massive. He reasoned they must be the result of genetic engineering.

Holding back panic, he pulled up his torn jacket sleeve and looked at his bloody left forearm. He was astonished at the sight of shredded flesh. The white of wet bone shone in the afternoon sunlight. He took just enough time to pull the lacerations on the nearside of his wrist open to check for spurting blood. He knew that blood vessels are close to the surface there, and vulnerable. There was plenty of oozing blood, but no spurting vessels. He was worried about the nerves and tendons. To his relief, he could move his hand and fingers. His arm was already starting to throb, but he had problems that were more pressing.

Let's see how nervous they are. He reached out and shook a bush. The boy was answered with a long burst of full automatic gunfire that hit nowhere near him or the log he was behind. After yelling out in faux pain, he crawled quietly to a place where a massive limb held the windfall's main trunk twenty inches off the muddy ground.

The boy positioned his rifle so he could shoot from under the log. After getting into the prone shooting position, he took time to get into his natural point of aim. He only had a vague idea where the last shots came from, but he was as ready as he could be while waiting for a target. He planned to fine-tune his NPOA when a target presented itself.

*   *   *

Although, he had been lying still for ten minutes, the government agent's heart was still pounding. Beads of sweat joined and formed rivulets that ran down his forehead, stinging his eyes. "Do you…think…you got…him?" He spoke in a labored hoarse whisper between heavy gulps of air. His eyes flitted nervously from tree to bush to log, not lingering long enough to allow his mind to register even if his eyes had seen anything other than tree, bush, or log.

Shaking his head, his partner mouthed the word *maybe*, and then shrugged his shoulders. His eyes made long sweeps across the swamp before him, too fast to see anything, but a blur of menacing woods: the wall of green.

Twenty more minutes of anxious waiting spawned nerve-fraying tension. The hoarse whisperer, whose heartbeat and breathing had still not settled down, stood up and announced in a normally loud voice, "I'm going over and check. You cover me."

His partner nodded solemnly, eyes expectant, foretelling his partner's death. He was sure not to break cover himself. "Go ahead, dumbass. I'll just stay here and see how long you live."

The boyish-faced agent tried to wipe stinging sweat out of his eyes. He inhaled deeply, swallowed hard, and with great effort, forced his lead-heavy legs to move.

Still lying under the log, the boy smelled the man's fear in the humid air and watched it sap his strength. He could feel the weight of it on the man's shoulders and smell his drenched uniform.

Someone is out here with a rifle, and he knows how to use it. No unarmed helpless victim, this one will kill your ass. You gutless murdering son of a bitch!

"I see fear on your face, you bastard." The boy spit out his words. He exhaled forcefully through his teeth in disgust, and watched the man rush closer to take cover behind a tree that was more than a foot too small to stop a bullet.

The boy kept his sights on the man and held his fire. Though he could easily kill him, he wanted more targets before he shot again.

The lack of gunfire was encouraging. The agent yelled over his left shoulder, "Cover me!"

His partner did not move. His eyes were busy scanning the woods for danger, carbine shouldered and ready. He saw nothing, but a blurred wall of green, his eyes sweeping in futile haste.

Bent over and hunched low, his head drawn down between his shoulders as much as possible, the agent, now in full sight of the boy, ran over to the water's edge and peered intently across the creek, meadow, and into thick woods beyond. He scanned the log the boy was hiding behind once, but his eyes could see nothing more than a mottling of multiple shades of color and light, all dancing gently to a mute tune played by the breeze.

Then the man stood up straight and turned around to face his partner, announcing at the top of his voice, "I think you got him. Come on. We'll go over and check."

His partner would have none of it. "What an asshole. I'm not going anywhere with you. Not until Chiang and Miles get here."

"Stop calling him Chiang," Hoarse Whisperer said. His real name was Robert. "It's racist to call him that just because he's Asian."

"Yeah well, that bitch mother who stabbed him in the ass while he was on top of her daughter had better names for him before he shot her. If not for his sore ass, he would be here already, and I wouldn't be stuck here alone with a dumbass like you."

The boy centered his front sight on Hoarse Whisperer's back and waited for him to coax one of the others into exposing himself.

"Okay. I seem to be the only one with balls around here, so you stay back there and keep wetting your pants while I go do your job for you," Hoarse Whisperer said.

Hoarse Whisperer stepped into the water.

The boy's eyes lit up. *Finally, I catch a break. Now let's sit back and watch the show.*

"Damn! This creek seems to be more mud than water." Hoarse Whisperer took two more careful steps and found he was armpit deep, but the water was not his problem at the moment, it was the fact he could not pull his boots out of the muddy bottom. He was already more than two feet into the sucking muck's clutches. Each time he put his weight on one foot to pull out the other, that foot would be pushed deeper into the swamp's sludge. Soon he was neck deep.

"Hey. Goddamn it. I need help!"

Silence.

"Come on now," Hoarse Whisperer yelled. "Don't be a shitwad."

"You should have known better than to try to cross that creek. I'm not going to get shot for you, dumbass. Chiang and Miles should be here soon."

"Bullshit. I'll be under in a minute. Get a rope or something."

"I don't have a rope. Maybe you can pull one out of your ass while we wait. Meanwhile, shut up. I can't hear if someone is walking up on me."

Five more minutes of soaking and sinking was all Hoarse Whisperer could take. The boy heard his voice lose all façade of courage. "I'm going under! Get me outa here now!"

Silence, but for the rumble of distant thunder.

"Pleeease help me. I don't want to drown in this goddamn mud."

A barking squirrel in a live oak forty yards away answered him. The man behind him remained silent.

"Come on," Hoarse Whisperer said. "Get me out of here. That boy's either dead or gone I tell you. Otherwise he would've shot me by now."

The boy watched the man's head bobbing over and around his scant cover, a small scrub oak. "Come on Shitwad," he breathed. "What's to think about? I'm just a Southern white trash farm boy. What do I know about an ambush?"

Shitwad took one last careful look across the glade. "Hold your shit together while I find a pole or something. I guess you're right. The boy is gone."

Now standing on the edge of the creek, Shitwad observed, "You're not that far out. Just stretch your carbine over this way, and I'll pull you out. There aren't any poles handy anyway."

Hoarse Whisperer turned at his waist as much as possible and pointed his carbine at Shitwad.

Shitwad jumped to his left. "Asshole. Now you're going to shoot me. Give me the butt end if you want me to pull you out."

Hoarse Whisperer glared over his shoulder. In silence, he simply turned his rifle around and held it out by the barrel.

Pulling only forced the stuck man under water.

"The angle is wrong," Shitwad said. "I'm pulling too horizontally. And with you facing away from me, pulling on the carbine just pulls you over backwards."

Each time they tried it, he came up spiting and gasping for air. "Enough. You're going to drown me, goddamnit."

"Look what happens when I leave you two alone."

Shitwad nearly fell over, until he saw that Robert was the one who had just walked up on them. He caught his breath, putting his left hand to his chest as if he thought he was having a heart attack. "Oh shit, Chiang. I could've shot you."

Looking incredulous and pulling himself back on his heels with a smug sneer on his face, Robert said, "Bullshit. If I were the boy I could have shot you." He glanced around and asked, "Where are the others?"

At that instant, a bullet entered and exited Robert's head. Pink mist exploded from his skull, and he fell on his face in the mud.

Shitwad opened his mouth wide in shock and horror one second before he too fell dead at the creek's edge, his head half submerged in the coffee-black water. Crimson gouts of blood spurted for a few seconds, spreading onto the wet mud, as his one eye visible above water, stared blankly at Hoarse Whisperer's back. Miniature wavelets produced by Hoarse Whisperer's shaking, lapped in and out of his half-open mouth.

Hoarse Whisperer forced himself to turn at the waist and neck and look over his right shoulder to see if what he feared had happened. "Oh shit!" He unloaded in his pants.

Waiting for another target, the boy guessed forty minutes had passed. The slight breeze of early afternoon, generated by a coming thunderstorm, gradually shook off its lethargy, exciting the green leaves of tree and bush to dance with more vigor. He lifted his nose. A trace of ozone wafted to his nostrils. Cooler air from high above washed over his face, drying some of the sweat beading up on his skin.

The squirrel in the live oak, encouraged by the recent silence, resumed a timid barking, soon turning into a chastising scold of things in general. Myriads of frogs croaked and bullied silence into partial submission with their monotonous love songs. Thunder, paled by distance, hung in the heavy air for a moment, and then faded to a weak hint of distant storms.

Hoarse Whisperer had sunk several more inches into the creek bottom. He could smell the swamp before, but now the lifeblood of this quaking liquid land was only three inches under his nostrils. Eons of frequent rains had washed everything of flora or fauna that had lived, died, and rotted to be reabsorbed by the liquid land from which it came into the creek. The after-smell of life and death, that which is temporary fermented and distilled into that which is forever, the quintessence of ever-present mortality, permeated his overloaded senses. He smelled his own death. His face was deathly white and he shivered violently. His teeth chattered, even though the water was bathtub-warm.

Farther back in the woods, someone was trying to sneak closer, but not having much luck with his intentions of stealth.

The boy continued to listen and watch, his lucent form still immersed in the green gloom of the jungle, now under the shade of heavy rain clouds and tossed ever more violently by the winds.

Hoarse Whisperer's ears discerned the rasping impact of someone moving through palmettos from the wind-tossed treetops and brush colliding in the gathering commotion. He yelled, "Miles, come help me. I'm drowning."

There was crashing in the brush and a blur of motion. Miles stopped behind a hickory tree. The voluminous midsection of his sweat-soaked body was exposed on each side of the inadequate tree trunk.

Miles timidly pulled his head out from around the hickory just enough to look at the back of Hoarse Whisperer's shivering head poking out of the water. His skin tingled with nervous tension, all senses on high-volume intensity, eyes funneling in and focusing the images before him in minute detail. He saw a two-foot-long water moccasin swimming upstream toward the head. Hoarse Whisperer's palpable terror and helpless state permeated the air, eroding much of Mile's intestinal fortitude. A suffocating feeling there was not enough oxygen in the atmosphere came over him.

The boy could see his eyes, and his eyes told him Mile's mind was slogging through a miasma of confusion.

You, with all the power of government, are the hunters. I am nothing—prey to be hunted down and killed. What happened here? What is happening now? Pull your fathead out from around that tree a little more, and I will show you.

Clouds that had rolled in earlier were building fast now, high and deep under the energy of the sun. The humid air could take in no more moisture. It started to rain, but stopped after a few minutes. A surge of wind, mixing hot air with cool, came down from the darkening sky and swept them without warning. The roar of a soaking downpour rolled across the woodland in an advancing sheet and hit all at once. In seconds, Miles and the boy were nearly as wet as Hoarse Whisperer. The crack of a lightning bolt assaulted their ears and set Hoarse Whisperer's bowels moving again. He moaned and looked about wild-eyed.

Already, the blood of those fallen soaked into the soil, and the boy's arm painted the ground crimson where he lay. As it continued to rain, the blood of the living and the dead washed into the earth. Soon, only God would know the blood of the oppressed from that of the oppressor.

Miles said nothing. There had been gunfire multiple times earlier; this was no time to take chances. Carefully, he pulled his head out a little so he could see more to the left. A bolt of lightning struck nearby. He frantically pulled his head back behind the tree. Regaining his composure, he timidly brought his head slowly out in the open and peered into the streaming slant of the downpour, shivering in the cold rain.

The bark of the boy's Garand reverberated among the trees and slowly faded into the drenching atmosphere. Miles lay on his back, carbine lying across his chest, eyes staring blankly at boiling storm clouds above.

The wind and the rain continued.

The boy had heard them talking. He knew Miles was the last. Still, he did not go carelessly to the creek. He took his time. There was no hurry. Why not make use of every advantage you have? There is always one more thing you can do to put the odds in your favor. Never take unnecessary chances.

He wanted this last one to see his hate before he died, to know why he hated them, to feel something of the value he placed on the two they murdered without thought or feeling. He might as well know before he goes to hell.

There was no way to tell how long the boy's face had been there watching him slowly drown. He was just there, or his face was, as if he had just emerged from the dripping wall of green as an alligator comes to the mirror surface of a bayou.

His impassive face contrasted with the heat of his eyes. They dominated his face, leaving no room, no capacity for emotion, all emotion in the eyes. They were too old for a young face. The heat of hate stared straight through the drowning killer and a thousand yards beyond at something hideous, visible to the boy only. It would chill anyone who felt it, but the boy was unafraid. He was past fear, past pain, past mercy. He had run all such things into the ground and left them far behind, gasping and dying, ran to death by force of will.

The boy was dead. In his place was born a wild creature of a primordial past, the green gloom of the woodland's trackless wilderness his environing haunt. The boy had relinquished himself to the shadow that had followed him all his life. The shadow had merged with the boy. They had become one.

In his heart lived the Human Spirit, the cumulative product of centuries of lives lived and lost, births and deaths, arisen from the smoke of long ago campfires by the echoes of past drumbeats.

Hoarse Whisperer closed his eyes. The water was now above his mouth, forcing him to breathe through his nose. The sucking in and exhaling of air through his nostrils against the intimately close surface of the water was the only sound he heard above the gentle patter of rainfall in the endless liquid stillness of time.

When he reopened his eyes, the face was gone.

Chapter 3

The old hotel convention room was overfilled with reporters, all trying to get the attention of the Director of Dissident Control. His hair was gray, with half a can of hair spray on his head. More than one in the room noticed the double chin was coming back, despite the nip and tuck job he had received only two years ago. The broad, open smile he flashed was without warmth. His teeth were perfect, though artificial. His waist was narrow. His shoulders were also narrow, but not as narrow as his mind, or so went his reputation. It was said he cared not about his shoulders or his mind. He would not stoop to carry more weight than the forty-caliber Glock pistol in the holster under his suit jacket. Muscles were for the lower class. The joke was, carefully repeated in private away from any government security cameras or microphones, his narrow mind was the product of always being right.

Even in this secured building, a bullet and blast resistant clear polycarbonate plate six feet high by six feet wide, and three inches thick stood in front of him. He was way too valuable to incur the slightest risk.

One tall man, thirty years old, with dark, sharp eyes that seemed not to miss much of anything, observed the DDC and his colleague reporters, a slight hint of humorous distain on his face.

A perky thirty-something blonde got to ask the first question. Her push-up bra accentuated her ample cleavage that was purposely left bare by leaving the top two buttons on her white blouse undone. Her blue skirt was shorter than anything the other women in the room wore, though most wore pants suits.

She was always assured an early question at such press conferences because she spent at least one night a month with the DDC. It was the price she must pay to make it in Washington, a suburb of Northeast City, as a top-tier reporter. Her husband did not know. Even if he did, there was nothing he could do about it. Marriage had long since been reduced to a contract of friendship.

Paul Garner, the sixty-eight-year-old DDC, smiled inwardly, a glint of expectation in his eyes. He pointed. "Mrs. Darnell, you have the first question."

Everyone else in the room suddenly became quiet and sat down on the cheap folding chairs, all painted gray and set in rows.

She gave a wintry smile behind a covering hand to practice her façade before raising her other hand to signal her readiness to ask a question. Suddenly the smile appeared sanguine and warm as she removed the veiling hand.

"Ah, Director, do you have any idea where the boy is now and how long it will take to apprehend him?"

"Mrs. Darnell, considering the fact he is on foot, we are certain the boy is still somewhere close to where he murdered the agents. The perimeter is quite large though. We are pulling in hundreds of agents from all over Southeast Province to keep him from escaping."

"Director, where did he get the guns? And what kind of weapons does he have?"

The DDC shook his head. "It is a shame really. It seems there are still a few holdouts out there in the sticks that refuse to stop clinging to their guns. And of course, some backwards types are still clinging to religion. Anachronistic Neanderthals all."

He was momentarily interrupted by a wave of giggles.

"Remember, the boy and his family were farmers living out in the sticks. The kind that refuses to accept the realities of the day. They should have moved into one of the six cities years ago."

He looked around the room with a confident, know-it-all look on his face.

"We have a relocation program in progress now to settle this question of what to do with people like this once and for all. Of course, a different department is handling the Removal Plan. But my Department of Dissident Control is responsible for security. Dissident Control, as you well know, has a monopoly on force, especially deadly force. It is the keystone to a civilized society."

His notorious, patronizing voice descended on his captive audience. "Everyone should live in the cities. We have a city for each of the six provinces. There are government farms to provide our food, so we don't need any freelance farmers. The Party has planned well. All needs are being met. Why anyone would want to provide for themselves and live out in the sticks, I do not understand. Nor do I want to understand such insanity.

"I do know World Law demands seventy-five percent of the North American continent be unpeopled so wildlife can survive." He lifted his finger in the air and waved it back and forth. "And we will not allow lawlessness. People can't just live anywhere they want. It matters not, how long the land they claim is theirs, has been in their family. What kind of anarchy would we have if everyone decided to just squat where they have lived for generations, just because they think they own the land? As if we have not cured society of that disease called private property. People must do what they are told, or else. And this boy is going to learn to accept authority the hard way. It's a shame, but he has forced this upon himself."

"Should he have accepted the murder of his mother and grandfather?" someone yelled out.

Director Garner pointed at the man who spoke, with his eyes full of hate. Two uniformed national police officers rushed into the crowd, knocking over and bodily throwing anyone in the way aside, man or woman. Chairs and bodies flew as they created a corridor of access. The man tried to run, but was shot in the back with darts from a stun gun. He screamed and convulsed on the floor for two minutes as the officer repeatedly sent jolts of electricity through the man's body.

Reporters moved back to avoid being kicked by the thrashing, convulsing, screaming man. Most watched with amusement. Only two reporters looked as if they had any empathy for the man's suffering.

Finally, the officer had his fill of fun. His partner slammed both knees into the man's back, and handcuffed him so tightly that his wrists were bleeding by the time they dragged him out of the room by his ankles, his face rubbing on the waxed floor.

The sound of heavy blows followed by screams could be heard through the door. Nearly every reporter in the room faced Director Garner and pretended not to hear and that nothing had happened since the DDC's last words. If a mouse had run across the room, it would have received more notice.

Director Garner continued. "The boy's antisocial behavior is probably because of him being raised in an isolated home, out in the middle of wildlife habitat where people do not belong. He is nothing more than an incorrigible homicidal wild animal. It is unfortunate his family abused him in such an uncivilized way by raising him like they did."

His voice was drowned out by a loud scream. He snapped his fingers at another officer, the last one in the room. The officer rushed out the same door and closed it. A gunshot rang through the door and down the halls of the building. Only a few reporters jumped. One woman held her stomach with one hand and covered her mouth with the other. The tall, dark-haired man clenched his jaw. The screaming stopped.

The Director continued. "Now the boy is past salvaging. There is nothing left to do, but put him out of his misery like a rabid dog." He smiled and capered with faux excitement and enthusiasm. "Sincere apologies to all rabid dogs."

There was a clamoring of nervous laughs. The dark-haired man looked around with a face as neutral as a calm deep sea, his rage now under control. He did not seem amused or disgusted. His eyes swept the room, observing.

The DDC's face hardened, and he slammed a fist down on the podium. "This tragedy is the result of illegal guns and a refusal to accept government planning over individual thinking. The Party knows best, not antisocial individuals. What is wrong with these crazies? How dare they ask that we go back to the Stone Age and reinstate the old obsolete

Constitution? We left that tired old baggage behind long ago, never to return.

"In order to care for the Redundant Headcount and provide for their basic needs, most important, their safety, and not leave things to a random chaos some miscreants still call freedom, we, the government, had to take control. After all, the great majority of any society is incapable of providing for the individual by the individual and must be husbanded by the government. No matter what their age, they are just children and would either starve or harm themselves and others like this boy has. The government simply must be their provider of all things and their protector from all things."

Nearly every reporter in the room stood, put down their recorders, cameras, and notepads, and began to applaud loudly and vigorously. The dark-haired man sat impassive, observing. One brunette did not stand or applaud. She seemed sick to her stomach.

The director smiled and put up his hands. "Okay, that is enough speechifying. Let us get back to work." Everyone knew the DDC loved approval. He soaked it up as a lizard absorbs the sun's heat. Now his face was glowing with pleasure.

The dark-haired reporter was allowed to ask the next question. This was because there had been trouble with him before. The DDC usually culled the troublemakers to neutralize them before they could do any damage. He had a crude, unabashed way of doing this. Everyone knew what he was doing when he did it. But what did he care? No one would dare report it or even complain. After what happened in the hallway, who would step over the line on this fine morning?

Standing to address the DDC, he held no notepad or camera. He wore no jacket or blazer, just a light blue shirt with a dark blue tie that could be mistaken for black and gray slacks.

"Sir, do you have any idea why he would murder his grandfather and mother as you claim, and then take out eight Dissident Control agents? And I would like a follow-up question like you gave Mrs. Darnell."

"The term is murdered, not took out." The DDC pointed a thin finger accusingly. "I know you. You use words as weapons to confuse the public. You're part Indian, a Nez Perce or some such, aren't you?"

James Joseph, independent reporter at large, sighed, raised himself to his full six foot two stature, and looked the director square in the eyes. "One of my ancestors was Chief Joseph. But let us get back—"

"Oh yes. That's right. I remember now: Chief Joseph. He was a packing chief wasn't he? He made sure your people's precious stuff like buffalo robes was packed on the horses properly didn't he?" He sneered and invited the others to join in by motioning with his arms. "Now that's what I would call a first-rate chief."

The director put his hands up in the air and looked up at the ceiling as if he were communicating with God. "From where the sun now stands, I will fight no more forever. My heart is sick and sad…"

A spattering of chuckles and catcalls rolled across the room.

"Sir, if you are finished, please answer the question."

The DDC leaned over the podium, looking irritated. "There were guns in the house. That says it all."

"But Director, it seems there were guns in the house for decades, and no one in the family had any history of violence. The question is what set the boy off?"

Garner said, "You have had your question and follow up."

"But you have not answered." He shook his head and sighed, then sat down. He could push it no further.

Ignoring Mr. Joseph, Director Garner looked around the room. His eyes fell on a brunette who was unusually pretty. He pointed at her. "Look at you." He smiled. "And here I was wasting time with that red-skinned bastard." His eyes appraised her figure. "Perhaps you are the kind of woman that is willing to do business." He motioned with his head. "Like Mrs. Darnell."

Mrs. Darnell's face turned red. She ran out of the room. Everyone knew, and she knew everyone knew, but he did not have to rub her face in it.

There was not as much as a gasp, much less a verbal protest from anyone. No one that is, but Mr. Joseph. Standing now, his voice reverberated in the room. "Director, your position and power far exceed your decency."

Garner swung his gaze on Joseph like a tandem-gun turret. "Sit down and shut up, or I will have you carried out by your ankles."

Mr. Joseph said nothing more, but did not sit down.

In her late twenties, and dressed in a smart tan business pants suit that looked good on her, or rather she looked good in it, she stood there indifferent to what had just been said. At the moment, her indifference was giving way to an expression of distaste.

"Miss—you." The DDC pointed at her. "I don't remember seeing you before. What is your name?"

"Maria Rodriguez. Reporter for the Patrick Henry Journal." She looked him straight in the eyes.

"Oh."

Miss Rodriguez was under the impression he found her employer unworthy. It was a small newspaper, one of the few that survived with no support from The Party. And it was often critical of governmental policies. On second thought, she realized she was mistaken. He probably had not heard of the paper. The historic background of the name was what bothered him.

"Continue, Maria."

"I have talked with many in the area of the family's farm who—"

"You what?" The DDC interrupted. "That area is off limits. It is full of Wild People. You are lucky to have gotten out alive. I've a mind to have you arrested right now." He gave a slight, lifeless smile. "But I am in a magnanimous mood, so repeat the question."

"Many in the area believe your agents summarily executed the mother and grandfather, and the boy retaliated. In fact, many believe that if the boy had not been armed, he too would have been killed as his unarmed family was. All the neighbors think well of the family, and they say the boy would never have committed murder. It must have been self-defense." She stared Director Garner down. "In light of this information, will you answer Mr. Joseph's question as to what caused a boy with no criminal history to suddenly act out so violently?"

The DDC shook his head up and down slightly, but rapidly. "So, you have been investigating on your own have you? Why don't you leave that to us? Your job is to report what we tell you and nothing more. We investigate. You report." He scowled at her. "You independent reporters need to get with it, before we put you out of business completely."

Director Garner looked her up and down. "If you were not so stupid you would know we run into lying Wild People all the time. This incident took place outside the six cities. They are hicks in the sticks, and they hate the government. They lie. They conduct free commerce with one another in defiance of our system and do not rely on the Unity Party's generosity. All those who practice free enterprise are antisocial. They don't care about the poor and ill, we do."

The eyes of many in the room started to glaze over. It was going to be another long news conference with the DDC.

Garner hesitated to continue, then began to say what he was thinking.

"Scientists tell us their research strongly suggests Wild People are subhuman. And we have reason to believe many practice cannibalism. How else are they feeding themselves without government help? They have been known to kill and eat citizens unfortunate enough to stray too far from the city limits. That is why the signs are there, to warn you to stay out of Wild People country. And I will not get into how they treat their wives."

A spattering of gleeful laughter erupted in the room.

Talking more to the cameras and others in the room than her, he continued. "Why would anyone want to live outside one of our beautiful cities anyway? They must be anarchists. Keep in mind that those living outside the cities are not eligible for government food and health care, much less housing and transportation. They claim they are living independently, but the fact is they hate the government, and that means they must hate us. Quite simply, they are animals. Living independently from the government, but interdependently among their neighbors, what a crazy, contradictory concept." He shook as if trying to shake the repulsive idea out of his head. "That in and of its self is antisocial. Only wild animals feed and take care of themselves and their offspring."

Miss Rodriguez hoped to end the tirade and get back to discussing the incident at the farm. "But if what the neighbors are saying is true...You do not deny the boy had a right to defend his family and himself do you?"

"I, I, I, don't believe you! Are you honestly asking...?" Hot blood flowed to his head. "Even if my agents did execute those two animals, the prime concept of our society today is that only the government has any right to self-defense. My agents have exclusive authority to use deadly force. We must demand full enforcement of our, meaning the Department of Dissident Control, monopoly on deadly force. This is a basic precept of World Government."

Miss Rodriguez just managed not to roll her eyes. "Yes Director, my wonderful, highly dedicated government teachers explained all of that when I was twelve. But I did not know government agents have the authority to summarily execute nonviolent, unarmed civilians on the spot for no logical reason." She did understand fully, but was trying to get Garner to tell the truth about the wholesale murder of Wild People. She glanced at the door that opened to the hall for a split second and back to Director Garner.

Garner's face showed full agitation. "Are you kidding? Are you that stupid? Go all the way back to the case in the nineteen nineties involving an agent of the now defunct FBI. The agent was charged with various crimes in a kangaroo court in what was then the state of Idaho. The area is still full of hicks to this day. But we will clean them out soon. It is of course now part of Northwest Province. The agent was charged with murder for shooting an unarmed mother while she held her baby in her arms. It was blown up into a big emotional thing just to fan the flames of antigovernment hatred. They screamed that it was a violation of human rights." His eyes bulged with passion. "You know, every time I hear that term, I want to reach for my pistol."

Garner pointed at her. "Do some real investigating, and you will find the government's lawyer, lawyers, another relic from the past, successfully argued the agent could not possibly have committed murder because he had administrative authority. It was eloquently explained that national law enforcement officers violated laws all the time in the performance of their duties. If they had to obey the law like common civilians, it would hinder their work. Furthermore, even though the director of the FBI admitted the agent had violated the now, thank The Party, obsolete Constitution, administrative authority provides all national law enforcement officers with blanket immunity." He leaned over the podium. "Do I need to explain it again?"

Most of the other reporters in the room looked at her as if they were wondering how she gathered enough intelligence to find the conference room in the first place.

Undaunted, she kept her chin up and spoke again. "Sir, would you suffer me and my acute IQ deficit disorder one more question?"

After the murmurings and chuckles settled down, Garner acquiesced, indicating so by simply nodding. Master of all beings in the room, a nod was sufficient. This young woman was not worthy of the energy it would take to verbally respond in a polite manner, unless she was willing to agree to an "arrangement," as Mrs. Darnell had. Now, his amusement of her willingness to allow him to demean her without so much as a protest was not difficult to see.

Her dark eyes shined with disciplined passion. What she was about to say would cost her life, and she wanted to get the highest value for the price she would soon pay. The courage of conviction bolstered her resolve and her face was calm. She was unarmed, outnumbered, and smaller than any man in the room was, yet she stood there, a sentinel of freedom. She did not expect to leave the room alive.

"The government asserts that it gets its authority from its might alone, and its might alone makes it right, always, and that nothing, no law, no former Constitution, no unalienable human right, not even our God-given conscience, should stand in the way of its might. Being that the boy has thus far prevailed over that might, does not your reasoning demand that we all acknowledge that it is now the boy who has become our government, simply by virtue of his own might? Perhaps, we should pronounce him king, since his might so far has proven to be mightier than the governments."

Sweat suddenly drenched Garner's face. "How dare you," he screamed, his wild eyes bulging. "You dishonor the fallen agents. It is treason to suborn violence against government authority. And you flaunt my agents' monopoly on deadly force." His face was deep red and frothy spittle flew from his mouth, spraying the polycarbonate plate in front of him. "Get out! Get out of my sight now before I charge you with sedition and shoot you myself, right here, right now." He subconsciously reached under his coat for his pistol.

Nearly everyone in the room sat dumbfounded. No one dared speak to a government official in such a disgraceful manner. It was just not done. Such disrespect. After all, it was by the grace of government that everyone there was still alive. And government was the only reason reporters existed at all, news agencies, being pseudo government entities and only partially dependent on a free market, something that barely survived the strangling restrictions of governmental power, a stunted flower precariously growing through a narrow crack in a concrete sidewalk.

In addition, the DDC had been gracious enough to take the time to fly in from Northeast City to this backwater Southeast Province suburb of Southeast City, just to reassure everyone the government was working hard to protect them all from a crazed mass murderer.

Miss Rodriguez calmly stood her ground and waited for a chance to speak again. However, that chance would never come. The director may have spoken in anger, but his was no idle threat. He might even shoot her and charge her dead body with sedition.

"Oh shit." Mr. Joseph rushed over and grabbed her by a wrist, then whispered in her ear, "Come with me now before the agents get back. They'll kill you."

She resisted, and he was obliged to use more force to pull her out of the room than his respect for women would have normally allowed. Still, she would not relent and took her last chance to speak her mind before he pulled her through the doorway.

She pulled against him, yelling, "You may kill the boy in the end, but you will never kill his spirit! He has proven that. Thank God, there is at least one man left in this country. That boy has more balls than any of the so-called men in this room. Free the oppressed."

Garner looked like he had just seen a ghost. "The woman is insane."

Once in the hallway, Mr. Joseph grabbed her shoulders. "If you don't let me help you, they will kill you. Do as I say. Now follow—"

She yanked her shoulders from his grip. "Yes, I know they will kill me. If that is what it takes, then so be it. Freedom! Is there no one left who remembers what the word means?"

"I would love to wax eloquent on how much I agree with you, but there is no time. Now, let's go."

After running down a stairwell and through four narrow dimly lit hallways, they came to a service door.

There was a guard sitting on a steel chair, resting his folded arms on his prodigious protruding stomach. The cheaply constructed chair, which now strained under the man's weight, had no armrests, so fortunately for him, he had brought his own. Bored from four hours of mind-numbing door sitting, he was nearly asleep.

Mr. Joseph smiled and held his press ID card out as he tried to walk by. "Hey Boss. Didn't mean to wake you, but the lady here is sick to her stomach. I guess meeting the DDC was too much excitement for her. I'm showing her a shortcut so she won't ruin the carpet."

The guard shook cobwebs from his head. With more volume than necessary for the circumstances, he yelled, "Hey, hold on there. You can't just decide on your own to exit the building this way. You will have to go out the way that you came in. The DDC is in the building. Security is paramount." That last sentence was a direct quote from his superior.

Miss Rodriguez could sense his dissatisfaction with the level of competent authority that he strained to instill in his voice. "Oh come on, Officer, give me a break will you?" she asked, giving him a warm smile while holding her stomach. He was only a "Green Shirt," a flunky wannabe, who couldn't qualify for the Department of Dissident Control, and not normally given the respect of the title "Officer."

He stuttered, "I have orders."

Still smiling, with a pleasant voice Mr. Joseph said, "I'm just trying to save the carpet in the hallway, Boss. And I'm doing the young lady here a favor." He winked at the unarmed rotund guard.

The guard's eyes lingered on her cleavage. "Well, you both have press ID cards, so I guess you can—" His radio interrupted. "Code red! Let no one pass your station. I repeat, let—"

Mr. James Joseph, whose family bloodline included Chief Joseph of the Nez Perce, a man who nearly gave the same U.S. Army that just won the Civil War its greatest defeat since the Battle of the Little Big Horn, plunged his right thumb into the left eye of the guard. The sharp, focused force put the eye out forever. Corpulent jowls quaked on impact, and his mouth grew wide as he screamed. Involuntarily bringing both hands to his eyes, he fell to the floor.

"If only you had sounded more authoritative, I might have been afraid to do that," Mr. Joseph said.

Turning to Miss Rodriguez, he said, "You can stop smiling now." He looked up at her queasy expression as he bent over to take the guard's keys and radio. "Oh, I see you already have stopped smiling, haven't you."

She looked down at the guard and swallowed.

After they were outside, Joseph closed the door, locked it, and broke the key off in the lock. They could hear the guard still moaning.

He held her hand to steady her. "Now you *do* look like you're about to throw up."

"I just might," she said.

He smiled self-consciously. "No. I don't think you will. This is just the beginning of what you started. In fact, it will never be over for either of us."

An unusual combination of alarm and stoic determination washed over her face. "I made my choice. Now, I'll pay the price. I just wish you hadn't gotten involved."

He smiled again. A still higher respect for her shined in his eyes. "You know, some people say freedom is not free. Well, neither is life. Every decision a person makes has its price. If I'd decided not to help you, I would've been forced to live with it. I chose the less painful route."

She raised her face and eyes, looked into his, and smiled at his obvious unease. "What now?" she asked.

For a fleeting second, a sad, brooding expression flooded across his face. The sadness washed away. "It's not going to be easy getting out of town, but I know where we can get help. We will have to hoof it. Our vehicles are being watched. Bet your life on it."

"And they have GPS transponders in them," she added.

"Big Brother must keep a close watch on us children," he said. They rushed down the sidewalk.

They ducked into a back alley half choked with garbage, sprinted as fast as they could, and then emerged onto a street to walk calmly along a sidewalk.

There were only a few cars on the street, and most of them were miniature electric cars with limited range, not much more than the golf carts of years past. City people did not go out much. When they did, it was to get basic necessities from government centers. Mostly they just sloughed in their government-supplied apartment and watched mindless government-controlled satellite television.

After a dozen more back alley sprints and sidewalk strolls, they reached a secondary, less-used road that led out of town. She was grateful they were on the outskirts of the city. In the city proper, there were cameras everywhere, and their chances of getting away would be nil.

They passed the signs warning travelers they were entering Wild People country. Here, they were forced to walk in the grass along the road's shoulder for nearly a mile. The occasional, rare, petroleum-fueled vehicle, mostly freight-hauling trucks, zoomed by as they tried to appear to be a couple out for a stroll. They held hands when they thought someone might be watching. This was the period that strained her nerves the most. She noticed he was as alert as she was. If a Dissident Control agent drove up on them now…

Chapter 4

Joseph and Rodriguez came to a large tract of woodland that appeared to be virgin forest. He waited for the last vehicle to get out of sight, quickly veered off the road shoulder, and ran into the woods with her in tow.

They walked four hundred yards. He said, "Okay, we can rest here a while."

He took his tie off and used it to wipe his forehead. "Whew! Being scared breathless for three hours sure wears you out."

She leaned a shoulder against a scrub oak, grateful for a chance to rest. "I don't want to put any pressure on you, being as I caused all this, and you jumped in with both feet to help me. But I hope and pray you have some kind of plan, because I sure don't."

"Like I said, I know some people who can help. We have about an hour of walking ahead of us. It's mostly woods from now on." He looked at her curiously. "Didn't you know that speaking out against the government not only can, but will get you killed?"

"Of course." She gave him a hard look. "Do you think I'm an idiot?"

"What prompted you to do it? And without as much as an exit plan."

"It was the boy," she said. "I'm sure he knows they will kill him in the end. But he won't stop fighting. If only we had a million like him. There may be a few more boys, and girls out there with the backbone to fight back. They just need some encouragement."

"They need some encouragement all right. What the people need is a shot of raw courage pumped into them, not just encouragement." Mr. Joseph's face showed disgust. "If there hadn't been so many people over the last three or four generations who expected the government to take care of them and keep them like pet cats or dogs, we would not be in this hellhole today. A government with the means to take care of you like a pet has the power to take everything you have, including your life."

"And freedom," she said. Her eyes lit up. "You know, you might be charged with plagiarism, or at least misquoting Honest Abe."

He shrugged. "If it's worth saying, it probably has been said before and more eloquently at that. Besides," he smiled warmly, "I thought it was Thomas Jefferson who said that, or something similar."

She tilted her head and smiled mischievously. "Never with more passion, I'm sure. Whoever it was."

He ran his fingers through his jet-black hair. "And to think I just saved your life."

She laughed. "Just kidding. Please go on. You're on a roll."

His sight turned inward. "You're right. If the resistance had a million like him, a million Patrick Timucua Paines, we would be free." He turned his eyes on her again. "That's his name you know."

She nodded. "His father died years ago. I wonder if it was his grandfather or his mother who put the steel in his backbone."

"Probably both." He took a step. "Come on, we have to go."

She followed. "Thank you for saving my life."

"You are most welcome, Miss Rodriguez." He looked over his shoulder.

"Please call me Maria."

"It would be an honor. By the way, you should have started calling me James a long time ago. Now let's finish this great escape and see about helping our friend Patrick, if he lives long enough."

"I'll put my bet on the boy."

*   *   *

James and Maria stood at the door of a small, modest home, waiting for someone to answer their knocking. Trees and jungle-like undergrowth surrounded the place. All outward appearances would cause a visitor to believe no one lived there. In fact, no one did. It was a "station" in the new Underground Railroad.

A voice from back in the woods bellowed out, "You're trespassing. Whatever you're selling, I don't want any no matter what it is, even if it's free. I don't give or take Unity Credits for payment anyway, just gold."

James stood still and continued to face the door. "I'm looking for a place to bow-hunt deer next season, heard you charged a reasonable fee."

"Well. Why didn't you say so? Go on down to the river and turn upstream. Someone will be there to talk to you about it."

James turned around and walked toward the river. "Follow me and don't make any sudden moves. For God's sake, don't reach into your pockets. We're being watched through telescopic sights. Let me do the talking. I've done this before."

There was an indistinct path down to the wet river bottom. They walked it, careful to step over the muddy spots. The slope was gradual, but it was easy enough to see they were heading down to a lower, wetter area. As they walked, James was careful to keep his hands in plain sight. When he got to the river, he turned downstream, not upstream. Maria noticed it but said nothing.

They came to a flat bottom aluminum boat tied to a cypress tree. There was just enough current to make the boat dance and strain slightly against the rope in the purling tea-colored river water.

James motioned for her to get in. He held her hand until she sat in the back seat. Then he untied the rope, shoved off, and quickly got in as the boat was caught by the edge of the river's main current. He sat down facing toward the stern.

The dripping oars swung back and forth, lifted and dipped, as he worked his shoulder, arm, and back muscles. Soon they were more than a quarter mile downriver. On the far bank, he turned into a creek and eased their way through a maze of submerged logs and moss-covered overhanging branches.

Late in the afternoon now, sunlight filtered through the canopy high above and rained down on them and the swamp at a forty-five degree angle. The sunlight's rays caught a mist in the humid air on the way down and left freckling blotches of infinite shades of colored light on whatever they landed on. Lichens grew from rotting logs, and mushrooms sprang up in gaggles here and there from the rich black peat bottom of the sun-shaded swamp. Star-like reflections shined from the rippling wavelets left in the boat's wake.

Maria found herself both amazed and somewhat alarmed by an uneasy feeling that, she had been propelled backward thousands of years, to a time before mankind had any ability to alter and transform the natural world. A time when mankind was at nature's mercy. A mixture of wonder and apprehension came over her.

What have I gotten myself into? I haven't had a thing to eat or drink in hours, I'm near the limit of my energy, and now I'm being taken into the bowels of The Great Dismal Swamp. And it is hotter than Hades. I wish I'd been able to dress more appropriately.

James smiled and winked. "It's not going to be as bad as it looks."

Just then, a cottonmouth slithered off a log into the water. Maria pointed, smiling.

He smiled back, shrugged his shoulders, and mouthed the words: *Trust me*!

She nearly laughed out loud, just catching herself in time.

He stopped rowing and gave her his penetrating gaze. "First impressions are not always accurate, but this time…I think you were worth saving."

"That must be the greatest compliment anyone has ever given me. Considering the price you have paid."

James continued to navigate the labyrinth of submerged logs and overhanging limbs.

A voice from back in the swamp startled them. "Come on in on the starboard side."

James did as directed. He caught an overhanging tree branch and pulled the bow up on a muddy clump of what passed for dry land.

They sat in the boat and waited, while a man in his sixties picked his way through a maze of cypress knees and mud bogs.

Maria noticed with some relief that he was not armed. For this, she was grateful. He looked to be about the scruffiest, scariest bum she had ever seen. She would not want to meet him walking down a sidewalk, much less in the middle of a swamp.

He wore boots that could not be seen through a thick layer of caked-on mud, faded, tattered jeans, also muddy up to the knees, and a sweat-stained T-shirt that had seen its better days. He stuck his head behind a cypress tree to spit out a wad of homegrown tobacco that he had traded off a friend in what used to be South Carolina.

He wiped his grizzled face. "Hope you didn't see that Miss. It's a bad habit I know. But I wasn't expectin' any ladies out here."

There was tension on her face. "Miss, don't be worrying about me. I ain't never harmed a hair on any woman's head in my life. Fact is, my late Susana used to put knots on my head once or twice a year, when I didn't get out of the house fast enough. God bless her soul. But I never laid a hand on her. She might a killed me if I had."

He waved his arm in the general direction he had just come from. "Come on along with me this a way, and we'll see what's what."

James got out and pulled the boat up onto the mud a little more, then helped Maria get out.

The stranger spoke up when James started to tie the boat to a tree. "Don't worry about the boat. It ain't going nowhere." He pulled up his jeans a little and started picking his way back through the mud. "Come along now, it's gettin' late, and you two have got a ways to go, unless you want to spend the night out here."

They walked fifty yards back from the creek and came to a platform made of rough-sawn cypress planks nailed to living cypress trees for posts. It provided dry, solid footing during times of high water. There were three steps to expedite getting up out of the mud and water and onto the platform.

After they were all three on the platform, the man motioned to a six-foot bench made of the same rough-sawn cypress. "Have a seat. You two look tired, and your day ain't over yet."

The man pulled a cooler out from under another bench, took two bottles of water out, and handed one to each of them. "I'm sure both of you could stand to wet your whistle right about now."

James and Maria enjoyed their first drink in hours. He put his bottle down after half emptying it. "We need to get far from the city and into Wild People country. The lady here kind of pissed off the DDC this morning."

The stranger rasped on his face with his knuckles and laughed. "Oh yeah? I wish you'd killed the bastard." He looked at her thoughtfully. "Don't worry Miss. We'll get you both out of this swamp by nightfall. If the government wants you they'll have to kill us first." He tilted his head and looked at James. "And don't be telling me anymore about you. It's better that way."

The man bellowed out into the swamp, "Hey, Hawse, got a couple pilgrims that need an escort and transportation."

James stopped drinking and looked over his shoulder.

Hawse was an apt name for the man. There was nothing subtle about him, from his wide ugly face to his six-foot-eight, three hundred pound frame. A living definition of a giant.

Unlike the older man, he was armed. An FAL rifle hung across his chest from a combat sling, and he had six twenty-round magazines on a load-bearing harness. Also on the pistol belt was a canteen and a holstered forty-five caliber Glock. He stood there eyeing James suspiciously.

The older man admonished his friend. "Don't be scarin' the lady now, Hawse. Remember, you look about as ugly as one of them sucksquash things. Except you're about twice as big and half again as hairy."

A giant smile spread across the big man's face. "Yeah, I might be uglier than you, but I'm smarter."

The older man laughed and slapped his knee. "You got me there, Hawse. You were home schooled. Remember though, while the government schools I went to were mostly a waste of time, they weren't as bad as them they got nowadays."

The big man's eyes focused on James. "Can you operate a jet ski Mr.?"

James answered, "Yes."

"If we leave now and ride fast, you two can make it to a shower, warm meal, and soft bed before dark. Let's go."

Hawse led them away.

The older man yelled out, "Good luck to you now. You hear?"

For half an hour, James and Maria followed the big man, slopping through the mud while slapping mosquitoes. Hawse ignored them. They came to a four to eight foot narrow, three to twelve inch shallow, black water creek. Hawse turned upstream. James and Maria found the big man, with his long legs, could move fast.

Six jet skis were lined up, and floating in only a few inches of water. All had been crudely over-painted dull green, flat black, and loam for camouflage.

Hawse got in the lead craft. "You two ride double on the one behind me." He put on clear safety glasses and revved the engine a few seconds after starting it.

James settled on the seat. She sat behind him. "Don't be shy," he said. "Slide up closer and hold on tight. I don't want you falling off." He took sunglasses out of a shirt pocket and handed them to her. "Put these on. They will protect your eyes from branches and bugs. And make sure you hang on tight."

They took off. The creek was just wide and deep enough to float them. Yet, Hawse was in a hurry. He would suddenly slow to navigate a sharp bend and then dump gas into the double-barreled carburetor, spraying a rooster tail in James' face.

Maria was concerned they may be forced to spend the night in the swamp. Where was the big man taking them?

With the hulk of powerful machinery under them, she no longer felt the frailty and the diminishment of modern man in wilderness so deeply. On foot, it had been different. In those long, uncounted yards, even with James in front and the muddy, tobacco-juice-stained man leading, she had felt it: not solitude, but ice-cube-in-your-stomach-cold loneliness. Weak and timorous inside, she had walked on her own unsteady legs and sunk her feet deep into the mud of Adam, her mind swimming through the murky liquid current of timelessness.

She imagined a juvenile boy alone in this, hunted by grown men, trained killers and a pack of dogs, knowing behind every tree, every bush, and every windfall, violent death might explode from a gun barrel at three thousand feet per second. Not for an hour or a day but for weeks, day and night. Imagine trying to lie in the mud and sleep at night, knowing you are being hunted like an animal. Yet, this boy had prevailed.

She became angry. What happened? How did we beget such a government? The boy had committed no *mala en se* crime. Violence to prevent the murder of one's self and family is not an evil act. But committing murder under the color of authority is still murder. The national police had committed the evil act, but he was the one being hunted down.

The sun was deeper below the horizon, and it was getting so dark she wondered how James managed to keep the Jet Ski between the dangerously close trees. She hoped they were near the giant's destination.

They came out onto a wide expanse of water that was a large lake. The engine roared and they gathered speed. She could see much better now, without the glasses.

The fading twilight hung high over them in the clear, starry sky. She could just make out the near and far shores across the glassy surface. The western shore was a ragged line of shadow. It seemed strange after miles of dark swamp creek.

Hawse turned left and skirted the western shoreline. The big man soon had his vessel gliding across the water at fifty miles an hour, staying in the shadow of the trees to escape the notice of anyone on the far shore.

A bug hit James in the right eye, but he managed to stay on course using the other eye only.

Hawse slowed to ten miles an hour and turned into a twenty-foot-wide creek. He stopped after going a hundred yards.

James idled up beside. "Let me wash my eye out. It's on fire." He leaned over and splashed water. "Got a bug in it a few miles back."

Hawse pulled something out of a compartment on his jet ski. He twisted a knob on it and handed it to James. "Don't drop this. They used to be expensive. Now they're just hard to come by. To get your hands on one, you have to kill a Dissident Control goon."

It was a night vision device. Hawse got another one out and strapped it on. "We're late, but we'll get there with these. Make sure you have yours set up so you can see."

James looked around. He gave Hawse the thumbs up. "Ready when you are."

Hawse took off again at high speed.

Maria estimated they had traveled three miles upstream when Hawse slowed, circled back twenty yards, and then took off on a smaller branch creek. After a half mile of slower travel, Hawse pulled up to a large cypress tree.

"This is as far as I go ladies and gentlemen. You'll need the night vision goggles to stay on the path. There is a small house up there about three hundred yards. You will be climbing uphill onto dryer land. I doubt there is anyone there. If there is, it will be a woman named Fran. Use the door on the near side of the house. It's unlocked. Help yourself to what you need. Give the goggles to whoever picks you up in the morning. Good luck."

James shook Hawse's hand. "Thank you. You know, you only missed one turn? You really know the route."

"Don't tell the old guy back there about the missed turn." Hawse revved the engine. "There's a rope over there to tie off the ski with. Someone will get it tomorrow." With that, he opened the engine up, throwing a rooster tail five feet into the air. Four seconds later, he was swallowed by the dark night.

They walked up the trail, Maria following along blind by hooking a hand in James' belt. He had no trouble staying on the well-marked trail with the night vision goggles.

After making their way up a cobblestone walkway in the backyard, they both stopped on the concrete pad back porch to kick and scrub mud off their shoes. They found the concrete block construction house to be deserted. It was stocked with everything one under their circumstances might need, including a gas refrigerator full of food.

Maria headed straight for the shower. "Will you see if you can find some clothes that might halfway fit me?"

James sat in an easy chair. "Sure. I need to look for some clean clothes myself."

He found jeans and a T-shirt for both of them, leaving hers outside the bathroom door.

After they both had showered, they enjoyed a large meal of steak, rice and gravy, homemade bread, and a salad of tomatoes, lettuce, cucumbers, black olives, and olive oil dressing, all washed down with home-brewed beer. They wolfed it down while a storm raged outside. James commented once on how good food is when you are really hungry. Maria just nodded and continued to eat.

Neither one felt like talking. They were too tired. Now that there was time to think about it, she realized they barely knew each other.

While cleaning up, Maria glanced over her shoulder to see him wiping the table down. She put a dish on the rack to dry and turned to face him. She stood there in a T-shirt that hung so loosely it constantly threatened to slip off one or the other shoulder. The neck was many times too large and the shoulders way too wide, so she bunched some of the superfluous cloth in her right hand and held it to her chest. The jeans were likewise too large and were pulled tight around her small waist with a wide belt that would appear more appropriate on a pirate with a long blade hanging from it. The rest of the jeans were so baggy on her she looked like a clown. Standing there barefoot, her raven hair not yet dry and still uncombed and pulled back behind her ears, clutching the front of her shirt, the sight would have made James laugh under circumstances that were more normal.

"I have something to tell you," she said, "and I hope you're not going to be angry."

James put the rag down. "I doubt that. But don't ever be afraid to tell me anything."

Looking sheepish, she asked, "Remember your sunglasses?"

"Yes. What about them?"

"When we were out on the big lake doing about a hundred, I turned my head slightly and the wind just whipped them off. I'm sorry, but they are gone."

James chuckled. "You've got to be kidding me. I'm afraid I have to sit down and laugh for a while."

She put her hands on her hips. "Well, what's so damn funny about me losing your glasses? They looked expensive. They probably cost you a lot of Unity Credits. I bet you worked hard for them."

James looked at her with the deepest expression of incongruity she had ever seen on a man. "Both of us gave up everything, and I do mean everything today, except for our lives. And you think I give a damn about those sunglasses?"

"Why *did* you risk your life and throw everything away for me, a stranger?"

"There is a good reason. At least I think it was a good reason. I was not just saving a pretty woman. I saw in you everything I value. And it damn sure was not sunglasses or any other material thing. This morning you put me to shame. I have seen what you're made of, what you believe in. So much you are willing to sacrifice your life. I had to do what I could. To do nothing would have been spitting on everything I value. I'm telling you I value you. And it does not matter that I barely know you."

Maria blushed. Her eyes bore into him, half expecting this to be a come-on. However, she did not think it was. "What about the man they killed? You did nothing for him."

"It was he who made saving you possible. The three agents were busy disposing of his body. That gave me time to get you out of the room." His face grew grim. "I don't know who he was, but he saved your life."

"Yours too," she said. "You probably would have tried to save me even if the agents had not left the room." She looked at him accusingly. "I'll bet it wasn't the first time you sat by and did nothing while others were murdered. Yet you saved me because I'm prettier than he was." She looked away. "I'm sorry. It's just I don't believe my life is more valuable than that man's."

"Don't apologize. You're right. I'm a sucker for pretty girls. The fact is though; the only thing I could have done for him is get myself killed. I saw a small window of opportunity and took it. Like I said if it wasn't for him…"

She looked at James, not sure what to say.

"For years I restrained myself when talking to that bastard and a hundred others just like him. Oh, I came close to the edge. And my reports got me locked up and beaten a couple times. But I never put it all on the line like you did today. I never had the courage, but you did. Just because of some kid you never met, his willingness to stand up to the bastards, no matter the odds. If they have not killed him yet, he is out there now, alone in the dark, in some place like we just came from." He moved closer. "And you were willing to die just to support him in your own way."

Thunder boomed outside. She ignored it. "He knows he does not have a chance, but he won't quit. He just keeps fighting."

"And so did you today. You did not know that I or anyone else was going to help you. You expected to die for your right to speak the truth. To *die* just because you said something someone in power did not like. Today you reminded me of what our people could be. That boy inspires you. Well, you inspire me."

Maria took a step back, catching herself on the kitchen counter. She looked as if she had just taken a blow to the stomach.

James put his hands up and backed away. "Oh, I frightened you with my sudden talk of…how I feel about you. I know we just met hours ago. I was talking about respect. I did not mean to be so sudden. I was talking about your courage. Don't think I expect anything to happen between us. I just thought it was so ironic, you worrying about those sunglasses."

Maria put her hands to her face, using her palms to check the rivulets running down her cheeks. "It's not that. It's just that your words reminded me of the worst day of my life; the day I saw my mother and father standing in front of the agents who were about to execute them. My father spoke many of those same words to her."

"Perhaps you're a lot like your mother."

"Never," Maria shook her head. "I'll never be as brave as her."

"I'm sure she and your father would be proud of you."

She turned her back for a few seconds, wiped her face and turned to face him. "I have been wondering these last few years if I were not insane. I seem to be the only one who thinks freedom is more valuable than anything the government can provide. Everyone you meet in the cities thinks the Unity Party is the best thing to ever happen to us."

"Well, now you know you're not alone."

Windblown rain assaulted the kitchen window.

"He is." She looked out at the night. Flashes of distant lightning, revealing storm-tossed trees, lifted the curtain of darkness intermittently. "Do you think it's storming where he is? He's out there somewhere, being hunted like an animal."

"No. He's a long way from here."

*   *   *

The boy shivered in the rain and wrapped his shredded forearm with cloth torn from his shirt. He guessed it was around midnight. He had no watch, but it seemed like midnight. He tied the ends of the cloth together and pulled the knot tight with his right hand and teeth. Somewhere nearby he had a cache hidden. He needed to find it. It contained many needful items: food, ammunition, military surplus wound bandages, and other items he did not need at this time. He planned to leave what he did not need.

His cache sites were calculated to be as easy as possible to find again. First, he always had a large target to aim for. For this one, a mile-long lake, and a creek that flowed out of it, the convergence of the two being the general area of the cache. Two giant cypress trees, much larger than any others in the area and easy to find in the swamp, were the next markers. Then the last marker was the skeleton stump of another giant cypress ten feet across that had died decades ago. Seven feet south of the stump, the bottom end of what was the cypress trunk was lying hollow and half-rotted on the swamp floor. In the hollow log, was a waterproof container buried under punk wood and leaves.

All of this made the cache easy to find in daylight, but he was worried he might not find it in the middle of a stormy night. He could wait for daylight, but he wanted to be miles away by then, so he pressed on wearily. He used a flashlight with a blue lens.

Using his compass and dead reckoning only, he systematically searched in a deliberate pattern until he found one of the trees. The storm was waning when he shined light into the hollow log to check for snakes before putting his hand in.

Chapter 5

"It's a hell of a thing, isn't it Merrick?" Sergeant Gurney Appleton looked around, appraising the kill zone. The scene of death stank of wet swamp and dead dogs. The creek had retreated to some degree now that the storms had passed. Horse Whisperer's head was exposed to the hot sun, protruding above the surface of the black water, looking as if he grew there from the muddy bottom. His head was speckled with flies, most clustered over his open, vacant eyes and crawled in and out of his mouth. The look of abject terror was frozen on his face. Those who ventured to look were struck with a sudden chill, incongruous as it was, standing in the jungle in heat and humidity around the man-invented number of one hundred. Man-things, things of civilization, seemed starkly out of place here in the timeless mud.

Merrick Raebyrne, a lieutenant in the Department of Dissident Control, District 13, of Southeast Province, remained quiet and continued to look at the-six inch-tall flags marking the location of each spent 30/06 and .45ACP cartridge case.

He stood among three dead dogs swarming with flies. His green and black uniform was soaked with sweat. He kept in shape, but too much time enjoying air-conditioning had taken its toll, and he was getting too old for this crap anyway.

Damn it's hot, he did not say. He swept the area, his eyes scribing a full circle. He saw only primal jungle. There was no sign of man or his modern technology. It could have been the Stone Age as far as his eyes were concerned. Ropes suspended from hovering helicopters had lowered him and his men into this jungle. Global positioning transmitters, both on the dogs and the national police agents, led them to the location. The helicopters had left and would return later to take them and the dead men back to the twenty-first century.

Raebyrne looked across the glade and beyond to the other side of the creek. There, he saw the flags on six-feet-tall poles. "What a place for an ambush."

The bodies of the three dead dogs were already bloated, but the smell was not quite unbearable, yet. Flies buzzed in the air, disturbed by the presence of the men and now gathering courage to return to the bullet wounds to feast and blow maggots once more. Raebyrne was glad there were no human bodies on this side of the creek. Nothing is more repulsive than rotting humans are.

Raebyrne sat down on the windfall the boy had used for cover to think, trying to guess where the rifle would have been when the cartridge cases were ejected. He looked up at his friend, Sergeant Gurney Appleton. A short, compact man of surprising physical strength that had been the undoing of many foolish enough to believe he presented an easy mark. "I need your carbine for a minute Gurney."

"Sure." The sergeant handed over the M4 carbine, muzzle pointed skyward, and then used his free hands to swat mosquitoes off his face and head. His military style "high and tight" haircut left little protection for his scalp. His white hair stood on end like a brush, and his light complexioned face had a peppering of acne pockmarks, reminders of his teenage years a decade ago.

Lieutenant Raebyrne kept the carbine pointed safely away from his friend. "Tell the others to get out of the kill zone for a minute."

After everyone was out of the area, he shouldered the weapon and aimed it at the flags on the other side of the creek seventy to eighty yards away. The flags were on top of six-feet-tall poles, marking the bodies that still lay where they fell. Resting the carbine on the log, he tried to aim at each flag.

"How did he see them through all of this brush?" Raebyrne muttered something unintelligible under his breath. Then he said, "Damn. The boy's eyes picked out small pieces of them through the woods. I don't want him hunting *me*."

Raebyrne lifted the carbine. "The first to die was flag number four."

He got up from the ground and then walked over to where two pistol cartridge cases and two rifle cartridge cases lay, small flags marking them. Once again, he carefully got down where he thought the rifle was when fired at the agents. He aimed the carbine over the log toward the kill zone at the flags that marked where the bodies were.

Pointing at the ground, Raebyrne said, "There is where he was when he shot flag number three. Then he shot one of the dogs with his rifle and two with his pistol."

If Appleton was uncomfortable with his friend's unfeeling way of calling their dead men "flags," he said nothing.

"Gurney? Look, this is where he killed the last two dogs. They were on him when he shot. Little chance they did not draw some blood. His mind was on the agents when the dogs came up on him from behind. He knew they were coming, but he was relying on his ears to warn him when they got close, while his eyes were on the agents. The only mistake he made was letting the dogs get to him, and that was because he did not know they were trained to come up so quietly, when they get close. I wouldn't bet my life on the boy making that mistake again."

He walked over to where the last shooting took place. After getting down in the prone position, his elbows sinking into the still rain-wet mud, he pantomimed shooting from under the log. "This is where he killed the last three. He saved the safest position for last."

"Smart. That's when the danger of him being shot was highest," Sergeant Appleton said.

"Smart or trained."

"Yeah, there is trained and untrained. The boy is trained."

"If he lives long enough to get some experience under his belt, he's going to make the devil's own demons look like kind old ladies."

Lieutenant Raebyrne walked back to the first position and handed the carbine to his friend. He sat down on the windfall, taking a full five minutes to think before saying anything.

A bald eagle circled overhead, screaming his displeasure with the intruders.

Raebyrne looked up.

Your grace has fallen. Now you're just another bird of meaningless feathers.

As if to answer, the eagle turned over and executed a high-speed dive, pulling out of the fall only two feet above the treetops, then coming up to a great height similar to a plane in a loop and then a barrel roll at the apex, spinning as it came back down. It continued its aerobatics for some time. Then, seemingly satisfied it had shown the world it is still an eagle, it leveled off, looked down at the men and screamed insistently for thirty seconds, finally swooping down to glide just above the treetops, disappearing out of sight.

Raebyrne brought his thoughts back to earth. "The boy repositioned every time he shot. Snipers do that. Even though he only moved a few yards each time, it was enough to throw the men off if they saw his muzzle blast move any brush, or perhaps the muzzle flash if it was dark enough in the shade of these trees. And it allowed him to stay safe behind this log."

"A sixteen-year-old boy...not only pumped with fear, but rage also," Appleton said. "And he has the presence of mind to waylay a squad of agents."

"Not only did he stay concealed, he took certain deliberate effort to stay behind bullet-stopping cover: this log."

"And he knew the difference between concealment and cover," Appleton said.

Raebyrne nodded. "If you had done what I just did, you would know how good he is at picking out targets through small shooting lanes in the brush. I don't think there's an agent alive who could do as well. There was one I knew of, but he's lying over there dead."

"He must have spent his childhood in these woods. Here, he is a shark in the sea, and we are a fish on land." Appleton scanned the scene. "He's going to be hard to ferret out of these woods."

"If we keep the pressure on him he may weaken from starvation, or just plain exhaustion," Raebyrne said. "On the other hand he may have caches of supplies all over these woods."

"He's young. I say keep the pressure on him and he'll break. Maybe even do our job for us."

Raebyrne swallowed, his face strained. "Maybe, but I don't think so. He intends to put a bullet in everything in uniform until we kill him." He pointed at the flags on the other side of the creek. "I think he has proven when he intends to do something he gets it done."

"This boy's a strange animal indeed."

"Strange or not, he can shoot. He left two dead agents back at the farm, both upper chest shots. He also left two rounds of empty thirty aught six brass exactly six hundred yards away up on a hill." He looked up at his friend with worried eyes. "He had the range already measured and marked. He was prepared, and you don't make a shot like that without knowing the come-ups on your rifle sight. There was not much wind when he made the shot, but I would not bet my life on the small chance he can't dope wind and adjust his sights. Two shots equaled two dead men, six hundred yards."

"You're right. He didn't stick around to try to kill more on the spot either. No. He knew they would outmaneuver him and call in reinforcements, so he led them here. He wanted them to come after him."

"You know why he wanted to take them here?" Raebyrne did not wait for an answer. "Because it's probably the best spot for an ambush in the whole damn district. That's why. Especially for someone alone. The whole ambush was military precise, as professional as it gets. He utilized everything in his environment to his best advantage. If he had been leading so much as a rifle squad, he could easily have wiped out an entire company here."

Appleton's eyes narrowed. "Hey, I admit he held his own, but this kid is just a farmer."

Raebyrne made a sweeping motion over the ground. "Look at the empty brass. Count them. Then count the number of dead men and dogs. One shot each. He doesn't like to waste ammo."

The senior agent took out a handkerchief and wiped sweat from his forehead. "He didn't waste a bullet on the one stuck in the mud. The boy knew he would die before anyone got here to pull him out. He and the new transfer who was shot through the chest were the only two who were not shot in the head."

After years of World Government, it was rare for Dissident Control agents to encounter an individual who had both a backbone and a mind. Such a thing could provoke a true believing Unity Party bureaucrat to wet his pants. Now it was giving Raebyrne concern, and he was not a true believer.

Raebyrne's face was a question mark. "This boy was already trained. Those lumps of rotting meat over there gave him the one thing he needed to put that training to use. Who trained him, anyway? How many more are there like him? The government gives them reason to hate, and now someone is training them to kill. The stuff nightmares are made of."

"Why do you think he shot the new guy, Simmons, in the chest and all the others in the head? You think he wanted the first one to suffer. Get it out of his system maybe?"

"Read Simmons' personnel records. He was the only one out here who knew what he was doing. Chances are Simmons never exposed himself enough to offer a headshot to the boy, so he shot what was available. Like you said, the boy is trained. Somehow, the boy knew Simmons was his greatest threat. That's why he shot flag number four first."

Appleton turned to look at flag number four. "Simmons."

Raebyrne stood. "Get on the radio. Issue an official order authorized by me. All personnel involved in the Patrick Timucua Paine case will wear full body armor at all times when in the field. Remember, that is an order."

"It's over a hundred out here friend. You know we'll probably lose some men to heatstroke."

"Before this is over, we will lose a lot more to massive trauma and blood loss."

"Yes sir."

While Appleton was on the radio, Raebyrne circled the area, deep in thought. He stopped short with one foot in the air, then turned to look at a tree. Something had caught his eye.

There was a piece of olive drab nylon cut from a poncho tied to an oak tree only fifteen feet away.

"Why didn't I see that before?"

The waterproof material was rolled up and tied with a length of vine. He unrolled it and found a copy of the Declaration of Independence and the original ten Amendments to the Constitution, formally known as the Bill of Rights. Worn and faded, it looked as if it had been carried around in someone's pocket for a long time.

Who carries something like this around nowadays? It can get you ten years for subversion.

He saw where part of the Declaration of Independence had been underlined: We hold these truths to be self-evident, that all men are created equal, that they are endowed by their Creator with certain unalienable Rights...

"Human beings" had been written above the word "men." He turned the document over. On the back, he found a note. Raebyrne, forty-five now, his eyes needing help for reading, he had been waiting four years to get laser surgery at the government clinic, put on his glasses and began to read.

> It has not been easy, but I have managed to live in peace with The Party and the government it controls for slightly more than sixteen years. This is because my family stayed in the shadows of society and we kept to ourselves. We were not worth your bother, until today.
>
> Now you have come to scrape out the bottom of the barrel, the last ten percent. You have already consumed the soft underbelly of what was the United States of America. I portend you will find the last tenth to be iron backbone. You will need strong teeth to chew it and a stronger stomach to keep it down.
>
> It took much work and sacrifices for my family to keep the last of their bloodline hid and therefore preserve what freedom I enjoyed. They

provided me with an island of freedom and light in a sea of tyranny and dark.

God shines his light with equal luster on all hearts, but you in government have worked diligently to deny that light to all mankind. Now, nine tenths of our people live in a cage, kept by the government like animals in a zoo. No human being can live in a cage and remain a human being for long. The moment a man is caged, the human being in him starts to die. You have turned most of our people into hairless apes, with no soul, no heart, no humanity, no decency, and no mind. You know this, as it was done by your design. You call these hairless apes you created the Redundant Headcount. This is what you have done to ninety percent of our people. Still! Your hunger for power over our people is not satiated.

Those who came this morning said if we went with them, we would no longer have to work the land, as we would be given free food. Do you in government think work is a bad thing? They said we would be given a place to live, but we had plenty of land to work and live on if you in government had stayed off it. They said we need you to take care of us. However, no one from The Party came around with a spare nipple when our crops failed. We got by with what we had. Your kind of charity comes with a price all free people must refuse to pay. So, it is as well you did not come to offer help, as we would have been obliged to refuse it. Last, they said we need protection, but your trained killers are the only ones that ever did us harm.

This morning, killers came to force us off our land and move us into Southeast City. They said they did not intend to harm us, but what would you call stealing our land, our way of life, and our freedom. You can keep your city and your World Government. What we had was better.

Still! My grandfather and mother raised no hand against those who trespassed and entered our home uninvited. Their only incriminations, harmless words of protest, were to entreat you to leave our home and land and leave us in peace. Even this was more than your killers would suffer. They murdered my grandfather and mother. With such a murderous people, I want no peace. I will kill you wherever, however, whenever I can, and my choices are varied and expansive.

My grandfather and mother represented the last two generations of my family before me, but for one other and hundreds of books, they taught me all that I know. You would say I am uneducated, as I have never suffered the brainwashing and perversions of your schools and other government programs.

I must admit you in government can be efficient instructors, for you have opened my eyes to a new subject this morning. I trust in the near future, you will help me hone a fine edge to the particular yet diverse art of killing. I have studied war, but until this morning, it was all academic. I have never studied hate, but you have led me to a new and useful passion. It will keep my heart warm in this cold world.

If the harmless words of the father of my father and the mother of all that I am should prompt you to kill them, let it be known that I, Timucua, will save my breath for the fight.

Let the gun speak!

Lieutenant Raebyrne stood holding the brown paper, an expression of bewilderment engraved on his face. He had never in his life read anything like this, a digest of the world according to a sixteen-year-old boy. A worthless piece of paper cut from a book. Fine, flowery thoughts printed on one side, but with nothing to enforce any of those proclamations, transformed into a document of true value by one human being's clear declaration of a willingness to fight, kill, suffer, and die for those flowery words, thus giving meaning and substance to them for the first time in generations.

"You are the freest human in America. Unfortunately your life expectancy is short."

Lieutenant Raebyrne felt a wave of chilling doubt flow from his gut to every extremity. He could not find fault in the boy's actions. If the boy was not wrong, then why was he laboring to kill him? He took no countenance of anarchy, but why use deadly force when not necessary? Surely, those agents did not have to kill the mother and grandfather.

Too much power. We agents have no limits. The government removed all of the confinements of the worst human traits. It's a recipe for disaster.

The killing of the agents was not murder. Even revenge is justified if it is congruent with self-defense. Forget the damn law. And piss on the government. It does not matter. The boy must be killed. It is certain that he will not un-declare his private war. He will continue killing until he himself is killed.

Raebyrne read the testament again. A feeling he had before returned, stronger this time. He had been concentrating on the words. Now he let himself feel the mood of the words, read between the lines. He felt himself being sucked backwards. He wondered if it had not been written in the twenty-first century, but perhaps the twentieth or nineteenth or eighteenth, or the seventeenth. The past became one with the present.

The question of freedom and human rights was not a new one. The immemorial darkness of soulless governments clawing more power from the flesh and blood of the governed continued. *God tells us man is born free.* He had been taught there is no God, and there is no such thing as a God-given human right. At this moment, his heart was screaming at his mind.

Raebyrne walked over to Appleton. "Gurney, get back on the radio. Tell HQ I want everything that can be found on the boy and his family. I mean everything. The smallest detail. Someone trained this boy, and I want to know who."

Chapter 6

The sun was high when Timucua ran to a canoe he had secreted on a creek months before. Upturned to shed rain, he kicked it over and stepped back. A four-foot diamondback coiled and rattled for a few seconds, then moved away, its belly undulating almost imperceptibly like a caterpillar as it pushed its thick body over the leaf-littered swamp floor with large belly scales, head lifted high, tongue flicking.

The boy could not make good time paddling. His left arm throbbed and shot bolts of pain into his shoulder. He had cleaned and bandaged the wound as best he could with a small first aid kit he kept in his "bug-out" pack, but it was inadequate for the seriousness of the injury. Despite his arm, he paddled all day and into the night.

When the night was two thirds over, a sliver of moon came out from behind the clouds, its image reflecting off the glassy surface of the bayou, creating its own stars in the rippling wake of the canoe. The glow of indirect light made it possible just to make out an alligator in an aggressive mood. It shadowed him for sometime as he paddled through the pain. He was learning to distance pain from his consciousness. He told himself that they couldn't hurt him anymore. They had done their worst on the first morning. Anything that comes after is nothing.

Mosquitoes buzzed constantly around him, but he dare not slap at them and make any noise. His enemies intended to hunt him down and kill him. He would need all of his skills to stay alive long enough to make them pay for his family's blood and his own life. A small mistake could be fatal. He must remain unseen and unheard until he strikes again. By false dawn, he was deep in one of the largest swamps in the South.

*   *   *

"Where is that background info on the Paine family I asked for? I should have had it yesterday." Raebyrne just walked in from the field, his uniform soaked with sweat, legs muddy up to his knees. He wasted no time when he had a case to work.

The helicopter ride had cooled him off, leaving his uniform a little less wet and stained white with a ring of salt on his back.

Now he was clammy in the air-conditioning. Up all night directing the search, he was dead on his feet. No matter. He had no time for a shower and change. The boy must be hunted down before he killed again. He did not ask for the job, but it was his.

A woman, looking official in her crisp well-fitting uniform, her auburn hair tied back tightly into a bun, got up from her desk and raised her petite form to its full stature, all 5' 2" of her. "Here Lieutenant." She handed him a thin folder, gave a perfunctory smile that lasted all of one third of a second and sat back down behind the desk.

It was just as well, his eyes were on the folder, and he made it a point not to be too friendly with the female officers. He was married, very married, and he had much trouble through the years with officers of both the opposite and same gender engaging in romantic fraternizing. It caused friction and discord among the ranks and created discipline problems, not to mention marital problems at home, which in turn were brought back to the agency that in turn caused... It was a snowball racing to hell, all starting with one thing and leading to another. He could not stop others from taking part in such juvenility, but he was married, and he took his responsibilities seriously, both professional and personal.

Raebyrne stopped in front of her desk long enough to thumb through the small number of pages. After a few seconds, he looked up. "Is this all there is?"

"Yes. That is all we could find on the family. What little we could find we had to dig up the old-fashioned way. There was nothing in the records, and I mean nothing. Before the killings, The Party did not know that family existed. Only a little on the grandfather was found, and that stopped decades ago. It's like he fell off a cliff."

"You have nothing here on the boy. You're right; it's as if he doesn't exist."

"He must not have been born in a hospital," the woman said. "And he never went to school. I think some of the anarchists call it freeborn."

He looked back down at the papers. "Not much on the mother either. She had a degree in history from way back before The Unity Party abolished the Constitution. I can't see where any of them have been in any trou— Hey! The grandfather was in the Army. Served two tours in Vietnam. Something called SOG." He looked up. "What is that?"

She shook her head and shrugged.

Raebyrne yelled out across the room. "Does anyone here know anything about what the Army calls SOG?" He got nothing but shrugs and a "What?" and "No. Never heard of it." He refocused his attention on the woman. "Where are the rest of his Army records? Damn it."

"Army says there was a fire during the two thousand sixteen famine riots. Some records were lost. The Vietnam War was a lifetime ago."

A janitor emptying wastebaskets on the far end of the office caught Raebyrne's attention. "Hey Gary, aren't you a Vietnam veteran?"

A nearly bald, white-haired, thin elderly man picked up a duster and started to walk out of the room. He was bent over steeply and taking six-inch steps.

Maybe he did not hear. It only took six quick long steps for Raebyrne to catch him at the door. "Gary, what can you tell me about an outfit called SOG? It was during your war."

For a few seconds Gary still seemed not to hear. "Why do you want to know about SOG? It was a long time ago. Why not let it be?" On his voice rode an air of musty, disused emotion, just taken off a shelf.

"I'm not asking you to tell me war stories and cause you to revive old nightmares. Just tell me what SOG was. What did they do?"

The old man's face suddenly showed more emotion than anyone had seen him express in years. His eyes cleared and began to look too young for his crevassed, hollow-cheeked face. He hawked to clear his throat. "So many young guys died. And for what? So The Party could destroy it all."

"SOG, what was it, Gary?"

"They worked in small RTs, recon teams, with indigenous personnel. They were ordered to go outside the law under Johnson and then Nixon. Took their orders directly from the Pentagon and the White House. It wasn't legal according to Congress, but they mostly worked in Laos, and Cambodia. There were US soldiers there long before the people and Congress knew about it, when LBJ was in the White House."

"What was their job, their mission?"

The old man laughed out loud, a haunting, crazy old man's laugh, a laugh that said he had seen it all before, a sneering laugh born of pain and the sickening irony of man's brutality to man. He had lived a small part of the profane sadistic limerick of human history.

His laugh reverberated throughout the room, and everyone looked at him. "Why the same thing you were doing this morning. They hunted the deadliest predator on earth, and they killed them by the thousands. Their main job was to disrupt traffic along Uncle Ho's trail. And they found targets for Arc Light missions."

"Arc Light missions?"

"Heavy bombers."

Raebyrne read from the paper in his hands. "How about Devlin Paine? Did you know him?"

The old man's eyes widened, and his bent-over back suddenly stiffened and straightened a little. "Dev Paine's grandson? Is he the one you're after? Didn't say on the bullshit news." He looked inward. "What are the odds?"

Raebyrne thought he might be getting somewhere. "Did you know the old man?"

"Knew of him. Met him two, three times." Suddenly his jaw clenched and became rigid as steel and his eyes flashed. "If you had sent those killers out to his farm when he was twenty-five, he would have killed them all. It doesn't take much to murder an unarmed old fart soldier and a woman, does it? His grandson showed them though. How old is he?

Sixteen they said on the news. Maybe they got that right. Just about everything else was bullshit."

"Well, what can you tell me about him?"

Anger flashed in the old man's eyes. "He's dead! I can tell you that. Heard you and your killers talking about it. Seemed proud of it. Well, the boy knocked all that hot air out of their lungs didn't he? How 'bout it, is your chest all swelled up with murdering a woman and old man?"

"Come on, Gary, you know me better than that." He swallowed. "Tell me about Paine's service in the war."

Gary appeared to want to go back to blissful, less painful, forgetfulness as soon as possible. "He was one of the best. A Distinguished Service Cross. Silver Stars, two, I think, and lesser medals. Written up for the MoH. Knew how to teach what he knew."

"Medal of Honor?"

"Yeah, but no President ever presented him with one. Made too many enemies in the Pentagon when he refused to follow illegal orders that went against his conscience."

"When was the last time you saw him?"

"Must have been about forty years ago. Ran into him at a lurp get-together."

"Forty years ago…well, thanks, Gary."

The old man seemed glad to be left alone and started walking away as fast as his six-inch steps allowed.

"Oh. Wait a minute. What's a lurp?"

Gary answered without turning around. "Means Long Range Recon Patrol. Don't ask me anymore about that. You can kill me if you want, but it's not any of your business."

The old man walked out of the room leaving Raebyrne ashamed.

*   *   *

Timucua slept late into the afternoon. When he woke, he ate a cold, tasteless meal of soup out of the can. Being "wet" food, it was needlessly heavy. He planned to eat the canned food first, saving the light freeze-dried supplies. There was no disappointment or surprise that the soup was tasteless. His heart was beating, but there were only two things telling him he was still alive: The hate burning in his heart, and the pain in his arm. To his eyes, the world was colorless. He saw only bleak shades of dark and light, varying degrees of gray. The world was dead and he barely alive.

He had to stay where he was in the canoe until sundown, so he had time to think. He did not feel inclined to travel yet anyway. Fatigue gradually forced pain and hate to back off some small degree. His arm did not seem to hurt as much except when he tried to move it. However, his body was drained, no more to give. It had to be recharged before he could go on. His internal tormentors must allow him to rest.

Timucua felt different in some strange new way. As he lay in the canoe and thought about his future, the things he planned to do were less fanciful, more concrete, and less fun. He saw with his eyes and felt with his heart, a cold, colorless world of ugly, heartless cruelty. What was there to live for but revenge?

His eyes saw this ugly world, but he seemed to fit right in, as he himself was just as ugly. The world he spent sixteen years in was dead, and his boyish spirit had died with it. He still found the swamp he had enjoyed as a child to be his friend, but for an inherently different reason. It was his environment, his advantage. It was what kept him alive by making them come to him on his terms. It was his killing ground.

Looking up, he saw an eagle circling. It had been there for thirty minutes. When he was small, his grandfather told him many stories of how warriors of the time of freedom could join the spirit of the eagle and watch over their loved ones while away from home. He told of how warriors of ancient times proved themselves worthy of the eagle's spirit with great deeds. Changing an enemy's heart and stopping a war, or saving the tribe's women from insult. All myths, he told himself, but good stories to tell a little boy. He remembered his father telling him myths usually expose much truth to those with a mind willing to see. "Many are based on history," he said.

"Remember," Grandfather added, "the eagle is the bird of freedom, and we people are its feathers. Without people of courage, freedom cannot fly."

Father told of the earliest Europeans settling in what was later called New England. A white man had killed an Indian woman and her baby. The chief, who had given the white settlers food, keeping them alive through their first season of snow, came to the settlement to inform them of the crime. A witness pointed to the man who was guilty.

The white leader said the murderer was too valuable to the settlement to lose. He was a good timberman and carpenter and a hard worker. They would hang another man who was lazy and of less value to the settlement in his stead.

The old chief walked away in silence.

The white leader ran after him. "Why do you leave?" he asked. "Are you not pleased with my decision?"

The chief kept walking. The white leader beseeched him to stop and answer.

He stopped. "I came here for justice, not to turn one crime into two. You have taught me here today you do not know what justice is. I have wasted my time."

"We are Christians," the white man said. "What do you know of justice?"

The old chief asked, "And what do you know of Christ? I know him by a different name, but I feel now I must know him better still than you."

He thought of how he had avenged his family's murder. It did not fill the empty cold in him. Still, he felt compelled to raise the price for his family's blood and his own life as high as possible.

His arm was oozing fluid through the bandages. He knew it needed more care than he had provided for it. He was not worried. He expected to be dead before the arm became a threat to his health. It did make him think of how his father and grandfather told him stories to teach him humility. The pain in his arm seemed much more effective than any of his grandfather's stories. He felt no pride in what he had done, but he felt no shame either. There was no room for shame or pride. He was full to the point of bursting with two of the ugliest of things, and there was more killing to do.

What had he become, and what would he become if he lived a month or two before they killed him?

Chapter 7

Sergeant Appleton stood before Lieutenant Raebyrne's desk along with a specialist from the crime lab. Raebyrne was impatient to learn the results of the analysis of the message left by the boy. The brown paper was in a clear plastic bag on his desk.

"Well," Raebyrne said. "What can you tell me about the person who wrote this?"

The short, slight man made an effort to stand taller, which gave him the appearance of having a steel rod up his spine. Half-glasses hung down to the near-end of his nose. He was not reading, so he did not need to be wearing them. To see, he had to look over them and that made it appear he was looking down his nose at people, though in physical fact, his nose was not upturned.

The psychoanalyst had been told little about the person who wrote the note. He began. "First of all, a boy did not write this monstrosity. It had to be someone at least thirty years old. And whoever wrote it must be educated to some degree." He waved his arm in a dismissive gesture. "The note says the author never went to school. The author is probably more traveled and experienced than he or she claims. The diction tells me the person is suffering from delusions of grandeur and is trying overly hard to be melodramatic." He smiled. "You know…the use of certain words for effect.

"Empathy for the human condition is expressed, however misplaced. I mean, blaming the government for the world's problems and all. This would suggest the author was a woman, but his propensity for violence suggests a psychopathic male in his mid-to-late twenties. Perhaps this person suffered child abuse and has many personalities, some male, and some female. Normally, I would advise a person like this almost never strikes out in violence, but you say he or she has already done so. In conclusion, I wouldn't place any significance at all on what the author says in this, ah, monstrosity."

Raebyrne leaned back in his chair and put his hands behind his head. "That is the biggest sack of bullshit I've ever been handed."

Appleton struggled to hold back laughter.

Though he was certain it would be a waste of time, Raebyrne decided to ask a question that might seem peculiar to the others. "What about the tone of the message? Doesn't it seem to be from...oh I don't know, it reminds me of something, but I can't get my mind around it."

The psychoanalyst smiled. "That's my job, to help you where you're weakest: your mind. Anyway, that does remind me of something a few of the others in the lab were talking about. We checked into the name, let's see here." He dug a scrap of paper out of his white lab coat pocket. Finally making use of his half-glasses, he read from the paper. "We looked into the background and history of the word Timucua. Unfortunately we could not find anything on it because of the purge of unnecessary history from all records back about fifteen years ago."

He slid his glasses back down his nose. "A couple of our older people think it might be a Native American tribe though. This jibes well with what one of them said about how she remembered reading a speech back when she was a little girl. An Indian chief that lived in the eighteen hundreds, before such garbage was purged from all records, spoke it. The note reminds her of that. Not the same words, just the tone, as you call it."

Raebyrne held his chin in his right hand, deep in thought. Coming back to the present, he leaned forward and put his elbows on the desk. "Thank you. You can go back to the lab and do some more thinking for us imbeciles while we do our jobs as automatons."

Appleton waited until they were alone. "What are you thinking?"

"I'm thinking the boy is more than he appears to be. Judging by his background it would be easy to jump to conclusions. But with him, you better be careful where you jump, it could be fatal."

He pointed at the note. "The person who wrote that is no psycho. Psychopaths do not give a damn about other people. Read that and consider his actions. Then tell me if you believe he doesn't care about what happened to his mother and grandfather. Justice. The boy is willing to suffer and die for it. He may not give a damn if his idea of justice meshes with The Party's, but that doesn't make him antisocial or a psycho, and he wasn't being melodramatic. His actions had already spoken before he put pencil to paper. He meant every word."

"You seem to have come to some conclusions about the boy already, without even meeting him."

"Haven't you?"

Appleton lifted his eyebrows and flashed his eyes toward the camera hanging from the ceiling. "I can't say yet."

"Yeah, well, I can."

Raebyrne got up from his chair and looked down at his pants. They were caked with dry mud. "I stink of swamp and bloated bodies." He rubbed his face, covered with red and swollen spots from many mosquito bites. "It's seven. I'm going home to dinner."

He had wanted to go home all day, to take a long shower, wash off the swamp, sweat, and spend some time with his family. Maybe it would make him feel better.

*   *   *

Ten O'clock that night, Gary was dusting. He should have been in his apartment asleep. However, he came back to work to finish a job he started earlier. It will be his last day as janitor.

No one was around, so he walked over to the lieutenant's desk. Gary had already checked the camera monitor room, and no one was there. He pulled out a miniature camera and started snapping photographs of any papers on the desk. Not daring to take time to read anything, he just took what photographs he could and slipped the camera back into his pocket. He turned, looked up at the ceiling camera and gave it his middle finger, then left the building.

*   *   *

Timucua crawled just close enough to the two-lane country road to allow him to see a quarter mile in one direction, half a mile in the other. Just at the nearside of a curve in the road was a roadblock.

"There you are, you SOBs. Grapes for the picking."

There was a patrol car, not armored, but a "thin-skinned" civilian-type car, parked sideways across the road. Anyone who wanted to could have simply drove around, but who nowadays had that kind of nerve. One must always be polite to the government, even when they are murdering people.

Two agents were sitting in the front seat with the engine running and the air-conditioner on high. It was hot, over one hundred degrees, and they had been ordered to wear bullet resistant vests and helmets at all times. So there they sat enjoying the cool air. With no traffic, they had nothing to do but put in their eight hours and then go home. There was no reason to believe the boy would be anywhere near. They were thirty miles from the boy's farm.

In the other direction, there was a hill. Timucua had already checked and found nothing but more woods on the other side for a mile, as far as he could see. He had also checked around the curve and found more woods. Not a house or person was in sight.

Timucua would rather have shot them when they were outside the car, but you cannot always have what you want. He did want the car, blood and brain splattered or not.

Estimating the range to be two hundred and seventy-five yards, he was confident he could make the shot. He confirmed the range by comparing the front sight to the width of the near agent's head as it appeared while looking through the rear peep sight. He had lowered the rear sight below normal battle-sight-zero for close-in woods fighting so he could take headshots at less than one hundred yards. His own battle-sight-zero and come-ups were for his hand-loaded rounds, not old military surplus that had already been used up, and was impossible to get even before all ammunition, and firearms had been banned. At this range, six clicks up would allow him to put the man's head on top of the front sight when he pulled the trigger. A small target, but he had done it before at longer range. This time the target was two human heads, not paper.

Timucua looked at the trees by the road where the patrol car sat parked to judge the wind. Then he checked the trees and brush across the road from where he lay. He judged the wind as light, about five miles an hour, perhaps six, at full value coming out of three O'clock. He moved the rear sight one click to the right.

Now he wanted to get the angle right, so he crawled to the edge of the pavement. The weeds and grass along the road had not been mowed since The Party cut Wild People off from all commerce and declared war on freedom lovers. He made full use of the concealment it provided.

Timucua worked rapidly. Someone might drive up while he was lying there beside the road. Even so, he still took the time necessary to get into his natural point of aim. The shooting sling caused considerable pain to his left arm, but shooting without a tight sling would decrease the accuracy of the shot. This he could not afford, not with such a small target at this range.

The Garand barked and kicked. He called the shot perfect. If his sight adjustments were right, he now had two dead men sitting in the car two hundred seventy-five yards away.

As soon as he could after the recoil, the rifle barrel had raised only two inches; he quickly looked through the sights to check the results of his work. Both side windows were gone, shattered, the near agent's chest was leaning against the steering wheel, the horn blaring its monotone wail. He could see that there was no movement.

After checking to see if anyone had driven up on him from over the hill, he crawled back into the woods. He stopped and took the time to reload his rifle and reset the rear sight. Then he made his way through the woods and back to the road where the car was parked. There was no movement from either of the two agents when he walked up to the car from behind with his rifle shouldered and ready.

They were both dead, their heads ruptured. He pulled them out of the car and dragged them into the weed-choked ditch. Ignoring the blood and brain matter, he slid behind the wheel and then laid the muzzle end of the rifle on his lap and the butt end on the seat beside him so he could get out of the car fast with the rifle ready. He left his pack on the floor.

Timucua was apprehensive about driving since he had never done it before. After a few miles though, he was driving what he considered to be reasonably well. "Good enough for government work," he said. He did not recognize the voice as his own.

As he drove, he listened to the radio, but there did not seem to be much going on with the agents in the area. He read the messages on the computer screen. There was nothing of any use to him. Everything seemed to be routine at the moment, but he was certain that would change soon.

The miles flowed by, to the boy seemingly at astonishing speed. Many ruins of once occupied homes stood rotting by the road, their former owners either dead or moved by force to Southeast City.

That is one advantage to the Removal Plan: Fewer people in the way means more room for my war with anyone wearing a green and black uniform.

Traveling at sixty miles an hour, he had gone more than twenty miles when he saw two agents on motorbikes coming from the other direction. The one closest to the centerline was in the lead by ten feet. At the last second, Timucua whipped the car to the left, striking the lead motorcycle with the left fender, forcing it into the path of the other. Both agents spilled onto the pavement, rolled, and skidded forty yards, rendering one unconscious and the other stunned.

Timucua slammed on the brakes and brought the car to a halt, tires smoking. He backed over one agent, stopping the car on top of him. The rear left tire caved in his chest, his intestines oozed out from under his soft body armor.

The other agent tried to lift his head. Both arms were broken, jagged bone protruded from his left, halfway between the shoulder and elbow. A crimson puddle was expanding on the pavement where he lay. Without getting out first, Timucua aimed his pistol and shot him in the face just under the helmet.

He decided to test their body armor to learn vital information for future use, so he got out and shot a dead agent through the head with his rifle. The bullet penetrated completely through the helmet. He then stood over the corpse and shot him in the center of the chest to see if the bullet could defeat the trauma plate in the vest. Timucua was disappointed when he found the plate had stopped the bullet. Next, he tried to shoot through the vest at an angle that would miss the trauma plate. He bent over and ripped at the Velcro straps. Taking the bloody vest off allowed him to learn the bullet penetrated the nearside of the vest and went through the chest to be stopped on the far side. "That will work," he said to no one.

Timucua did not believe a .45 hardball round could go through a helmet, but wanted to be sure, so he took careful aim and fired. The bullet sang a raw, earsplitting tune, descending in both pitch and volume as it flew away after ricocheting off, leaving a deep gouge where it hit.

His experiment finished, Timucua got back into the car and drove off. The left tire spun in the gore of the other agent's body.

Driving down the road, a thought came to him. His mother's childhood friend lived nearby. He decided he must warn her family that his actions probably put them in danger. Ill-tempered agents will be swarming the area soon. A foreboding feeling washed over him, compelling him to drive faster.

The dirt road they lived on was in bad shape. Only horses and wagons had been down it for more than a decade. He was forced to drive no more than ten miles an hour. Evidence of recent use by a large vehicle, probably an armored personnel carrier, set his heart to racing.

Timucua had not been to the home in years and was not sure how much farther it was. Passing a curve, he realized too late that he was already there.

As he looked through the windshield, a scene assaulted his eyes so violently it felt to him to burn eternally in his retina. He forgot to breathe. Part of him, the tactical warrior in him, tried to take in the scene of sadism so he could effectively react. However, the human side of him was tripping overloaded emotional circuit breakers, so repulsed, sickened, he could think of nothing but throwing up. Suddenly, he felt near to blacking out from not breathing and began to gag for air.

Her piercing screams cut through the humid air, a sickening combination of animal terror and human suffering. Her name was Haleigh, the last time he saw her she was eleven. Now her red hair was matted with the deeper red of blood, and her face was contorted with pain and terror. She was nude and completely helpless. She was fourteen years old and was just starting to be less of a girl and more of a woman.

There were five men in the green and black uniform of the national police. Four of them were holding her stretched out on the tailgate and bed of a pickup. Two in the bed of the truck were each pulling on an arm. Two more stood behind the tailgate pulling on her legs. The one holding her right arm had a knife, was cutting gashes into her arm, and shoulder repeatedly, each cut deeper than the last. A fifth was raping her violently.

By shear unthinking instinct, Timucua grabbed the Garand and slid out the door. The range was an easy one hundred yards. He fired from standing, offhand. The one raping her was the first to die. The two holding her arms were sprayed with blood and heart as the bullet exploded from his chest. All five were dead in half as many seconds. Their minds barely had time to register what was happening before they in turn were shot. The last one was just starting to jump out of the pickup when he was shot through the right lung. Timucua did not realize he was screaming as he shot.

A man ran out of the front door of the house, holding his pants up with his right hand, an M4 carbine in the other. He tried to make it to the personnel carrier. Timucua almost missed, he had given too much lead to the shot, but he did nearly remove the man's left arm three inches above the elbow. The man screamed, dropped his carbine, and grabbed his broken arm. His pants fell to his ankles, tripping him. He raised himself on his knees and his right hand, but he was shot through the right lung, heart and out the left lung. He fell dead from an instant loss of blood pressure.

Timucua ran for the woods twenty yards away. Someone fired from a window on full automatic. He dove behind a large hickory as bullets chewed at the tree, throwing chunks of bark. When he was able to look, Timucua saw the agent standing in the window while reloading. He remembered the lessons of his grandfather: "The key to hitting what you aim at in a firefight and doing it before he does it to you, is to take all the time necessary but no more. Remember, you can't miss fast enough to survive a firefight. You must get there the 'firstest with the mostest'!" He put a bullet through the center of the agent's heart and was already reaching for a fresh clip before the pinging empty hit the ground.

His mind worked on the problem he faced, taking in what data was available. First, it was obvious to him the personnel carrier parked in the yard was empty, useless to the remaining agents. Otherwise, its heavy machinegun would have already been used. Second, right now those inside were wishing they were in the personnel carrier and not in that house. Third, there was zero cover between the house and the personnel carrier. They would never make it past his rifle. His fourth thought was there could be no more than three or four agents left in the house, unless it was a reinforced squad, even then, no more than five or six.

They will come out the back.

Staying behind cover at all times, he repositioned so he could cover both the front and back of the house.

Timucua settled down for a nerve-fraying wait.

He did not have to wait long. Two agents exploded from the back door, heading for the barn. Timucua was surprised by his calmness after the revolting shock he just had. He swung on the lead agent and fired. His head exploded and sprayed wet pink matter into the eyes of the agent behind. Blinded, he staggered and tripped over the other man's body. Timucua shot him in the buttocks and then both knees, finishing off by removing both his elbows, leaving him screaming and squirming on the ground.

That same old fire was building, heating up, burning his soul, and boiling the blood in his heart. God help him. He hated them.

Let the bastard lie there and bleed. Let him hurt his last moments on this earth. Let him hurt all the way to hell.

Movement at the front door caught his attention. An agent tried to make his way to the personnel carrier, keeping Mrs. Tenerson between him and Timucua's rifle. He was taller than she was and was forced to crouch to keep his head behind hers. More of his grandfather's words echoed. "Shoot what is available while it is available." Timucua adjusted his aim and shot him in the foot.

The naked Mrs. Tenerson screamed. Her eyes were large and wild with fright and pain. She saw her daughter lying under the personnel carrier, weeping, and watching her mother in horror. She reached up to the hand around her throat, bent the index finger back until it broke at the first joint, and continued to bend it until the agent was forced to release her. The instant she pulled away, creating space between her body and his, Timucua fired, hitting the agent in the right shoulder. He fired again and again until the man lay helpless, all four limbs hanging by threads of flesh, the bones shattered. Timucua's ears heard him screaming, but his heart could hear only the cries and sobs of the two bloody human beings.

He yelled at the mother, who was crawling to her child, "Are there anymore in the house?" She continued to make her painful way to her daughter. "Please, Mrs. Tenerson. Are there anymore in the house?"

The girl crawled out from under the personnel carrier. Mother and child shook with terror as they held each other. The girl caught her breath. "I think it's Mrs. Paine's boy, Patrick."

The woman's eyes darted over to the woods. "Patrick?"

"It's Mrs. Paine's son. Are there anymore in the house?"

"No. That's all of them."

"Get in back of the APC and wait for me."

The two helped each other up and walked on weak legs.

Timucua walked out of the woods.

The agent's face was white with fear and blood loss. Pain and shock evident in his eyes, he said, "Please."

Timucua sensed he could not believe a teenage boy had just wiped out a squad of trained killers in less than five minutes.

Timucua ignored him, but sent a silent message by stepping on the rapist's shattered left elbow "accidentally" as he walked by.

"Oh, God," he moaned.

Without bothering to look back, Timucua said, "God is not here. So shut up and lie there and hurt until I get back to you."

Timucua cleared the house, finding it empty. He then checked on the agent in the backyard. He was alive and conscious, but just barely. He found two blankets in a closet and brought them out to the personnel carrier.

The mother and daughter wrapped themselves in the blankets and Timucua grabbed a medical kit from the back and then helped them out.

Mrs. Tenerson looked down at the man as she walked by, her face contorted with rage and hate. "You're a piece of shit! And I hope you die slow, you bastard." She gathered up what dignity she had left and raised her head as she walked by.

Timucua remembered his mother telling him Mrs. Tenerson never cursed. He kicked the prone agent's right knee. The man screamed. He was forced to half-carry Haleigh. She was still terrified of the wounded man although he was obviously helpless.

"He can't hurt you now. He will be dead soon," Timucua said.

She released a lung full of breath, her eyes rolled back and she fell to her knees and would have fallen to the ground if Timucua had not caught her up in his arms and carried her into the house.

Damn them.

He was surprised by how light she was.

She's just a kid.

Then he realized she was only two years younger than him. Still, she seemed so much younger. He wondered if she would be afraid of men the rest of her life.

Timucua looked into the girl's pain and shock-filled eyes. "I'm sorry." He looked up at the mother. "I'm sorry. I wish...It's my fault. They were looking for me." He put her on the couch and handed the medical kit to the mother. With no further words, he walked out the back door.

A pistol shot rang through the house, causing both mother and daughter to jump. He walked by them. "He won't hurt anyone." A few seconds after he walked out the front door, his pistol spoke once again.

It took him nearly an hour to drag all of the bodies into the personnel carrier. He walked into the front door and stood across the living room from them. "Is...Is there anything else I can do for you?"

His arm was bleeding again and hurting. The pain was pounding at the door of his mind, but to no avail. He had learned to put distance between physical pain and his consciousness. The exertion of dragging so much dead weight up the ramp of the personnel carrier had turned a dull throb into a sharp, screaming demon in his arm. He paid no heed. Mother and daughter saw only concern and thinly veiled shame on his face.

Mrs. Tenerson had bandaged the cuts and was wiping her daughter's face with a wet towel. "I know you have to go, don't you?"

"And so do you," Timucua said. "You can't stay here now. It's too dangerous. I put all of the bodies in the personnel carrier, and I'm towing the car, but you still can't stay here. They have GPS transponders in all of their vehicles. They will know the vehicles have been here. They will retrace...You don't want to be here when they come." He turned his face away. "I'm sorry. I brought this evil down on you."

"No!" Mrs. Tenerson's voice was sure and strong, so much so that he was surprised. "They brought themselves here. If they were so intent on finding you, why didn't they just leave when they saw you were not here? Your mother was my friend. They murdered her. That was evil and it was not your fault. What those out there did today was evil. You stopped it. The shame is on them, not you."

"Where is Mr. Tenerson?"

"He is with some men who decided to fight when they heard about you. A lot of people are angry about what they did to your family."

Timucua started to tell her he should have stayed home to protect his family, but felt no good could come from speaking such words. They would have killed her husband anyway. "Is there someplace not too far away you can go?"

She walked over to him. "Yes, we have a place to hide. I think she is strong enough to make it. When Ben comes back and finds us gone, he will know where we are." She ran her fingers through his dirty hair. "I always knew you were a good boy. There was something different about you. Your mother...she was a good friend. The finest woman I ever knew." She swallowed and took a deep breath. "Don't let them kill you inside. They haven't yet. I can see that. But they will if you let them. Don't. Because then evil wins."

"Oh, they're going to kill me, either from the outside in, or the inside out. But it will be a hollow victory. First, they have to pay and pay and pay. I'm going to see just how many of their own they are willing to feed my grandfather's rifle just to kill one half-grown kid." He started to walk out the door, stopped and turned back around. "I would leave here as soon as possible. I wish..."

"I know. God be with you."

Chapter 8

The personnel carrier had a heavy chain wrapped around brackets on the front, so heavy it was difficult for Timucua to lift even a small part of it at a time. He dragged it around to the back and managed to tether the patrol car to the personnel carrier by hooking the chain to the undercarriage.

As he drove down the dirt road, engine whining, gravel popping under massive bulletproof tires, weeds brushing down each side of the vehicle, swooshing and snapping, breaking their backs against the armor, he began to cry. It was the first time. He had not allowed himself outward emotion over the murder of his mother and grandfather. Now that he started, he could not stop. He did not stop until he became so angry with himself he got out, stood in the dirt road, and screamed at God. No words, just a primal roar. God it seemed, was not listening. Perhaps He was busy giving the human race the gift of more sadists. Or was it God's fault? Could God even be faulted? Was it Satan? And what about Timucua? What had he become? No answers came to him. All he got for all of his bellowing was a sore throat.

He wiped his face and swore he would never do that again, got in, put the beast in gear and drove on.

Timucua thought seven miles was far enough from the Tenerson farm. They were marked for death anyway. Only one of many things he would have to live with. Moving the vehicles would just slow the agents down a little. They could never live on their farm again. He stopped to unchain the car and drove it in the weed-choked ditch by the two-lane road.

Before he started traveling again, Timucua took the time to ready the Browning M2HB fifty-caliber machinegun for immediate use and practiced firing it. Two short bursts were enough. He cut a pine tree in half. "This thing will cut a thin-skinned vehicle to pieces." He swung the barrel around and shot the engine of the patrol car up.

Thirty minutes later, he topped a hill and saw an opportunity before his eyes. What had been a county park and public boat ramp before The Party, sat below him nestled against the Black Water River. The place was teaming with four utility vehicles, a van bristling with satellite dishes and radio antennas, and two patrol cars. More than thirty agents were milling about among the vehicles. Many were eating at dilapidated picnic tables or just talking and resting.

Staging area. Got to be at least a lieutenant or maybe a captain there.

He stopped in the road one hundred yards from the entrance to the small park.

A few of the agents seemed puzzled about why he stopped and were waving for him to drive on up. He answered by working over the van with three six-round bursts from the Browning machinegun and then ripping the other vehicles up, along with those taking refuge behind them.

The van burst into flames when the generator's liquid petroleum tank strapped to the rear corner exploded. Two men rolled out of the back doors onto the ground as screaming balls of fire. Six darted from cover and tried to run for the woods. Timucua risked overheating the gun when he laid on the controls. His eyes drank in the sight of their bodies flying apart as they were punched by bullet after bullet. In his mind, he was not slaughtering human beings, but needless sources of misery.

He was not aware of the pinging and clanging of bullets as they bounced off the armor until the machinegun grew silent. The belt of ammunition was exhausted. He removed the empty ammunition box and slid a full one into the bracket. Timucua swung the lid open and removed it, letting it fall to the floor below with a clang. Sweat shook from his dripping face, and it landed on the smoking barrel near the receiver, hissing and spitting.

Timucua soon had the "Ma Deuce" Browning machinegun speaking again, cutting a large oak tree in half and the man taking refuge behind it. Another broke for the woods, but he was shot down fifteen yards from the tree line.

The last man jumped into a patrol boat and started the engines. In his frantic haste, he kept trying to put the boat in reverse before the engines had idled down enough to disengage the safety mechanism designed to prevent just that. The windshield shattered. A burst from the Browning removed his head, and he fell back onto the floor of the boat. Blood ran down the deck in a racing flood and out the holes that gave the deck its "self-bailing" feature.

Timucua continued to work methodically over anything that might offer cover to any agents left alive and chopped up all of the vehicles thoroughly. The ammunition belt consumed, he returned to the operator's seat, drove into the driveway, and stopped by the boat ramp.

Time to head back to my own neck of the woods.

He grabbed his pack and rifle. Looking around at the carnage, he kept his rifle at the low ready position as he walked.

After throwing his pack on a bench seat, he jumped in the twenty-five-foot boat. Its twin two hundred horsepower outboards were idling.

The man's hair was too short to offer a handhold. Grabbing an ear with each hand, he tossed the severed head overboard. Then he lifted the headless body over the gunnels. It fell with a splash.

Timucua took one last look around before backing away from the dock. Not wanting to dwell on the magnitude of what he had just done, his mind's eye flashed to the face of the girl he carried in his arms little more than an hour ago. The burning image of what he saw when first driving up to the farm, and the carnage he now gazed upon compelled him to shake his head.

My, how we Homo sapiens have advanced. Hairless apes? It is an insult to apes.

Speeding away upriver, he said to no one, "Now that I have my boat, this hairless ape will be a true fisher of men." He turned the wheel and traversed a sharp bend. "I am become death…Well, the killing will stop when they decide to leave my people alone."

The river was wide at first, but it reduced in width after ten miles, forcing him to slow down. Along the water's edge on each bank, junipers, cypress, and hickory stood in a chaotic distorted scrim of trunks and limbs draped with Spanish moss and festooned with leaves. Adding to the brooding mass of flora was the undergrowth of saw palmetto, thorny vines, and cabbage palm. Impenetrable and forbidding to his enemies, that subtropical jungle was Timucua's only chance, and he knew it. One step off the boat, and he would be walking in the mud of his warrior ancestors.

Many were the snakelike curves, some doubling back on themselves. One such switchback allowed Timucua so see the river upstream through the trees where he saw another patrol boat speeding at him.

Timucua knew they saw his boat and he was ready to act before they could see who was driving. The two boats met on his side of the bend. He rammed their port bow with his; it was a glancing blow, forcing the other boat to veer off course, wedging itself between two cypress trees. The boat stopped at an odd angle; listing to port, bow pointing up at a thirty degree incline.

The driver was knocked unconscious when his head hit the windshield frame. He draped over the starboard gunwale motionless, blood poured from a gash on his forehead. The other agent flew over the port side into the river when the boats collided. Timucua tried to run over him, but he somehow survived. He was heading for the bank as fast as he could swim, but was struggling with the weight of body armor.

Timucua put the boat in reverse, backed up, and shot both agents. Then he shot the last six rounds into the gas tank of the other boat. The empty clip pinged out of the Garand, landing in the river. He set the gas ablaze with a flare gun he found in his boat.

A column of black smoke rose, boiling into the hot, humid air. "See that assholes? Come and get me."

They're not likely to hurt any innocent people out here.

"Oh yeah, you will kill me, but first I'm going to teach you how to hunt."

Timucua drove another seven miles. The sun was low in the sky, and he was in full shadow of the western tree line. He pulled to the outside of a sharp bend in the river where the water was deepest near shore. Already, the crickets and frogs were beginning their nightly chorus.

The first items he put in his pack while searching the boat for anything of value to a man on the run were two night vision goggles with spare batteries, then a medical kit and some emergency rations. The medical kit had its own pack, which he tied to his. Unfortunately, it was red and not a proper color for someone trying to stay hid in the woods. He planned to dump the pack later, keeping its contents. For now, he needed to get away from the boat and river as soon as possible.

Digging into a compartment, he found a packet of six aluminum-ized "space blankets." He had a use for those. Many other items were on board, but nothing he felt he needed.

In a compartment near the transom, he found a five-gallon plastic container of gas. After piling any flammable items he could find near the transom, he poured gas over everything. Timucua then put his pack on and jumped out onto the bank. One shot from the flare gun set the fumes ablaze with a loud "woof," raising the items he piled on, off the deck several inches for a second. When the pile settled back down, it was a roaring mass of flame.

Smoke billowed vertically before being caught by the wind to stream horizontally two hundred feet above the river. Timucua searched the sky with a stony face, half-expecting to see a Dissident Control helicopter circling.

He walked into the graying river swamp. When it got dark, Timucua used one of the night vision goggles to travel most of the night. An hour before dawn, he was in his old haunts again. There was little wind, and the mosquitoes were swarming and feasting on his blood. For some reason, though the air was hot and humid, he felt chilled. Hour after hour, day after day, layers of fatigue were piling up, weighing him down. He had to rest.

His arm now gave him long periods of numbness, contrasted by sharp, intense throbbing. When numb, he found it difficult to hold anything with his left hand, often dropping it on its own, with no signal from his thoughts. During the moments of pain, he willed his mind to think of his family and Mrs. Tenerson and her daughter. At least he had his life and his dignity. They had not taken that yet.

He found a good place to sleep under some thick brush. He was certain Dissident Control would have helicopters in the air soon, so he draped one of the blankets from the boat on overhanging brush to cover his heat signature. This would make it more difficult for their airborne forward-looking infrared, or FLIR, to detect him while he slept. A bonus was it protected him from the damp morning dew. The ambient air temperature was higher than his body heat, and he thought that might also help.

*   *   *

Captain Tory Voisselle had Lieutenant Raebyrne in his office and was in the middle of another one of his raging eruptions. "Goddamn it all to hell. Why haven't you killed that little bastard? We lost several dozen more agents yesterday and numerous vehicles *and* two patrol boats."

With his face red from rage and frustration, he continued. "The little bastard is rubbing our nose in shit. We look like goddamn fools to the public, and we cannot afford to look like fools. I don't give a damn about the Redundant Headcount. They don't know their ass from a hole in the ground and are fed nothing but shit for news anyway. Not to mention the fact none of them has any balls. It's the hicks outside the cities, the wild asses, who will learn of this farmer's little bastard through their underground news network. I would not be surprised if he becomes some kind of folk hero to those anarchistic morons."

Voisselle glared at Raebyrne, who looked back impassively. "Need I remind you of the modified Removal Plan that is just beginning to be implemented? The final removal stage must be carried out with no more delays. Those damn hicks have been a thorn in our side long enough. It's time they be exterminated. We gave them a chance to move into the cities and get with the program, but they refuse to be reasonable.

Reasonableness is beyond their mental capacity. They're Neanderthals. Evolution has passed them by. Just kill them."

Lieutenant Raebyrne waited patiently for the eruption to subside. He knew the captain was under a lot of pressure. If the Removal Plan did not go well, World Government was likely to send in soldiers. If that happened, the North American Union would lose what little autonomy it had left. "Sir, we have three helicopters in the air at this very moment. A dozen dogs are on his trail. One hundred fifty agents are following behind in a long sweeping skirmish line. We will get him. There is no way he will survive the day."

Voisselle sat in his chair behind the desk. "Are you sure those dogs are on the little bastard's trail, not chasing a coon or something, Merrick?"

Raebyrne looked disgusted, but chose his words carefully. He was too tired to argue with the captain. "Yes sir, I'm sure the dogs are on his trail. We picked up his scent not far from where we found one of the boats. Of course if you hadn't called me back here, my information would be more current."

The captain's chest deflated, he put his elbows on the desk, his face in his hands, and began to rub his eyes with his palms. "For our sake I hope you're right. Recent level-three interrogations of captured terrorists suggest that a state of general rebellion is close at hand. All it will take is one spark to set them off. Something like this boy can do it. Those in Washington were hoping to be further along with the Removal Plan before they found enough balls to fight back."

Raebyrne looked at the captain with cold, hard eyes. "We've had this discussion before. I warned you these people still had millions of guns and hundreds of millions of rounds of ammo in their possession. Don't make the mistake of believing the boy is the only one who knows how to use a rifle. They pride themselves in marksmanship. It's part of their culture. I'm telling you the government is slapping a hornet's nest. Leave them and their children alone."

Voisselle ignored him. He shook his head in wonderment. "They don't even believe in abortion. They actually care more for their children than they do themselves. Now that's self-hate, or pure animal instinct. Like a bitch biting anything that hurts her litter. They're animals."

"Animals or not, they have rifles, and they know how to use them."

Ignoring Raebyrne again, he continued. "Merrick, if a little puissant boy can cause this much trouble, how would you like thirty-five million of those animals up in arms. We're going to kill them. More to the point, we're going to kill their children, all of them, if they find out what we have planned for them this early in the process…W.G. will send soldiers in for certain."

"What did I just tell you? Convince The Party to leave them alone. If enough high-ranking officers got together and warned them of the likely results, maybe they will change their policies. I hear that's already happening in the military. Generals say it will be a bloodbath. And it won't be one-sided."

Voisselle stopped rubbing his eyes. "I don't know about you, but I like my job. It's the best job in the world. I can kill anyone I want, just because I feel like it. And I intend to keep it." His face was strange and sickening. "Haven't you felt it? Those surges of power when you pull the trigger and watch them die. I'm sure you have felt it when you killed."

Raebyrne's face became white granite as he fought an overpowering urge to throw up and then put his pistol to the captain's head and pull the trigger.

Chapter 9

"Yeah I hear you, you yelping bitches," Timucua muttered under his breath. He had gotten little more than three hours sleep before the noise of helicopters woke him, but what he was listening to now was not helicopters. There had been a large pack of dogs on his trail since two and a half hours after sunrise. He first learned of this fifteen minutes ago, when they got close enough for him to hear their excited full-throat caterwauling. Twenty minutes before noon found him on the edge of a large bayou he knew well, and he had plans to use that knowledge to its fullest advantage.

Timucua took an eager drink from a five-quart collapsible canteen and filled a half-empty one-quart canteen with it, afterwards pouring out the remains over his overheated, sweaty head. He then filled the empty five-quart container with air, blowing it up like a balloon. He held it shut so the slightly pressurized air could not escape while he screwed the lid on tight.

He tied the five-quart canteen to his pack so it would be between his pack and his back while wearing it. He also had two twelve-inch-diameter artillery weather balloons, procured by a friend of his grandfather's years ago. He blew them up and tied them together with two feet of rope.

Nearly ready to go for a swim, he put both rifle and pistol in a clear plastic military rifle bag and blew it up, then tied it off. He placed the bag in the water, letting it float while he carefully lay on his stomach so he would not sink into the mud and slid into the stinking water. The rope he had tied between the two balloons was across his chest and under his arms. Ever mindful of the fact he had enough weight strapped on his upper body to drag him under without flotation, he silently thanked his grandfather for showing him how not to, "drown your ass like I saw many overloaded soldiers do in 'Nam while trying to cross a river."

Timucua swam over half a mile using a modified sidestroke, powering through the tea-colored water with his legs only, careful to avoid splashing in order not to attract alligators. A helicopter buzzed by just before he crawled out of the water. He was in waterweeds by then and not detected. He knew the spot well. It was the only place for a mile where a man could crawl out of the water safely. Here, a myriad of roots solidified the quaking shoreline enough to give purchase to hands and feet while hauling body and heavy load out of the water.

Before moving on, he removed his rifle and pistol from the bag and deflated the two weather balloons and canteen, putting them back in his pack.

"The only thing that got wet was my ass," he muttered, ignoring the fact his throbbing arm was once again soaked with filthy water. Everything in his pack he did not want to get wet, he kept in a rubberized nylon waterproof pack liner bag that he always kept tied off at the top, the bag itself giving some amount of flotation.

"The yelping hellhounds sound frustrated," Timucua said to no one. The dog's vicious raging had changed to yelps. He listened while he took the wet, dirty bandage off his arm.

When the dogs reached the water's edge, they smelled the disturbance of the muddy bottom and, as trained, jumped in. Several alligators had already been attracted to the loud barking. Now, the dogs' splashing aroused the reptiles' primal urge to hunt. Two dogs were pulled under. Yelping shrilly, the others started for shore.

The water was too deep anyway. The bottoming sludge of the swamp still lay in slumber, as if the boy had never been there, leaving nothing distinct to be of any use for the dogs' nose.

Though trained to be vicious, the alligators were too much for them. Water was not their element. As they turned to head back to the near shore, paddling franticly, Timucua's ears detected the difference in their voices. The excited hysteria was now abject, higher pitched. Fear. Timucua heard it, smelled it, and tasted it in his guts. He knew it well. It had been his constant companion for more than a week now. Gone was the previous unchallengeable vicious courage in their voices. Courage not born of real bravery derived of concern, friendship, or love for one another or their handlers, the kind that compels a human being or dog to give his or her life for another. For genuine bravery normally attributed to man or his beloved dog had been bred and beaten out of them from birth. No, they cared not for any living thing, not even themselves. Their viciousness was as natural as breathing, born of hating the world for being born. When hunting prey, it was their only chance to strike back, and they never failed to take advantage of that chance with all vigor. There are men like that. Timucua knew this. He had killed many of them.

After running five miles, his body regained that familiar salty rank smell of the unwashed, mixed with the decaying vegetation, rotten egg smell of swamp mud. He was living like an animal because he was being hunted like an animal.

At sundown, a helicopter flew by at low speed just above the treetops. It was such an easy shot Timucua could not stop himself. He put a bullet through the right window into the pilot's shoulder then pumped three more rounds into the engine before the pilot could veer off.

Banking to the left in a tight half circle, gaining altitude, the pilot seemed to be in control until the aircraft nose-dived into the swamp's canopy of treetops, resulting in a thunderous crash, screeching shredding steel, and a roaring ball of fire. He was pleased with both his marksmanship and the results.

An idea formed in Timucua's mind. It would be risky, but he felt the risk worth the objective. The only way to get to the downed helicopter was by using more helicopters. There was no road for miles and as far as he knew, no one on the ground was close enough to get to the crash site before dark. He did know there was more than one helicopter in the area, and the fireball could be seen for miles from the air in the dimming light of sunset. Why not use the crashed helicopter for bait. He just proved they are easy to shoot down with a battle rifle.

Timucua waited.

He did not have to wait long. A helicopter came in fast. The pilot changed prop pitch and turned sharply, the prop's whop, whop, whop, and air-beating whirling roar filled Timucua's ears. He watched through the scrim of treetops as it circled at two hundred fifty feet altitude and then backed off, the image of a dragonfly looking for its mate.

Five minutes later, it came back, hovering above the blazing wreck. Flickers of orange, red, yellow, reflected off the fuselage. Its wafting patterns swimming and dancing along the dull green and black logo: "Dissident Control."

Timucua took careful aim, resting his weak hand against the vertical edge of a cypress tree, willing his throbbing left arm to do what it must. The pilot turned the rotorcraft's right side to him. Aiming for the pilot, he squeezed the shot off. Instantly, he pumped the remaining rounds into the cockpit.

Before he got a fresh clip out of a Korean War military surplus pouch and in the rifle, the aircraft turned on its side in midair and arched downward from the sky, ripping itself apart among the treetops. Another roaring fireball erupted, lighting up the twilight.

That night he circled back around after getting the dogs off his trail, hearing, more than seeing, the long line of agents hunting him. They were not exactly quiet in the woods. Twice, he allowed them to pass by unknowing. Both times, he felt he could have killed one with his knife without alerting the others, but that would have been risky. He was becoming ever more drained for some reason. He felt it was more than fatigue.

Not pushing his luck further, he traveled most of the night, making use of night vision goggles. His left arm ached and was weak. It took considerable will just to get his arm to hold the rifle steady. Certainly, he had made the right choice.

*   *   *

James was standing at a table strewn with reports from militia members. He had a dozen accounts of government atrocities he planned to include in an article he was just starting. His article would be part of the next issue of the underground newspaper Maria and he published with the help of seven others: The Patrick Henry Pamphleteer. It was popular among resistance fighters.

When Maria walked into the room, his eyes lit up. Not an unusual occurrence whenever she was near. They planned to marry soon. "I just got something on the boy."

"Is he okay?" Maria asked.

"First of all, he's still alive. He shot down two helicopters just at sundown yesterday."

"Yes!" She appeared to want to jump up and down with joy. "They sure stepped in it when they murdered *his* family." Her face changed from happiness to melancholy in a second, thinking of the murder of her parents.

James read her mind. "Oh, come on, you're using your skills to fight back in your own way, just like he is. Don't get all gloomy on me. I have something here you will want to see. It's copied from photos taken from the desk of a lieutenant at the headquarters of District 13, Dissident Control."

She walked over and stood beside him.

"This is a copy of the note the boy left at the scene where he killed those on the first day," James said. "We're in the process of making thousands of copies."

"Thousands of copies?"

He brought a chair over. "Here, sit down and read it, and what is on the other side, too. Then tell me how many copies you think we should make."

She read it. "How about one?"

"One?" James looked at her, puzzled.

"One copy for every man woman and child on the North American Continent."

"You don't ever think small, do you?"

She shrugged. "Well, now that we are part of the resistance, it's our job to tell the truth about the government. And this is more than that, much more."

The expression on James' face changed. "Here we are cheering him on, but we both know how it's going to end for him. What they're doing to him is sick. He has done nothing wrong. In their arrogance, they don't see it that way. So now, he's being hunted like an animal. It's gone on so long they must make an example of him. And the longer it goes on…How much do you think a boy can take before he becomes the animal they claim he is?"

"I know. I know. When we were in that swamp with the big man, I thought about the boy as I looked through the trees and brush. I can only guess at what it must be like, what he's going through."

*   *   *

Lieutenant Raebyrne watched through a camera monitor as the interrogator broke another one of Gary's fingers. The old man moaned for a few seconds and then tightened his jaw, not making another sound until his tormentor broke another finger. This time the moan was lower, not lasting two seconds.

The interrogator had been emotionless, now he grew angry. "Oh. You're starting to like it, are you?" He backhanded the old man across his face with enough force to knock him out of the chair if he had not been strapped in.

"I told you," Gary said, his voice calm, nose and mouth bleeding, eyes looking past his tormentor at something only he could see, "I don't know anything about the person that I gave the note to."

"Was it a man or a woman?"

"Like I told you, it was dark, and I was the only one who spoke."

Raebyrne stood beside Captain Voisselle. "I don't see why this is necessary. Gary gave a copy of the note the boy left at the scene of the ambush to someone with the underground newspaper. We know that already. Why this?"

"He has been working with the terrorists, and we need to learn everything he knows."

"Did you know Gary is a veteran?"

"So what." The captain became irritated. "He's guilty of spying for enemies of the state. He must be shot."

"Well, then shoot him. He fought for this country. He deserves some respect."

"He fought for the United States of America. That country does not exist."

Raebyrne felt himself losing control. He knew he would regret it, but he felt a great tidal wave crashing in on him. He could not hold it back. "Goddamn it! What have we allowed ourselves to become? Our men made the boy what he is today when they stupidly and needlessly killed his family."

"The only stupid thing they did was let the boy get away. The more we kill now, the sooner the job is done."

Raebyrne turned to the captain. "There are two kinds of people in this world: those you can push and those you can't. Sometimes you can't tell what kind you're turning into an enemy until it's too late. This boy has a button inside him. You push it, and you're dead. And with him, once it's turned on there is no turning it off. That's why you don't go around needlessly fucking with people like the government has, like we have, for many years now."

Voisselle frowned. "They should have moved into the cities and got with the program years ago." He appraised Raebyrne with a cold stare, suspicion in his eyes.

Raebyrne was not finished. "These people, Wild People, are not Redundant Headcount, not hairless apes without any heart or soul, as the boy put it. We have been rubbing their nose in shit for decades, and for the most part, they have backed off and backed off. Well, if you start killing their families wholesale, you can expect a reaction like your worst nightmare."

"You're afraid of them, aren't you?" Voisselle had a smirk on his face.

"Yes," Raebyrne said. "You would have to be insane not to be."

Voisselle's eyes grew wide, but he said nothing.

"Consider this Paine kid, just one boy. We kill his mother and grandfather before his eyes. What's his reaction? What's his kill ratio now? Five dozen to one? No. So far, it's five dozen to zero. How's that for a kill ratio?

Voisselle frowned and waved Raebyrne's words away. "He had help. I warned you others would be encouraged by his example if you didn't kill him soon."

"He was alone at the creek and the road, the farmer's house, and the river."

"Bullshit. He had help from the militia."

Raebyrne's face contorted with distain. "The militia? Few in the militia could stand in that boy's shadow in their wildest wet dream. They don't have his skills, his knowledge, and his drive. They don't have his heart."

"You will never convince me one boy caused all this."

"You know, Wild People are not always predictable, but you can bet there are millions more out there like the boy. You kill their families and they will react just like the boy. How would you like ten or twelve million hate-filled nightmares hunting you night and day?"

"That's why we're going to kill them all." The captain smiled.

"Easier said than done. I don't believe the boy stops long enough to rest or eat, much less get any sleep." He flinched when the interrogator broke another of the old man's fingers. "First, he kills two at the farm, runs six hours straight, stops to kill five men, leaving another to drown and—"

"You admire the little bastard don't you?"

"He shows up thirty miles away, obviously traveling by foot, kills two, taking a car. Twenty miles farther, he kills two on motorbikes. A few miles down the road, he kills ten, taking an APC this time. Thirteen more miles, and he kills three dozen, using our machinegun. Ten miles downriver, he kills two more in a boat. He's circling around now, back to his favorite happy hunting grounds. Twenty-two or three miles away in a swamp, the last fifteen miles he's back on foot again, he shoots down two choppers, killing everyone onboard. Near as I can tell he must have traveled thirty-five miles one day, on foot. He's nothing less than a well-trained combat-hardened soldier. A sixteen-year-old farm boy? How? He must be one fast learner!"

"Are you trying to claim all Wild People are like him?"

"You might say he's not human, but he is. It's his human love for his family and his human hate for us that drives him. He's more human than anyone you will ever meet in your life. The human heart: The Party has been trying for decades to kill it. Well, they failed."

"Human heart, my ass. He's just a crazy kid."

"If he's crazy now, we did it to him. We pushed that button in him." Raebyrne turned away when the old man's pain-filled eyes looked at the camera. He swallowed and turned to Voisselle. "I say we've got to convince The Party to leave them alone. I'm telling you, we don't want to push them any further. An all-out fight with them will be so bloody even if we win we lose.

"And if we're going to lose, why torture an old man whose only crime is actually giving a damn about another human being? Or have we allowed the government to turn us into nothing more than sadistic animals?"

The captain pushed Raebyrne around ninety degrees by hitting him on his right shoulder with the palm of his hand, the sound of the impact echoing in the small room like a rifle shot. "You're starting to piss me off, Merrick! So you want to just lie down and give up, do you? Well, I'm not made that way. I worked hard to get where I am, and no one is going to take it away."

Raebyrne's jaw tightened and creases in the flesh of his face that were not there only a year before deepened. "It would be different if there was something worth fighting for, but The Party has turned this country into an overflowing toilet. Maybe someone needs to pull the lever and flush it."

His voice lowered, compressed, Raebyrne was not exploding; his discipline would not allow that. He was imploding, like the triggering force of a nuclear bomb that produces high-pressure heat to spark the chain reaction. "And don't ever put your hands on me again."

Captain Voisselle took two steps back, his eyes ice-cold. "You have always done your duty, Merrick, otherwise I would have you taken out back and shot right now." He nodded his head slightly. "All right. You take the old man out back, and shoot him yourself. Let's see how devoted you are to respecting the old fart."

Raebyrne stormed into the room, interrupted the interrogation, and started removing the straps constraining Gary.

The elder man looked at him through swollen eyes over a broken, bloody nose. "Are you going to kill me now?"

Raebyrne gently lifted him to his feet and said, "It's the best I can do for you Gary."

"Thank you, Merrick. Let me die with some dignity."

Raebyrne said nothing. He pretended his face was chiseled stone, or prayed it appeared to be, as other agents watched him take another victim to his death. They all knew Gary. "Goddamn the Unity Party! Goddamn them all!" Raebyrne's voice echoed in the hallway.

Behind the building, there was a walled-in courtyard. On one side, there was a mound of dirt. It was pockmarked with bullet holes.

He stood Gary on a grate-covered drain, four by six feet in dimension. A water hose was coiled nearby. The area was wet from a recent spraying. Water dripped into the drain, the drops mingling with rusty-red water below.

The smell of gun smoke still lingered in the air. At the spot Gary stood, his back now straighter than in years, was a concentration of dirge.

"I smell death," Gary said. "It's brought back memories from a lifetime ago. I've fought death before, and I know this time I'll lose."

"I'm sorry, Gary."

"I see no reason for you to be sorry. Death always wins in the end. When I was a cocky young rooster right out of high school, I fought death. And I won. Proud to have faced it down and smiled at it." His chest rose as he gave a sad smile to himself. "But death is always waiting for you to let your guard down. When you do, it rushes in to take you away from this world. Well, I'm tired, and I'm sick to my heart. This country was good to me once. It wasn't perfect, but it was as good as you could expect in this world. You could open a business, or farm your land, work hard and support you family and have some dignity. Now you're expected to grovel to the Party for scraps, roll on your belly and piss your stomach like a whipped puppy. I'm too old and proud for that. I refuse to give them my pissed-on belly; I'd rather give them my teeth."

Raebyrne said nothing.

Gary had been placed facing the mound of dirt. He turned his head a little to the right. "I guess I'm going to die for what I believe in. The difference is that boy out there is young, and I'm an old man. God bless him. And God bless America!"

Raebyrne held the pistol up two feet from the back of Gary's head. His right arm became too heavy. After struggling for some seconds, he gave up. His hand was shaking as he lowered the gun.

Gary turned his head just slightly again. "It's okay, Merrick. You have to do it. If your hands are shaking, calm yourself. I don't want you to screw it up. The brain is smaller than you may think. Put it against my head so you can't miss no matter how much your hand shakes."

"If what you were trying to do is start a civil war, you will get your wish. The words that boy wrote drew a sharp line between The Party and the human spirit. Socialism is not humanitarianism, it is inhuman, the enemy of humanity. Human beings should take care of one another, not government. I know that now. The boy taught me that. It wasn't government that stopped the rape and torture of that mother and daughter. It was him, a human being."

"He is right about his people. They will fight," Gary said. "They did not allow their children to be brainwashed and turned into soulless animals, and they will not allow them to be slaughtered. Wild People are not Redundant Headcount."

"No, they are human beings, like you," Raebyrne said.

"Well, I guess I've fought my last battle. It may not seem like much to some, but I know what I started. The funny thing is, I didn't have to fire a single shot."

"You and that boy are brothers who never met."

"Help them, Merrick. I know you're not like your Captain. Help them. Believe me; you will be glad you did. Nothing can be as bad as the hell you're living in now. Help them, and you will know the contentment I'm feeling. Take your wife, children, and join them. Save your family and yourself. I'm trying to give you one last chance before I go. You did me a kindness, now I'm trying to return the favor."

The old man turned and faced Raebyrne squarely, standing straight, in a military brace. "You did not kill me, they did. Remember that. Do it now, Merrick, I am ready to go."

Raebyrne pointed the pistol at Gary's head, but his index finger would not move. His hand shook. "I am a blind fool. I never knew. You have been working here for years. I thought it was to keep from being put to sleep like an old dog. Make yourself useful to The Party. But you, you were waiting for a chance to give, to strike back. I never knew the man who dusted my desk and emptied the wastebasket. I was blind. I can't," Raebyrne said. "I would rather put the bullet in my own head."

"No! You can help them. Don't throw that away. Wild People will protect your family if you show them you are human. Help them. Ask them for refuge. They will forgive you of your past."

Gary reached out his right hand, knotted and twisted with age, scarred, missing the little finger, taken by a bullet from an SKS rifle when he was twenty years old. His eyes flashed, belying his age. "You see? You're not an animal. This proves it. You can defy them, Merrick. You don't have to do what they say. I would offer to do it for you, but you know the Captain is watching. The camera, remember?"

Raebyrne put the pistol in his left hand and took Gary's hand in his. "I promise I will do what I can." Instantly, he swung the pistol up and pulled the trigger. For a millisecond, Raebyrne's hand was nearly crushed as the old man's hand tightened with great force. Then suddenly, his entire body relaxed as all life left it. He crumpled onto the grating in a heap. Before, a living man, now nothing.

The report of the pistol was a signal for two men to come out of a small building nearby. They carried a stretcher.

Raebyrne ran between them and the body. "Don't touch him. Don't you dare touch him!" He still held the pistol in his left hand. They looked alarmed, staring at the pistol and then Raebyrne's face. "There is going to be a funeral. I am calling someone right now. Go back where you came from."

The two men looked at each other, then without saying a word, turned around and went back into the building, closing the door quietly.

Chapter 10

Timucua had been traveling in a daze for three days. Each day found him weaker and more ill. He used hydrogen peroxide to clean out the wounds on his arm whenever he could, and put antibiotic cream on it. However, in less than an hour, the bandage would be soaked with sweat. In addition, two or three times each day, he was forced to cross a creek or bayou, getting the wound wet and dirty again. He had a hard time keeping flies off it. It stunk, even more than the rest of his body. Now yellow and white pus, mixed with red blood, oozed from inflamed flesh. His forearm was deep red around the wounds, fading to pink farther away.

There was an old man, nearly as old as Timucua's grandfather, who was his grandfather's friend and had become Timucua's friend since he was small. The old man would come and visit or his grandfather would take Timucua to visit the old man, until they both got too old to walk far. The last four years, Timucua had to hand-carry letters between the two friends. Distance and the infirmities of old age separated the two, but the boy kept them in touch with each other.

Timucua fell. The third time in the last half hour. His fever high, it took all of the strength his weak body could muster to keep walking. He wanted to lie down and die. It would be so easy. Dying would be an easy way out, but he had more to do before resting. He was just beginning.

There is the spring.

He wondered if it really was, or if he was just dreaming. He dropped his rifle and squirmed out of his pack, letting it fall. Then he unbuckled the belt on his load-bearing harness, shook his shoulders out of the straps, and let it fall to the ground behind his feet.

He dropped to his knees and bent over to put his head in the cool, clean water and wash the grime off a little before he went up to the shack, and maybe get a drink.

Before he knew it, he lost his balance in his dizzy state of delirium and fell over, headfirst. The shock of the fifty-five-degree water took his breath away. He sank six feet. His left shoulder bounced off the bottom. Finally coming to his senses, he kicked up puffs of white powdered limestone silt, digging in six inches with his boots before he hit firm limestone rock, the force of his desperate driving kick bringing him out of the water nearly to his waist.

Timucua inhaled a deep lung-filling gasp of air, then another. He found his arms and legs would not do what he demanded.

Damn it, swim! Am I going to drown in Mr. Ironwood's spring?

He was barely aware of something grabbing him by the collar of his jacket, then being pulled to the bank.

"What's the matter, Patrick? Have you forgotten how to swim?" The old man had pulled him out onto the bank only up to the waist. He did not have the strength to pull him out all the way. He yelled over his shoulder. "Bart! I need your help, come a running!"

A tall, lean man in his late twenties with light brown hair, cut so short it did not need combing, stood and watched as the old man cleaned Timucua's wounds. There was a hole, a large pucker an inch wide, and a half-inch deep in the right side of his otherwise handsome face. The aftermath of a spent bullet catching him just above the jaw and knocking out three of his lower teeth and then the infection that set in because it was two weeks before he could get to Doctor Stevenson.

His slate-gray eyes appraised the boy. He stood out of the way and observed the pulling of the lacerations open and his friend wiping deeply into flesh with antibiotic-soaked gauze. The old man laid the arm on a clean towel, leaving the wounds open and uncovered to drain.

Bart Bithlow said, "So that's him. The one everybody's talking about. I half expected him to be ten feet tall. But then it's the size of the heart that separates the counts from the no-accounts."

The old man's face was creased with more than age. His gray hair, thinning on the top and crudely scissors-cut on the back and sides, was the same color as the day-old stubble on his nine-decade-old, long, thin face. His gnarled, spotted hand shook as he ran it over the crevices of his cheek. Thin all over, only his stomach gave any hint he had eaten lately, protruding slightly past his belt buckle. His hips so narrow, the tattered blue jeans he wore would surely fall down immediately without the military-style web belt pulled tight.

Timucua's grandfather always insisted on bringing as much food with them as they could carry whenever they visited. "We brought some calories with us," he would say, and then he would joke, "If you get any skinnier you'll have to stand in the same place twice to cast a shadow."

The jeans' right front pocket was worn through and patched. Under the patch, there was a bulge: a Taurus .44 Special revolver with two-inch barrel and shrouded hammer for fast removal from the pocket. He carried it with him always. He would never be taken alive.

Now, he was not about to watch the grandson of his late friend die in his own bed. The boy was nearly unconscious, burning with fever. Only minutes ago, he had cried out something unintelligible in delirium.

The old man rose, his knees creaking almost as loud as the chair. He grabbed the younger man by the shoulders. "Bart, I need you to run to the Blackwelders. Tell them we need Doc Stevenson. If he's not available, then get Doc Hightower, or anybody. We need a doctor here fast." He looked at the younger man with intense eyes. "Can you do that? Will you do that for me?"

"Of course. You know I will. You've been in the freedom struggle longer than any of us have. You taught us how to fight."

The old man went into the main room of the shack, found a piece of paper on the large table there, and wrote a note on it.

The younger man followed and stood beside him.

"Give this to the doctor so he'll know what to bring," the old man said. "You will have to carry the stuff for him. Otherwise, he'll take forever to get here. Time is running out for him. The infection is spreading. He needs lots of antibiotics now."

He stopped writing and handed the paper to Bart. "Tell the doctor to come prepared to save the arm. He won't want to live without it. There is only one thing keeping him alive now. He needs that arm to do it." He thought for a moment. "Get Mathew and a few others to help you. It's going to take a lot to save him. I want plenty of manpower here to get more supplies. And I don't need to tell you what happens if the government finds out he's here."

"Don't worry, I will only tell those we can trust above all others."

"Go now. Run as fast as you can."

Bart put on a load-bearing harness, homemade web gear that held six twenty-round magazines, and took an M14 in his hands. Without further words, he ran off into the woods.

Late that night, an alcohol lamp lit the small bedroom as fifty-eight-year-old Dr. Cornelius Stevenson wiped his bald black head, put the handkerchief in his left back pocket, and checked the intravenous drip to make sure it was at maximum flow. "I am giving him all his body can take of this. I'll need some more in about four hours, so send a runner to get it now."

Mr. Ironwood nodded. A man in his early twenties took a list from the doctor, grabbed his rifle, and disappeared into the night, using a flashlight to illuminate his way.

The doctor sat down on a steel-folding chair to rest for the first time since he had arrived. He arched his aching back and rubbed his neck. "Rex, you know the arm will have to come off. I don't think his body can fight off the infection otherwise."

Rex Ironwood flinched slightly and inhaled, his chest rising. "If he wakes up and sees that you cut it off, he will just lie there and die. He will have no reason to live. And without that, his body will not want to fight because his spirit will die."

"Many people live full lives with only one arm."

"Not him."

"Why not?"

"Because he has only one purpose in life now."

"And what would that be?"

"Kill Dissident Control agents."

"How many?"

"All of them."

The doctor ran the palm of his hand over his forehead. "That is quite an undertaking the boy has placed upon his shoulders. How far along on this mission is he?"

"They say…well, what they say is hard to believe. I will believe it when the boy tells me. Until then, it's just talk coming from those who were not there. Let's just say it was more than a handful."

The doctor was silent for a moment. "I presume he has become important to your cause, hasn't he?"

A flicker of fire flashed in the old man's eyes, then he turned away to look at the boy. "He's the grandson of the best friend I ever had. We served together in our war. I watched the boy grow up. He is practically my grandson or nephew."

"I apologize, I misspoke, but the fact is the arm is going to be nearly useless anyway. I had to cut away a lot of dead muscle."

"He won't know that until he is nearly well, and I wouldn't count on him not being able to use that arm, not just yet. I know him. If he thinks he has a chance, any chance at all, even if he is the only one in the world who can see that chance, he won't quit; he will keep fighting. But he needs that arm to *want* to keep fighting."

"Well, I will do what I can for him, Rex, I promise."

*   *   *

Timucua thought he must be insane. He was flying. Far below were the green woodlands and fields of the farm, above, a clear blue sky. He saw everything sharp, bright, and clear. There was the swamp and the river. Turning to follow the river, its surface reflecting sunlight like a silvery snake, he saw a young man in a canoe, no, a dugout, looking up at him signaling, his right hand making a circling motion.

He tried to will himself to swoop down lower, but just as he got close enough to see the man's face and recognize him as his father, a gust of wind carried him aloft again. It was his father, but he was too young. At least fifteen years younger than his father was when he died.

Timucua had not seen his father since he was seven, and he desperately wanted to be close to him, to hear his voice.

A thought came into his mind that his father wanted him to circle, to look down, and see all that his childhood consisted of. There were black stains, first where his mother and grandfather died and the two agents who shot them and then the others. He could see where all of them died, their life's blood spilled out onto the ground, leaving the stains.

Looking at the stains made him feel sick inside, but he enjoyed looking at the horizon as he flew. Circling again, he looked down and saw the stains were gone. Something told him to worry about the stains no more. There were no stains. There never had been.

He gasped when he recognized the voice that told him this. It was his father's voice as he remembered it at the age of seven. He had forgotten what his father's voice sounded like, but now it seemed only seconds since the last time the voice entered his mind and heart through his ears. He felt safe and protected. The way only a loved child can feel when near his or her mother and father. It had been more than half his life since he felt so contented and safe.

Once, his father told him you couldn't control under what circumstances you are born or when, where, or how you will die, but in between, a good man will always do the right thing as he sees it. There *are* core values engraved in the human heart, live by them.

Cool water washed across Timucua's face. He opened his eyes, but could see only a blur of motion in front of him. Someone was wiping his face with a wet cloth.

It must be Mr. Ironwood.

He blinked. With some effort, he was able to see a little.

Brown hair. No, light brown hair, long.

A face he had never seen.

Well, that settles it. I must be dead. An angel, with the light of Jesus in her eyes. What? And I thought I was going to...

The back of a small hand touched his forehead. "Fever's broke," someone said. "He's waking up."

Timucua blinked, then again, trying to clean away the blurring film on his eyes. The angel was still there, but he now understood she was mortal, and he was not in heaven. He had never heard of heaven hurting like this, but then, he had never seen a living angel before either.

A young girl sat by the bed, maybe seventeen or eighteen, smiling at him as if she were happy to see him awake, though he did not know her. His eyes did not want to be pulled away from hers. They were blue and illuminated by some mysterious power that could only be good. He finally pried his eyes away and decided her face went well with her eyes.

The skin looked so smooth and soft. How could she come from the cruel, brutalizing world he had been immersed in since that day? She must have been protected from it all somehow, otherwise there would be visible scars cut deep into her heart, her soul, and he could see both, but no scars, no hate. What he did see was…not possible, not in a mere mortal human.

He tried to lift his arm to touch her face and prove to himself that she was real. Pain shot to the tips of his left fingers and back up his arm into his shoulder to reach the back of his head where it swam around in his skull until it faded enough he could think of something other than the pain. It was still there but he could now push it to the back of his consciousness again.

This time he lifted his right arm and let his left lie as it was. He lightly brushed his fingers down her left cheek, holding his hand for a second under her chin. "Beautiful," he muttered. He was touching the softest, smoothest thing he had ever touched in his life.

"Now kid, that's enough of that." A small, feminine hand held his for a second and then put it back to his right side.

Mr. Ironwood stood behind the girl. "Yep. I would say he's getting better all right. All it took was one look at your face girl. Should have asked you to help with him sooner."

"Yeah, right. Maybe you should've warned me about him before he woke up."

"Didn't know there was anything to warn you about. You got to remember, he's been out of it for days. I expect that if the first thing I saw after what he's been through was your pretty face, I might have been trying a lot more. And I'm an old man."

"Now Mr. Ironwood, I can forgive him, but you need to watch your mouth." She smiled.

"I meant no offense, Sharon."

"None taken."

Timucua's vision cleared and he looked at her intensely for a few seconds as if he had never seen a girl before in his life, then the world went dark again.

*   *   *

"Patrick, you're not going to be able to use that arm for a while. Don't be rushing yourself. It's only been a month." Mr. Ironwood spoke to him from across the small dining table.

"Six weeks," Timucua said. "And it takes everything I have just to lift a glass with it."

"That's not bad, considering."

Timucua looked at his bandaged arm. "Where's my rifle?"

"One of the boys cleaned it for you, the pistol too. In fact all of your stuff has been cleaned and put in my closet."

"There seems to be a lot of helping hands around here, while I lie around and do nothing."

The elder man scratched his face. "Yeah, well, don't be thinking you're taking advantage of anybody. We all owe you. Tenerson was here a few days before you woke up. After what you did for his wife and daughter, believe me, if he could he would give you his left arm to replace that one. Instead, he left some food. Said he would be back sometime after you're well to thank you to your face."

"Well, I don't see what that has to do with me laying around at other's expense." He got out of his chair. "I need the rifle. I want to practice dry-firing in prone position."

Mr. Ironwood started to say something, caught himself, and then began to speak. "I try not to think of you as a sixteen-year-old boy. I know the boy is gone, dead perhaps. Either way, you're not a boy anymore. I saw...felt...that thousand-yard stare the moment you started to get better. I saw and felt that same dehumanized, used-up inward stare into the depths of hell many decades ago; knowing the rest of the recon team in turn saw it on my face."

Timucua sighed impatiently. "Have I traded one nosey grandfather for another?"

"Calm down now and humor a senile old man for a minute or two, will you? You have the rest of your life to live with the consequences of the last two and a half months. Listening to me for a minute isn't going to hurt you."

Timucua stood silently.

"The only time I see any of the old Patrick, and then for a fleeting moment or two, is when you're with Sharon. Part of your soul, your spirit, has been replaced by something. I do not know what it is, but I'm afraid it's hate."

"What do you expect?"

"It isn't about what I expect. I was your grandpa's friend and I'm your friend. Do you believe that?"

"Yes."

"Then listen to what I have to say. There is a war coming. That war is about freedom, not revenge. Those who killed your mother and grandfather are dead. Let the hate die with them. I am the last surviving member of my family. Dissident Control killed them all. Including great-grandchildren and in-laws, twenty-one of my kin were murdered by the government on the same day. Four were babies. I think I know about pain and hate."

His age-filmed eyes looked around the room. "I've been living in this shack since they burned my home down the day they killed my family. Except for your grandpa and you...and a few militia members coming around, I've been a hermit since. Ten years now.

"The land around us, fifteen hundred acres, has been in my family's possession since eighteen eighty six. Government claims that it's part of the World Biosphere, and only animals can live here. They can kiss my ass! It's mine. If they knew I was here they would send a murder team to kill me." He looked at his young friend. "And if they knew you were here…"

"They'll get me sooner or later and you know it."

"Later is better. This land, I need someone to leave it to when I die. I thought maybe Sharon…or you."

"I'm likely to die before you. Give it to her or anyone you want. I won't need it where I'm going."

Mr. Ironwood leaned forward in his chair. "Now you remember these words because there will come a time when you will need them." He paused, his eyes distant. "Hate leaves you with nothing. You got to have more than hate to live for. You might not let those words sink in right now, but there will come a time when that fire in you starts to cool a little. If you're smart, that's when you will remember those words and let them sink in."

Timucua looked out the open door. "The national police left me with nothing already. And you and I both know it won't be long before they kill me."

"You're hard to kill, you proved that." He gave Timucua a wintry smile. "It wasn't that you were afraid of dying. You probably weren't even sure you wanted to live. You just wanted to show them they weren't tough enough or smart enough to do it. I knew a young man just like you once. He was death on two legs in a fight. He was your grandpa."

"I just wanted to make them pay first."

"Yeah, I know. If they want to see the show, first they have to buy the ticket. Well, think about what I said."

"In the meantime I want to find out if I can still hold a rifle."

"It's in the closet if you want it."

"Good." Timucua started to leave.

"Hold on a second. One more thing. Sharon, the girl who has been helping me with you. Have you thanked her?"

"I—"

"No you haven't. In fact you've been mistreating her."

"I never did anything to her."

"You've been cold to her even though you know she likes you."

"How can she like me if I've been mistreating her? What's there to like about me anyway? Then there's the fact I'm not going to be around much longer. She should set her sights a lot higher."

"I don't know, but you seem to be the only one around here who can't see that see likes you. Bart will tell you the same."

"I don't believe you. Why would a girl like her have anything to do with me? You're just playing with me because she's so pretty."

Mr. Ironwood laughed. "You seem to be full of questions. Why don't you ask her? She's the only one who can answer them. Just don't be cold to her. You hear me? I love her like a granddaughter, and she has nothing to do with you hurting inside. It's not her fault, so don't take it out on her."

"For God's sake. I've been treating her same as you."

He laughed again. "I hope not. Just thank her for taking care of you."

"I can certainly do that." He disappeared into the bedroom.

Timucua came out of the room holding the rifle by the barrel with his right hand, the muzzle pointed skyward, and walked out the front door.

Mr. Ironwood got up and followed him, grabbing a chair off the front porch to set under the shade of a tree while he watched. He was tired. He had not slept much since the boy arrived. The first two days and nights after the doctor left, he took care of him alone, except for two or three of the militia members who were usually busy with either picket duty or running for more supplies.

The old man asked his young friend Sharon, to help, and since then he had gotten more sleep, but he was still bone-tired. She had been a Godsend though. She bathed the boy and cut his hair, even shaved him, all while he was unconscious. She once nicked him on the chin with the old man's straight razor, and he was amused when she became so upset, acting as if she hated herself.

Sitting in the chair, he watched Timucua check the rifle's chamber and receiver to make sure it was empty. "I bet you're glad your grandpa bought that synthetic stock for the Garand, aren't you? Makes the rifle more accurate in all weather. You've already been through swamps at high water with it. Imagine worrying about a wood stock soaking up water and warping, throwing the point of aim off all the time."

Timucua fell to his knees and tightened the sling on his upper left arm, his face showing a slight hint of pain. "You got that right. Not as pretty as wood, but pretty doesn't do much killing."

The elder man looked over to the other side of the clearing. Sharon was walking up. "Oh, I don't know about that, sometimes pretty can kill."

She took a backpack off and let it swing from her right shoulder, hooking the strap with the crook of her right arm and then letting it swing to the ground in one motion, the contents hardly jarred. Her eyes flashed in the sunlight. "What in the world do you think you're doing? That arm is still nothing but proud, raw flesh, and you're out here rolling around in the mud with it." She turned to Mr. Ironwood. "I thought you wanted the boy to get well. Can't you keep him out of the mud?"

"No I can't. I tried, but he won't listen," Mr. Ironwood said.

Timucua was on his stomach, grimacing in pain, trying to hold the rifle steady and "shoot by the numbers," the way he was taught. He was aiming at a one-inch knothole in a board on the chicken house twenty-five yards away.

The more he tried to shoot the way he always had, the more his arm hurt and the more the rifle moved. Finally, the firing pin clicked. By then sweat was pouring off his face. "Damn. I've got to do better than that." He pulled the bolt back to cock the rifle. Once more, he tried, with the same result. "This is going to take a while."

When he reached to pull the bolt back again, he thought he heard someone yelling in his ear. He looked up to notice Sharon was standing beside him looking down.

"A lot of people worked hard to get you well," Sharon said, "and this is the thanks you give us."

Timucua, still looking up at her, trying to ignore how pretty she was, said, "If I can't shoot I might as well have died anyway."

She tilted her head and gave him a look that made it clear she thought he was insane. "If you think revenge is all there is to live for, you're dead already." She picked up her pack and stormed off into the shack.

Timucua resumed dry firing the rifle. The firing pin clicked again, and he glanced over toward the shack to see her looking through one of the only two windows on that side of the building. Instantly, she turned as if she were doing something and not watching at all.

Mr. Ironwood chuckled. He had been watching the whole thing with amusement as if he had seen it all before, and he had. "Patrick, you don't want to be overstressing that arm. I'm not trying to boss you, but I've been through it a few times myself, starting when I was about five or six years older than you. What I'm saying is, you don't want to be rushing things. Take your time."

Timucua had been focusing on the top edge of the front sight, trying to ignore the pain. He only caught the last sentence. "Don't worry, I'm not sick now. I won't touch her again." He had been told about what happened when he woke up for a few seconds that time.

Mr. Ironwood looked perplexed. Then he began to laugh more than he had in years. "I wouldn't bet on it."

Chapter 11

"You've been pushing yourself too hard again," Mr. Ironwood said. "You won't admit it, but your arm is hurting isn't it?"

"What makes you think that? Do you hear me bitching?" Timucua asked.

"I don't have to hear. Common sense tells me without you saying a word. All day, you've been patrolling the area with a heavy pack on, carrying a full combat load. Then you spent two hours dry firing from prone, sitting, and standing. Now you're paying for it."

"It's okay."

"Okay, bullshit. I know why you didn't take care of your arm before. I was hoping maybe you learned something from that."

"What are you talking about?"

"When you were out there waging your private war, you didn't concern yourself with that arm because you thought you would be dead before it got so infected and rotted, and you got sick and weak. Well, you were wrong weren't you? You did live long enough." The valleys and crevices on the old man's face deepened. "Now you're itching to get back to your war and don't care about that arm so long as it can hold the far end of the rifle steady enough to shoot straight." He shook his head. "It's not your natural-born inclination to be a hater, Patrick. I know. I saw you grow up and know how you were raised. If they kill you with a bullet that would hurt me. But it won't hurt anywhere near as much as knowing you let them kill you with hate."

"I remember you saying they had already killed the 'old Patrick,' as you put it."

Mr. Ironwood rubbed his chin with a shaking hand. "I was talking about the innocent boy, not the man. Now I'm talking about the human man in you."

"Well, I don't think they have turned me into an animal yet. And my arm is okay." Shooting bolts of pain ran up and down his arm. He would not admit it, as he did not want to be reminded of how many times he had been warned. He just sat there in the dark on Mr. Ironwood's porch, swatting mosquitoes with his good hand, trying to pretend his arm was fine.

The two grew silent for many minutes.

Frogs in the distant bayou were belching out their lamenting love songs that only a frog could find romantic. Even they seemed to have little hope of success tonight. Fortunately, the few frogs ambitious enough to suffer the cold water of the spring run were relatively quiet. However, the crickets in the nearby brush were making up for their neighbors' quietude. It was a warm humid night in the Southern woods. So humid you could smell and taste it. Only in winter, when the temperature is near freezing or below, are the Southern woods ever quiet at night.

Mr. Ironwood spoke from the other end of the porch. "I thought I should mention I've been receiving reports of many people being forced out of their homes and taken to the cities." He hesitated a few seconds. "Unfortunately many of those people aren't making it to the cities."

"What do you mean?" Timucua asked.

"I think you know what I mean."

"I don't understand why they call it the Removal Plan anyway. They did not even try to remove my mother and grandfather. They just murdered them."

"Young friend, I have a suspicion the Final Removal Plan is just another term for Final Solution."

"It was before my time, but I read about it. I also read about another Removal Plan, here in America and what they did to my ancestors."

"I'm not quite that old either, Patrick, but my father and uncles saw firsthand what was done to the Jews in Europe."

"Sometimes I'm ashamed of what people do."

"What governments have done?"

"Yes, but governments can't do a damn thing that the people don't let them. It was not just the Nazi government that hated Jews. It was the common folk. And there was plenty of that here in America at the time."

Timucua paused to listen. His ears determined it was an armadillo digging in the grass. He laid the Garand back in his lap and continued. "Roosevelt sent European Jews who made it here by ship back to the Nazis, knowing they would all be murdered. Most of them were small children. I think all but about two hundred and fifty were saved by other Jews later, but that doesn't reduce Roosevelt's shame."

Timucua shook his left arm and rubbed it. "What I'm most ashamed of are our own people. For years, we just wanted to be left alone, thinking if we stayed out of their way, they would respect us and return the favor. I can understand wanting to believe in the best of others, at least until their actions force you to do otherwise. But I cannot understand why more of our people are not fighting back now. Our people are not going to make the same mistake as the Jews, are we?"

Mr. Ironwood ran his hands over each other as he tried to work his aching joints. "Cooler weather will be coming soon. Just as well, I'm too old to do much fighting in the heat. It's time for us Wild People, as they call us, to face reality. The big fight is coming. One way or another, this thing is going to be settled. Your question will be answered, soon."

There was a moment of silence. Then Mr. Ironwood continued. "You can help."

"How can I help?"

"By staying alive. If you were killed in action, so to speak, you would be a martyr, but you are actually ten times more inspirational alive. Being only sixteen, you have deeply shamed some of the men; maybe enough they will grow a pair and fight now."

The old man looked into the dark distance between them. "And everyone now knows about the declaration of war you wrote to the government. I don't think you will ever fully understand how much those words have affected people. It explains the situation completely, both on the individual personal level and our people as a whole."

"I just told them why I'm going to keep killing them, until they kill me."

"If you had just threatened them," Mr. Ironwood said, "it would have meant little if anything. You said a lot more than that."

"I didn't write the Declaration of Independence."

"It's what you wrote on the back I'm talking about, and you know it. So our people need you alive, and to tell you the truth, I'm sick of outliving all the good people I've known. Do me a favor and let me die before you."

"I'm not going to give my life away free," Timucua said. "They'll have to pay for it, but I will not stop killing them until they leave our people alone. When I learned they like to kill so much, I resolved to give them more killing than they can stomach. I have just begun."

"You've got to control that fire Patrick. It'll burn you up from the inside out."

"You might as well come to terms with the fact you may outlive me. I'm the last of my family too, so I know what it's like. But people have to play the cards they are dealt, and that's what I'm doing."

Timucua heard the armadillo scurry off toward the spring run. "Now if you think you can trust me, I would like to know more about your organization. The number and location of your observation posts, how many trained and armed fighters you have available, most important, how committed are they to being free. Are they willing to pay *any* price?"

There was silence for a few seconds.

"Anything else you want to talk about?"

"Yes. Why haven't your fighters stopped the government goons from killing our people?"

"How?"

"Have ambush teams on every road that leads to Wild People country, as they call our land. So far, they're using ground travel more than aircraft. That will change, but for now, we can kill them on the roads before they get to the farms. Of course, we need anti-armor weapons and explosives. Maybe we can rig up what they call a fougasse."

"Foogas? Oh yeah, I remember what a fougasse is. In 'Nam we used gas. We set it off when the NVA got inside the wire of an FOB or firebase. Burnt their ass up like napalm."

"It means different things, any improvised weapon for instance. What I'm talking about is a homemade cannon set up to fire at an APC as it goes down a road. You can even bury it pointing straight up so when an APC, or maybe even a tank, drives over you shoot it up into the bottom of the vehicle where the armor is weakest. We can use six to twelve inch diameter steel pipe to make the barrels with."

"Yeah." Mr. Ironwood smiled in the dark. "A Titan-sized shotgun like that could rip an unarmored vehicle to shreds."

"Fortunately most of their vehicles are not armored, just thin-skinned utility vehicles and the like." Timucua patted his rifle. "Battle rifles shoot through them easily. It's the armor we will have trouble stopping."

"We have some homemade black powder and some modern bulk military surplus rifle powder in twenty-five-pound cans."

"Black powder may not produce enough velocity to defeat armor, but it's worth a try. We need to capture an APC and use it for experiments. I had one, but I couldn't bring it with me."

Mr. Ironwood laughed. "Yeah, I heard about that."

"Who told you?"

"We get information like that in different ways."

"You know that fifty I used on them by the river might work on some APCs. John Browning sure knew what he was doing when he designed the Ma Deuce more than a century ago. I doubt he had any idea the Army would still be using it at this late date though."

"How'd you learn about the Ma Deuce and Browning? You have studied this stuff? I knew your grandpa was teaching you small unit tactics, but I didn't think he was teaching you about machineguns."

"I read every book I could get my hands on until the day they killed my family. My grandfather taught me a lot also. I think I could headspace and time a Browning after reading about it and then asking my grandfather a few questions. Anyway, now I'm sure I can operate one."

The old man chuckled. "Yeah, I think so. They tell me you burned down their roving command post with a couple belts of .50-cal."

"That reminds me. Sharon told me they burned my grandfather's home and barn and killed all the livestock."

"Uh, yeah," Mr. Ironwood said, "that's what they do. The idea is to appease World Government so they won't come in and take over completely. They have decreed seventy-five percent of the North American Continent be depopulated and returned to nature."

"Kindhearted of W.G. to be so concerned about our wildlife, isn't it?"

"Yeah," Mr. Ironwood said, "they're bighearted people."

"And it has nothing to do with them wanting all of us in the cities so we will be completely dependent on them for all necessities like food, making it easy for them to control us. Anyway, I think you know the elephant in the room is W.G. They'll send soldiers as soon as our government gets into trouble."

"Those damn Europeans will stick their nose in our mess, that's a certainty."

"They don't have enough balls to even know what freedom is; much less understand us Wild People."

The old man laughed.

"Mr. Ironwood, how are you organized? In triads, three man rifle teams?"

The old man looked at the voice in the dark. "Yes. How did you know?"

"Makes sense for a guerrilla force. Three triads make a rifle squad. Three rifle squads make a platoon. It's safer to use no more than three or four triads on any one mission right now, at least not until we're stronger and they're weaker. Don't want to make the mistake of acting like a conventional army. That can get a lot of us wiped out fast. What we need to do is, use swarming tactics. Hit and run. Stay dispersed. Even though Mitchell and Douhet's theories on airpower proved wrong during World War II, it's a good thing we have no population or industrial centers for them to bomb. They have depopulated the rural areas to a great extent with their Removal Plan over the years, so we're already spread out on our little farms. But we need to disperse even more and go to ground, hide as much as possible and still produce enough food to feed ourselves."

"You have studied guerrilla warfare too?" Mr. Ironwood seemed surprised.

"Of course. Even that communist, Che Guevara, had some ideas."

"Okay, I'm going to spend the next few days showing you what is going on in the world I have lived in for decades, and I want you to offer advice to me freely. But once those three days are over, keep in mind that most adults are not going to take kindly to a teenager telling them how to fight this war. Be political about it, otherwise you'll bend some egos and cause friction. Understand?"

"Yes. But you cannot expect me to let stupidity get good people killed just because I'm supposed to be too young to know my ass from a hole in the ground, do you?"

"Happens all the time in warfare, Patrick. Whether it's youth or rank. You're new, and you're young. They won't like you butting in and telling them they know less, even if they do, *especially* if they do."

There was a moment of silence as they sat in the dark. Timucua used the opportunity to listen for approaching danger. He heard nothing but woods sounds.

"I tell you what," Mr. Ironwood said, "you have a reputation already, and there are plenty of young people who want to fight alongside you. Why don't you lead three triads of volunteers? Remember, the first item on your agenda is to bring them all back alive. That may not always happen, but it's number one. You understand?"

"I'm not sure I want to be responsible for other people's lives."

"Yes, I know. Otherwise, you wouldn't be fit to lead at all. Patrick, were you afraid when you fought those agents the morning they killed your grandfather and mother?"

"Of course I was. What kind of question is that?"

"I asked because I needed to know. Because a man who is never afraid is not a man. And a man who does not do the right thing despite the fact he is afraid, is a coward."

Chapter 12

"Call me Timucua. Only Mr. Ironwood calls me Patrick." He stood before nine volunteers who expressed a desire to fight alongside the boy who had declared war on the Department of Dissident Control. The sun had risen only twenty minutes earlier. Thin, translucent, orange, and red clouds flared in multiple feathers across the glowing blue sky behind him. Humidity was in the ninety percent range. He smelt and tasted the swamp when he inhaled the sixty-eight-degree air, which felt relatively cool to him. Still thin, pale, and not as strong physically, as he was before his life changed, he wondered how many were disappointed with what they were now seeing.

He was somewhat distracted by their expectant faces. They were looking at someone who could not possibly be him, someone much more experienced and competent than he was feeling.

They stood before him in a line, not military style, in a brace or at ease, but the way high school kids might stand in front of a coach. All of them were fit; no fat bodies among them, ranging in age from eighteen to twenty-eight. Three were women.

"Mr. Ironwood says I am to lead you in our next fight." Timucua looked from face to face. "That does not make me better than you, and it damn sure does not make me God. But I need to know what to expect from you, and you need to know what to expect from one another and me. Only our lives depend on it."

He started walking down the line, quickly looking over their equipment, especially their weapons. "We must fight in an organized, coordinated system that supports one another. All we're going to have when it hits the fan is each other." Stopping and turning back at the end of the line, he continued. "No reinforcements. No supply lines. Almost no medical care for the wounded. Just one another and what we can carry on our backs. If we fail one another, we are just

SOL. For that reason, we must know each other's strengths and weaknesses. We all have them both. I know I do."

Standing before the nine young people whose lives he would soon be responsible for, Timucua felt their eyes assessing him. "I have been told stories have been spread about me. I don't know how much of it is true, but I have managed to survive more than one fight with the murderous bastards. That much at least is true."

Bart spoke up. "Don't worry; I don't think anyone here expects you to be our Joshua."

"I hope not. I'm not so sure God is on my side. What will be on our side is accurate shooting and supporting fire and maneuver techniques. A properly-trained fire team, a triad, is not three times more effective than a single fighter, but ten times." He looked them each in the eye. "At least ten times, and a squad, three triads and a squad leader, is a hundred times more effective than a fighter alone. Maybe you already know that. If you don't, you will before you fight with me."

His eyes lingered for a fraction of a second on a girl at the left end of the line. "I understand that all of you have been with the resistance for some time." He turned to his right. "I'm sure many of you know more than I do about certain subjects, so don't hesitate to give advice, but there can be only one person in charge. If not, who are you going to blame when something goes wrong? That's why they always find some poor bastard to put in charge. Unfortunately, for now at least, I'm that poor bastard."

There was a murmur of laughter. Someone yelled out, "I know what you mean: Many of us have been there."

Walking down the line, he stopped and turned around when he reached the other end. "Who among you can put a bullet in an eighteen-inch circle at five hundred yards shooting from prone? Every time?"

There were no hands raised.

"Then all of us have work to do."

Timucua walked over and stood before the oldest. He was Mr. Ironwood's friend, Bart, who carried an M14. "Bart, you and—"

A teenager with an FAL spoke up. "Mathew." He was three inches shorter than Timucua, thirty-five pounds lighter than any man in the group was, and had a face that made him look even younger than his actual years.

Timucua nodded. "Mathew." He looked at Mathew's clothing and equipment. "How old are you?"

"Older than you." Mathew eyed him.

"In years." Timucua's face was unreadable.

"Almost nineteen."

"Where did you get those boots?" Timucua asked.

"Off a dead Dissident Control agent. The same place I got this big-ass backpack and the boonie hat, and a lot of other stuff that's in the pack."

Timucua smiled. "It's those weird tie-dyed camouflage pants I was wondering about."

Everyone laughed, including Mathew.

"My mother made up a half dozen for me with blue jeans and green and brown dye. They might not look pretty, but they help hide me in the woods."

"Point taken." Timucua became serious. "How far can you kill a man with that FAL?"

"Four, five hundred yards but not every time. With a scoped bolt-action yes, but not with this."

"Is the barrel good?" The tone of Timucua's voice made it clear the question was important.

"Bright and clean."

"Then you will be killing men at five hundred yards all day long before I'm through with you."

Timucua walked past two men with carbines and stopped in front of one with a rifle. "And you with the Garand."

A man in his early twenties stood a little straighter. He was exactly six feet tall. His shoulders strained to rip his olive drab fatigue jacket apart, and he looked as if he could break a man's back if he wanted to. Timucua doubted it would take much to put him in the right frame of mind to want to. He wore his jet-black hair down to his shoulders, kept it tamed, and out of his eyes with a sweatband cut from the pant leg of a military uniform in woodland camouflage. He looked more like an Indian than Timucua did. The homemade boots of thick leather soles and twelve-inch buckskin uppers that he wore over his pant legs put the finishing touch to his Indian patina. "My name is Tel," he said.

"Okay Tel. Is the M1 chambered for thirty aught six or has it been converted to seven point six two?"

"It's GI issue."

"Good," Timucua said. "The Garand it not designed to take the higher pressure. It never made any sense to me to alter a classic anyway. How much ammo do you have for it?"

"I've got ammo and clips buried all over; about two thousand clips and fifteen thousand rounds."

"You won't need any of my ammo then. The question is how far can you reach out and kill a man with it?"

Tel looked him in the eye. "The chamber throat is half gone, but it still gives me four MOA, so I can kill a man at four hundred, five, if I get lucky."

"It's still a five-hundred yard rifle, and you will soon be a five-hundred yard rifleman."

He walked over to the end of the line where a teenage girl stood holding a Savage bolt-action rifle. He needed to know if it was chambered for a long-range caliber. "What caliber is the rifle, Sharon?"

Timucua was standing there looking at what he still considered the prettiest face he had ever seen and thinking about the time he made her blush. It was the first week after he became conscious but was still too weak to get out of bed for anything but using a "honey bucket" that had to be placed in the bedroom, because the outhouse was too far.

One day she insisted on giving him a sponge bath. Of course, like any self-respecting boy, he refused. That is when she informed him the event had taken place twice before while he was still helpless.

"You had half of every swamp in the Southeast on you," she explained.

"Did it take more than one time to get me clean?"

She laughed. "You were sweating so much from your fever you needed cleaning again after only two days." He remembered her saying, "Mr. Ironwood is going to have to throw that mattress out. It's soaked with sweat, blood, and tears."

"Whose tears? It damn sure wasn't mine."

He remembered how Sharon put her hands on her hips, her feet wide, her upper body leaning to her left from the waist, and gave him a cold stare. "Mr. Ironwood's. He was worried about you."

It seemed to him she had appointed herself his official nursemaid and guardian angel. For some reason, all his protestations did nothing but encourage her more.

He was able to dissuade her from further efforts to bathe him. "I'm claiming rights to return the favor, and you already have at least two such baths coming." He tried to make his face unreadable. "Maybe three." It did manage to cause her face to turn red for a second or two. That alone made the argument worth the trouble, a small measure of revenge. He was not completely successful in his attempt not to smile at her blushing face.

That is when she revealed to him that the angel did indeed have a temper, and he had a dirty mind if he thought she had any interest in him at all. "I'm just doing my civic duty by helping out a wounded freedom fighter. My brother was one, and I believe in the cause." She added, "I hope you would have the decency to take care of anyone under the same circumstances." This ended the argument, as he did not want to think of her going through what he had.

Now, he stood before her, already under a handicap, because he admitted that time while still semiconscious that she was beautiful. Despite what Mr. Ironwood said, he was not sure what she thought of him or what her motives were. Perhaps she was just doing her civic duty as she saw it. Either way, he considered her a distraction from what he had made up his mind to do, a very pretty and alluring distraction, but a distraction nonetheless.

He promised Mr. Ironwood he would thank her for taking care of him when he was sick. Now he remembered the day he did. When he saw the reaction on her face, he almost regretted it. It seemed to release a coiled spring in her. "It's an honor to help you," she gushed. "After all, you've fought harder than anyone. People are calling you a hero."

His response, he spoke before he thought was, "Bullshit."

Her face turned pink and then red. "Bullshit what? Me?"

"No. Hell no. I wouldn't say anything like that. I meant the idea of me being a hero."

"You can't take a compliment. Or is it just me you can't take?"

"Come on. You have to admit you were laying it on thick."

"What? The bullshit?"

He rolled his eyes. "Will you stop taking offense to everything I say? Look, everybody likes you. Why are you so defensive?"

"Everybody but you it seems."

"Okay, I like you. Will you stop acting as if I just insulted you or something? Who doesn't like you?" He quickly decided he had better back up a little. "Now don't take an inch and stretch it into a mile. It doesn't mean we're engaged or anything."

"Of course not. You must think you're really something." She tilted her head and looked at him as if she thought he was crazy. "*Engaged!* You're so stuck-up you can't even open up to me this much." She held her hand up, thumb and forefinger an eighth of an inch apart.

"Stuck-up? You're too good for me. But none of that matters anyway."

"Why not?"

"I would rather not talk about it," he said.

Now, here she was distracting him at a time like this. His reminiscing ended when she gave him an embarrassingly warm smile and said, "It's a thirty aught six."

A girl doesn't smile like that unless she's up to something. "Ah, good. What kind of scope is it?"

Timucua could not believe it. Her smile got more warm and enthusiastic. He had not thought that possible. She had her high beams on. Her blue eyes were burning right through him. Every time she bathed him in the light of those eyes, he felt himself melting and he would find some excuse to escape before she saw through his cold exterior. At this moment, he had nowhere to run.

His forehead began to sweat, though the morning air felt cool only moments before. After what seemed to him three lifetimes, she finally answered, "It's a ten power Leupold with a Mil Dot reticle. My brother told me that much anyway."

He needed an excuse to look at something besides her face. The few times he had allowed himself to look at her, he found her face flawless. She had a few light freckles on her nose that gave her just enough of a "flaw" to help remind him that she was human after all and not the angel for who he first mistook her.

By now, he was certain she was just trying to embarrass him. She knew she made him nervous, and now she was rubbing it in. Unfortunately, he could not think of any defense at the moment. For the life of him, he could not come up with any smart-ass remark that would redirect the discomfort to her. "May I examine it more closely?" Timucua asked.

"Sure." She handed it to him.

He shouldered it and aimed at the top of the tallest tree in the area about a hundred yards away. Looking through the scope, he saw that the lenses were still in good shape, no scratches, and it still appeared to be watertight. He tried to twist the scope in its mount to check if it was tight. He could not move it.

Timucua opened the receiver and found the rifle empty. After removing the bolt, he looked down the bore to check the rifling. It was clean and bright. He replaced the bolt and noticed half the bluing was worn off the receiver and barrel. It had a black synthetic stock that had been spray painted here and there flat green for camouflage. Its receiver had been carefully bedded in the stock to enhance accuracy. The rifle was four decades old and heavily used, but well taken care of.

Nodding approval, he said, "This is a sniper's rifle. The bore is good, and it has a heavy barrel. It should be able to kill a man at seven, eight hundred yards. If you know how to use it, you will be our designated marksman or sniper. On the other hand, if you can't use it, you should trade it with someone who can."

"I was hoping you would teach me how to use it." Sharon looked like she was smiling at a private joke.

Timucua was almost afraid to look up, but he had to. At first, he was relieved. Her big warm smile was gone, but it seemed to have turned into a kind of smirk, which was not so bad, but her blue eyes were burning into him like never before. Never in his had life had he felt more helpless and vulnerable, and that scared the hell out of him. Her smirk seemed to be telling him she was scheming against him in someway. What a sly girl she must be. But then again, he might just be seeing things that are not there.

He thought he was thick-skinned and did not care about anything but killing anyone who wore the green and black uniform of the enemy of everything he valued and loved. He was not interested in wasting time on anything else. He was Timucua, not Patrick, and even Patrick had no experience with girls. So, why in the world was he letting her bother him? There are lots of pretty girls in the world, so what was it about her?

Suddenly he realized what it was. Take everything dark, cold, and ugly in his heart and send it to hell. What you would have left would not be worthy of basking in the light of the warm human goodness of her. She was his opposite.

Until recently, he believed nothing in this world had ever hurt her, as he could find no scars on her heart. He was so surprised when Mr. Ironwood told him her brother had been killed, he could hardly believe it. Where was the bitterness, the hatred?

It had been only six months since he first saw her that day. The world can turn on a dime. When it comes to moving the world or a boy's heart, Atlas is weak compared to this girl.

To his everlasting embarrassment, it came out of his mouth before he knew it. In fact, they were already laughing before he knew he had said it. "I would rather you shoot at me with this than those eyes. They scare the hell out of me."

He would never remember hearing himself say it, but the laughter was a clear sign he had, and he knew those words could not be recalled. They would just keep marching on.

His face turned several shades of red. He said nothing. What was there to say? He just handed the rifle back to her. She took the rifle, standing there with a knowing look on her face, telling him with her eyes that she *owned* him. If he had said it out loud on purpose, it would not have meant much: a boy getting fresh with a pretty girl, just a little joke. However, she knew by his red face that he did not mean to say it out loud. That is what did it. She had broken his back with her spindly little fingers without even breaking a sweat. From then on, he knew he had lost and she had won, but worst of all, she knew it. Leave it to a girl like her to suck you in like a whirlpool no matter how hard you swim.

How could he explain to her that despite everything, no matter how deeply her warmth penetrated him, he could not give her what she needed? It just was not in him. He was Timucua, not Patrick; a killer, not a teenage boy. She might be able to live in this cruel world and remain undamaged, but he obviously was not as strong as she was.

It was time to deflect the whole thing. "All right, let's get back to work."

Timucua walked down the line of young freedom fighters, focusing his attention on those who carried carbines not suitable for long-range shooting of men. "Though some of you are carrying M4s that I assume you took off dead government goons, you should still be able to kill a man three hundred or more yards away, so you will be undergoing marksmanship training also." He looked at a woman standing by Tel. She had an M4 carbine slung from her left shoulder. "The problem with Stoner-designed carbines is not accuracy; it's the lack of long-range killing power of the caliber it fires. Still, we must be able to utilize our equipment to the very edge of its capability."

"You believe in basics, don't you?" Tel said.

"You bet," Timucua answered. "Accurate shooting equals dead men. Dead men don't shoot back. We're going to start by practicing getting into your natural point of aim, NPOA. Those of you who already know this stuff should not mind the practice. Practice: There is no substitute for it."

Timucua pointed to a rope two feet above the ground and stretching thirty-five feet long. "All of you make certain your rifles are not loaded and get into the prone position on this side of the rope. There is a target for each of you exactly twenty-five meters from the rope. The targets have a one-inch square in the middle. Later, when we use live ammo, you will learn to put every round into that one-inch square. Once you can do that, and learn to adjust your sights, there is no reason why you can't put a bullet into a man's chest at five hundred yards. The rifleman's quarter mile."

Some of them started to take their backpack and load-bearing harness off. "No," Timucua said. "When you fight, you'll be shooting with your combat load on. Always practice the way you will do it while fighting."

Everybody got into his or her idea of the prone shooting position. Timucua stood at the end of the line so he could watch them all at the same time. He saw only one close his eyes and then open them to look through his sights, afterwards adjusting his position by swiveling on his left elbow. He did this three times before he was satisfied.

Timucua yelled out. "Does anyone here know what natural point of aim is?"

The teenager named Mathew raised his hand and spoke up. "I do."

Timucua nodded. "I need you to be my marksmanship training assistant."

"Okay." Mathew stood up, leaving his rifle on the ground.

"Good. Go to the other end of the line where Sharon is and work your way down, explaining to each of them what NPOA is and watch them find it until you're sure they know what you're talking about and how to do it. Also, show the ones who have a shooting sling how and why to use it."

Timucua did the same, starting with the person on his end of the line.

Mr. Ironwood sat in a chair on the porch of his shack watching. He nodded his head, a look of approval on his face.

Timucua noticed most of them were not putting their left elbow as close to directly under the rifle as possible. "You guys need to get your left elbow under the rifle more. The time to stretch your muscles so this becomes second nature is now. The last thing you want is to be forced to learn this under fire. After a few days, you will find the prone position natural and comfortable."

Sharon flashed a look at him. "A few days? We're going to be too sore to move."

Timucua walked over to her. "You'll get over it, but if you can't shoot under fire they will kill you. Remember, you're going to be the designated marksman. If you can't prove to me that you can keep all rounds in a man's chest at six hundred yards, hopefully seven hundred, I will ask you to trade that rifle to someone who can. So if you want to keep it, learn to use it."

Sharon tilted her head defiantly, her upper body propped up on her elbows, and her face showing resolve. "This rifle belonged to my late brother. It's more than just a rifle to me, and I'm not parting with it."

"Fine. Then learn to use it or transfer to another triad that I'm not responsible for."

She snapped her head around and faced the target. Timucua saw hurt and anger flash across her face for a fleeting second as she turned her head.

She was not aiming, just lying there angry. He noticed, and began to fear she might believe he was not going to give her a chance to learn to use her brother's rifle.

He lay down beside her. "Look, I'm not going to take your rifle, but for God's sake, learn how to use it. I'm sure Mathew won't mind helping you. What boy wouldn't want to be close to you?"

She continued to look toward the target. "Evidently you. You seem to want to get rid of me."

"That's not true." A whirlwind of thoughts formed in his head, thoughts he felt he had no time for. "But I do need to know that you and everyone else can shoot. After that, we're going to go over small unit tactics."

"Well then," Sharon said, "why don't you teach me? They say you're a good shot."

"I never said I was not going to give you a chance, or that I won't do my best to teach you. You've been good to me. What kind of person do you think I am?"

When Sharon turned to look at him, she had that smirk on her face again. "I don't know what kind of person you are, yet. You're hiding yourself. I know that."

Timucua felt it was time to change the subject. "Let's stop wasting time. If you want to learn to shoot, first you need to look downrange, not at me. Now put your elbow back the way Mathew taught you." She did so. "Okay that's good. Now find your natural point of aim again."

It took her several tries to find her NPOA. He was pleased to see that Mathew had done well. She knew how, but did she understand why? "Do you understand that trying to shoot while forcing yourself into an unnatural position will decrease your accuracy at long range? Since as a sniper you will be shooting at extreme range, it is doubly important for you to use your shooting sling and always shoot from your NPOA, except in an emergency when there is no time."

She shined her high beams on him, nodding. "Yes, I got that."

"Uh, don't look at me. Look downrange at the target. That's where the action is. Unless you're planning on shooting me and not the target."

She laughed under her breath. "Only with my eyes. Admit it, I make you nervous, don't I?"

He sighed. "Do you want me to teach you how to shoot or not?"

"Yes. Are you angry?"

"No. You do realize I'm not convalescing anymore."

"What are you talking about?"

"When I was sick I had plenty of time for your games. Now that I'm well, it's back to getting ready for the war. And right now, I'm trying to teach you how to shoot so you won't get yourself or someone else killed."

"Games?" she huffed. "You didn't have much time, or should I say, use for me, when you were sick."

He put his hand on her shoulder. "Look, the answer is yes. But I'm sure you make every other guy here nervous to some degree."

She giggled almost inaudibly. "But they would never admit it. You're honest. You hide most of yourself, but what you let people see is real." She was smiling at him again, but this time her mood was sad. She turned back to the target. "You're an enigma. I never met anyone like you. You don't think you want to be my friend, but you can't force yourself to tell me to get lost."

"You think you have all the answers, don't you?"

She turned her head to face him, and once again, her eyes burned through to him. Her smile was warm but sad, not playful or girlish as before when she had giggled. "If I'm wrong, show me. Teach me how wrong I am, but there's the rub, isn't it? To show me I'm wrong you would have to open up to me. Then what? I would learn all that steel is on the outside, hiding warm human flesh, and that you're a sixteen-year-old boy who feels. Not just as much as any other, but stronger, deeper, than any ten boys."

His jaw tensed for a few seconds. "Sharon, you are naïve. You may be older than me, but you have no idea how ugly and cruel this world is. And I am of this world. You say I have armor around my heart, but you have Teflon around yours. Cruelty and ugliness cannot stick to your beauty. I hope it never does."

She looked deeper into him and slowly let a lung full of air escape. For a short time, he thought she might be going to cry, but he could not believe he had said anything as melancholy as that. Finally, she turned back to the target without a word.

She worked the bolt on the empty rifle and aimed at the target. "And by the way, you make me nervous sometimes." She squeezed the trigger. The firing pin clicked. "No one who's ugly inside would say what you just said."

He pretended he did not hear her. "If you're going to shoot with your legs stretched straight like that, which is fine, then you should keep your feet further apart so you will be more stable. Or you can pull your right knee up and leave your left leg straight. Try it both ways and determine which works best for you. Then stay with that method and practice, practice, practice. Dry firing is actually better practice than live firing, and it does not use up ammo. Remember, consistency is extremely important when shooting long range. Always do everything exactly the same, after you learn what works best for you."

Timucua readjusted her left elbow slightly. "I know it's not comfortable, but it will get easier after your muscles stretch. I'm not picking on you. It's important. If your elbow is not directly under the rifle when you exhale or inhale, the rifle will not only move up or down, which is what you want, it may move horizontally also. That you don't want. Your off-hand simply will not hold the rifle as steady." She threw a glance at him. He continued. "By the way, you will find with practice that after going from standing to prone, you won't be far from your NPOA. It's a pain now, but it all gets easier with practice."

"And you do believe in practice, don't you?" Sharon asked.

"Think of it this way, hunters like to do all their hunting before they pull the trigger, not after. That's why they believe in learning how to shoot accurately before they go hunting." He looked at her grimly. "Animals don't shoot back."

"So it's a lot more important to practice before going into combat."

"Yes. A lot of people have spent many generations learning this stuff. Believe me; they know what they're talking about. They learned the expensive way: Their tuition was blood. Everything I'm showing you is important, no matter how trivial or even silly it may seem now. These little things add up fast at long range. Two inches off at one hundred yards means fourteen inches off at seven hundred, a miss. And a miss could cost you your life."

"Seven hundred yards," Sharon said. "Do you think I will ever get that good?"

"Yes. Certainly. If you're willing to work at it."

She turned her high beams on him again. "So you are going to help me become a sniper like my brother."

"I can teach you to shoot, but I can't turn you into a killer. That must come from within."

She sighed and turned back to the target. "I know this is not a game. My brother is dead."

"And a lot more of us are going to die before this is over."

Sharon aimed at the target and slowly pulled the trigger. The rifle's firing pin snapped. She worked the bolt. "What next?"

Chapter 13

Mr. Ironwood sat in the dark on his front porch. Timucua was in another chair eight feet away. "So you're satisfied with their shooting ability now?" Mr. Ironwood asked.

"Yes," Timucua said. "They're all capable of killing a man at five hundred yards, the rifleman's quarter mile. Though most have carbines that are limited in range, they're all able to ring the last yard out of the weapon they carry."

"You seem to be spending extra time with Sharon. Is she having trouble learning how to shoot?"

"No," Timucua said. "She's doing fine. It's just that the standards are higher for her."

"Why is that?"

"Because of the accurate rifle she carries. She is certainly a five-hundred-yard killer, but she needs to be able to reach out to seven hundred yards. She's actually a better shot than most of us. It's just that I believe everyone should be able to shoot more accurately than the rifle he or she carries."

"So you're trying to make a sniper out of her."

"Well," Timucua said, "more like a designated marksman."

Mr. Ironwood coughed. "She says you don't want her to fight."

Timucua did not hesitate. "I don't."

"But you're teaching her to shoot."

"I owe her that. I can't stop her from fighting, so all I can do is give her a better chance to survive by teaching her what I can. As long as she's willing to learn, I'm willing to teach." Timucua paused. "Do you like the idea of her fighting?"

Mr. Ironwood did not answer.

"Well?"

"No," Mr. Ironwood said. "No, I don't."

"Anyway, it took a lot of extra time and work, but I taught her how to use the Mil Dots on her scope reticle, judge range, and dope wind. I taped her come-ups from battle-sight-zero out to one thousand yards on her rifle's butt stock; but I have stressed the use of Mil Dots for range and wind compensation to keep things fast and easy for her."

"Good idea. She's smart enough to learn the come-ups by rote in a short time anyway. For now she can use the Mil Dots."

"I think in the real world of combat it's a lot faster to leave the scope set at battle-sight-zero. Set and forget. To help her learn to use the Mil Dots for range finding, I had her look at men standing, sitting, and prone through her scope at fifty-yard increments from two hundred out to one thousand yards."

"She'll need a lot of that. In fact, they should all get used to seeing a human man in their sights. It's not the same as a paper target."

"Of course," Timucua said, "she took the bolt out of the action first for safety. You know, it's a lot to learn all at once in a short time, but she's smarter than you would think."

"It sounds like she has impressed you."

"Well, I never did take those dumb blonde jokes seriously anyway. A joke has to be about something I guess. So why not pretty girls?"

The old man laughed. "I never thought of it that way, but now that I think about it, you're right. A joke about pretty girls is certainly more interesting than one about a mouse and an elephant."

"Anyway, in time she may be able to make one-thousand-yard shots on a calm day. She seems to be really motivated, and her hard work has paid off. I guess she wants to avenge her brother. Or maybe she just wants to fight for freedom."

"What are your plans for tomorrow?"

"I'm taking them out on patrol." None of Mr. Ironwood's questions surprised Timucua. "I need to know how well they understand what it takes to survive in the woods when men are trying to hunt you down and kill you."

"What about tactics?"

"I'm going to go over the usual small unit stuff. You know, movement techniques such as traveling over watch, bounding over watch, immediate action drills, hasty ambush, immediate assault, break contact, fire and maneuver; a rifle team's interlocking fields of fire. All the stuff my grandpa taught me and a few things I've learned on my own."

"That could keep you busy for a month."

"I'm also going to swing over to one of my caches. I've got to dig up some more ammo for my Garand."

"Sharon shot it up in her bolt-action, did she?"

"Yeah, she went through four hundred rounds. There's another man with an M1, but he has plenty of his own ammo.

"That would be Tel. He's a good man. Don't let him get to you with his sarcastic remarks. He doesn't mean anything. How about your grandfather's .45? Got plenty of ammo?"

"I still have ten thousand rounds of .45 stuff. I'll never use that much since we can't practice much nowadays anyway. That reminds me. I need some nine-millimeter ammo for Sharon."

"I've got some I'll give you in the morning. Where did she get the pistol?"

"Since that rifle of hers, with its ten power scope, is not suitable for close shooting, I scrounged up a Glock and helped her learn how to use it. But I could only find one hundred fifty rounds for her. She shot most of that up. That's only a start. She needs to shoot several thousand rounds before she will even come close to real competency with the pistol. Unfortunately, we can't spare that much for practice. I just hope she never has to use it."

"Looking out for her, are you?"

"Well, sure, her and all the others."

"So you think she's the best choice for sniper?"

"Her rifle kind of dictates that," Timucua said. "But there is no way to know for sure how she or anyone else will react when it hits the fan, until it does. I do wish we had at least one more sniper though."

"I doubt you could get her to give up that rifle anyway."

"I'm glad it worked out that way now, I mean her being a sniper. Government goons are generally poor shots, and she will be back out of range at least some of the time. The only thing standing between what I saw at the Tenerson's farm and her is a gun. She's so damn small and...She does not belong anywhere near evil. But I have no right to tell her she can't fight for her brother or her freedom."

"I know, Patrick. It's not easy, is it? To let her walk into it. Even though it's her choice. Knowing all the while what's awaiting her. But I also know there is going to be a lot more than her rifle standing between her and them."

After some hesitation, the old man spoke again. "Patrick, did you know Sharon has never killed a man?"

"No. You said they had all been fighting for some time."

I thought so, Timucua did not say.

There was a loud moment of silence. "What do you think?" Timucua asked. "You know her better than I do. The day after tomorrow I was planning to take them out on a real ambush. We need to know if we can count on her."

"Like you said, no one knows until the moment of truth."

"Yeah, but can't you tell me something? What's your estimate of her? Well...I mean...can she kill a man?"

"I think she has more good in her than any hundred of the ugly gender, but I'm not sure if she can pull the trigger on a man. There is no way to know. If she does, it will be out of love for someone and not hate for the one she kills."

Timucua's chair creaked as wood rubbed against wood. The weight of his body shifted when he leaned forward to look up at a full moon. There was a ring around it, reminding him of the old adage that you can foretell how many days before rain by counting the number of stars in the ring. He did not believe it. Nothing is that simple.

"She won't allow herself to hate," Timucua said. "It's easier if you hate them."

Mr. Ironwood looked across the porch. The darkness separating them disappeared. He was looking at himself.

*　　　*　　　*

The ten freedom fighters just walked nine miles in three hours. Too fast for safety, but Timucua wanted to be set up for ambushing Dissident Control agents by that afternoon. The enemy had never been much for getting too far from a road on foot, and he felt the risk relatively low. He stayed alert nevertheless. The woods were too thick to walk in two wedge formations, one fifty yards behind the other. Instead, they walked in two single file groups fifty yards apart, each person seven yards behind the other. Even that forced Timucua to work at keeping them on course and in proper formation.

Still, he was proud of their patrolling skills less the result of his teaching abilities, he felt, than their own experience as backwoods farmers and hunters.

His life was no longer in his hands alone. Now, in his hands were the lives of nine young people whom he had already grown to respect. How can you not respect someone who is willing to sign a blank check with blood? A check drawn on his or her personal life account. These people were willing to pay the price of freedom.

He considered this trip to be a training exercise, a trial run, and a chance to see how well these young fighters could work together and stand up to the strain. However, if they made contact with the enemy, people were going to die.

Several times during the day, he reminded himself that he had not asked to fight with them, and he certainly did not ask to lead them. They were the ones who had asked to fight with him, but the weight on his shoulders was already growing heavy.

Timucua admonished them often about the dangers of making too much noise in the woods. Now, someone behind him had developed a case of "battle rattle." He stepped aside and motioned for them to keep walking by him. Timucua learned the person who had not packed her load so nothing would make noise as she walked was the second from the last in the leading group.

Once he discovered who it was, he turned and with long, quick steps got back to the head of the line and raised his left fist, giving the signal to stop and freeze. Then he opened his hand and twisted it, giving the signal to gather around him and "go to ground."

We walked back to Sharon. Trying hard not to be too disapproving, but still displaying a hard glare, he whispered, "Sharon, you're clinking and clanking as you walk. Figure out what it is and do something about it. The rest of you form a tight three sixty and rest while she does it. Mathew, go back and tell Bart to do the same with his team."

She gave him a look that made it clear she thought he was picking on her and then pulled half a dozen loose cartridges from her right fatigue pocket. She was wearing a sun-faded olive drab military surplus fatigue jacket that had a profusion of pockets, and the rifle rounds were being given a good shaking as she swayed her hips.

Sweat-soaked hair stuck to her forehead. She looked as out of place as anyone could in the heat and humidity. The other two women were obviously hot, tired, and uncomfortable, but they seemed to be nowhere near as out of place as Sharon. Still, looking at her sweaty face gave him the feeling he could smear it with mud and she would be no less beautiful. He half expected the mud to refuse to stick to her skin and just fall off anyway.

Timucua wanted to tell her to go home, but he would just as soon put his hand in front of a diamondback rattlesnake and let it bite him. She wanted to be with them, and she had a right to fight for her freedom. As long as she did not endanger the others with incompetence, he could not deny her a chance to fight in memory of her brother. This was simply not enough of an infraction to shame her by sending her home. He was afraid she would join another group and fight anyway, and then he would not be able to look after her safety.

Kneeling in front of her, Timucua whispered, "Put them in your pants pocket for now. Your jeans are tight enough your pocket will keep them from rattling."

She knelt on her knees and put them in her pocket.

Her displeasure of his demeanor was easy to read on her face. Her discomfort from the heat and humidity added to the effect. He could not help but notice that even angry, she was beautiful. Did *everything* about her have to be so endearing? Even when angry with him, what he called her "girliness," seeped into his soul like a warm fire on a cold night.

"I don't understand why you're being this way," she whispered. "No one could hear that more than ten feet away."

Timucua looked down. He was afraid she would read his mind if she saw his eyes at that moment. What was it about this girl? He sighed as if he was losing patience with her, though that was not the case. "I was on point, and I could hear it. But the problem is, I can't hear if there are enemy in the area, if all I can hear is you."

Sharon glared at him. "You're just used to being alone in the woods and don't want to put up with us. We're only human and not the great Timucua warrior."

Timucua shook his head and put his right hand up. "This is not the time or place for that. There could be people in these woods who want to kill us. Concentrate on holding up your end of the load."

Sharon's reaction told him his words had stung her. They were not meant to, but he had no time to be unduly concerned about hurt feelings. Hurt feelings won't kill you. She turned her head slightly and looked away, her eyes still shining, but not brilliantly, as when they looked right through to his soul. It was a look that he had already come to know and experience, anytime he hurt or disappointed her in some way. He did not like it. It made him feel that he had committed a sin. After all, hurting or letting an angel down had to be a sin.

Timucua was not able to decide if it was his youth and inexperience with girls, or if there really was something special about her. Perhaps it was a little of the former and a lot of the later. Either way, he would just have to deal with it along with everything else.

Though he liked girls from as far back as he could remember, he had never experienced lust the way he had since he first got to know her. Then he had never been around a girl who had so much to lust after, in both personality and appearance. She had everything in all the right places with the right size, shape, and curves, all covered with the most beautiful skin he had ever seen. Everything about her told him she was a girl, from her voice to the sway of her hips. He could not admit to himself he wanted her, and he dare not admit it to her. However, he was afraid she had already seen it in his eyes.

Now, he realized more than ever she was not the kind of complication he needed in his life, not in the middle of a war. He also felt privileged to have met her, and blessed to have attracted her attention at all. He knew there would never be another Sharon, not in his life. That knowing was the only thing that kept him from driving her away, for her and his own good. Caring about someone in time of war just leaves you open to more hurt. Chances are some of them would be dead in a few weeks or months, perhaps her, perhaps him.

If he had been a little older, he may have been strong enough to do the smart, sensible thing and not let her under his skin. He had and was resisting that warmth radiating from her, but it was persistent, relentless, and had already started to penetrate the armor he had built up around his heart. She was who she was, and he found her irresistible.

He put his hand on her shoulder. "Hey, this is not a big deal. I'm the one who told you to keep extra rounds always ready for quick reloading. I'm just doing the best I can to keep us alive. You're doing okay."

Timucua stood, walked to the head of the line, raised his right open hand, and swept it forward, giving the hand signal to resume the patrol.

Later that afternoon, Timucua found a good place for an ambush. He looked down the road. Sharon crawled up between him and Bart, where they lay just inside the edge of the woods. Timucua started to tell her to go back where he told her to stay with the others, but instead realized he was glad to see her. "Sharon, I want you and Bart on that rise over there to the left."

She smiled and nodded.

He pointed down the road and to the right to get her to look the other way and stop making him nervous. "That's where the kill zone will be."

Sharon turned her head to look down the road, squinting. "What will the range be?" She turned to look at him again, her face serious but beautiful.

Timucua wished she had not. "The three of us will figure that out when we get up there."

"Oh, you're going to be there too?" Sharon seemed at ease.

Timucua wondered if she truly understood what they were about to do. "No. I'm going to be a hundred or so yards closer and further down the slope."

"I thought maybe you were going to protect me." She gave him that disconcerting smile/smirk.

Timucua looked down the road. "If it were true, you can't blame a guy for that."

Bart chuckled. "I think all the guys are in love with you. Maybe even me."

She giggled. "I thought chivalry was dead."

"I'm not so sure he was talking about chivalry," Timucua said. He started crawling backwards from the edge of the woods. "Come on, I've seen enough."

When they got far enough back in the woods to safely stand without being seen from the road, she pulled on Timucua's jacket sleeve.

He stopped and looked at her.

She pulled on his neck and brought her lips close to his ear. "You can't hide it, so stop trying."

He froze and tried to swallow but found his throat constricted. She kissed him on his cheek, snickered, and walked away. He stood there watching her sway, not exaggerated, naturally, as she walked. Slowly, she turned and looked over her shoulder, smiling, her eyes burning him. He could not help but smile back. She turned and walked back to her triad.

"Oh shit. I can't even think straight. Let's   see...position those with full auto carbines near the kill zone."

He followed her back to the others.

"I will fire the first shot," Timucua said, "signaling you to lay down as much accurate fire as possible. You guys with full auto carbines, remember, I said accurate fire, no spraying and praying."

"I can't spray much with my Garand," Tel quipped.

Timucua shot a glance at him but did not reply. Everyone else ignored him. "When the leading driver is well within the kill zone, I will kill him. Sharon and Bart will shoot the second driver. If there is a third vehicle, all three of us will shoot that driver. Of course, the rest of you will probably have killed him by then. Since we have no anti-armor weapons, if an armored personnel carrier is in the convoy we will let them go by."

"You've got these guys positioned directly across from the kill zone, now where do you want those of us with long-range rifles placed? And where will you be?" Mathew asked.

Timucua sighed. "Okay guys. Try not to interrupt me while I'm setting up an ambush. Mathew, you should know I'm not through yet. Someday there will come a time when we will have to set up a hasty ambush, and we won't have time to waste on questions. Ask questions after I'm through."

"Sorry," Mathew said.

"No problem," Timucua said. "We're all still learning. That's what this trip is about. Just remember though, this is the real thing. If government goons show up people are going to die."

Timucua pointed up the slope. "Sharon will be positioned five hundred yards from the kill zone. I know she is fully capable of taking a man's head off at that range." She could over watch the entire kill zone from that position, and more important to him, she was relatively safe there.

"Bart will be fifty yards closer, downhill," Timucua said. "I'm going to position somewhere between Bart and the kill zone, about a hundred fifty to two hundred yards closer. I will have to be closer to the woods line to see from prone because the elevation there is lower."

Timucua turned to Sharon and Bart. "Because of the angle, you may be shooting over my head, so when the ambush is over, don't shoot me when I stand up."

Bart nodded.

Sharon said nothing. She looked worried.

Timucua continued. "Mathew, position one hundred yards from the kill zone to cover the rear. Remember, stay fifty yards back from the road. Search out a place where you will have a firing lane to the road like I did for the carbine shooters. And keep behind solid cover."

"I won't be able to see much through the brush," Mathew said.

"I already checked," Timucua said. "You will be able to see about half of the kill zone. That big live oak, get behind it."

Mathew nodded. "Why didn't you just tell me that in the first place?"

"I was hoping you would figure it out on your own."

"Oh," Mathew said. "You're trying to train me."

"That's the idea."

"Do you want me to figure out where you want me on my own?" Tel asked.

Timucua turned to Tel. "I want you two hundred yards farther down the road. You will take on the last vehicle in the convoy, if it manages to back out of the kill zone or turn around and come back your way. Don't fire unless that happens. And wait until they are less than a hundred yards from you."

Timucua turned to leave with Bart and Sharon.

Tel spoke up. "You know, there's a big oak on the other side of the road too, do you think I should position behind it? Or do you want Mathew and me on the same side of the road as the rest of you." He had a smirk on his face.

"Staying on this side would be a good idea Tel," Timucua said. He turned around. There was no smile on his face. "Remember, everyone but you and the three of us up the slope will be fifty yards back from the road. Because of the shooting angles, Mathew and the carbine shooters here will be safe from fratricide. None of us on the hill can possibly hit any of them accidentally, but if any of the vehicles come back at you, you will be on your own. If any of us except me try to back you up, they may hit you."

Timucua saw Tel's smirk dissolve. He pointed. "That big pine, there's a rock beside it and another between it and the road. Ensconce yourself in there and you will have bullet-stopping cover on three sides."

Tel nodded his head imperceptivity, a slight smile on his face. "Thanks, that was thoughtful of you."

"Yes, wasn't it?" Timucua kept a straight face and walked away with Sharon and Bart.

Sharon was on a small rise near the top of the slope that allowed her and Bart to see over the brush. A two-foot-thick pine tree offered cover from fire. All but her lower legs, head and right shoulder would be protected from bullets. It was the best Timucua could do. There is no such thing as complete safety in combat.

"Make sure you keep that boonie hat I gave you on, so your face and hair won't be so easy to see from the kill zone," Timucua said.

After she was satisfied of her shooting position, he asked Bart to help him improve her camouflage. They stuck brush cut from the other side of the rise in the ground and wove leafy branches into living brush, making it appear the cut brush was growing there.

She smiled at them as she watched. "You guys are going to smother me with camo. And Dad was almost as afraid that our own men would mistreat me as the government goons."

Bart said, "That won't happen. No one is going to hurt you. Anyone who tries will be shot."

Timucua added, "Just remember that your father is right. There are evil men in the world." He looked at her. "And not all of them wear a uniform."

"You have a low assessment of people don't you?" she asked.

"I have a very high assessment of some people." He summoned enough courage to gaze back into her eyes. "But I have learned there are some who need a damn good killing bad." He turned his gaze away. "You may soon see me do things that turn your stomach. Just remember we are fighting for our lives; and I don't hurt innocent people."

"Why do you care what I think? I'm not God."

"You haven't seen anything yet." He turned away, purposely not looking at her face.

She did not know Timucua had placed Bart only fifty yards from her because he was the oldest, most experienced, and the second strongest among them. It would take a hundred men to get up that hill and past his M14, and he was strong enough to carry her for hours if she were wounded. Putting Bart close to her instead of himself also made it a little less obvious that he was so worried about her.

It was not as if he did not take equal pains to position all of the others behind bullet-stopping cover and camouflage. He in fact, racked his brain trying to come up with just one more idea to put the odds of survival more in their favor, even smart-ass Tel. Such as insisting they position no closer to the road than necessary to allow them to see and have firing lanes through the brush.

He himself was positioned just inside the brush line. He did have good cover and concealment behind a thirty inch high by forty-inch wide limestone rock.

Everyone settled in for a long wait.

Chapter 14

Timucua knew the chances of a raiding convoy showing up were slim. There were many roads for them to take, and he had no intelligence reports from Mr. Ironwood to cause him to believe this road was more active than the others were.

Boredom soon became everyone's constant companion. Modern man is not accustomed to dealing with the volatile combination of mind-numbing inactive waiting, coupled with the anticipation of sudden violent death. Like all warrior skills, waiting in ambush is a skill one must learn. Timucua knew this. It was why he led them here. Even if the enemy did not show, it was a learning experience for them all. Dealing with the psychological stresses of combat requires exposure to such stresses. Like a muscle, courage and mental strength must be exercised regularly to build endurance.

On the first day, there was no traffic at all. Timucua spent most of the day on his stomach. Every two hours he sat up and tried to stretch his muscles. While sitting up, his eyes caught movement in the brush below.

You guys need to be more careful when taking a leak.

He told himself to remember to warn them later. Occasionally, someone would have to move back from his or her position a few yards where they had dug a small latrine to relieve his or her self. That was agreed to be permissible, but they were warned no more than one could leave their position at a time and then not for any longer than necessary.

Timucua lay on his stomach and looked down the road. Nothing.

He checked the woods where his people were. He was spending as much time checking on them as the kill zone. Worry compelled him to reassure himself they had not gotten restless and were still maintaining proper discipline. Uphill, there was too much brush in the way to see Bart or Sharon. He knew that well enough, but had to look anyway.

Eating was allowed only just after sunrise and before sunset. One out of three ate while the others kept watch.

The sun sank behind the tree line. Timucua sighed, sat up, and opened a can of tasteless beef and vegetable soup with a small pocketknife that had a swing-out can opener. No fires for cooking were allowed day or night. No one dared light a match or turn on a flashlight. He sat and looked around while eating the soup straight from the can.

Sleeping was scheduled at night, and rotated so half slept while the others stayed alert. On average, they got five or six hours sleep. They each were given an hour out of every twenty-four, to stretch and move to get their blood circulating and relieve sore muscles.

Three hours after sunrise on the second day, a blue Ford crew-cab pickup rolled by at low speed, coming from the country toward the city. The pickup was fueled by home-distilled alcohol. Gas and diesel had not been available to anyone outside the cities for more than a decade. Everyone watched as the truck went by.

Timucua wondered if they were all thinking the same thing: It must be a family that had given up. They were moving into the city on their own. A few Wild People were so weary of living in fear and sick of worry for their children, some of them were trying to appease the government by voluntarily moving into the cities. Word had not gotten out yet, that all who did were slaughtered. The true purpose and intent of the Final Removal Plan was only suspected by some and not yet confirmed by any.

Not long after the truck went by, they heard automatic gunfire. Timucua judged it less than a mile away. He sighed, resigned to the reality of an entire family being murdered down the road. He and the others strained to listen, knowing fully the tragedy that was taking place just out of sight. Finally, three short bursts of gunfire echoed in their ears. Then silence.

The heat of hate-generated rage began to boil the blood in Timucua's heart again. He saw plainly that there were small children in that truck. He and the others had come to protect their people. For those just murdered, it mattered not that they were so close. Timucua and his fighters had failed them.

After hours of inactivity and boredom, everyone suddenly experienced a doubling of their heart rate. High-pressure blood pulsed in their heads as they trembled with rage. All aimed their rifles or carbines at the kill zone, and clicked the safety off, praying the killers came their way. They were the young lions of the Wild People and did not believe in turning the other cheek. All their lives they had seen the other cheek bloodied as well as the first.

The first vehicle in the convoy came into view. Cold, murderous intent surfaced on the faces of those who waited for their chance to give the murdered family the only justice they would ever receive.

Sharon's breath came in gasps. She aimed at the driver of the second vehicle. The high quality ten-power telescope allowed her to see the features on the man's face. He was smiling and laughing. Her face turned pale. She steadied her aim and nervously waited for Timucua to fire the first shot.

When the lead vehicle reached the pothole he had designated as the near limit of the kill zone, Timucua squeezed off a round. The hundred sixty-eight grain full metal jacket bullet crashed through the windshield, took off the upper half of the sergeant's head, turned downward slightly and yawed off center thirty degrees, then continued on at slightly reduced velocity to take out one inch of spine in the neck of the twenty-four-year-old corporal sitting in the back seat.

Before Timucua had the Garand out of recoil, Sharon had shot, and everyone was pouring bullets into the vehicles. The Dissident Control agents were dead in ten seconds, but many continued to fire for nearly one minute.

Those with M4s, including two young women, Elizabeth and Linda, went in and put a round into the head of each of the enemy while the long-range shooters over watched for security.

Elizabeth, a rawboned redheaded woman in her early twenties, approached a moaning agent in his mid-twenties. Somehow, he had managed to get out of the vehicle on the opposite side of the ambushers. Now he lay on the faded yellow centerline of the road. He coughed up blood, turned his head away from her, and closed his eyes. His left shoulder and arm had taken multiple rounds from an M4. In a fit of rage, she kicked his upper arm with all the strength in her right leg. The arm was hanging by thin strips of flesh, and the blow completed the amputation. It flew five feet and landed on the cracked pavement, now painted crimson.

The agent opened his eyes and screamed. Elizabeth said, "Look at me child killer. I want you to see the one who pays you back."

He endured silently, his eyes filled with pain.

Elizabeth looked over the sights of her M4. "You've been killing my people. But today is your turn." She pulled the trigger.

They quickly collected weapons, ammunition, and anything else of value to their cause. Most prized were the night vision devices. There were twelve of them.

When everyone in the kill zone was back in the woods, Timucua stood and signaled for Bart and Sharon to come down the hill and join him. The three of them met up with the others.

"Leave the battlefield loot here," Timucua said. "We will pick it up on the way back." They had been out for three days, and he was ready to get them back home. So far, they had taken no casualties, and he did not want to push their luck, but there was still one more thing he wanted to do. "I think we should check on that family in the truck. One of them might be alive. I don't want to think of leaving anyone wounded if we can help."

Elizabeth said, "If any are badly wounded, we won't be able to get them to a real doctor in time anyway."

"That's true," Timucua said, "but they may not have shot the smaller children. I don't want to take the chance of leaving a baby or toddler behind to die of thirst and hunger."

There was no further dissent among them, so they headed for the site of the massacre. Timucua insisted they walk slow and quiet, taking careful, deliberate measures for safety.

Because of his precautions, it took them thirty minutes to reach the site.

As they approached, the cries of a baby echoed in the woods. This put them all in a sour mood, but the sight that greeted their eyes turned the stomach of even the most experienced fighters among them. Sharon was not the only one who threw up.

A three-year-old boy and a five-year-old girl had been beheaded. The other bodies were also mutilated. The parents and two boys, a ten-year-old and twelve-year-old, lay in their own blood. Flies were just starting to swarm.

Timucua wondered why they did not kill the baby, still strapped in a seat in the truck cab. They certainly had no qualms against killing the other small children.

Mathew found some blankets in the back of the truck and began to cover the bodies. Elizabeth reached into the open passenger side door to take the baby out.

Timucua's eyes widened. "Wait! Liz! Don't go near the—"

A tremendous blast knocked everyone to the ground. All of Elizabeth above the floorboard of the pickup vaporized, leaving her booted feet and lower legs in the grass by the road. There was nothing left of the baby or the seat she was strapped in. The roof of the truck cab was ruptured, opened like the petals of a steal flower. The interior of the cab was plastered with bloody flesh. The windshield shattered. Myriads of pieces of glass sprayed outward in a widening shotgun pattern forty yards down the two-lane road. Some of the sharp-edged glass pellets shredded Tel's backpack, right fatigue jacket sleeve, and shoulder, leaving his right arm and side bloody. His rifle was torn from his hands, and he was blown to the pavement, knocking him unconscious.

Several in the group besides Tel were still too stunned to move when Timucua, Bart, Mathew, and Sharon pushed themselves to their feet, shaking their dazed heads and blinking rapidly. Those who could, immediately administered aid to the wounded. Everyone on security duty and thus farther back from the explosion ran to help, their faces ashen.

Not a one of them could hear a thing but loud ringing in their ears, so they communicated with hand signals and tried to lip-read when someone yelled instructions. Five had minor wounds from flying metal and glass fragments and two lay unconscious.

Tel was already on his feet, leaning against a tree fifty feet away, and picking glass out of his flesh. Linda helped him remove his backpack.

"I'm okay," Tel said. "My pack took most of the glass." He blinked, opened his eyes wide and then collapsed to his knees.

"Someone help me," Linda yelled, her face glistening.

Everyone was busy with other wounded.

Sharon saw Tel struggling to stand while Linda tried to convince him to sit down. She had just finished with an unconscious twenty-three-year-old man named Boon. She ran by Timucua, stopping long enough to pull at his load-bearing harness to get his attention and point toward Tel and Linda. He saw, grabbed his meager first aid supplies, and ran after her.

After removing Tel's load bearing harness and jacket, Linda pulled his T-shirt off. Timucua handed Sharon his canteen. She poured water on his shoulder and down his back and right arm to wash the blood off so they could see, closely examining each wound where the glass had penetrated his flesh. Most of the glass was only half buried in him. However, there were six places where the glass was deep.

Timucua poured alcohol on a pair of tweezers and started pulling glass out of the shallower wounds as fast as he could. He worked on his back, side, and shoulder first. If the glass was too deep for him to see it, he left the wound alone.

Tel held on to a small pine tree and stood on his knees. "Just get some of the glass out of my neck and head and I'm good."

Timucua said nothing. He finished with his back and started on the back of his head and neck. Then he moved around behind Sharon over to her right side and started on his arm.

Linda asked, "What about those deeper ones?"

Sharon was cleaning his head and neck with antibiotic-soaked gauze. "Near as I can tell, there are no major blood vessels damaged. I'm judging by their position on his body and the amount of bleeding. Anyway, they will have to wait for a doctor. More than likely the glass will be left in."

"I've got all the glass out that I can," Timucua said. "Are you dizzy?" he asked Tel.

"I was only out a few seconds," Tel said. "I'm okay."

"Blurred vision?" Sharon added.

Tel blinked and looked around. "My eyes are fine."

"It's your head I'm worried about," Sharon said.

Timucua cleaned the tweezers off with alcohol and put them back in his first aid kit. He slid his right shoulder and then the other into the straps of his pack and stood. "I've got to get them out of here."

Sharon unrolled a sheet of gauze. "Go ahead. We're almost done anyway."

Two stretchers had already been fabricated from ponchos and poles cut from small pine trees, and the unconscious men were placed on them. Timucua ran over and quickly looked everyone over. "Are those two the only ones who can't walk?"

Bart answered, "Everyone else is ambulatory, except maybe Tel."

"Tel is okay. You take charge and get everyone back in the woods seventy-five yards. Set up a defense perimeter and wait there for us."

"Right."

Timucua ran back to the others. He tied a cord around Tel's pack.

Tel put his load-bearing harness on over his jacket. "Give me my pack."

Timucua held it up behind him so he could slip into the shoulder straps. "Why don't you let me carry it?"

"You have to get these people out of here," Tel said. "That's enough on your shoulders."

"I tied the pack together where it's ripped so the stuff won't fall out." Timucua helped Tel with the pack straps.

"Thanks. Let's make tracks before another patrol comes up on us." Tel took three careful steps. "I'm a little wobbly but I can walk."

When they reached the others, Timucua took the lead. They picked up the weapons and equipment they left behind and headed home. He waited until they were three miles from the ambush site before he stopped and turned around. The walk gave their minds time to think about what had happened. He did not know Elizabeth. Everyone else knew her well. What he saw caused him to turn and continue, until he had time to think of the best way to help them through it.

A combination of shock, disbelief, grief, and horror, turned the face of most into tragic examples of humanity. Sharon and Linda were silently crying, so were some of the men who knew Liz well. The rest, Timucua included, wore clenched jaws under blazing eyes of rage. Nearly half the team was inconsolable, the others could think of nothing but revenge.

Timucua raised his left fist, signaling them to halt and freeze. He turned, walked back along the line, whispering to each of them, "Tight-three-sixty around the wounded." He continued until he came to Mathew who was covering their six. "Tight-three-sixty. We will stop a few minutes." Mathew nodded and kept walking.

Timucua searched the woods behind for any sign of pursuit. After waiting until the others were out of hearing range, he stood and listened while searching for movement in the brush and in the shade of tall trees.

"You want them, don't you?" Timucua spoke under his breath. "Well, you can't have them. Not today. You have hurt them all you're going to on this day. Soon it won't be so easy. My people's blood is not free." He turned back, dreading what he must now do.

Bloodied, grieving, enraged faces greeted him when he arrived. Their misery washed over him and nearly overtook his own self-control, but he was not going to let them down. For whatever reason, they had asked him to lead them, this he would do to the best of his ability.

They looked up at him expectantly. He put on a stoic mask and saw them for the first time with his heart, not just his eyes. The core of their most elementary beings now shined through their exterior appearance. He saw young people, the salt of the earth, born into a world of insane brutality, doing the best they could, trying to hold onto their humanity and sanity while dealing with an enemy that had neither and were under the intoxication of absolute power.

If you want to test a man's character, give him power. If you want to test a man's character absolutely, give him absolute power. He could not remember where he read that, or even if he had read it somewhere.

Timucua knelt beside them and began to speak in a subdued voice, trying his best to be the glue that holds them together. "At a time like this we need one another more than ever. We all feel the same pain, though each of us deals with it differently. Never forget that each other is all we have. Look around and recognize your brothers and sisters, remember not their faces, but their hearts. It is only at a time like this when you can truly see the person in front of you. Remember what you now see, because those you see here with you on this day, are the only ones who will ever understand what we are going through at this moment."

He thought of the redheaded woman. "Liz died because of her concern for the baby. They used her humanity against her, against us, our people. They can call us Wild People, but we do not kill babies. We do not behead children. We are human beings, endowed by our Creator with undeniable rights. We prove it by holding true to our values and beliefs, and acting on them."

Everyone's eyes on him, he continued. "Our enemy has drawn an ugly, bloody line between them and us. Good. There *should* be a line between us, an unapproachable chasm. As for us, I say we resolve to never allow them to turn us into the animals they are."

Their faces changed.

"What we do now, how we react, will lay the foundation for the rest of our lives." He looked back at each of them. "Yes, they think we are animals. You can stand or fall under the weight providence has placed on you, but if you fall now, I or someone else will pick you up. You are not alone."

Sharon looked up at Timucua and blinked. He saw the disillusionment on her face.

I told you, he did not say. *Pity does not exist out here.*

"Now take some time to support one another as best you can. Cry, scream, cuss, pray, or whatever you need to do. Reconstitute your inner strength, because we have to go on."

A few held on to someone and cried. Others just turned away and looked inwardly at their own hearts. Bart pulled out a KA-BAR knife and stabbed it repeatedly into a nearby pine tree.

Timucua stepped back and saw them looking at him as if he had the answer to some question they desperately wanted to ask. He shook his head imperceptibly. *I don't know. I don't know why.*

Sharon and the other girl, Linda, were holding each other, their deep sobbing and grief-contorted faces broke down yet another layer of Timucua's stonewall. How could anyone think of those two girls as animals? He remembered watching them drag his dead mother by her feet, her head bouncing on rocks, long black hair trailing in the dirt, as if they were dragging a bag of trash to the dump. Still, he kept the mask on.

Then, Sharon and his eyes locked. His face turned white. A heavy weight pressed on his chest, leaving him breathless. The light in her blue eyes had gone out.

Quickly, he turned and walked away. He checked to make sure no one had followed him, fell to his knees, and closed his eyes. He was sixteen years old again. He was Patrick again, and Patrick was not as strong as Timucua.

He felt a warm presence. Small, delicate hands held his face. He looked up to see Sharon kneeling in front of him. For the first time since the murder of his family, Patrick allowed himself to need human warmth. He pulled her to him and held her as tight as he dared. They held each other in silent grief until Timucua started reemerging, and Patrick became strong enough to release her.

Holding her face in his hands, he kissed her forehead. It was his first expression of affection since the day he became a killer. For months now, she had been knocking at the door to his heart. He had deceived himself all this time, believing that door would stay shut, bolted, locked tight, and barred, if only he refused to answer the persistent knocking of her human warmth. He understood now how silly it all had been. From the moment he first saw her, that door had been blown off its hinges.

He had tried to treat her fairly and with respect, but had not encouraged her interest in him in any way. Now she was supporting him in his weakest moment. He saw the irony in the fact it was his concern for her that had broken him down. He was going to get through it, or so he thought, until he saw what they had done to her.

He tried to tell himself the storm of thoughts and emotions he was dealing with, was just because of him being so young and in a weakened state and her being so damn pretty and openhearted. However, somewhere back in that deep, dark pit he had pushed Patrick into so many months ago, he knew he placed a higher value on her than anything on earth.

Dreading what he might see, but hope compelling him, he looked into her eyes once more.

Sharon saw the joy on his face. It was the first time she had seen him actually smile. "What?" she asked, more with her face than words.

"I was afraid they had killed you inside. When I saw you crying before…"

Before he knew it, she locked her arms around his neck and head and she was kissing him. She finally released him and stood, wiping tears from her face.

He wanted her, and he prayed it was not as obvious as he feared. It was his first kiss. And it had not been like it is with most boys: that she was just some girl who was available because she lived nearby or went to the same school, some girl he was not in love with, but who was just handy for exploring his hormone-fueled emerging new world of desire and lust. She was not the beginning of a long search. He had found her before he started searching. The warmest place on earth was basking in the light of her blue eyes.

"We better get back with the others before they start talking and spreading rumors." He caressed her face lightly, holding the side of her face in the palm of his weak hand. "Just don't let them kill you, or change you. I can take anything else, anything but that."

Her face begged an answer. "I've known you for six months, but still, these last few minutes are the only time you have allowed me to see the real Patrick."

"It would have been safer for both of us if I hadn't let my guard down. Emotions can get both of us killed. I guess I'm not as strong as I should be. It's just that when I thought...you're the counterbalance. Don't you know that? The opposite of what happened on the road. Both what they did and what we did." He turned away. "This world we live in would be a cold, ugly place without you."

"But I'm just a girl. What gave you the idea I counterbalance anything?"

An understated half-smile came over his face. "Maybe I'm crazy, but that's how I feel about you. I don't know if all men can see it, but I know some men can see a woman's inner beauty. I just know I can see something beautiful in your eyes. From the first time I saw it, it has stayed with me. I see it whether my eyes are open or not, whether you are near or not."

"And you never told me any of this before."

"No. Of course not."

"I don't get it."

"I expect to be dead soon or maybe you. Why invite more pain?"

"I thought you were brave."

"Who told you that?"

She smiled. "I never met anyone like you."

"Same here."

"Patrick…I've been trying to get you to open up to me. And I knew there was more of you… But I had no idea. You hid it well. It's all or nothing with you, isn't it?"

"Now don't start fearing me. I'm not obsessive. I know you don't feel the same, and I don't blame you. I'm a hater. Hate isn't exactly fun to be around, and I'm certainly not pretty like you."

"Oh? I think you're pretty."

"Come on girl. Don't make fun of me."

"I wasn't, and I do think I feel more than friendship. It's just I'm surprised of the depth of…I'm not a symbol Patrick, of good or anything else. I'm a girl. If you're going to love me, love me for that."

"You're a girl all right. You have so much girly in you, it radiates from you."

She laughed. "I thought it was my eyes."

"It's everything. Your voice, mannerisms, everything, but yes, it's your eyes. I hope I say this right. Once my grandfather told me of his wedding night with my grandmother who died when I was three, nothing lurid now. They were only eighteen and nineteen, and they had waited until they were married." He paused and went on with his Grandfathers story.

"He said, damned if it isn't true. I said, what Grandpa? He said, what my father told me about the first time you see your wife naked. I asked him what he meant. He said, the prettiest thing about a naked woman who loves you is her eyes. Don't get me wrong, I'm not so delusional to think you're in love with me. Your inner beauty exists even without that. That's why you're having such a hard time learning to hate."

She started toward him with a look in her eyes that warned him.

He put his hand up. "Whoa. We've done enough of that for now. I'm still drunk from that kiss. We have to get back to the others."

Holding her chin up, she walked by him with a slight smirk on her face. As soon as she got in front of him, she turned and stood in his way. Her smirk turned into a warm smile.

"Oookaay, but two things: First, I'm going to find out what your real age is. It can't be sixteen. Twenty-five maybe, and I'm not the first girl you've kissed. You can't plead innocent with me. Aaand, I refuse to call you Timucua. It may be your middle name, but I will call you Patrick from now on, just like our friend, Mr. Ironwood does. Your name is Patrick, and since I'm your friend, I'm going to call you that, whether you like it or not." She put her hand under his chin. "But I'm quite certain you will." With that, she walked away with a girlish swing to her hips and a confidence in her stride that made him nervous.

He waited a full sixty seconds before he rejoined the others. However, Tel and Linda noticed the difference in their demeanors, especially Sharon's. Patrick glanced at the group, not wanting his eyes to linger on any one of them. "If you guys are ready, we have to go."

Chapter 15

Patrick led the wending procession of ragged souls past Mr. Ironwood's front porch. They trudged along, shoulders sloped, and heads bowed. The booby trapping of the baby and butchering of the other children brought an ugly truth out into the open. This is much more than a disagreement with government policies, and whether or not people have a right to choose where they live. The government considered Wild People to be nonhumans.

Family, friends, and lovers who had been waiting their return, ran to them. A couple in their fifties rushed to Sharon and held her with tears of joy. A half dozen people administered aid to the wounded.

Mr. Ironwood watched, noticing first their despondent demeanor, second, the wounded on stretchers, then, the absence of Elizabeth. Patrick walked by within feet of him, looking straight ahead, saying nothing. He stopped and leaned his rifle against the porch; shed his pack, then the load-bearing harness, letting it fall at his feet behind him. Next, he squirmed out of his olive drab fatigue jacket, letting it slide off his shoulders onto the harness in a pile. He sat down on the porch and pulled his boots off.

Leaving everything as it lay, he trudged to the spring. On the water's edge, he remembered the elastic sleeve he wore over the wounds on his left arm. It was still proud red-raw vulnerable flesh. He pulled it off with one motion and slung it behind him. It flew twenty feet and landed on the grass. With a preparatory, lung-filling gasp, he simply stepped off terra firma into the water.

He did not come up until he was on the other side of the boiling spring where the bottom sloped up to within three feet of the undulating crystal surface. There, he just lay back, partially floating and partially sitting on the bottom, and looked up at the blue sky until his eyes hurt. The water was cold but invigorating. The hot afternoon sun shining on his face was a stark contrast. Appropriate and fitting, for his life had no middle, only extremes on both sides of where the larger middle should have been; the middle that was hacked out of his life by the government. Recently, he had experienced the filthy and the pure and clean, the ugly and the beautiful.

Already, the sweat and grime of four days in the woods was washing away, and he hoped at least that some of the ticks were finding his body to be less inviting than previously. The blisters on his feet were stinging at first, but now the cold water was numbing his outer extremities enough that he felt little of them and his sore muscles.

He had insisted on carrying one end of a stretcher most of the way as soon as he was certain they were not being followed. It was a tactical mistake and he knew it. He should have been leading, not carrying, but he did it anyway. Now the cold water relieved the pain in his left arm.

However, he needed the cleansing affect most. The filth and ugliness of man's cruelty to man, and the hate it bred, repulsed him. His heart too, was not without guilt. He hated them, and they continued to give him ever more reason. If only the cold water could put that fire out, but without hate, could he do what had to be done? How could he stop them without killing them? How could he kill without hate?

For the first time since the day his family was murdered, he knew who he was: a sixteen-year-old boy named Patrick. And he now let himself admit what he always knew: Revenge is the poorest of reasons to wage war. The only decent excuse for war, the only sane reason, is freedom and the defense of yourself and your people. All other excuses for killing a human being are profane.

"Hey, your arm is bleeding!"

Patrick had over-stressed it while carrying one of the wounded. Blood capillaries and small veins were near the surface of his flesh because of the surgery, and often would burst if he abused his arm. There had been no skin graft, only a thin layer of protection had grown over the carved-out flesh.

Head tilted back, eyes closed, Sharon's voice sang in his ears like bright, shining globes of sound floating through the air, penetrating his consciousness, soothing his aching soul, and resonating in his mind. Even her voice was endearing. Not high-pitched, but girly, just like everything else about her.

Sitting more erect, his face dripping, he looked over to the far bank where he saw Sharon standing, an arm over the shoulders of each of the middle-aged couple. "Those two your parents? Or are they just holding you up?"

Sharon beamed. "Can't you see the resemblance?"

Patrick sidestroked over to their side. It was the exact spot where Mr. Ironwood pulled him to the bank when he was floundering. It seemed half a lifetime ago. The water was deep there. He had to hold onto the bank with his left arm. Thinning blood ran down dark pink dimpled flesh and onto the grass. He raised his right hand. "I would like to shake the hand of the man and woman who raised Sharon. I don't know what you did, but it was done right. Tell me, how did you put the light of Jesus in her eyes?"

The man leaned down slightly, a look of pride on his face, as if he were happy that someone besides he and his wife had noticed how special their daughter was, and shook Patrick's hand. "The name is Sam. And my wife's name is Sharon also."

Looking up at all three, Patrick smiled. "So Sharon is a junior. Or does it work that way with mothers and daughters?"

Sharon rolled her eyes. "I don't care if it does or not. If you start calling me Junior, I might drown you.

"You will have to join me to do that."

"No thank you. I'm going home to take a shower. That water is cold as ice."

"You know, I still don't know your fine daughter's last name. She's an introvert, she don't tell me nutthin."

Mother looked perplexed. Sharon hugged her neck. "He's not retarded, Mom. He just gets that way when he's in cold water."

Mother's eyes sparkled and Patrick saw some of the origins of Sharon's inner beauty. "It's no secret, our name is L'Amour."

Patrick laughed boisterously. "Of course it is. What other name would fit as well? I should have known."

Father looked suspiciously at his daughter and Patrick. She pulled him closer with her right arm that was around his neck and kissed him on the cheek. "Why Patrick, you are full of surprises. I never knew you had so much, personality."

"And I never knew your name is L'Amour, though your eyes told me that the first time I saw you. I should have listened to them. Is your middle name Angelique? Angelica? Or how about plain old Angel? Sharon Angel Love. Now that would be perfect."

Suddenly he became serious. "If I seem different Sharon, it's because I am. On the day they killed my family, I decided the government would never take my freedom. And if they want my life, they will have to pay for it."

"Oh, Mr. Ironwood told me how stubborn you are," Sharon said. "Not that I hadn't noticed it already."

"But you taught me something: When they killed my mother and grandfather, I forgot my humanity." He shook his head, resolve in his eyes. "They're not getting that either. They're not taking one more thing from me, or our people. To hell with them. As long as there are people like Sharon L'Amour in the world, I can fight them, I can kill them, I can even hate them and be a human being at the same time."

Sharon's eyes were brilliant.

"Hold my hand, Sharon Angel Love, will you?" She walked closer to the water's edge and reached down. As soon as she bent over and grasped his hand, he tightened his grip and pulled her over into the water. She just had time to inhale and brace herself for the shock of the cold before she went in.

"Come and be baptized in the tender L'Amour of God's eternal water," he said, as she went over his right shoulder.

She came up sputtering. "It's freezing!"

He took her right hand and pulled her to the bank beside him. Caressing her face and looking into her eyes, he said, "You're not cold. You're warm. Ninety-eight point six degrees. That means you're alive. And so am I."

Speaking to Sharon's parents, he said, "I'm going to talk to Wild People's warriors. And I'm going to be profane, so cover your ears if it offends you." He turned to the others who had not left yet and yelled out across the clearing at the top of his voice. "Fuck the heartless, soulless government! We are human beings! We win! They lose!" His voice reverberated across the yard, past the glade and penetrated deep into the forest of pines and rang in the air, buoyed, sustained, for a lingering age, by the sheer force of will and strength of a human heart that would never stop loving freedom.

A cheer rose up from Bart, then Tel, then Linda, and soon most of the crowd was cheering. Members of the triads walked over to the edge of the spring and its run, cheering. Wild People or no, they were free human beings.

Patrick was not finished. "Come. Wash the stench of the heartless, soulless, government off you. For they have failed to enslave us, dehumanize us, or kill us on this day. As long as L'Amour lives, the government is pissing in the wind!"

Nearly everyone was cheering and laughing, the spring was filling with people who were jumping five and ten at a time.

Sharon yelled above the roar of the crowd. "Have you been drinking?"

"I am drunk on life and L'Amour," he said and kissed her cheek.

Her eyes were brighter than he had ever seen them as she smiled at him happily. "Whatever happened to you this afternoon, I like it!"

"No. It was not today. It was when I saw that even though you are beautiful and girly and feminine, your beauty is stronger than the ugliness of their diseased hearts. It's not going to be easy or fun, but the only way they can win is if we give up. And you won't let me quit." In mock military sternness, he saluted her. "So it's all on your shoulders now girl. Don't let us down."

She tilted her head, her eyes burning him again. "Have you lost your mind? There is a war coming, and it's not going to be a tea party, in Boston or anywhere else. You better not count on me to win it."

"Oh, contraire, Madam. It is the gentlest of souls like you who will inspire vicious bastards like me to be the protectors of the best of our people. Need I say the best most definitely includes you?"

It did not take long for most of the crowd to get enough of the cold water. They were pulling out onto dry land and shaking the chill off themselves, laughing and chattering, slapping one another on the back, heading home, leaving Patrick and the L'Amours in quietude.

Sharon shook her head. "You're still a little boy at heart and you have read too many books. Chivalry is dead."

He held her face in his hands, kicking to stay above water. "What I see in you, and what it inspires is not death; it is life. Real men know with no need to be told, because it is carved by the hand of God into their hearts, women and children civilize real men, and anyone who purposely harms either is not a man."

Mr. L'Amour's mouth was slightly agape. He whispered in his wife's ear, "He must be older than he looks."

Sharon pushed the wet hair plastered to his forehead aside. "I wish someone had told the men who murdered those children on the road that."

"Don't you understand what I said? They were not men. I don't kill men, and someone did tell them, God. But they listened to the government and maybe the devil instead, and they reaped what they sowed. If what I believe and value is immature, then I will die a little boy. And I value what I see in you."

Her saddened, blinking eyes filled. "But I'm not...I am not what you think I am. Just because I don't show it like you, doesn't mean I don't hate."

Patrick saw that she was upset, though he could not believe it was anything he said.

She pulled him to her and pressed her cheek to his. "You have trusted me to hold up my end of the load, as you put it. But I let you down and the others too. You're going to be disappointed, but I have to tell you. It wouldn't be right not to. I don't want you to think I'm more capable than I am. People could get hurt."

"What are you talking about?" Patrick asked.

"I'm not sure I hit that driver at the ambush. I didn't call the shot, and others were shooting before I was able to look through the scope again after the recoil to check. I was so angry when I saw him laughing minutes after they killed that family, I forgot everything you taught me. I guess I'm a miserable failure as a freedom fighter. And you yourself said I can't walk quietly in the woods."

Patrick chuckled almost inaudibly. He looked up at Mr. And Mrs. L'Amour. "Is she in the habit of flogging herself for being human?"

Mrs. L'Amour's eyes told him she wanted to hold her little girl. "She has had to handle a lot in recent months. She is struggling with…She wants to do her part, but the thought of killing…her heart is not built that way."

Patrick felt the shadow in him retreating further, back to the ancient campfires and drumbeats of long-dead warriors whose blood now flowed in his veins. Timucua was resting. This was not his day. There would be other days. She was so human and so girlish and so irresistible Timucua might as well take a nap.

Sharon heard Patrick's smile-muffled chuckle, as he pantomimed ironing out the slight worry wrinkles on her forehead with his thumbs. "You really should be more careful. Those wrinkles might not go away next time." He kissed her on her forehead as if to make the wrinkles disappear.

"Haven't you been listening girl? What I'm talking about has nothing to do with you killing anyone. Now I know it's difficult and takes a lot of heart on your part. I guess it's a twenty-four-seven job, and I'm sure you have to work extremely hard at it."

Patrick held Sharon's face in his hands, wiping tears from her cheeks with his thumbs. "All I'm talking about is you being you. Can you do that for the cause of freedom?"

She looked at him with that half-smile, half-smirk he first saw when she knew she had gotten past the hard crust he had built up to protect himself from the world when Timucua was in the forefront, and said nothing.

"You know, those eyes are making me uncomfortable." Patrick covered them with his right hand.

She pulled his hand away. "Are you still afraid of me?"

"Yes."

She giggled.

Her father said, "He's an honest man Sharon. Your mother scared the hell out of me when I first started letting her under my skin, but I never admitted it."

"Oh Dad, he doesn't lie that way. He lies by omission."

Mr. L'Amour laughed. "You have to allow a man *some* place to hide girl. There is not one man in a million who would admit he was afraid of you, especially at his age."

"Well, he can't hide from me. He should not even try. Someday he will realize that."

*　　　*　　　*

Patrick finished giving his oral after-action report to Mr. Ironwood, explaining how those he was entrusted with were killed or wounded. The elderly man shook as if he had Parkinson's disease, or some other palsy. "Goddamn them! I can't believe that even they would commit such a damnable crime."

"Will you see this gets to the newspaper the resistance puts out?" Patrick took a folded piece of paper out of his pocket, unfolded it, and put it on the table.

"Maybe, let me read it first." Mr. Ironwood put on his glasses.

> My name is Patrick Timucua Paine. This is my testament as to the events others and I witnessed three days ago.
>
> We were waiting in ambush to kill Dissident Control agents when a truck conveying a family consisting of mother, father, and five children,

ranging in age from six months to twelve years went by.

We believe they were attempting to move voluntarily into Southeast City. They passed our ambush site in peace and safety. However, they did not get far before government agents attacked them. This happened out of our sight, but we could hear the gunfire.

A few minutes later two government vehicles, each occupied by six uniformed Dissident Control agents, drove into our kill zone. We were successful in killing them all. Later, we went to the site of the massacre. There, we found all but one of the family dead. The parents and the ten and twelve-year-old had been shot. Their bodies suffered postmortem knife wounds. Two smaller children, age estimated at three and five, had been beheaded. There were no other wounds on the bodies, so unless they were strangled first, the children were alive when the blade was put to their necks.

As we took in this ghastly scene, a baby wailed from a seat in the truck. One of our people, whose last name I do not know, but whose first name was Elizabeth, attempted to remove the baby from the truck. This triggered a bomb that had been set by those who murdered the family. It killed the baby and Elizabeth and injured many of our people.

We know the final phase of the Removal Plan, otherwise known as rural cleansing, is now underway. However, the crimes against our people I just bore witness to, and many other equally inhuman crimes prove to us all the real goal of the government, is the total nullification of our people as human beings. They no longer think of us as "Wild People," but as wild animals.

My brothers and sisters, the last survivors of the United States of America, we have one last chance to give our children life and freedom. We will never be stronger. Tomorrow we will be fewer. They are killing us by the thousands. I implore you to fight now. Every day we hesitate, more of the most vulnerable among us die.

We have no choice. They will remove us from the face of the earth if we do not stop them. If we fight and fail, it will be a bitter end to our people, but we will die with no shame. If we allow our people to be slaughtered without a fight, I fear God will turn His grace from us. He is not likely to abide a cowardly people and according to my murdered grandfather's beliefs, our ancestors will not greet us when we cross the Great Divide. They will turn their backs and bow their heads in shame.

I reject with all my God-given soul, any contention that I, or my people, are not human beings endowed by our Creator with undeniable rights. I reject any contention that I, or my people, are not free. I reject their system of government because it has proven to be antihuman and anti-freedom. I reject it because it is in disputation with God.

I hereby pledge to devote my life to the protection of our people from all enemies, be they our own government, or World Government. I implore that you do the same.

Kill them before they kill your children.

Mr. Ironwood put the paper down. He began to wipe his glasses with his shirttail. "You're quite a firebrand, aren't you Patrick? Once again, you've identified the monster and described it for us all. Then you stepped in its path and declared war. But this time you ask others to join you."

"Do you think there's any other way?"

"No," Mr. Ironwood said. "Like I told you sometime back, it's time for our people to face reality. But there is one problem: I need not mention that this will put you in the center of the government's attention like never before."

"People have been talking about rebellion all of my life. This is nothing new. Besides, they already want me dead. They want all of us dead."

"*You* are what's new, and they know it. Not all of them are mentally blind. Someone near the top of that shit pile called the Unity Party is telling someone below him or her they have to kill you soon." Mr. Ironwood looked at his teenage friend, his eyes intense. "And they're trying to get information from spies. It's only a matter of time before they find you. No matter what precautions you take, you're vulnerable. And you will be a much more valuable target than I ever was if I send this to be published."

"All already thought of and pushed out of my mind," Patrick said. "People have died. People will die because of that shit pile you mentioned. None of us are going to get out of this world alive."

The old man nodded. He stood there and looked across the table. "I want you to know your grandfather was the best friend I ever had. But you, Patrick, I've never been more proud to call friend." He pointed at the paper on the table. "It should be all over the Southeast in less than three weeks."

Patrick decided it was time to say something he had wanted to say for months, and he realized there might never be another chance. "Mr. Ironwood, maybe you don't know, maybe I should have told you before. But I've known since I was ten why my grandfather and you were such good friends." The old man jerked his head to the side and looked away. Patrick continued. "He told me what happened in Cambodia."

Mr. Ironwood stood taller and looked across the table at Patrick. "Did he tell you he saved my life?"

"No. He said—"

"Then he did not tell you about Laos."

"He never mentioned Laos."

"He wouldn't. The only hero was your grandpa. Remember that."

"But—"

"No. I don't want you calling me a hero. The hero was your grandpa, not me."

"I just wanted you to know what he thought of you."

"I know, Patrick. Thank you."

Patrick took up his rifle and walked out on the porch, stopping to put on his pack.

"Where are you going?" Mr. Ironwood asked.

Patrick jumped off the porch. Walking backwards as he spoke, he said, "To bask in the heavenly light of L'Amour."

Mr. Ironwood laughed through the open door. "Tell her I said hello."

Chapter 16

James and Maria leaned over the table in their office and pored over the packets they just received from the resistance. They contained many reports of an increase in atrocities committed by Dissident Control agents. Some descriptions sickened them.

Maria picked up a piece of paper and she immediately became animated. "It's from the boy." Their heads touched as they read together. "Oh my God." She clasped a hand to her mouth.

When James finished reading, he walked to a window. "He believes we might as well go for broke, all or nothing. They're going to kill us all anyway." He watched the nineteen-year-old boy who delivered the field reports wash sweat and grime off with a garden hose fed from a water tower. "Maria, come here a second." He put his arm over her shoulders when she stood beside him at the window.

"It's probably the first chance he's had to wash in a week, yet he did not ask to use our shower. It's people like him, kids, who are standing between holocaust and us." He turned and held her tight. "The Unity Party is proving that a socialist is a socialist, whether they call themselves Nazis or members of the Unity Party. Call it the Final Removal Plan or the Final Solution. It's all the same by any other name."

Maria's eyes were locked on the boy. "Find some clean clothes for him, you know, something greenish for hiding in the woods." She walked outside.

James watched as his wife asked the boy to come inside and use their shower. Their voices could just be heard through the glass as the boy declined the offer, shaking his head. "No thank you. I must be on my way."

She took him by the hand and practically pulled him toward the house. "The war can wait that long and while you're in the shower, I will prepare something for you to eat. James is looking for some clean clothes for you."

The boy protested. "But I'm dripping wet now. I'll get your floor wet."

"Not if you run on into the bathroom. This is not our house anyway. We're just using it temporarily. It's more your house than ours. Go on in and take a shower."

James led him to the bathroom. Returning to the kitchen, he found her already preparing to cook. He stood there watching her until she saw him.

She stopped short. "What?"

He shrugged. "Nothing."

She went back to work. "Well, stop staring at me like that and go find some clothes for the boy." She put a loaf of home-baked bread on the counter. "James, we owe them more than words on a piece of paper. I agree that we're doing more good at the moment by informing the people, but there will come a day when we will pick up a rifle and fight alongside people like him. Until then, not a one of them is going to leave here without a meal, or anything else within our power to provide them."

"You will get no disagreement from me. Except for the part about you picking up a rifle."

Maria turned from her work to face him, ignoring his invitation to another argument about her fighting. "Do you know what it's like to live in the woods like an animal for weeks, months at a time?"

"No, but I can imagine."

"Well, why don't you interview him while he's eating? Ask him what conditions are like out there for the fighters. I would do it, but he may not feel comfortable with a woman. He may not feel free to be as, descriptive, with me."

The look on her face told James he should listen. "They need, deserve, someone like Ernie Pyle. They need to know that we give a damn. That we are backing them. That we know what immersion foot is. What swamp mud does to you when you stay in it for days or weeks at a time. That we know they go for days without food or rest. That they walk twenty-five miles, fight, and then walk another twenty the next day. That the wounded suffer and die with little or no medical care. We owe it to them. It is something we have not done enough of."

"Okay," James said. "You're right as usual. Let me go find some clothes for him first. He will be done soon."

After the boy left, James helped Maria clean up. "That boy was so hungry he didn't want to talk while eating. I did get him to agree to take me with him tomorrow morning when he heads back to his 'outfit,' as he calls it." James paused when he saw the look in her eyes. "I'll bring a miniature recorder with me. I hope it will survive the weather and mud. I've got waterproof bags to keep stuff dry in my pack, including paper to write on." His face became serious. "Maria, if I go, I won't be back for several months. Understand that."

Maria threw a spoon in the sink. Soapy water plashed on the counter. She turned to face him squarely and shot a scorching look at him.

"Now, hold on," he said. "It was your idea. And someone must stay here to keep the paper going."

She sighed forcefully, growing angry. "I should have kept my mouth shut. You're just using this as an excuse to go on one of your adventures you told me about, half accusing me of ruining your life by tying you down with connubial responsibilities."

"Oh, come on. I never—"

"One of them comes around once a week. Why don't you interview them right here? I know, and you know the answer. It's your chance to go on another adventure like you did before you married me. I'm sorry I made your life so boring."

He threw his hands up. "Will you stop? You're inventing things that don't even exist. You and our marriage have been nothing but good for my life. This has nothing to do with our marriage."

"Oh?" Maria put her hands on her hips. "You're going away for months. I think that involves me and our marriage."

"You just gave a very convincing argument for a modern-day Ernie Pyle. Well, Ernie Pyle lived with the soldiers and reported firsthand what the soldiers were going through. And firsthand is the only—"

"And he died with the soldiers."

"All I can do is promise I won't take any unnecessary chances. I intend to come back to you."

"Intentions and plans often get blown away in the winds of war."

James walked out of the kitchen to return with the paper Patrick wrote his testimonial on. He held it in front of her. "Maria. I'm going to interview the person who wrote this. If I can, I will spend a month with him, sending back reports for you to disseminate among all our people. I will get to know him, and through my words, you and our readership will get to know him. That is worth the risk. You say he inspires you, well let's find out if he inspires thirty-five million Wild People."

"How are you going to find him?" Maria leaned against the counter behind her and crossed her arms. "People will be reluctant to tell where he is. They won't trust you. They may even think you're a spy."

"They know us both. We've been reporting on the war for them for months."

"All they know is a name."

"The boy will introduce me," James said. "Then I'll go from his group to another. I will work my way closer. Until I find him."

"That could take months, or a year!"

"I'm sorry. I don't have to tell you we must all be willing to sacrifice. You'll be reading my reports regularly, and I'll have a letter for you in every one. I promise."

*   *   *

Captain Voisselle's face turned bloodless white. Reports were coming in from all over District 13. In the last fifteen hours, he had lost two dozen men, and the tempo of killings was increasing by the hour. At this rate, he would be out of men in a week. Reports of the deaths of agents in other districts were starting to reveal a pattern. It started in District 13 and was spreading, the closer to the epicenter, the faster the rate of killings.

Voisselle glared at Raebyrne. "Our intel failed us on this one. That old man you protected probably knew about this. I place it all in your hands."

Raebyrne could take no more. The execution of Gary was eating at him day and night. He had been close to suicide for months. Only the thought of what it would do to his family stopped him. "You can place this up your ass as far as I'm concerned. Don't you get it, you dumb shit? The music just quit and so do I. I've got twenty-five years in, and I've had enough."

Voisselle jumped out of his chair. "Don't think you can hand me this turd and just walk away. Dream on. You can't retire until I say you can. And if you fail to follow orders or do your duty for The Party, I will have you shot."

Raebyrne's jaw tensed, chained rage was straining for release, just under the surface. He took a piece of folded paper out of a breast pocket and threw it on the desk. "I suppose you have not seen that yet, have you?"

Voisselle looked down at the folded paper with slight amusement. "Now what is that?" He sat back down.

Raebyrne shrugged. "I thought you wanted intel, but I guess you're too busy to read it. It's why the shit has hit the fan, why we are all going to die." All blood suddenly drained from Voisselle's face again. Smiling slightly at the sight, he continued. "It's from the boy. Evidently, he's not as stupid as you thought. He has put the pieces of the puzzle together and gotten a glimpse at the whole picture. He knows the Final Removal Plan is actually a plan to remove all of them from this world. More to the point, he has played Patrick Henry and told the rest of his people about it."

"So what? We knew they would find out sooner or later."

"I'm afraid we're going to learn what it's like to face the wrath of thirty-five million people who have been taking shit from the government most or all of their lives. And now they learn they have been adjudged nonhumans and are slated for death." Raebyrne glared. "Rebellion? The Party has given them no choice. Don't you true believers have enough brains to understand? When a man has nothing to lose, he has nothing to lose."

Voisselle deflated to the point Raebyrne thought he might be melting, or perhaps melting down. Voisselle looked around the room, panic on his face. "They have no education, no trained officers to lead them. Why, they don't have a chance. We have modern weapons, artillery, and aircraft. They have old rifles and pistols only." He stood up, looked like he was going somewhere, and then sat back down. "They're nuts." He tried to swallow his Adam's apple. "They're kidding themselves."

"Maybe so, but they have no choice. Don't you understand that? You stupid son of a bitch. Their back is against the wall."

"Good," Voisselle said. "I've shot many who were lined up against a wall."

"And I wonder why you continuously underestimate these people. I take that back. I do know. It's arrogance. You think they're hicks in the sticks, like the DDC says. Well, we will see."

Raebyrne sat in his chair, stomach churning at the thought of what was coming. "Already they are systematically denying us access to their people. No longer will you be able to drive into the countryside and hunt Wild People as they work their farms unarmed. Drive into the countryside now and you won't come back alive."

Voisselle slowly rose from his chair. He suddenly appeared worn down to a smaller man. He began to pace the office, sweat staining his face and running down his neck to soak his uniform collar. "Why, you talk like this is my fault. I'm just following orders. If we don't depopulate the designated biosphere areas, W.G. will send in soldiers and take over our government completely. You know that as well as I do." He stopped pacing and looked at a portrait of the DDC on a wall across from his desk. "That's what those damn hicks don't understand. Even if they did defeat us, they can't possibly defeat W.G."

Raebyrne looked sick. "Leaving World Government out of it for the moment, just do the math. Most of our population is Redundant Headcount, societal parasites in the gut of our nation. The boy is right: They're nothing more than hairless apes, useless in peace as well as war."

Raebyrne continued with distain on his face. "And most of our government consists of egghead paper pushers who cannot kill a cockroach. They rely on Dissident Control for all force, and thanks to W.G., we're not allowed to maintain more than a token military. That leaves us, Dissident Control, to handle thirty-five million pissed off Wild People."

"Merrick, what's wrong with you? I once thought you had some sense." Voisselle talked as if he were the only adult in the room. "Those wild ass animals can't possibly take on the most sophisticated society in history. We're *socialists!* The Party has planned for everything. These anarchists can't compete with us. And these particular wild asses are Southerners to boot."

"Then there is the most important factor in the equation: The quality of our people as a society." He stared Voisselle down. "Standing side by side with them, we don't measure up, not in our wildest dreams. What little I have learned about life in general and Wild People in particular, tells me character matters. It's a rare treasure unevenly dispersed among the human race. Virtue and character cannot be inherited, it must be learned, and their way of life demands both, ours demands neither. What it does demand is selfishness and callous cruelty."

Voisselle appeared to blow a gasket. "Bullshit. Socialism is about spreading the wealth."

Raebyrne's eyes grew distant. "What was it the infiltrator said in his report? What was it he heard the boy say?" He scratched his chin and nodded. "Oh yes, now I remember. He said, 'Fuck the heartless, soulless government. We are human beings. We win. They lose.' "

Voisselle snorted. "What the hell are you talking about? Who gives a damn what the boy said?"

Raebyrne sighed sadly, his spirit suddenly deflated. "Yes, I know, it's all beyond you, over your head. The sickening truth is you're not alone. That is the tragedy of the Unity Party, of Socialism. I see that clearly now." He stood up from the chair. "Yes, there will be a bloody war, and many of them will die, but we can't beat them. They are better than us, more human."

"Whaaat! Why, you gutless bastard!"

Ignoring Voisselle, he turned to the door. "I'm going to check on my men. I still have duties to perform, since you're not going to allow me to resign." He stopped at the door and turned to face Voisselle. "Or are you going to do me a favor and have me shot?"

Voisselle just stood there staring at him as if he were insane.

"Speechless, are you Captain? Your own twisted mind has deceived its self." He pointed at a plaque on the captain's desk. On the front was engraved: "Unity Party forever!" On the back was a dirty joke. "The real dirty joke is on the front." Raebyrne walked out the door.

*   *   *

Patrick sat on the couch across the living room from Mr. L'Amour. Mrs. L'Amour and Sharon were in the kitchen preparing a Sunday dinner. The smell of fried chicken wafted into the living room. The men could hear the sizzle of cooking grease, some of which would later be used in gravy for rice. A pail of fresh milk Patrick had just coaxed out of the L'Amour's cow sat on the kitchen counter. Salad of tomatoes, cucumbers, and onions he and Mr. L'Amour picked together, was waiting in a large bowl. Behind him, there were a dozen family photos on a shelf, many figurines and knickknacks on another. One photo was that of a U.S. Marine captain standing by a cave on Mount Suribachi. He held a smoking M1 Garand, across his chest hung an empty cotton bandoleer. It was taken two hours before the famous staged photo of the flag raising. The Marine was Mr. L'Amour's grandfather.

"Patrick," Mr. L'Amour said, "I have been meaning to talk with you about something important. The relationship between you and my daughter has been something of a whirlwind affair. It seemed to get serious fast. Too fast and too…heated…to my thinking."

Here it comes, Patrick thought.

"In many ways you demonstrate maturity beyond your years, your mind comprehends much more quickly and thoroughly than most men twice your age. Still, you're not quite seventeen, and I remember those olden days when I was young."

Mr. L'Amour coughed and squirmed in his easy chair, obviously uncomfortable with the subject. "Well, Patrick, I was young once. Now I know that's hard to believe, but I was sixteen like you."

Mr. L'Amour glanced toward the kitchen door. "Anyway, I know testosterone can prevent you from thinking things through and allow you to make a life-altering mistake." He sat up straight in his chair. "I don't think I must remind you the last thing Sharon needs is a premature pregnancy at this time in her life. And the problems with the government lingering over our heads…"

He ran his fingers over his thinning hair. "And, also, I know you can't understand this, but she's still my little girl. She's almost eighteen, but she is not a woman yet."

"No, you don't need to mention that's the last thing she needs right now," Patrick said. "But I would have been surprised if you hadn't…mentioned it. I expect perhaps you have a shotgun hidden behind that easy chair within reach."

Mr. L'Amour smiled and chuckled.

"And I too sometimes think of her as a girl rather than a woman. She has a heartwarming girlish way about her. I have noticed she leaves herself exposed and vulnerable to the pain of life and often pays for her openness."

"She's my sweetheart."

"I know you think of her as innocent and worry maybe I'm out to take advantage of her. If I were her father, I would be worried too, but she has complete and full control over our relationship. Believe me, she's the boss."

"That's the way it should be Patrick," Mr. L'Amour said. "But in her case it may be the blind leading the blind. She is inexperienced. And it's obvious she is smitten with you, her first boyfriend."

"Look, I will never lie to you, and I must tell you right now…I want her. I want her and need her in every way a man needs a woman. I must also tell you just as honestly, I will never hurt her. I will always treat her with respect and I mean that in every sense of the word."

"Thank you. That is also the way it should be."

"Believe me when I say what you have seen us do in public is what we have done in private. In fact, now that I think about it, we haven't even been alone more than four or five minutes since we met. That is an accurate and complete account of our physical love life together."

"I should hope so. You two have not known each other long."

"I expect over time to learn to love her even more. She is teaching me. Once I let her under my skin—well…"

Mr. L'Amour smiled. "She's an extraordinarily lovable girl. It will take a mature and unselfish person to handle the emotions she invokes, but I think you may be the one. I hope so anyway. She seems to have her heart set on you."

"On that subject, I cannot give you an accurate and complete account of my spiritual and emotional love for her, not unless you want to set in that easy chair and listen to me talk about your daughter in sometimes embarrassingly frank ways for the next ten hours."

Mr. L'Amour's mouth was slightly agape, a look of astonishment on his face.

Since Sharon's father did not seem to have anything to say, Patrick continued. "I told you before: I will not lie to you, so believe me when I tell you we will not consummate our love until or unless, we are married. Until then, I will not even ask her. Not once. Besides, I don't want to find myself looking down the barrel of that shotgun."

The slightly agape mouth slowly turned into a smile and Mr. L'Amour began to laugh loudly.

Sharon and her mother rushed in from the kitchen, wondering what could have made the usually reserved man laugh so much.

He looked at his wife and daughter and pointed. "He is remarkable. Damned if he doesn't beat all. You're right girl. There is something different about him. You're not months older than him; he is years older than you." He turned his gaze on Patrick. "You're amazing boy." Suddenly the father's face grew stern. "But I'll hold you to your promise."

Patrick returned his gaze with unblinking earnest. "Why of course, Mr. L'Amour. I expect you to. Nothing I said was in jest."

Chapter 17

Raebyrne stood in the late night black, beside a fully loaded five-ton military truck. Mosquitoes droned and crickets chirped. A gar splashed in the river ten yards away, just beyond the crumbling concrete boat ramp. A bright falling star streaked across the sky at a descending angle, suddenly lighting up the immediate scene, creating multiple moving shadows under the tall trees. Raebyrne ducked under an oak. He looked up just in time to see the meteor fade to nothing, still high in the sky. The flash of bright light and moving shadows looked just like the searchlight of a helicopter. He waited for his heart to stop galloping then walked back to the truck.

The truck and its contents had been stolen from a military base that afternoon. He drove in with his friend, Sergeant Gurney Appleton, and a forged acquisition order from Captain Voisselle. The commanding officer looked the order over, checked Raebyrne's identification carefully, and ordered a sergeant to detail a dozen men and load the truck with the list of items. All branches of the military had recently received orders to cooperate fully with the Department of Dissident Control.

Raebyrne had made arrangements with the resistance. For five tons of high explosives and shoulder-fired anti-armor and antiaircraft missiles, he and his family would be given refuge in the countryside, one year's supply of food, and a modest home and land to farm. He and his family would also be taught how to survive in an agrarian society and economy. After that, he would be on his own.

"Don't move." Patrick's voice was low but clear.

Raebyrne stiffened.

"If you are being honest with us, we will hold up our end of the deal and more, even if it costs us our lives. On the other hand, if this is subterfuge bullshit, you and I are both going to die tonight. For now, you need to do exactly what I tell you. Nod if you understand." Raebyrne nodded his head. "Good. Now put your hands on the truck and put your feet out so you are leaning at a forty-five degree angle, and then spread your feet as far as you can."

Patrick's instructions were followed explicitly. Raebyrne could barely make out someone approaching him from the side wearing a night vision monocular. The man put a belt around him and tightened it until it was uncomfortable.

Patrick spoke again from farther back. "You now have a radio-controlled bomb strapped to your ass, so I hope you don't have any government goon friends nearby playing with radios. It could prove embarrassing to both of us if a stray RF sets the thing off."

Two men started unloading the truck, carrying crates down to the river's edge. By the time they had made three trips, boats started arriving. One person, who had been carrying a device around the truck, went out to the crates and passed it over them. Afterwards, he walked over to Patrick and whispered something in his ear.

"Check him out too." Patrick said.

The man with the device waved it over Raebyrne. "He's clean."

"Well, so far it seems we might live to see this through, Raebyrne. We have not detected any GPS transmitters or bugs yet. The ice is just starting to melt."

It took more than three dozen small boats and half as many men to unload the truck.

After the last boat left, someone walked up to Patrick. "Everything looks copasetic so far. Bill says there was a hundred each of electric and fuse-ignited blasting caps. Also, plenty of wire and fuse, even a couple power sources to set off the electric caps with. Oh, and there was a crate of Claymores."

"Great," Patrick said. "Now get everybody out of here, and don't forget to recheck everything for transmitters again. In case they have some on a timer, to be activated later."

Someone removed the belt from Raebyrne's waist, disappearing into the night with it. Patrick waited several minutes to give the others time to put yardage under their feet. "Okay, Raebyrne, it's just you and me now. We're both ninety-nine percent free. The ice has melted, and we're almost friends. Do not move for three minutes. Afterwards, get back in that truck and drive off. If by the appointed time everything still checks out, you will have fulfilled your end of the bargain. Then you and your family will be some of the most protected Wild People I know. Considering you have probably committed uncounted crimes against my people, you have brokered one hell of a deal."

Two days later, Patrick and nine of his freedom fighters, including Bart, Linda, Tel, Mathew, and Sharon, were waiting by a dirt road. They had positioned as if it were an ambush, and they had observation posts a mile down the road in both directions. They would warn of any approaching danger by radio.

A car conveying a man, woman, and two children came into view almost to the moment of the appointed time. The car slowed, and then stopped where a quart of white paint had been poured out across the road only fifteen minutes before. For security reasons, Raebyrne had not been told exactly where to stop. His instructions were to turn onto the yellow sand road and keep driving until he came to white paint.

Patrick watched from the woods. "Yeah, that's him. Bart, go out to the edge of the brush and yell for him to leave the car where it is and walk into the woods on this side. Don't get any closer than you need to for him to hear you. Have them walk straight into the woods and then head this way." He pointed. "Don't let them walk down the side of the road those hundred yards. Make them walk back from the road in the woods. I don't want them visible from the air. Whatever you do, don't go to them, make them come to you."

The first thing Patrick noticed when they arrived with Bart following was the woman was frightened nearly out of her mind. Raebyrne was carrying a backpack but did not appear to be armed.

Patrick glanced at Tel and motioned with his head. Tel took a transmitter detection device out of his pack and waved it over each of the Raebyrnes. Then he had them empty their pockets and turn them inside out, piling the contents on the ground in front of them. To Raebyrne's disgust, he was told to take his pack off and empty it also.

Tel smiled as he handed the little girl back the only thing she had in her pockets: a bag of costume jewelry. The boy had a small penknife, a rabbit's foot, a cheap compass, a box of fishing hooks with a roll of line, and two candy bars that were already half melted.

"I can see we're going to be friends already." Tel handed the items back to the boy.

It took longer to examine the items in the pack. It was mostly food and clothing for the mother and children. When finished, Tel stood up. "Okay, you can repack now."

Raebyrne said, "You don't think I'm stupid enough to try anything with my family here?"

Patrick got Tel's attention, then hand-signaled for him to take the lead. "Keep all of your senses working fulltime. We're not out of danger yet."

Tel nodded. "Is it okay if Linda follows behind me?"

"Sure, as long as you two don't distract each other too much." Tel turned away from Patrick and rolled his eyes at Linda, whose chest shook from an inaudible snicker.

Patrick turned to Raebyrne to watch him repack. "Hurry it up. The longer we stay here, the more danger we are in, and keep in mind I don't know what your family looks like. They could be here under duress, forced to pose as your family." He glanced at the thin brunette. "The lady is scared stiff."

Raebyrne finally got repacked and slid into the backpack. "That's because the government has told her all her life that you Wild People are animals."

One of the men Patrick barely knew said, "Yeah, that's right, we're animals, and we might as well act like it."

Sharon's eyes blazed. "That's enough, Harry. She is already so scared she might do something stupid like run off into the woods." She stood in front of the woman. "Don't worry, your husband has kept his end of the deal, and we will keep ours."

The woman seemed to be reassured by the tone of her voice.

Patrick stood by Sharon. "Do we look like animals to you Mrs. Raebyrne?"

She glanced nervously at Raebyrne. "No. My husband tells me the government has almost never told us the truth about anything."

"Well, your husband should know. We need to move out now."

As they walked, Patrick decided he might as well make use of the time and pump Raebyrne for intelligence. If he was willing to talk. The four were making so much noise a company of soldiers could have walked up on them without him hearing anyway.

"Raebyrne, you have already paid for what you bought in full, but I would like some information if you are willing."

"I have no objection. I have already burned all of my bridges behind me. There is no turning back. It won't take them long to find out who absconded with the truckload of goodies I traded you."

"Okay," Patrick said. "Who is in charge of District 13?"

"I don't know."

"Oh shit. You're already lying to me."

Raebyrne stumbled on a root. "I know who it was, but I don't know who replaced him."

Patrick walked alongside Raebyrne as they talked. He cocked his head. "You killed him. Before you left, you killed him. Didn't you?"

"I see why the others allow you, a teenager, to be in charge."

Patrick watched Raebyrne appraising his own unremarkable appearance and saw the man's interest jump to a higher level. He nearly laughed at the look of astonishment that came over Raebyrne's face.

"Ah, yes, I killed him. He was a psychopath. He threatened to have me shot several times in the last few months. And he ordered me to do things that have caused me great emotional anguish, things that I find hard to live with."

Tears welled in his wife's eyes, but she said nothing.

"Yeah, I bet," Patrick said. "The government has forced me to do things I did not want to also, but I never hurt any innocent people."

Raebyrne grabbed Patrick by the shoulder. "You're him, aren't you? The boy. Timucua."

"You don't need to know my name."

"Well, okay, but I know you're him. It's true, what I thought. You're not just a teenage boy. I could see it, sense it, in your writing. Now that I've heard you talk…You're not normal. Not for a grown man, much less for a teenager. You're a trained killer. I know things about you your friends here don't. I know what you did at that creek, how you set those men up, but how could you be trained? Who trained you? That's not normal."

Sharon interjected. "Watch your mouth. He has treated you and your family with respect."

Raebyrne shook his head. "No. That's not what I meant. Maybe I should have said special or unique."

"I'm just a scared kid who struggles to do the right thing as he sees it, while playing the cards he's dealt. None of my friends here, as you call them, created the cesspit you have been part of all your life, but they and I have to swim in it."

Patrick tried to keep his sense of hearing working as they walked. "I want to get back to the point of this conversation. We're going to stop to let your children rest soon, and feed them. They look exhausted already. When we do, I would like you to tell me where you got those weapons. You know what we need: Their security measures, safest way in and out, best time of day, week, month, to raid the place."

"Yeah, okay. I'll draw you a map, both allegorically, and literally. I know where there are three warehouses full of the kinds of weapons you need less than seventy miles from here in two locations. One has ten thousand M14s and nearly two million rounds of ammunition, all slated to be destroyed, but we have been busy thanks to you. Another has more missiles and HE like I traded you."

Patrick's eyes caught the motion of a squirrel scurrying up a pine tree. "Of course you will not be insulted if we take everything you say with a large grain of salt."

"No, of course not. But I think you have a pretty good Bravo Sierra detector on your shoulders anyway."

"That's right. And don't forget it."

*   *   *

"Here kid." Harry handed the girl a candy bar and then gave the boy one. He stood up from stooping low for the children who were sitting against an oak tree resting. Turning to Patrick, he said, "I'm going to cut poles and make a stretcher for the girl. She is too young to walk the distance we have to by tomorrow afternoon. I and Mathew will carry her."

"Sounds like good thinking," Patrick said. "But you're going to spoil your reputation."

"What does that mean?"

Patrick threw a look at Sharon. "Being concerned about someone else's little girl: that does not sound like an animal to me."

Sharon's gaze shot from Patrick to Harry, an amused smile on her face.

Harry turned away and started walking. "Don't be fooled, I can be as vicious as they say you are, when I have to be."

*   *   *

Mrs. Raebyrne failed to hide her disappointment when she saw the small Spartan home. Because of the government denying Wild People commerce with the cities, modern building materials had not been available for decades. The wood shingle roof and heavy timber doors made the small house look like something from centuries past. All work exhibited craftsmanship almost unheard of for generations, but to someone coming from her background the home was bare and entirely anachronistic.

The front door was opened, and they were bid to enter. Inside, there were sparse but adequate furnishings appropriate for each room: a furnished bedroom for each of the two children and one for the parents.

A comforter on the girl's bed had feminine design patterns and coloration. On shelves, were dolls and books written and published with young girls in mind. Nearly all were forty or fifty years old and the stories much older, by long-dead authors. In the closet and chest-of-drawers, there were clothes and shoes of various sizes because her exact size could only be guessed.

Similarly, the boy's bedroom possessed design patterning and coloration more suitable for its young occupant. A rustic outdoorsy theme prevailed. On one wall, fishing equipment hung from a rack made of deer antlers. Clothing, including boots and shoes fitting for outdoors work on the farm and play in the woods, again of various sizes, reposed in a closet and chest-of-drawers.

The master bedroom contained a bed with a headboard of intricately detailed design. Three large pillows sat neatly across the bed in front of the headboard, their cases made of silk. A bereaved mother whose daughter had been murdered by government agents donated them. Stored for many years, they had been intended as gifts in hopes of a future wedding for her beloved daughter. A dream shattered by an agent's bullet. The mother no longer held any value to them and thought it fitting as a gift to a former agent who had seen the error of his ways. Sharon, who knew the slain sixteen-year-old girl, did not say anything about the silk pillowcases.

In the days before the Unity Party, when there was still a real economy and a real United States of America, the handmade furniture would have been worth a year's income for the average worker.

Mrs. Raebyrne whispered in her husband's ear, "This is beneath civilized people."

Mr. Raebyrne sighed impatiently. "Actually, I'm surprised so much thought and effort has been put into the place. Taking all things into consideration, they have gone beyond the requirements of the bargain." The two walked into the kitchen. "They have proven by their actions once again that common decency is much more common among their people than ours."

"At least the children seem to accept the whole thing as a grand adventure," she said.

"I think they will adjust. It will depend on your attitude as much as anything." He gave her a stern look. "We should be grateful for their kindness and consideration for our children.

They, after all, are the children of a lieutenant in the hated Department of Dissident Control. Yet they have treated not only you and them as human beings and not as enemies, but also me. Keep in mind, until the deal was agreed on, we were deadly enemies." He looked into her eyes. "They have ample reason to hate me."

She held him. "You did what you could to stop it."

"No I didn't."

"It's not your fault."

Tel walked by the kitchen and heard them talking, then walked outside into the front yard, shaking his head.

"What?" Linda asked.

"I almost feel sorry for the bastard."

While Sharon helped little Suzy get acquainted with her new room, Patrick took Raebyrne on a tour of the farm. "The land is fertile. With hard work, you will have a surplus of crops you can trade for needed items. There are a few tools and other farming equipment stored in the barn, and plenty of food to feed your family for a year. It's all put away so it won't spoil and vermin can't get to it."

"Remember, we will need instruction on farming," Raebyrne said.

"After you're settled in, in a week or two, a teenage brother and sister, about thirteen, fourteen years old, will come around to instruct you and your wife, at least enough to get you started."

Patrick stopped walking for a second, smiling while rubbing his chin. "Those two are kind of rough around the edges. They're backwoods farmers and they have lived a hard, demanding life. Don't take offense if they consider you to be dumbass city folk. All they have known is rural life, and your family might as well be from Mars. You would do well to warn your wife."

"I will."

"Keep in mind also, you're a former enemy. Try to convince them you have reformed, and you'll get along fine. Don't worry about your children at all though. No one will hold kids responsible for wrongs adults perpetrate."

"What makes them more backwoods than you or the rest of your people?" Raebyrne asked. "You're all farmers."

Patrick looked up at the sky for a second. "You're smart enough to answer that question yourself."

"What do you mean?"

"Do I speak with what you would call a hick accent?"

"No."

"That's because those who raised me did not either. If you knew their parents, you would understand why they are more backwoods. And if you saw Sharon and her parents together it would take you only five minutes to understand why she is who she is."

Raebyrne nodded. "Family."

"Yes, family. It makes all the difference."

As they neared the barn, Patrick spoke again. "There are books in the house on farming, animal husbandry, and canning food. I would read them and write down any questions they bring to mind before those two arrive. In time, two mules for plowing, some pigs and milk cows, along with chickens and the like will be brought to you."

They walked to the back end of the barn. "Let me show you something," Patrick said. He reached up, took a key down from the top of a beam, and then opened a tool cabinet. He handed the key to Raebyrne. On one end were various hand tools, on the other was an M4 carbine, seven magazines, boxes of ammunition, and a nine-millimeter Beretta military issue pistol with three magazines and more boxes of ammunition.

Raebyrne was surprised. "You trust me with weapons?"

"My conscience wouldn't allow me to leave you here with nothing but an ax and knife to defend your family with. The government wants you dead as much as the rest of us. Also, like all societies, we have a small percentage of criminals and psychotics among us, perhaps one tenth of one percent."

"Only one tenth of one percent?"

"Or fewer."

Raebyrne was incredulous. "Come on, there is no way you have so few criminals and crazies. I had to work under a psycho for the last two years."

"If your way of life does not poison your heart and soul, your mind is much less likely to be diseased. We even live longer, twenty years longer on average, and healthier lives than you city people, especially the Redundant Headcount."

"I can see that your way is better than the government's, but it's no Utopia."

"Of course not. We do get more exercise working our farms and eat healthier natural food. Not that garbage your government forces down your throat. I'm afraid this war may cause more psychological problems among our people though. I'm talking about the children in particular."

"Would you be a farmer if not for the government forcing it on your people?"

"Probably not. An agrarian economy was all that was left us. We had to survive."

Raebyrne followed him outside.

"Look, I know this place is not what you and your wife are used to," Patrick said. "But we did the best we could. The house is not fancy, but it's clean. I'm sure in the end you will find getting used to the buildings a lot easier than learning about and coming to terms with the new way of life you and your family are now entering." He stopped under an oak and turned to Raebyrne. "We will do what we can, but we are busy with the war, and we cannot be here every day to hold your hand."

"Yes, I realize that and so does my wife. It's been quite a shock for her, but she will adjust."

"You might want to mention to your wife that most of the people who escorted you here have no home, family, or anything else, thanks to your government. Many gave until it hurt to do this much for you."

"I was given to believe your people do not believe in charity."

"We believe in charity given by choice. The government cannot possibly be charitable because everything the government does is implemented with force. That's not charity; it's armed robbery. Name a single time the government has ever given anything to anyone without first stealing it from someone else. Government charity comes at the price of the priceless: freedom."

"It doesn't have to be that way."

"It always has been so far. Think about it. Why didn't President Roosevelt allow people who wanted no part of his unconstitutional government mandated retirement program to opt out?"

"Because the people who wouldn't want to participate are the very ones needed to fund it."

"Precisely. That takes you right down the path to armed robbery, legalized plunder. Before the government could give away free land in the eighteen hundreds, it first had to steal it from Native Americans. Before the government can give away free food, healthcare or anything else, it first must take those things from someone who worked harder and or smarter in the free market. The free market that no longer exists outside of Wild People country thanks to the government. Governments cannot create wealth, but they can give away worthless Credits that amount to IOUs with nothing but force to back them. Wild People are rich compared with anyone in the cities, and not just the Redundant Headcount."

Raebyrne nodded. "They can't tolerate a free market. It allows the people to have too much financial freedom and that takes power from the government."

"And a free market cannot survive without the concept of private property. Private property rights had to be abolished in order to confiscate wealth to pay for social programs. At one time income was considered private property, the same as the fingers on your hand. Without tax or labor slavery, Socialism cannot exist. And even with tax *and* labor slavery, it is unsustainable because there are few in society creating wealth. Even worse is the loss of freedom because it leads to Statism, putting government first, which leads to tyranny."

"You're saying you believe in charity given by choice, not at gunpoint."

"Yes. If the government can commit armed robbery in the name of charity, why can't I? Perhaps I should steal your boots in case I come across someone who is barefoot. You know, it would have been a whole lot easier if we just stole that house, land, food, and other things we traded you for the explosives and missiles. Instead, we asked for donations. The government doesn't ask."

"I stole the weapons from the government."

"Yes you did. And you will have to live with it. The government has declared us not fit to live. I have no qualms about confiscating weapons from an enemy before they use them on my people. We are at war."

"But isn't it true you can't always count on people to do the right thing and help the poor?"

"The only difference between government officials and common people, is government officials yield the power to have you jailed or killed. They are endowed with no more generosity, kindness, morals, or concern for the suffering of strangers than anyone of us. If you can't trust people in general to do the right thing, then you can't trust those in power either. You have only made matters worse by giving people who have all of the same flaws as the rest of us, in reality more, the power to take people's freedom and property in the name of charity."

Patrick continued. "On top of that, the more you depend on the government, or even your neighbors, friends, relatives, or spouse, for basic necessities instead of yourself, the more you are subjugated, and enslaved by others."

"Aren't you enslaving the one you are leeching off?"

"Yes. But you are also turning yourself into a dependent, which is a form of slavery."

"Explain."

"A wife who depends completely on her husband for the basic needs of life may soon find herself controlled and abused by him. If you can't always trust your spouse, presumably someone who loves you or at least once did, in a relationship of dependence, how the hell can you trust an all-powerful government? I'm not an anarchist, but government must be limited in size and power." Patrick shrugged his shoulders. "That's what the old Constitution was for."

"I understand. The mess we are in now, proves much of what you are saying. Listen, I want to help you as much as I can because you have been so kind to my family. I'll write down any information I can think of that may help. When the two teenagers arrive, I'll give it to them."

"Thank you. It may save lives."

Chapter 18

Patrick and Raebyrne stood under the shade of a wide oak, enjoying the cooling breeze. Two former enemies were becoming friends. Raebyrne knew the boy would be leaving in a few minutes and, for some reason, felt compelled to try to understand him. It was a feeling he never had before. He was taller than the boy but was certain who was standing in whose shadow.

"Who taught you how to hunt men?" Raebyrne asked.

"My grandfather taught me how to use a rifle and pistol, small unit tactics, and most everything else he learned in the Army and serving in Vietnam."

"Did he teach you what you did at the creek?"

"Some of it. The rest came naturally as the result of a childhood spent in those woods learning the differences and similarities of prey and predator."

"Soldiers in modern armies are conditioned mentally to kill, to overcome their natural inhibition to kill another human being. And you're so young. How did you learn so fast?"

"I watched them kill my mother and grandfather from a hill six hundred yards away. I could do nothing. My rifle was hidden in the woods in a waterproof cache under a log. By the time I got back with the rifle, they were dragging my dead mother to the APC by her feet. I learned how to want to kill fast. Your people taught me."

"I understand. And I'm sorry. I wish it did not happen. It was stupid and needless. But there is more to your abilities. What you have done is impossible, yet you did it."

"I have thought about it. I think perhaps I was born a killer. Something happened to me that morning. I don't know what. But the killer in me came alive. Don't get me wrong. I don't like it. And I have no romantic childish delusions about war being noble or some kind of adventure. If your government would leave my people alone, I would go back to being a farmer in a second. Those who killed my family are dead. And I might add, they were easy to kill because they were stupid. I was lucky that day."

"What do you mean something happened to you?"

"I can't explain it. I'm not sure myself. I just know something did."

"I will tell you something I do know." Raebyrne paused. "There are only two kinds of individuals who would declare war on a government, stand alone against it and ask no quarter, with the odds of a million to one: an insane person, or you. The amazing thing is you are a sixteen-year-old boy."

"Not anymore."

"I guess you're saying you have aged a lot because of what you've been through."

"No. I'm not whining. I believe whatever woke up inside me that morning is much older than me. And I don't think it is atavism."

"I don't understand."

"Neither do I. So we might as well leave it alone."

"Okay. I have to ask you a question though. When did you stop being motivated by hate?"

"How do you know I'm not?"

"Because I can tell by the way you treated my family that you, and the people you are with today at least, have a kindness in you that overshadows hate, even though you have plenty of reason to hate me."

Patrick looked away. "This is too personal for me to talk with a former enemy about."

"Wasn't what we were just talking about personal?"

"It's not the same." Patrick looked around to see if anyone was near. "I have a question for you. Have you ever been humbled by someone so much that you were changed forever?"

"Yes. Yes I have."

"If you are fortunate, that person is your wife."

"I understand. You're talking about the girl. She does seem to be special. She is in love with you. You know that don't you? It's obvious."

Patrick turned and faced him squarely. "I don't want to talk about her."

"I just wanted to understand what caused you to be...who you are. It's not her we are talking about."

"Like everyone, I am a product of my genes, family, environment, and experiences. If those killers had not invaded our home and murdered my family that morning, I would not be the person I am now. If I had not met someone who taught me...Well, I would still be breathing in air and exhaling hate with every breath."

"So now you fight for freedom and not hate."

"But don't think I'm satisfied yet. Not until the Unity Party is as dead and despised as Hitler, and no more than a footnote in history. Every man should try to do one thing before he dies: win some victory for humanity. If he can do that, his life will have not been a waste."

The man began to envy the boy for what he was. He could see clearly now through the scrim around the boy's heart. Only justice and honor and empathy and love of family and of a woman, all of the things indelibly engraved in the heart of a man, were worth living, killing and dying for. And these verities were made possible only by those with the courage and heart to be a real human being and not a hollow shell of one called a Redundant Headcount.

"You don't have to say it." Raebyrne had been warned. Now he hesitated. "Your actions speak for you. You love her more than you hate the government."

Patrick looked at him and said nothing.

"I wish I could have been on your side from the beginning. But I was not born free like you. They molded me into what I became. I am as much a victim as you."

Patrick looked past the field and across the glade. "They had your mind but not your heart. I hope there are more like you in the cities."

Raebyrne looked beyond the boy, over his shoulder. In the glade's tall grass, he could see his wife and children playing in the green of nature, chasing one another and laughing with joy. He watched as they turned to something and ran toward it, their faces shining. He saw it in their eyes: what it was that gave them hope, what they were running to. Tears stained his cheeks. How many years had it been since he had felt alive? How long since he valued his wife's love? How long since he had treasured the time his children had before they would be adults?

Thank you God, for giving me another chance!

The boy saw his face. "You see something out there, don't you?"

He turned from the boy, not wanting anyone to see his tears.

"I too see, with my own eyes, in my own way. What I see is the land my people were born and lived and died and are buried on. In my mind's eye, right now, I see my ancestors living on in the freedom they lost to invaders from across the sea. They have been thawed from earthly bodies and are now even freer than before the first enslavers came. Someday, if I am worthy, I may join them."

The new man looked with opened eyes. And yes. He could see. He closed his eyes and reopened them. The image was gone.

Raebyrne turned to look at the boy and then across the glade again and felt the outer fringes of distant warmth, radiating like flickering fire feathers, the afterglow of the light the boy now walked and breathed and lived in: freedom, human dignity. He now understood the one thing that made the boy who he was and felt cleansed of the filth of his past life.

What he could not understand until this moment, what had kept him up long mind-stormy dark hours, walking blindly down the halls of his conscience, what it was about the boy that so frightened him on that morning when he stood at the beginning of it all in the swamp by the creek, standing by the dead dogs and across from the flags on the other side, was the boy's foreknowing. First, the warrior in him, preborn and prebloodied and preskilled in the crafts of the death hunt; and the mind, strong from use, not from age; and the heart, stronger still from use and not from age, a free human being, God's greatest creation. He feared him on that day as demons of the dark fear light.

The boy was born into a nation now barely alive, left prostrate and wailing in agony; the aftermath of a heart operation where the heart of its heart had been hollowed out of all light and warmth and life, without benefit of any easing of pain, but instead with the sadistic purposeful infliction of torment of the kind unnecessary for the completion of the operation. And then the lobotomy, performed with a dull, rusty ice pick of intentionally injected ignorance yielded by government schools, calculated to remove all things human, leaving only the animal instincts and coarsest of selfish inclinations. The government claiming all the while their handiwork to be an improvement, better than what was before, though what was before was a man, or woman, or child; and what is today is a soulless, heartless, mindless animal. Wild People, the new man now realized, may be the only true human beings left in America.

The last hope of a nation and a once promising and glorious, though never completely fulfilled dream, lived on in a people he once looked down on, and a boy who had relinquished himself to, and therefore breathed new life into, the unconquered spirit of a murdered people who did not let the limitations of flesh stop them from joining the constant current of the endless river of time, to live on as a free people, more free than before. The ancient blood of patriots of many races who died for their people was somehow willing and able to reach out and embrace a living soul once again to help flesh and blood be more than it could otherwise.

Why him? The new man asked himself.

Character is fate that is why.

Ancient blood of the cast-off mortal bodies of unconquered spirits flowed in his veins, but it was his belief in and total acceptance of their love of freedom that allowed the immersion and bonding of the boy's shadow with the living boy. The new man did not know why he felt these things in his heart, but he did. Perhaps freedom allows your heart to believe in what your mind tells you would otherwise be impossible. The boy is, after all, more than a boy; there must be a reason for it.

Not atavism, the boy said. No, Raebyrne thought. It was spiritual, not spiritualism, spiritual. Not the blood of his ancestors, but the heart.

Raebyrne asked, "When did you stop calling yourself Timucua?"

"I...Sharon insisted on calling me Patrick. After that just about everyone else followed her example. I guess they figured she must know better than me what my name is."

Raebyrne laughed. "Maybe she does."

"It's my middle name. I have not used it until recently, since the day they killed my family. Now I guess I'm Patrick again."

"I was told it was the name of an ancient Indian tribe."

"Yes. They were a Stone Age people. Very primitive. But they were people, not animals. They were wiped out by the Spaniards, partly by disease and partly because they resisted slavery. At least some of them did. When I was seven, I read about them and memorized the declaration of war sent to Hernando de Soto by a Timucua chief. His name was Acuera."

"Do you still remember his words?"

"Yes. But the declaration is four paragraphs long. I can tell you the first paragraph if you want."

"Please do. I have been interested since...for some time now."

"Okay. Let me think for a second.

" 'Others of your accursed race have, in years past, poisoned our peaceful shores. They have taught me what you are. What is your employment? To wander about like vagabonds from land to land, to rob the poor, to betray the confiding, to murder in cold blood the defenseless.

No! with such a people I want no peace—no friendship. War, never ending war, exterminating war, is all the boon I ask.' "

Raebyrne said, "And these were Stone Age people?"

"Like I said, they were people, not animals. They fully understood the concept of freedom. I said they were Stone Age simply because they had no metallurgy or any other technology. They were human beings."

"You feel a kinship with them, don't you?"

"Of course. Don't you? They lived and died for freedom, their people and their land. I feel a kinship with all people who love freedom, not just the Timucua."

"Patrick, we should be going now."

Sharon had walked up on Raebyrne unawares.

"I heard you walking in the tall grass." Patrick smiled at her. "Anyone ever tell you, you walk like a girl?"

She shrugged her shoulders. "Is that bad?"

"No."

Raebyrne's demeanor stopped her in her tracks. He seemed different. He was not the same man who left the small home earlier. He was genuinely smiling at her, as if she were an old friend. He was happy, probably for the first time in many years.

Now he was relishing in the sight of a beautiful young girl, simply because God had given mankind the gift of beautiful young girls. There was not a perverse thought in his head at that moment. He was just happy for God's gifts. She could have been a small child or a baby and he would have felt the same.

As Patrick turned to her he saw Raebyrne's transformation, but his eyes did not linger. He leaned his rifle against a tree, then walked to Sharon and said, "I take it you've already said good-bye to them for both of us."

"Well, if you want…"

Patrick shook his head, stopping beside her. He put his weak arm across her shoulders and pulled her to him. "If they're not satisfied with you, I'll just be something the cat showed up with in her mouth."

Her eyes darted to Raebyrne. His beaming smile was so out of character, his eager eyes so unexpected, she began to blush. "Patrick, what have you two been talking about?"

Raebyrne sensed her discomfort. Suddenly turning his head and looking away for a moment, he said, "I apologize. It's just that I find myself looking at the world and all of its beauty in a new light now that my family and I are free."

Patrick chuckled under his breath. "I don't think he's mentally undressing you Sharon, he is just allowing himself to really see you for the first time, along with the rest of the world. And you have to admit; even other girls can see that you are full of life."

Sharon did not take her eyes off Raebyrne. "I still want to know what you said to him."

Patrick gave a muffled laugh through a closed-mouth smile. "We were talking about freedom and what is worth living and dying for, it had nothing   to... Actually, it had everything to do with you." He pulled her face gently to him and kissed her forehead. "He wanted to know why I stopped hating, and I guess I gave him a long speech, I don't remember. I should have just said: Sharon." He held her face, covering most of the left side with his hand and kissed her forehead again.

"I really do apologize," Raebyrne said. "Honestly, I was not leering, just admiring God's handiwork. I'm a happily married man. Or at least I am now. Thanks to you and your people."

Sharon smiled with her usual warmth. "Well, God gave you a beautiful family. I hope your rebirth of enthusiasm for life will allow you to admire and appreciate that also. It will make you happier than staring at me."

Patrick said, "I think she's giving you a gentle tongue-lashing. But as usual, there is wisdom in her words. I'm not trying to get rid of you, but aren't you eager to start your new life?"

Raebyrne looked toward his new home and saw his family gathered out front, waiting for him. He turned back to Patrick and Sharon. Stepping forward with his right hand out, he said, "Thank you. Thank you both. I wish you two a long and happy life."

He and Patrick shook hands. Raebyrne turned and walked through the uncut grass, slowly at first, and then faster. Halfway there he was running.

They watched as he held and kissed his wife and children as if he had not seen them in months. Sharon's eyes were as bright as Patrick had ever seen them, and her face was glowing. Nothing made her happier than seeing others happy.

She looked up at Patrick, still smiling and beaming with joy. "I don't know what you did, but he is not the same man."

Patrick just looked at her face with brilliant intensity, marveling at her inner beauty.

Sharon noticed it in his eyes, suddenly her face washed over with mock sternness. "Oh! Now you're doing it."

He laughed. "Yeah right. I'm mentally undressing your face. I've got news for you girl: your face is always naked. And your face is the window to your heart. What do you think I'm looking at?" He looked over at the family again. "The man is the same, Sharon. What has changed is you and I, and the others unlocked the cage door." He turned his gaze back to her. "One down and millions to go." Looking around, he asked, "Where are the others?"

"They left thirty minutes ago. This area is safe so far, and there was no need for them to stay around."

"Well, it's time for me to get you home before your father comes after me with his shotgun. You know, I like that long and happy life stuff he mentioned."

She waited as he picked up his rifle. "You do huh?"

"Yeah, I think he may have something there."

*   *   *

In Mr. Ironwood's shack, the fate of the Wild People was being debated. Mr. Ironwood looked tired as he sat in the old wooden chair. "This is way too large an operation for a guerrilla force to take on Patrick."

"I believe ten thousand M14s and two million rounds of ammo are worth the risk. They will destroy the surplus rifles and ammo as soon as they can get around to it. The only reason they haven't already is because we've kept them busy.

Raebyrne says that's why they were brought to this particular warehouse in the first place."

"The M14 is the best all around full-powered battle rifle ever made," Mr. Ironwood said. "Basically a modernized M1 Garand. But I still think it's too much of a risk."

Patrick continued. "The explosives, anti-armor and antiaircraft missiles are an absolute necessity if we are to have any chance at all of denying them access to our people. And if we can't stop them from getting to our people they will continue to slaughter them."

Mr. Ironwood rubbed his forehead with his shaking hand. "You're talking about planning and executing two major operations at the same time, involving hundreds of people. Too many things can go wrong."

"We have a small opportunity in time here. They're still reeling from the fact we are actually fighting back in an effective way. Once they get the cobwebs out of their heads, they will beef up security on all installations where heavy weapons like missiles and HE are stored. And they will destroy the M14s. We have a chance to get our hands on some great equalizers. Please don't let it slip between our fingers."

"You do understand we're likely to lose forty, fifty people if we do this?"

"We are going to lose more if we don't. The government does not have that many aircraft capable of close air support. Shoot down enough of them with those missiles and they lose that advantage fast."

"Well, even if I agreed to this plan, I don't believe I'll be able to get any of the other militia leaders in this area to go along with it. It's too large and ambitious."

Patrick looked across the table at his elderly friend, bracing himself. "Actually, it's a small fraction of what I had in mind."

"What!" Mr. Ironwood looked as much afraid as angry. "Now you're letting this war crap go to your head. I have listened to you in the past because you have made sense, but now…You know good and well we can't go acting like a conventional army. We will lose way too many people."

"I'm not talking about one or two large operations. I'm talking about a thousand small unit operations on the same day and a thousand more the next and the next. Most will involve no more than one rifle team. We can hit them everywhere at once, all over Southeast Province. Ambush and hit and run. Hack at the branches of tyranny and then work our way to the roots."

Patrick saw the reaction on his elder friend's face but was not deterred. "Better yet, if every fighter in every province were to constantly harass and kill them and take or destroy their tools of death, we can pull some of their teeth and claws before this war really gets started. Anything we do in the next week or two will save lives later."

Mr. Ironwood held onto the table for balance. "We must be cautious. Your ideas are too flamboyant." He shook his head.

Patrick sighed. "We need to show them that we can really hurt them, not just a pinprick, but really hurt them. We have to make them fear us more than W.G."

The old man threw his hands in the air. "Oh Patrick, now you've lost it. If it were that easy, we would have finished it a long time ago. We have to be careful. You're too young for this."

"I never said it was going to be fun. This is just the beginning. But what we do now will save lives later. Incrementalism when fighting for freedom and the lives of your people is insanity. They have already decided to wipe us out. For what? Because we are free. Simply because we live on the land of our grandparents. Do you think killing a few hundred of their murderers is going to change their minds?" He did not wait for an answer. "They don't give the slightest damn about their pawns. There is no cheap way out of this. We're likely to lose one hundred thousand of our people in the next month."

"Good God! We can't take that kind of loss."

"Why not? We probably lost that many unarmed women and children this summer to the Final Removal Plan. We might as well get it through our heads we are going to sustain damage and suffer pain, trying too hard to avoid it now will do nothing but cost us more lives later. It was our people's concern for human life that allowed the Unity Party to slowly take over in the beginning."

"What do you mean?"

"Allowing ourselves to be robbed of our own country by the tyranny of the dumbass majority that the government itself created with its own schools was suicide. We once had a Constitution to, if not prevent, at least slow down the destruction of undeniable God-given rights by mindless mob rule. Unfortunately, it was almost never respected in the aggregate. Every special interest group picked the small part of the Constitution it liked and said screw the rest. Proving the validity and wisdom of those who warned a pure democracy is worse than two wolves and a sheep deciding what to have for lunch."

"You're right there."

"The first time they started talking about annulling the Constitution our people should have started killing the bastards."

"The people chose safety and free things over freedom."

"And now we have neither."

"All of that is true," Mr. Ironwood said. "But I don't think you understand how weak our people are militarily."

"I apologize for preaching at you. Keep in mind I've been dealing with the mistakes of your parent's generation my whole life. This should have been stopped long before my generation was born. Well, we have inherited this festering cancer, and we are going to clean it up. It's time to love what is right and to hate what is wrong enough to fight, kill, suffer, and die to cure our people of this cancer called the Unity Party and its Socialism."

"I agree with everything you just said, and I am ashamed of our people for allowing it to get this far out of hand. But a hundred thousand people in one month!"

"Mr. Ironwood, I was only talking about here in Southeast Province. We will lose four or five times that many across the continent. It is either that or lose all thirty-five million of our people. I suppose they may allow a hundred or so of us to live, so they can keep us in a zoo behind bars for exhibition."

The old man stood up and looked across the table at the grandson of his now dead best friend, his face pained. "I have no doubt you are serious. I know you mean every word. And I know you're right about one thing. Things have been allowed to degenerate to the point the price required for our people's freedom will be grievously high."

Mr. Ironwood sat back down and sighed laboriously. "Patrick, I will try to convince the others to agree to the two raids on the supply depots, but you might as well forget about anything larger. They will never agree to such a massive operation. Security would be impossible. It's bound to leak out, and the government would be waiting for us."

"If we hit them everywhere at once, how are they going to be waiting for us? You won't tell me, but I guess we have ten or twelve million fighting-age militia members including teenagers of both genders. There is no way the enemy can be everywhere at once. That is the whole idea. As far as security is concerned, the plan is for everyone to attack whenever and wherever they can. That's not exactly a state secret."

"But the thought of sacrificing our people like that, Patrick. It's a desperate move, and mature, deliberate, reasoning people do not do desperate things. I think you're letting your hatred cloud your judgment. We can't just throw lives away like that."

Patrick slammed his fist on the table. "Damn it! Can't you see that all of us are already condemned to die? I'm trying to save lives! If we go at this timidly and let this stretch out for years we will lose millions to starvation and disease on top of those killed by the government. Because of The Party, we have been forced back into a totally agrarian society. It takes long hard days in the fields to feed us. If the war lasts too long we will starve."

Patrick's face changed, turning hard. "You told me once that you love Sharon like a granddaughter, prove it. Convince the gutless, selfish bastards at the top of the militia to fight for once in their lives. Maybe you're not the man my grandfather thought you were. But I am telling you right now, though I won't be with her to help her through life, before I die, she *will* be free of the government's death sentence!"

"Patrick, we are more than friends, nearly family, but show some respect for your elders." He held his chest for a second. Patrick noticed it and the pain on his face. "You don't have to tell me I have failed. I live with it every day." He held his shaking hands out, open and empty. "What God-given alchemy of the human heart turns a boy into a man in one morning? Can you turn a thirty or forty or fifty-year-old coward into a man like you Patrick? For the most part, that's what the militia is made of. This war will be fought by people like you and Bart and Tel and Linda and Mathew, and Sharon." He looked at Patrick, his body shaking. "Your capacity to hate is exceeded only by your capacity to love. I pray you don't grow to hate me for my failure."

Patrick shook his head. "No. You are my other grandfather; the only family I have left. If not for you my grandfather would have died not much older than me. I'm not being disrespectful. I'm just arguing my point forcefully. Please don't make a mistake that will cost us millions of lives. Pride be damned. I am young and inexperienced, that makes me an easy target for calumny. If I fail to convince you of the only moral course of action now, it will cost the lives of millions of our people because if you do not listen to me no one else will. I don't blame you. I just want you to convince them to fight. At least put it to them as forcefully as you can. If they still won't fight, I won't blame you."

"I was once an RT leader," Mr. Ironwood said, "not much older than you then. I saw boys turned to men by the crucible, the combination of the jungle and the enemy, the hammer and the anvil. But there had to be material to work with. You understand? The Army helped. I mean the noncoms. But it was the crucible they were thrown into that did it. That crucible was a man-made hell created by governments. And so it is today." His old shoulders slumped and he lowered his head. "The crucible. Over and over again, throughout history.

The crucible. The hell. Created by governments." He raised his head and looked at Patrick. "You went through that alone. My God. Alone."

"Oh, forget about me. I'm not long for this world. The important thing is to leave it a better place for our people."

Mr. Ironwood stood taller, staring at his young friend. "No time for self-pity, Patrick? And you damn sure don't want mine. I know. I know." He stood stiff as a statue, looking inwardly. "An army of crucible graduates...of Timucuas." He shook the thought from his head. "You're dreaming old man."

"Are you going to try?" Patrick asked. "At least try? Maybe I'm wrong. So convince me my way will cost us more lives than any other. I do know this nightmare is not going away if we do nothing. Remember, W.G. will come in as soon as The Party is in trouble. Speed is of the essence."

The old man sighed. "No guerrilla army in history has escalated hostilities so soon so fast."

"No people since the European Jews have faced the total nullification of their people as human beings. I hope we don't make their mistake. I pray we fight back with everything we have."

"But there must be a way out of this without paying such a terrible price. If we use our heads—"

"Take their farms."

"What?"

"I said take their farms. They are outside the cities and not all that well protected. Cut the cities off from their food sources and the Redundant Headcount will riot in the streets when they get hungry. Most of their power plants are outside the cities, destroy them. Ditto their water supply. Anything to make life miserable for the city rats. They have been brainwashed to rely on the government for everything. What do you think will happen if The Party no longer does provide everything? They are nothing more than hairless apes with no balls or brains, but they will go nuts."

"Yeah, I agree, they will go ape all right. The government will have to use soldiers to keep order in the cities, which will dilute their strength."

"Mr. Ironwood, we must do it all and more, and we must do it all at once. We have enough fighters. What we need more of are leaders. I know I'm just a teenager, but think about it. Being bold early on and accepting losses now will save millions of lives later."

"I'm growing weary. It's age catching up with me. I may be able to get the others to go along with the two raids. I can't promise you anything more."

"I don't need promises you can't keep. But I hope you at least give them the gist of what I have said here today. I don't have all the answers, but I do know I'm not likely to see the end of this and neither are hundreds of thousands of us. Our freedom demands a price. For our people's sake, we must be willing to pay it."

"Let's start with the raids. Afterwards, we will talk about more operations."

Sensing the elder man's fatigue, Patrick thought it best to leave it alone. The old man appeared more exhausted than his words let on. He regretted pushing his point so forcefully. "Will you let me know when the meeting is? I would like to be there. I don't plan to say anything, just listen."

"Okay, Patrick. Day after tomorrow will be as soon as it can happen. Late afternoon."

"I will be there. And I will try to keep my mouth shut."

When Patrick was outside, he walked over to Bart. "Ask someone to cook something for him and keep an eye on him, will you? He seems tired."

Bart nodded. "I'll stay with him tonight and see that he gets a hot meal in him. I think he's losing sleep over the fact the war is heating up. It's one thing to know it's coming, but something else entirely when it comes to those you know and care for. He's worried about us, not himself."

"I know. Thanks."

Chapter 19

"Mr. L'Amour, I wonder if there is some way you can keep Sharon home for the next four or five weeks." Patrick looked over his shoulder toward the L'Amour home. "I would prefer she not go near Mr. Ironwood's place for a while. There's something she does not need to get wind of."

"So this is why you asked me to go for a walk with you. Something big over the horizon?"

"That's nothing that should be talked about," Patrick said. "Nothing is set in stone anyway. Some may not have the stomach for it, so it's fluid at present. But I would like her kept somewhere safe until it's over."

"She's going to be madder than ever if she finds out you and I connived to prevent her from doing her part. She loved her brother and feels it's her duty to use John's rifle to carry on the fight. Personally of course, I want her safe and healthy right here at home."

"As far as I'm concerned," Patrick said, "she does her part everyday just by being herself."

Mr. L'Amour smiled. "Yes, well, you and I both know she may not agree with that."

"Right now she is the only thing keeping me sane and connected to the human race. Even if I never saw her again, the idea of her being alive and well is enough for me to go on. But there will be no going on if anything happens to her. Even if she hates me for it, I can't risk her life."

"Is it that you love her that much? You see, I'm her father. I know how special she is. And I know how a boy your age can become infatuated with a girl like her."

"I'm not going to stand here and try to convince you what I feel for her is more than infatuation, or lust for that matter. Only time will change your mind."

Mr. L'Amour turned, faced him squarely and looked him in the eyes. "You misunderstood me. I believe your feelings for Sharon are as deep and mature as you are. You have kept your promise, haven't you?"

"There was more than one. I've kept them all."

"I thought so. In fact, I know so, because I know you."

"You probably don't know me as well as you think. She deserves a lot better. I still don't know what she sees in me."

"That's exactly what I thought you were feeling. It is the way I felt about Mrs. L'Amour and still do." Mr. L'Amour's eyes lazily swept across his freshly planted fall crop. "I'm not very good at lying to her, but I will try."

Sharon walked up, stopped ten feet from them, and put her hands on her hips. "Okay, what is up with you two, sneaking off like that?"

"Why, my lovely daughter, we're just out for a walk and a talk. Sometimes the two go together in sunny weather."

"Well, how about that Dad, you made a rhyme." She smiled that half-smile, half-smirk that could be a sign of trouble, but mostly it meant she was thinking private thoughts too warm and human for words. The look was always endearing anyway, as were most of her mannerisms. "It's no wonder your heart is aflutter when you begin to stutter and put truth asunder."

Her father laughed. "See what I mean?" He walked to her and hugged her. "You have been one of the brightest lights of my life. You and your brother and mother. Just remember, even when you are eighty, I will still be watching over you from above and will know if you are not behaving yourself."

"When I am eighty, I will be a grandmother and most likely a great-grandmother."

"Is that right?" Mr. L'Amour asked.

"Yes, I am certain." She looked at Patrick, the smirk gone. However, her eyes were brighter than even the sunlight, and Patrick knew she was doing it again: seeing right through to his soul.

*   *   *

Patrick saw many armed men around the shack as he approached. He did not make it to the porch before Mr. Ironwood came out to meet him.

The old man was excited. "It's on, Patrick. The whole plan, it's on!"

Catching his breath first, Patrick stepped up on the porch.

"Come on in," Mr. Ironwood said. "There are some people here I want you to meet."

When Patrick entered the shack, he found it overflowing with men of various ages, mostly between forty and fifty-five, a few ten years younger and more ten years older. He counted two of Mr. Ironwood's age.

Mr. Ironwood spoke with a certain pride in his voice. "This is the boy who declared war on the government and then fought Dissident Control on his own with no help for four weeks."

There were gathering volumes of applause and cheers, fading away in a moment to a clatter of encouragements, many profane slogans insulting the government, and cries for revenge, all partially drowned out by still others.

"When?" Patrick's voice was nearly drowned out by the noise.

The clattering clamor continued for a few seconds more.

"I want to know when."

"What did you say boy?" a man in his forties asked. The clatterers' noise faded into the nothingness it had always been.

"Mr. Ironwood says you have agreed on a simultaneous attack all over the continent, at least that's what I discussed with him. The question is how soon? A matter of days I hope."

A short middle-aged man complete in camouflage pants and jacket, abounding with fake military insignia and medals, including the eagle of a full colonel above his left breast pocket and the stars of a general on his shoulders, stood next to a man similarly dressed. His friend had a revolver that seemed three times too large for him strapped loosely around his waist. The "general" chafed his knuckles over three day old gray and black stubble and spoke with incredulity. "Come on boy, get real. That's not possible. It'll be spring at the earliest."

Patrick's voice sounded much older than his years. "Then you might as well go back to doing whatever it was you were doing when Mr. Ironwood asked you here. It should be done within the week at the latest, before the enemy has time to react to our action, before we even start the action you are so happy to postpone until it becomes inaction."

One of the youngest in the crowd wore an angry face. "You haven't been here five minutes and you're already pissing me off boy. Where do you get the idea—?"

"What is wrong with ending this as soon as possible? Not ten or fifty years from now, but as soon as possible. Look back in history. We are a guerrilla army fighting a civil war. Guerrilla armies and civil wars throughout history have made conventional armies and nation-state wars look like a little girl's birthday party. Hell on earth is an entirely inadequate description."

"It's going to take many years whether you like it or not boy." The camouflaged man sneered at Patrick. "We've been at this longer than you."

"Yes, you have." Patrick stared the man down. "We can either use the violence and velocity of our action as a force multiplier, or we can piss around and watch millions of our people suffer and die from starvation, disease, and bombs."

Patrick looked around the room. He did not try to hide his disappointment. "You men have taken on the responsibilities of leadership. Now is the time to lead."

"Why you little punk!" Mr. Camouflage rushed at Patrick.

Several of the men threatened to "stomp" him or throw him through Mr. Ironwood's front window.

Mr. Ironwood's eyes shot darts at Patrick. "All right! That's enough!" He raised his arms as if holding back their rage. "Everyone settle down. Patrick has a straightforward way of speaking, but he doesn't mean anything by it. Settle down now."

The clatter gradually lowered in volume down to a murmur.

Patrick stood closer to his elderly friend. "I apologize for not keeping my promise to stay quiet Mr. Ironwood, but we only have one chance to get this right. What we do now will dictate the character of the entire war. And the window of time is closing fast."

"What do you mean?" a man about Mr. Ironwood's age asked.

"At the moment we have them backpedaling, but that won't last long. We have never fought back in such numbers before. They are momentarily stunned. This moment is the best and only chance we will ever have to end their raids on our people. W.G. will be here with soldiers soon, and we must have Dissident Control wiped out before that day comes. When those soldiers arrive death comes with them."

"And while we're at it, why don't we cure cancer," the short man with the large pistol snickered. Half the room joined him with a glee club of snickering laughs.

Suddenly someone spoke up from behind Patrick. It was Bart. "You know, the walls of this place are thin, and there are nearly a hundred of my friends outside listening. We're thinking Patrick should come outside and join us, so that we can have our own meeting and make our own decisions on how to fight for our freedom. You older men have been pretending to fight the government for twenty years, yet in eight months this teenager has not only killed more government goons than any one of you, he has killed more than half of you put together. We want to hear what he has to say."

One of the "generals" sneered. "Yeah, I hear he's the descendant of some great war chief Indian like Osceola or something. Give us a speech boy. We'll build a bonfire outside and we can all dance around it."

Mr. Ironwood's voice cracked in the room. "Get out! I won't have it. First it's Jews and now it's Indians. You and your two friends get out now!"

"It's okay Mr. Ironwood," Patrick said. "Whatever Indian blood there is in me is of a plebeian strain. There are no great orators or war chiefs in my ancestry. Does it matter? Wherever the seed of our genes first sprouted, whether this continent or another, we are all human beings and endowed with immutable rights. I don't know about the rest of you, but that is what I fight for."

The short man with the large pistol glanced at two men to his right. One of them was the colonel/four-star general. "Hector, Earl, let's go. They don't need us. The oracle prodigy punk has all the answers."

Earl stood in front of Patrick, sneering. The others moved to the door. "My name is Earl, Patty boy. If you ever want to show me just how ferocious a killer you are, let me know."

Bart started to stand between him and Patrick, but Patrick put his arm out and stopped him. "Stay back Bart, I'm curious to know what Earl has in mind."

Earl stammered. "Well, just what I said."

"Are you challenging me to some kind of duel? Because if you are it's customary for the challenged to choose the weapons and location of the fight."

The man in his late thirties sneered and snickered. "You got to be kidding. Customary my ass." He glanced nervously at Bart. "I wasn't talking about no duel anyway."

Patrick continued. "I choose rifles and that swamp on the other side of the bayou. I will give you a fifteen-minute head start. Then I will hunt you down."

Earl's face began to drip sweat. "I heard about you. You're crazy, but I don't believe half of what they say. That bullshit about what you supposedly did at the river is a lie."

Patrick looked the man in the eye. "I never told anyone about what happened at the river or any place else."

"Why don't you tell us what did happen?" Mr. Ironwood broke in. "Earl seems to be concerned about it."

"There was some killing," Patrick said.

Bart blew out a lung full of air and laughed under his breath. "And then some."

Patrick gave Earl a cold stare. "It was your idea. Personally, I would rather use the time and energy killing the enemy, but since we're friends, I will make time for you if you insist. Unless of course you have changed your mind."

The man's heaving chest betrayed his fear, though his face displayed incredulous contempt. "Forget it. I don't have time for punks like you anyway."

Earl tried to get by Bart and to the door, but he found Bart unwilling to move out of the way.

"Earl," Bart said. "You were wise not to take Patrick up on his proposition. Someone would have had to bury you by morning. And you would be wise to never threaten him again. You understand?"

Earl nodded nearly imperceptibly and swallowed hard, then stepped around Bart and through the door.

Mr. Ironwood said, "I don't want any more of that crap. Patrick is my friend, and he makes sense. We should at least listen to what he has to say."

"I'm almost done," Patrick said. Everyone settled down to listen. "A few more minutes, and then I will walk out of here and let you decide on your own what you want to do."

Patrick thought for a moment. "W.G. allows the North American Union only a token military. That is in our favor. The fact we have military bases within striking distance is also to our advantage. They are a good source for heavy weapons. But it will take more than a few triads to attack a military base. That does not mean we go conventional. It just means there are targets that require the massing of a larger force at times."

Expecting to be thrown out before he got halfway through the next sentence, Patrick continued. "In the next ten days, we should attack every military base in Southeast Province, better yet, every base in all six provinces and Alaska. All armories and depots and as many Dissident Control stations as possible should be attacked and raided at the same time. As much as possible, we must destroy their aircraft on the ground."

No one said anything, but a few rolled their eyes or shook their heads. "There are thirty-five million of us Wild People. We have the manpower. We just need the leadership and organization. We must do this before they realize we are finally fighting back wholeheartedly, instead of just half-assed the way we have in the past. Because once they know what is happening they will harden every valuable target, and that will cost us in blood.

"By the time this action is completed, we should actually have more heavy weapons in our hands, artillery, anti-armor and antiaircraft missiles, than they do. We will need them for W.G. troops when they arrive."

Patrick could see fear on many of the men's faces. The idea alone was panicking them. He knew now the doing of it was out of the question. They did not have what it took. He suspected it, but until this moment, he held on to hope. "We have a short window in time to pull their teeth and claws and take what we can for ourselves. Then and only then will we have a chance against W.G." His words were useless. He knew it. Dread pressed on his chest. "I realize I'm thinking big, but this is the time to think big. Later will be too late."

With no further words, Patrick nodded to Mr. Ironwood and walked out the door. He sat on the edge of the porch, his legs hanging, feet just touching the ground. Bart followed him out and walked over to Tel, Linda, and Mathew, where he began to converse with them quietly.

After a few minutes, Bart walked over to Patrick. "Will you come with me? We have something to talk about."

Silently, Patrick got up and followed him to where the others stood by a gnarled old oak tree.

"What's up?"

"You know they're not going to follow your suggestions," Bart answered.

"Yes I do." Patrick spoke in a matter of fact tone with no emotion.

The four looked at him astonished. "Then why did you go through that whole spiel with them?" Bart asked.

Patrick sighed and looked up at the darkening early evening sky. "I could not live with myself if I didn't at least try." Eyes filled with resignation, he said, "It's going to be a long, bloody slog. A slugfest. It could have been avoided, but that is the way it's going to be. I thought if I asked for the whole pie maybe then I would get a slightly larger slice."

Tel leaned closer, looking toward the shack furtively. "We need new leadership. We need you." He looked at the others. "We can have a hundred more fighters here by morning."

"I appreciate that Tel, but what we need to do will require millions. The fact is we are screwed guys. I'm too young and new to this militia stuff. You guys are nearly old enough, except Mathew, but you have not pushed for leadership positions in the local organizations." He shook his head and sighed wearily. "Of course I'm using that word loosely. Organized ain't the word. Anyway, we're forced to play the cards we're dealt. It's a big, bloody pile of crap, but there is no other way."

Linda's eyes filled. "People are going to die needlessly."

Patrick nodded. "Yes. I'm sorry guys, but the militia as it has existed has never been much of a threat to the government. Mr. Ironwood has been trying to change that for years. He told me how most of the men in that shack right now are useless. I've known it for months. Most of them just like playing militia. They have no hope of actually defeating the enemy."

Bart pulled a piece of paper from his shirt pocket and began to read.

> "…But if this catastrophe can be used to further the public welfare, it will be only by virtue of the fact that we are cleansed by suffering; that we yearn for the light in the midst of deepest night, summon our strength, and finally help in shaking off the yoke which weighs on our world."

"The White Rose," Patrick spoke wistfully, softly, as if he lacked the breath to speak it.

Bart was surprised. "You know about the anti-Nazi group called the White Rose?"

"Read about it. Evidently so did you. We will fare better. But it's going to cost us dearly."

Mathew lobbed a question among them like a grenade. "Do we have a chance? I mean in the end, are we going to win?"

Patrick found all eyes on him, pleading for the one answer they desperately wanted to hear. "If a wave of revolt rolled across the country, Dissident Control would be history in weeks. We have the manpower. The question is do we have the men.*" He smiled at Linda. "And women.

"Look guys, if we had enough like you and the rest who were with us on that ambush our victory would be a certainty. I've seen what you are made of, and I could not be more proud to call you friends. Count the number of real men and women among our people and give me a number, then I can answer Mathew. Until then, I can only say that we have no choice but to fight. They are going to kill us all anyway."

"Pleasant thought." Linda sighed sardonically.

"Yes, isn't it?" Tel smiled and winked at her.

Joining in, Bart shook his head in mock despair. "Guys, it looks like we're fucked."

Everyone exploded in laughter, including Mathew who smiled sheepishly.

*   *   *

Patrick walked out of the shack, stepped onto to grass wet with morning dew, and joined his friends. "Mr. Ironwood is sick, but there's nothing he could do."

Linda glared at one of the militia leaders as he walked into the woods, heading home. "Son of a bitch!"

"Well, I have ten triads, thirty fighters, to bring to bear against the enemy," Patrick said. "Last night, the militia leaders agreed to a tiny fraction of what I asked."

"Gutless bastards won't give you a chance. It's not just that you're so young; they don't want to do anything. Anything at all. If they have their way, there won't be enough of us left to fight before the war even gets going," Bart said.

"Yeah," Patrick said, "I tried to tell them last night. We're in a situation where a man sits as many risks as he runs. Doing nothing is at least as deadly to our people as fighting."

"How much of your plan did you get?" Tel asked.

"Across the Southeast, a half dozen Dissident Control stations and four military bases will be raided. I got my raid on the two depots, which was my first objective anyway. Our group will go after the M14s and ammunition. A second, larger force will attack the other depot. The fact they agreed to that much was a testimony to the respect Mr. Ironwood commands among many of the older leaders. All in all, it was more than I expected."

"Damn. We could use those missiles and HE," Bart said.

"How much you want to bet we never see any of them?" Tel asked. "Just like the missiles and HE we traded off that turned Dissident Control lieutenant."

"Well, we're all in this together, whether some of the leaders know it or not," Patrick said. "You guys gather up the most trusted fighters you know. Cheat a little. Pretend you can't count. And stretch those ten triads to eleven or twelve. Most of our fearless leaders went home last night anyway."

"They won't bother counting. That would be too much work," Bart said.

"If they do notice, they better not say a word," Tel added. "I've had enough of them."

*   *   *

Standing before his volunteers, Patrick waited until everyone was seated on the ground. "We're going to spend the day going over the task each of you will be assigned. Questions are welcome. Everyone must understand the overall mosaic, not just the part of the plan pertaining to your particular task. Otherwise, if something goes wrong the whole plan will fall apart. Your triad leader may be killed, so you all must be able to take the initiative on your own." He nodded to Bart, signaling for him to take over.

Bart stood by a map tacked to a tree. "Every triad leader has a topographic chart showing the departure point, objective rally points, emergency rally point, and the retreat route. However, they were not marked in such a way the enemy could glean intelligence from them if the maps fall into their hands. That's why you're going to memorize them. Everyone, especially triad leaders, take a long look at this map. This is the last time you will see it, so learn the location of the RPs and retreat route as they are marked. Here, here and here." He used a stick to point. Everyone leaned forward to get a better look.

Late in the afternoon, Patrick told the triad leaders to prepare to travel in five minutes. Just as they assembled fifty yards from the shack, and were about to start out, Patrick saw a flash of movement in the woods. He froze and cringed as if expecting a fatal blow. Emerging from the woods and standing in front of him panting from a long run, stood Sharon with her now familiar smirk/smile. In all outward appearances, she was fully equipped and ready for combat.

Naked fear showed in Patrick's eyes. "No! Go home! It's the best you can do for me. Just go home."

The smile on her face washed away, a slight tremble of her lips as it did. It was replaced by shock. She staggered back as if he had physically struck her across the face. Confusion, hurt, then anger, manifested on her face with deep wrinkles and creases grossly out of place on such a young feminine face.

She does not understand.

Patrick handed his rifle to Tel. "Go on, I will catch up."

Tel took the rifle. "You know, she has a right to—"

The look in Patrick's eyes told him it was time to shut up and start walking.

When Patrick walked toward Sharon she backed away. He held his arms out and started for her again.

"Stay away! Don't touch me!" She backed against a pine tree.

"You don't understand. I can't let them hurt you. I can take anything they do to me, anything but that."

"It's my right." Her chest was heaving. "I'm a good shot now. And I don't make any more noise than the rest when I walk through the woods. I'm not like you, but I'm as good as the rest. I have worked hard to live up to your standards. Why do you think so little of me?"

"You of all people must know…it's not that. Just thinking about what might happen to you drains all my strength and leaves me nothing to fight with."

He had hurt her, in his mind the most evil sin he could commit. "I'm not strong enough. I can't do it. I'm just too weak."

He rushed to her. She tried to dodge him, but he held her against the tree. She struggled to free herself from his arms.

"Get away," she said. "Let me go. I hate you! I'm going to fight for my brother. They murdered him." She did not look at Patrick. Her eyes were moving in her head with a frantic fear. He was in love with her and she did not look. She would not look at his eyes. Not now. "I never asked you to love me. You think I did it on purpose. But it was some kind of an accident, a force of nature." She continued to struggle. "I'm not ready for you. I have to fight first. For John. If I don't, I'll be spitting on his memory."

He touched his forehead to hers. "You're going to kill me." His mind was racing. "No! I can't take the chance."

She continued to struggle but was growing tired. "If you don't let me fight for John it's over. You hear me? No man is going to boss me and neither are you."

"That would hurt me, but as long as you are alive and well, I will go on. But don't ask me to let them hurt you."

"Why do I even have to ask? You never asked me if *you* could fight. Why doesn't it work both ways?"

Patrick held her.

"Well?"

"I can't."

"Because I'm a girl, that's the only difference. What do you think it will do to me if they kill you? You think I don't care?"

"The difference is I'm weak. I know that now."

Her face washed over with a coldness he had never seen in her, and it chilled him.

Velvet-covered iron.

"Well then, I can be weak too. You stay with me tonight and promise me you will never fight again, and I will hold you to it."

For the first time, she looked into his eyes and saw it. She allowed him to hold her face in his hands and did not move. No longer was she trying to escape his embrace.

"Do you understand what I'm saying?" Sharon asked. "If you stay with me tonight and promise to never fight again you can love me with your heart and your body. You will have me completely, and I will marry you whether Dad and Mom likes it or not. I'm eighteen now, and you have no parents. Either that or you let me go with you and fight. It's your choice."

He began to kiss her, holding her face in his hands.

Her eyes were sad, disappointed.

By the time their lips parted, she was holding back more tears.

Then he kissed her on her forehead. "I may be inexperienced, but I can tell when a girl is not kissing back. Your lips are lifeless. Don't play games girl. I know what you're doing."

She turned her eyes away when he looked at her. Her eyes flashed back to him only for a second, then suddenly to the side again. "I should have learned by now not to be surprised by you. Your instinct is to do what's right no matter the price." In a surge of courage, she grabbed his neck and pulled him to her, this time showing him that she meant it.

"Sharon," he said through smiling lips. "You're going to kill me. You know I can't. I have responsibilities. You don't just call off a war. What would I tell those people who just left? But then you knew that, didn't you?"

He took out a handkerchief. "This is clean," he said and began to wipe her wet face. "Okay, you win. You always do. I don't know what you're going to do, as you have not even been a part of the planning or briefing. Maybe I can find a place so you can over watch from long distance."

She gave him a disapproving look.

"Well, you are a sniper. We have to put your skills to best use."

She smiled her broadest, warmest smile and kissed him briefly. "On our wedding night I'm going to put your young heart through nothing like it has ever experienced, so make sure you eat right and don't clog your arteries."

"Wedding?"

"That's what we feel for each other is leading to. Isn't it?"

"I—"

"You don't want me?"

"I didn't say that."

Sharon laughed. "You're not saying much of anything."

"About that heart attack. You promise?"

She nodded. "Cross my heart—"

Patrick put his hand over her mouth. "And hope to live to be a hundred." He pulled her away from the tree. "I need one last hug before we go."

They held each other and heard the woods listening to them.

"Listen," Patrick said. "Can you hear it? Even God knows I love you. And God knows I will do my best."

"Do your best?"

He released her and stepped back. While reaching with his open hand and lightly touching her face, as was his habit for some time now. He said, "On our wedding night, when our flesh is talking to flesh, I hope to teach you it's not a one-way conversation."

Chapter 20

The sky was as clear as Patrick had ever seen it, an October sky, showing blue and bright as if God had moved his soothing hand over everything, calming the airs above it all. Down on earth where people live, hearts were not so calm.

Riding in the back of a pilfered green and black pickup, "Dissident Control" proudly proclaimed on each side in big bold black letters, Sharon's hair flowed in the invisible slipstream, her wheat-colored strands rippling waves on a sun-bronzed sea. The cool air collided against her cheeks, distorting them into ripples and then glided over her rosy skin. She pulled her head down and put her left hand over her face to warm and protect it from the windchill. Those behind the cab were protected to some degree from the biting wind, those near the tailgate where she was were not so fortunate. Following them were three more bullet-riddled, bloodstained pickups, also overloaded with freedom fighters.

Her eyes had caught Patrick's looking at her several times. Linda and Tel sat beside her. They had coupled and become an "item" months ago. Tel had his arm over Linda's shoulders and both were looking with desperate intensity at the fading sunset.

Sharon slid over to Patrick's side and hugged his neck, resting her forehead on his right cheek. She cradled the scope sight of her brother's rifle in her right arm, protecting it so it would not be jarred out of alignment or damaged. The barrel leaned against her right shoulder, the butt of the rifle resting on her right thigh to protect the scope from vibration. It must shoot to point of aim, or it would be useless and so would she.

He cradled her face in his left hand and kissed her forehead. Moving his lips closer to her ear, he whispered something and she blinked and pulled him closer. Together, they watched the landscape race by as the bright colors of the day gave way to slowly darkening gray.

Clouds would later settle in on the warm waters of the bayous and sink into the low places to lie in wait for the warming dawn. Surely tomorrow would come, for the fog and the now gray woods, but would it come for those who braved the night?

Patrick suddenly tensed and held her tighter. The trucks stopped to allow them to jump out as one mass of motion. He held her tighter still, two, then three seconds longer, his reluctance felt fully by her.

Not a word was spoken and barely a sound was made, only some scuffing of boots when they hit the asphalt. They each waited their turn as they formed into their triads, ten yards behind the one in front, each man or woman in the triad separated by five yards. They must be close enough to see the person in front, despite the darkening woods. In sixty seconds, the gray woods that seemed to open a passage to allow their serpentine progress and then immediately close in behind, swallowed them. Only yards away, no evidence of their presence could be discerned.

After walking six hundred yards, Patrick raised his left fist and then dropped it by his side: the signal to stop. It was just barely visible to the one behind in the quickening dark of night and black shade of trees. One-by-one, the signal was relayed down the line by raised fists. When he strapped on his night vision monocular, the one behind him did the same, the act repeated as it worked its way down the long line.

Turning on the night vision devices allowed them to see nearly as well as in daylight and caused the one half inch by one inch reflective tape each had placed on the back of their packs to glow brightly: a low-tech identify friend or foe method to help prevent fratricide.

The woods became colder and darker as they walked, but the heat of their bodies accumulated and increased, by both their physical exertions and the tightening of their nerves. With each step, they voluntarily walked closer to death. With each step the weight of anxiety, that leaden burden, parasite of strength and confidence, the dirge of them all, grew heavier. So pervasive, it is an intimately known monster born anew for each to face, to coldly stare down and come to terms with. Only the insane ignore it.

Into the night, the line continued to slither serpentine and silent down the immemorial path of warriors, each one respecting the others more deeply as they grew ever nearer to death. And that respect became love of brother and sister, in many ways as deep as that of lovers. Into each other's hands, they were entrusting their lives. They may live. They may die. It will not be alone.

Patrick raised his left fist. The line stopped. He took his pack off and pulled a poncho out. With a miniature flashlight, he checked a topographic chart while under his poncho to shield the light from enemy eyes. After he was sure of the location, he tied a reflective tape to a nearby tree. The others knew he was marking an after-action rally point. After the fight, they would all return there to gather for the retreat.

When they got near the target, Patrick stopped the triads. He turned to Bart and said, "Put Mathew in charge. Have them form a defense perimeter and stay behind while you, Tel, and Linda, come with me to look over the installation."

Using Bart's seven-power binocular/night vision device, Patrick examined every inch of the area outside the fence line. The others squatted by him in thick brush.

By the guardhouse just outside the front gate, two soldiers gestured while talking, their voices spent by distance. He could not hear, but he knew one had told a joke when he read laughter on both faces.

There were two more soldiers casually strolling along just inside the fence, talking, neither had night vision devices on. They relied on dim illumination from generator-powered lampposts. He searched between the buildings and found three more soldiers. They appeared to be as unconcerned as the others were. Some of the soldiers inside the ten feet high chain-link fence, topped with three rows of concertina wire, had only pistols, others kept their carbines hung comfortably across their back. Only the two guards in front of the gate had their carbines slung across their chest for ready use.

"I don't see any sign of Claymores yet," Patrick said, "but of course I wouldn't at this distance. The fence is electrified as we expected. They could have land mines planted outside the fence, but Raebyrne says no."

Patrick trained his eyes on the installation itself for a few minutes. "Can't see anything unusual. Only a small contingent of guards armed with M4s and pistols. They're not very alert. Just another boring night for them."

He handed the night binoculars to Bart and pulled his monocular down to his left eye. "Okay guys, take turns looking things over. And remember to remind them about the Claymores and motion detection devices and cameras just inside the woods line. Don't let any of them jump the gun and head for the buildings until that APC gives us a clear path through those Claymores."

They all nodded in the dark as he watched them with his night vision monocular.

An hour later, Patrick stood by Bart again. He had just placed the fighters of seven triads where he thought they would have the best advantage, while Bart stayed with his own triad.

"How are they holding up to the stress?" Patrick asked.

Bart looked through his night vision binoculars, watching the changing of the guards at the fence line. "Near as I can tell they're acting normally. In other words they're scared shitless but more afraid of letting one another down than dying."

"Yeah. If it wasn't for that dread of letting your friends down, it might just be impossible for a free society to wage war."

Bart lowered the binoculars and raised his eyebrows. "This is no time for philosophizing."

Patrick smiled in the dark. "You're getting to be as smart-assed as Tel."

Bart snickered. "They'll be okay."

"Yeah. The government has unknowingly hardened our people and created a perfect guerrilla warrior society."

Patrick checked the eastern sky for the earliest signs of the coming dawn. "It took a little longer than I expected to place everyone where I wanted. In many places the brush was too thick to find firing lanes to shoot through, so I had to search for a while for suitable positions. Anyway it's done, and I still have time to stand here and complain."

"Got about two hours before the others initiate the attack at the gate," Bart said. "Don't worry; the guy leading them is reliable. They removed the GPS transponder from the captured APC of course." He swatted a mosquito. "The party starts when they drive right up to the gate with it. Everyone has christened it the Trojan Horse."

Patrick looked over at Sharon who was sitting quietly on a log. "Well, I've got to find a place for our sniper. See you when the party starts."

Twenty-five feet up in a pine tree, Patrick and Sharon were busily tying a camouflage net across two strong limbs. He had managed to find a hill on the topographic map and then in turn this tall tree on top of the hill. It was five hundred yards from the near side of the warehouse, but she could see over the surrounding trees to future targets. At his insistence, she wore a harness that was attached to a rope. During her training, he had taught her how to lower herself quickly and detach the rope so she could depart the sniper hide fast.

"Tell me again, what's the heading for rally point A from here?"

"One five zero magnetic," she sang out.

"Good. What about the emergency RP?"

"Two three niner mag."

"Great. How long should it take you to get to RP A from here if you jog?"

"About ten minutes."

"How about the emergency RP?"

"Twenty minutes."

"What did I tell you about not firing more than one round every thirty seconds?"

"If I fire too often they will find my muzzle flash."

"And?"

"I'm a sitting duck up here in this tree."

"If the shooting starts after sunrise, they won't see your muzzle flash. But I want you to keep this camouflage netting draped over you until you get down. Do not, and I mean do not, bother taking anything with you but your rifle and pack. Leave the rest of this stuff up here. Do you understand?"

"Yes Papa."

"This is serious now kiddo." Patrick checked her safety line again. "It's a good thing I taught you how to shoot off your pack. It's impossible to shoot from the normal prone position while lying on this net. Remember, your job as sniper is to shoot only the most important targets at the most important time."

"Yes Papa."

"Well, I have to go. Just remember they're going to be shooting real bullets." He held her chin in his hand and turned her head to face him. "The first sign they have found you, get your ass down out of this tree, and get to the rally point. Promise me."

"That's okay for my ass, but what about the rest of me?"

"Come on, if you take a bullet you will not think it's funny."

"Okay, I get it. I promise. I'm just relieving the tension."

He put on a pair of leather gloves and slid down the rope, then made his way to a position where he could see most of the action between the gate and the building. As he waited for civilian sunrise and the arrival of the personnel carrier, he thought through many scenarios and what his correct response would be, dreaming up as many problems and their solutions as he could come up with.

There was a drainage ditch just outside the fence, and the gathering light of day illuminated misting vapors as gray fog awoke with the warming sun. It would be late in the morning before the fog blanketing the woods lifted completely, and the warm ditch water would continue to mist longer still.

Patrick's pant legs were soaked from walking in the dew-wet brush. Now they misted too, and he shivered in the cold. The air was crisp and clean. But there was an aftertaste in his lungs. He had learned to smell blood before it was spilled.

Whining and drumming of deep-tread tires on the two-lane country road warned them all the real war was about to begin.

This will not be an act of defense, but an act of deliberate war. The drumming grew louder for some time and then changed in pitch and subsided quickly. A personnel carrier slowed and turned into the driveway, coming to a smooth stop at the closed gate. Two guards walked out of the guardhouse and approached casually. Both left their M4s hanging untouched across their chest from combat slings. A man popped up from behind the machinegun on top with an M14. He threw down on them and fired twice. Almost simultaneously, their heads jerked back violently and the back of their helmets erupted in a crimson flood. The guards collapsed where they stood without a quiver.

A puff of dark smoke from the armored personnel carrier's exhaust foretold watching eyes. Even before the roar of the diesel reached their ears, they knew it was time to pick their targets. Seventy-two hands tightened on thirty-six rifles, waiting for Patrick to fire the first shot.

The gate gave way with a clanking crash and the armored vehicle went through unhindered.

A dozen men poured out of what must have been a barracks of sorts. The first two died in their tracks when Patrick's Garand spoke. Instantly, a barrage of semiautomatic rifle fire roared from out of the woods, every shot connecting with flesh. In less than six seconds, twelve bodies were piled in front of the barracks door. Nine more died just inside the fence on the far side of the compound. Patrick's warriors had run out of targets.

The personnel carrier continued to gather speed, running over many of the fallen. An opening was punched into the front of the warehouse. The personnel carrier skidded to a stop and withdrew from the building in reverse. Then the driver circled the warehouse. Someone fired several times from a gun port on the side of the vehicle when a target presented itself.

Coming back around to the barracks, the driver rammed the back end and went all the way through. There was firing inside. The vehicle came out the front, running over more of the bodies piled by the door.

The driver turned the vehicle toward the front corner of the fence closest to the fighters in the woods and smashed it flat. The back ramp came down and men poured out, running into the nearest building. Firing erupted inside. The ramp was raised and the personnel carrier came around the end of the ditch and looped back toward the woods, clearing a path, setting off three Claymores in the process.

Ten of Patrick's warriors scrambled into the open personnel carrier and caught a ride to the front of the warehouse. Patrick ran behind the vehicle until he got past any danger of Claymores and then veered off to jump across the ditch. Landing on the other side, he slid on wet grass, winding up on his side. While still pushing up from the ground, a distant rifle shot rang out from deep in the woods and bounced off the side of the large buildings. He looked up to see a man fall from the roof of a warehouse. Two more men were aiming carbines at him from the same roof. He lay on his stomach and brought the Garand to his shoulder in controlled haste, trying not to panic.

Another shot rang out. The man Patrick was just starting to put his front sight on jerked with the punch of a thirty-caliber rifle bullet. He swung on the other man, who was already firing at him on full automatic. Dirt flew in Patrick's face, but he concentrated on aiming and squeezing the trigger. A rising roar of rifle fire came from the woods, drowning out both the bark of his Garand and the third shot from six hundred yards away in a tall tree in the woods.

Patrick had felt the bullet punch his pack but he did not think he had been hit. Now the searing pain in the back of his right shoulder told him he was mistaken. He used his rifle for support as he got up from the ground. The pain caused a slight, involuntary pulling back of his shoulders and head when he took his first step. After that, no one could know anything was wrong.

Four soldiers lay under a five-ton truck and made a gallant effort that did not last two minutes. Picked off one at a time before they could manage to hit anyone, they were the last to die. After a thorough sweep of the installation, some men removed debris from the hole in the warehouse wall to allow for loading the crates onto trucks.

Bart ran into the building where Patrick was carrying one end of a crate of rifles and pronounced the other buildings clear. "No injuries to report," he said.

"Good. That's the result of accurate shooting. Dead men don't shoot back. Get the trucks in here."

Mathew heard. He was standing just outside. He spoke into a low-powered radio. "Send them in."

Two and a half ton military trucks came in at high speed from where they had been hidden down dirt roads. Two backed up to the opening torn by the personnel carrier, juxtaposed so they could be loaded at the same time.

There were four men in each truck, they rushed out and helped load. Everyone, including Patrick, loaded as fast as they could while those in the woods kept watch. There were also observation posts down the road in both directions to give warning by radio if Dissident Control agents or soldiers arrived. Mathew kept a handheld radio near his ear, ready to yell a warning.

They loaded crate after crate, working feverously. The sooner they were out of the area, the safer they would be. However, they knew it would take time to load ten thousand rifles and two million rounds of ammunition in trucks.

When the first two trucks were overloaded, the drivers took off and two more were backed in. They took everything, including a ton of high explosives. It totaled twenty-eight "deuce and a half" and nine five-ton trucks, all fully loaded, requiring nearly nine hours of hard labor. They also stripped the dead soldiers of their weapons.

The last truck was pulling out of the gate when Patrick yelled, "Time to go."

Everyone ran into the woods, following the path created by the personnel carrier to avoid Claymores. Patrick took the rear position, keeping an eye out for pursuit. After they were a hundred yards into the woods, he ran to get in front.

Sharon was waiting anxiously at rally point A. Her eyes were flaring when she ran to him and demanded he take his pack off and sit down.

She seemed to be angry with him and Patrick could not understand why. He said, "Sharon, fall in line with the others. All hell is going to come down on our heads at any moment. We have to get out of here."

She pulled at his pack. "Not until I see where you were shot."

Mathew yelled ahead at the others. "Hold up! He's been hit."

This was the last thing Patrick wanted. "Everyone keep walking. I'm fine."

He knew arguing with her would just waste more time, so he took his pack off, and then load-bearing harness, jacket and shirt.

She quickly searched over his chest, shoulders, and stomach, finding no sign of a wound. Not satisfied, she took two quick steps around him to look at his back.

Patrick had been careful not to let her see the bloody backside of his clothing when he removed them. He wanted everyone out of the area as soon as possible and that included her and him. There was no time for this. He knew the wound could not involve anything vital, or he would have been incapacitated within minutes, and dead hours ago.

Sharon saw his back painted in crimson and gasped. "Sit down!"

Tel, the last triad leader, walked by and saw his bloody back. He stopped, but walked on when Patrick said, "Keep going. We will catch up."

"Damn it! I said sit down," Sharon yelled.

Patrick dropped to his knees. "Don't panic, I'm okay." He pulled a canteen out of its carrier attached to his pack and drank from it. "I'm going to wash the blood off so you can see." He reached over his right shoulder and poured some water over his shoulder blade area. "Can you see it now?"

"You dumb ox. I can see the bone of your shoulder blade." She examined the wound more closely. "Let me have that."

She took his canteen and poured more water on his back while pulling the wound open, trying to ascertain if the bone was shattered.

"Well, we don't have all day girl."

"Just shut up," Sharon said. "You don't have any pity at all, do you? I've been waiting for hours, knowing you were hit. I should have climbed out of that tree and come down there, but I was supposed to stay and provide cover. I did what you told me. But now I feel like kicking your ass." She set the canteen down and pulled the wound open further. "Raise you right arm."

He raised both arms. "Do you want me to squawk like a chicken too?"

She stopped examining the wound and dug into her pack. "Well, you're right. You will live."

"It went through my pack; that slowed it some. It was mostly spent by the time it hit me."

She continued to dig in her pack. "It hit at a sharp angle and bounced off either your shoulder blade or your hard heart, probably the later."

"What are you talking about girl? It didn't go anywhere near my heart."

"Nothing."

The tone of her voice put the lie to the word. "Nothing" could be a pregnant word.

He fished around in his pack and pulled out a military surplus battle wound dressing his grandfather had given him. "Well, rip this open and put it on, will you? I have some duct tape to help hold it on if you can't make it secure with the ties that come with it."

Sharon took first aid items out of her own pack and ripped a plastic bag open with her teeth. Then she pulled a piece of gauze out of another package and dipped it into the orange colored liquid.

"What's that?" he asked.

"I should have washed my hands first, but this will clean the wound and the surrounding skin."

"Sharon, we have one minute, then we're leaving."

"I'm almost done. If you try to leave before I'm finished, I'll shoot you in the leg."

"Now that makes a lot of sense."

"I'm making more sense than you are. Remember what happened to your arm, because you didn't take care of it? You nearly died." She rubbed on the wound with the gauze as if she were cleaning a cooking pot. He flinched and pulled his shoulder away a fraction of an inch. "Hurts, don't it?" she said. "I hope so anyway."

"You're a mean little thing, aren't you girl?"

"Oh, shut up and hold that strip of cloth over your shoulder while I put this stupid contraption of yours on." After tying one strip of cloth across his chest and the other over his shoulder, she used some of his duct tape to secure the dressing to her liking. "Okay, Timucua, I'm done."

He put his shirt on and then his jacket, hesitating a little at the last because of the pain. "Whatever you did, it sure didn't make it feel any better."

She was violently stuffing items back in her pack. "If it hurts too much I can always put you out of your misery. What do I care? Timucua!"

While putting his load-bearing harness on, he said, "I thought you were not going to call me that."

"That was before."

He helped her with her backpack. "You just handed me a puzzle that will take way too long to solve, but I must ask. Before what?"

"Before you started acting like an ass."

As was his habit, Patrick tried to touch her face, but she slapped his hand away.

"I wasn't going to hurt you," Patrick said. He had not noticed before, but she had been crying the whole time she was with him.

"I know that. You wouldn't think of hurting me…physically anyway, would you?" She jogged away to catch up with the others.

Patrick was left standing there to ponder what had just happened. Shaking his head, he ran after her. "Girls," he said, "the great mystery of mankind."

Chapter 21

Patrick kept his freedom fighters walking all afternoon until the sun was below the tree line. They stopped to rest for ten minutes and went on, walked four more hours, then stopped and set up a night defense perimeter. "One third sleeps while the others pull security," Patrick said.

Bart and Tel started to carry out his orders.

When Bart walked by Patrick said, "Those who have to take first watch should be allowed to eat while others handle security for thirty minutes."

Bart nodded and made it happen.

Patrick searched for Sharon. She had been avoiding him all afternoon and evening. He found her sitting against a magnolia. "Sharon, you should stand watch for thirty minutes so the first watch can eat first."

She said nothing. Patrick started to help her up but she protested. "Stay back. You're the one who's wounded. I can stand on my own."

"Okay. Follow me while I show you where you need to stand watch." She could not leave her post and this would afford him a chance to talk to her.

He stood beside her, but she turned her face away, looking out into the woods. He spoke quietly so he would not disturb the others' rest or interfere with anyone's ears trying to listen for approaching enemy.

"Sharon, I never had the chance until now to thank you for saving my life. I know it scared you when I was shot. I guess you saw it, but it's not like I did it on purpose. This kind of thing is one reason why I didn't want you with us."

Without turning to face him, she said, "If I hadn't come with you, you would be dead."

"I can't deny that's a possibility. That first guy on the roof may have gotten me. I didn't notice them up there."

She turned so swiftly she became a blur for a second. "Oh, you can't deny that. Here, hold this rifle while I slap you!"

"Will you stop acting crazy? Has it taken until today for you to understand how dangerous war is?"

"No, but I learned something else."

"Let me guess, I'm an ass and a dumb ox."

"Oh no, I didn't learn that today. What I did learn, or it just came to me, is that all we have are our yesterdays and today, tomorrow may never come."

"That's certainly true, especially in time of war."

She slung her rifle on her shoulder. "You say we're not going home for three or four weeks."

"That's right. We'll pick up more supplies while on the march so to speak. We're just getting started."

To his surprise, she rushed to him, put her arms around his neck, and kissed him. She did not seem to want to let him go. Finally, she stopped and released him.

"Wow. It's about time you came up for air girl. What is it with you? You've been pissed all afternoon and now this."

Her eyes were somehow different from any look he had seen before. She pulled his head down so that she could speak in his ear, "It's time to get married."

"What!"

She held his face in her hands. "You heard me, so don't act like a dumb ox. I don't care how young you are or how young I am or what my parents think. I want to marry you while we're both still alive. The idea of you dying at sixteen and never…"

"Never what?" Patrick asked. "Oh, now that you mention it, we need to get right on that. It really should be the first thing we do when we get back. Normally, I'm not one to play on a girl's sympathy, but in this case…"

"Okay, now you *are* acting like an ass."

"Just kidding. You're being kind of…forward, and I'm a little surprised."

She looked exasperated. "You shouldn't be. You know I love you. What do I have to do? Hold up a sign?"

"I'm just a dumb ox, remember?" He shook his head. "I'm learning, though. When a girl threatens to shoot you in the leg it means she loves you."

"Oh shut up. You know I wasn't going to shoot you."

"You know your parents are going to raise hell. I hope they don't disown you or something. I wouldn't want to be the cause of that."

"They like you."

"Not enough to let me marry their little girl."

"If I'm a little girl, why do you look at me like you do?"

"I'm not the only one, and yes, you are still your father's little girl. If I was him, I would shoot me."

She laughed. "You know, at first I thought you were arrogant. Then you admitted you were afraid of me. Now, you're telling me you're afraid of my father. Maybe you are just looking for excuses not to commit to a relationship."

"I'm not afraid of your father. If he did shoot me, it would be worth it. But I am still afraid of those eyes."

The look in her eyes changed. She stood there looking at him, saying nothing.

"And without being too cold-hearted or practical about it, the fact is, I have no way to support you right now. There is a war to fight and I have nothing but my grandfather's land. And of course, the government would say that, not even that is mine. Your parents are right. I'm not good enough for you."

Sharon rolled her eyes, the spell broken. "That's not it. They just don't want to believe their little girl has grown up. They were only nineteen and twenty when they married. I think I can talk them into going along with it. In times like these, you have to live while you can."

"People should always live while they can, as long as they use their heads and don't cause unnecessary pain for others. The way I see it, the only way your father would agree to us marrying so soon, would be if he decides you're safer pregnant and home, than virginal and out here fighting."

She shoved him away with both hands. "Oh that is sooo romantic, Patrick!"

"I'm sorry. I guess I think too sensibly sometimes. At least you're calling me Patrick again, though."

"That was just out of habit—Timucua."

"Sharon, please don't let my awkwardness…Look, if I were as selfish as you seem to think, I would not be thinking about whether you marrying me is going to be a plus or a minus in your life. I would much prefer it be a plus."

"So it's all about arithmetic?"

"It is all about you being alive, healthy, and happy, in that order."

"So you might marry me, but it would just be out of kindness. Make an honest woman out of me or something."

Patrick was exasperated and thought about his grandfather telling him not to even try to understand women when they get like this. "How long has it been, Sharon?"

Her face flushed. "What? What are you talking about? I think I *am* going to slap you!"

"How long has it been since I told you I love you? Has it been so long that you've forgotten? Or did you not believe me, that time or the time before?"

Sharon quickly turned away, the way she often did when he said something that burned her. "A little advice Patrick: the next time a girl whispers in your ear she wants to marry you, give her less logic and more romance."

He put his arms around her waist from behind. "I'm always happy to take advice from a girl named L'Amour. But that advice will only be put to practice with you. I doubt any other girl is going to be whispering in my ear. Both of my ears are spoken for. I just got engaged."

She turned around and held him. "I guess maybe you're not a total ass. But you're still a dumb ox."

"A dumb ox that loves you."

The distant sound of a helicopter spurred him into action. Patrick clutched his rifle with one hand, and Sharon by her upper arm with the other, as he forcibly dragged her to the four foot wide trunk of an oak tree, her feet barely able to keep up.

"Keep this tree between you and the helicopter at all times," Patrick said. "Do you hear me?"

She nodded. "Yes."

The helicopter flew over them at a high rate of speed and it kept going.

Someone nearby yelled, "Do you think they saw us?"

Patrick yelled at the top of his voice. "Everyone find a large tree and keep it between you and the helicopter."

Someone spoke up in the dark. "They didn't turn around. I don't think they saw us."

"If they had their FLIR on, then they probably did see some of us," Bart said.

Patrick yelled, "Everyone put their night vision on."

Ears were straining to hear and eyes were looking skyward. Someone said, "They're coming back. I hear it. It's coming back."

"From what direction?" Tel asked.

A ripping sound, not unlike a giant sheet of canvas being torn apart by a powerful wind, raced toward them. Patrick jerked Sharon a little more to the left and pressed her against the rough bark of the oak. He put his left arm over her face and told her to close her eyes. He had never heard a mini gun fire before, but he knew what he was hearing.

Patrick looked around the tree and saw mini gun barrels spitting gouts of flame from each side of the aircraft. He strained to see through the branches of the treetops. The glow of the moon revealed the size and shape of the helicopter, and told him it was not an armored military aircraft, but a thin-skinned type.

As he tried to determine the helicopter's course so he could fire at it when it flew over, he saw thick pine trees cut in two, the projectiles destroying everything in their path. This put him in a near panic, afraid not even four feet of living oak wood could stop death from taking Sharon. He wanted to trade places with her to put his body between her and the hard rain of death. But it was too late. He had done all he could.

The terrifying sound quickly grew louder. Dirt flew up from the ground, tattooing two lines of craters in the forest floor in three-feet-high explosions, passing on each side of the tree and Sharon, whose arms he now had pinned behind her back to insure she did not accidentally expose them to danger. He prayed the pilot would fly straight. A few feet to either side and only the oak tree would stand between her and death.

With dust and chunks of wood still in the air, he released her, turned and shouldered his rifle. While his left eye looked through the night vision monocular, his right eye looked through the rifle sights. The light of the moon silhouetted the sights in the dark. His mind merged the two images, and he fired on the helicopter as it gained altitude, banking to the right. He hit it four times in the engine area and then held his fire until the craft had turned enough he could pump bullets into the cockpit. It was the pilot he wanted. When the angle was right, he fired until the empty clip ejected with a ping he did not hear.

Reloading, he heard the report of a rifle and then a bolt being rapidly worked back and forth. Just as he was aiming again, the rifle next to him fired, and he saw the helicopter suddenly turn on its side and dive into the treetops.

Over the explosion and roar of the fireball, someone exclaimed, "Damn! What a shot. Timucua blew the pilot's head off. I saw it."

Patrick yelled out into the dark woods. "All triad leaders check your people for wounds." He turned to Sharon who was reloading her rifle. "Are you okay?"

"Yes," she said, in a surprisingly calm voice.

He reached out to touch the right side of her face, but she jerked away. "What's wrong?"

"I…have a little bark rash."

"Oh. I'm sorry."

Bart ran up to them, panting. "We have three dead and two wounded."

Patrick put his hand on Bart's shoulder. "Where are the wounded?"

They followed the path of destruction left by the mini guns' projectiles until Bart stopped. A woman in her early twenties was lying on the ground bleeding. Patrick and Bart did not know her.

"Violet!" Sharon ripped off her pack and dropped to her knees. She looked around. "Where is Leo?"

"He's working on the one who's hit in the stomach," Bart said.

Violet was holding her right wrist as tightly as possible. "I could not find a big enough tree in time."

Patrick dropped to his knees beside her, putting his rifle down. Then he took hold of the woman's arm with both hands, squeezing her wrist, trying to stop the blood loss. Her hand was missing. "I got it Violet," he said calmly. She released her hold, turned away and moaned slightly, while covering her closed eyes with her bloody left hand. Her lips were drawn tight as she endured with no complaint.

Patrick looked up. "Bart, there might be more choppers coming. Get some stretchers made for the wounded. Strip the dead of equipment and try to give them a halfway decent burial. Mark their graves so we can come back and get the bodies later. But do it fast." Bart ran off without a word.

Sharon put a tourniquet on Violet's wrist just above Patrick's hands. "Grab the end and hold it." Patrick did as directed. She ripped a plastic bag open. Violet had been mostly silent until now, but she moaned loudly as Sharon poured the contents of the bag on the nerve endings.

"It won't hurt for long. This is coagulant. The bleeding will stop soon." Sharon stood on her knees and looked around. "Where is Leo?"

"Over here!" A man came running. "I'm afraid I've done all I can for the other one." He immediately started an IV. He asked Sharon, "How much blood do you think she lost?"

She shook her head. "I don't know. I've only been here five minutes, but she lost very little while I was here."

Violet moved her hand from her eyes and looked at Leo. "I'll be okay, give me something."

Leo hesitated. "Give the IV more time."

"I've been holding my wrist and then him. I didn't lose that much blood. Give me something."

Patrick looked at Violet and saw a girl in a lot of pain. He hated those in the helicopter. He hated war. He hated the fact that so much human misery is caused by other humans. He moved her black hair out of her eyes. "Violet, you wouldn't be lying to him, would you?"

"No. I want to live. I know you have morphine, Leo. You can stop this."

"Give it to her," Patrick said. "Now!"

Leo's eyes jumped from Violet to Patrick's. "All right. Without morphine, she may die of shock anyway. There is a risk with or without the morphine."

Within thirty seconds, he had given her a small dose. The effect was immediate, but she was still in too much pain, so he gave her a little more.

After a few minutes, Violet calmed and even smiled slightly. She looked around weakly at their faces and said, "I think that morphine did more for you guys than me."

Sharon sighed and said, "Oh Violet."

"God help us," Patrick said, "but you put us all to shame."

Despite the murmuring and low talking of the others, and the sound of the burning helicopter, the smacking and crackling of the small woods fire it ignited, a night chorus of insects started, as if they too had been holding their breath.

Bart came running up with two men Patrick did not know. "We've got a stretcher for her. We only need one now."

Patrick turned to Sharon. She nodded. "You can let her wrist go, I got it."

He grabbed his rifle and stood up. "Have you buried the dead?"

Bart pointed over his right shoulder with his thumb. "Back there. They're side by side."

"Then as soon as she is ready we'll be getting out of here. I hope before another chopper comes. That fire can be seen for miles from the air."

By morning, Patrick and those in his charge were within three miles of what was a county road before the Unity Party came to power. All but those on security were lying under trees, trying to catch a few moments of sleep. Mathew, who had become by his own choice, the RTO or radiotelephone operator, squatted beside him.

Patrick looked up from his topographic chart. "Mathew, get on the radio and arrange a pickup at these coordinates." He handed Mathew a notepad. "Make it as soon as one hour if possible. And I don't need to tell you not to stay on the radio one second longer than necessary, do I?"

Mathew gave a smile and shrugged. "They're still going to get a fix on our signal unless they're damn busy elsewhere."

"I'm hoping they *are* damn busy elsewhere," Patrick said. "That's probably why only one chopper came after us last night. Nevertheless, take someone with you and go for a walk, north, before you key the mike."

"And it's why you argued for as many fighters as possible to attack at the same time all across the Province. To keep their asses backing up, back peddling, taking punches from all directions." Mathew looked in the direction of Violet. "It's a shame the militia leaders didn't have the balls to do it right, but this operation may be large enough to at least put Dissident Control out of the killing business in this area for a while."

Mathew stood but did not walk away. "I may not be so smart, but I can see what is going on now, and it has your fingerprints all over it. You knew we could not save all Wild People, so you are concentrating on this area. A lot of people around here are not going to be murdered because of you. It won't last forever, but they're safe for a while. You did that."

"We have several more weeks of fighting before what you just said will be even remotely true," Patrick said. "But if it works, we'll be able to travel a hundred miles in any direction from where we now stand and not have a single Dissident Control goon take a shot at us. The military is a different matter."

Patrick looked around at the others, some of whom were listening. "And don't be making me out to be something I'm not. We all did this, are all going to do it, over the next month. I did not exactly come up with an ingenious idea anyway. I stated the obvious. My main purpose at the meeting was to expose the frauds, the cowards. They're more deadly than the enemy."

"That's what Bart said. I mean you shining a spotlight on those who just play militia and don't give a damn about the people or freedom. You see, we are getting to know you and how you think."

"I hope the enemy doesn't."

Mathew paused. "I'm just a kid, but I want to tell you there would be a lot more dead and wounded, like Violet, if you had not shot that chopper down last night. You know it's not your fault, none of this is. We all know you're taking the blame for every drop of blood. But it's not your fault. And it's not our fault. It's theirs. They declared war on us."

"Mathew, you are older than me. If you're just a kid, then so am I and thank you for trying, but if none of this is my fault I have no business being here. And I want to set the record straight. I did hit the chopper many times last night, but I did not shoot it down, Sharon did." Patrick watched her. She was listening. "Evidently, I'm a better shooting instructor than I thought. Now take that walk and get on the radio, then get back. I want to get Violet to better help than we can give her here."

Mathew and another man ran into the woods.

Sharon squatted in front of Patrick as he put the map away. He looked up and saw her face was smeared with spaghetti sauce. It was an MRE taken from the warehouse. She was eating it cold right out of the pouch without a spoon or fork.

She ate the last of the spaghetti and put the pack down. "You should eat something now before we start moving again."

He chuckled. "Well, I know where I could get a pint of spaghetti sauce, off your face."

She wiped her face with her fatigue jacket sleeve.

He laughed. "You've been in the woods so long you have lost all your civilized manners."

Her face started to bleed slightly where she rubbed the scab off.

"Damn it girl. Why did you let me push your face up against that tree so hard? You should have broken my nose with your elbow or something."

Sharon shrugged. "At the time we both had more important things on our minds." She bent closer and looked intently at him, her eyes sparkling. She had that familiar smirk on her face. "You're not going to cry over it, are you?"

"I might. A pretty face like yours should be treated better than that."

"Don't take me wrong. But I've noticed you can't stand to see a girl hurt, especially if she's young and pretty."

"I don't want old and ugly girls hurt either. And I've seen all the blood I want to see on your face for the rest of my life. Although, I don't mind the sauce so much. How is your friend Violet doing anyway?"

"I think she's unstoppable. In fact, she's a better match for you than me. She's as strong as an ox, and you're as dumb as an ox. Neither one of you lets pain get in your way."

"She's as strong as any man, more than about ninety-nine percent."

"You don't seem to mind admitting that," Sharon said.

"I just tell the truth as I see it. Both you and your friend are stronger in many ways than I am. I mean you in particular. You're strong enough to wade through all this sewage and not hate. I can't."

Sharon's eyes burned him.

"But even my weak arm is stronger than both of yours. I'm bigger than you are physically, but in other ways, smaller than you are. By the way, you don't think my reluctance to allow you on this trip had anything to do with my ego, do you?"

"I think I understand. You're an ass and a dumb ox, but you can't stand to see a pretty girl hurt. It's a weakness of yours. Didn't I just mention that a few minutes ago?"

She gave him that smirk as she used a stick to dig a hole to bury her food packages in, the way he had taught her. She looked up from her work, the smirk gone. "I bet you feel guilty about scratching my face, don't you? If I were to make a big deal out of it you would probably lose sleep over it."

"That might have been true a few moments ago, but it's too late for that now, so you have lost your chance."

She laughed. "I heard you tell Mathew I was the one who shot down the helicopter. Why didn't you just leave things as they were?"

"Why would I want to do that?"

"It might help your standing as a great warrior."

"I'm not going to start building my life on a foundation of lies. And I'm sure as hell not going to use you as a footstool. You shot the pilot, bringing the chopper down, that is just the simple fact. And you did it standing by my side, hours after you saved my life at least once. I'm proud of you. My head is large enough already. I don't need any more pride."

She stopped pushing dirt over the pouches. "You mean I'm more than just a pretty face?"

Patrick gave her a smug smile. "I just answered that question before you asked it."

He stood and walked behind her, lightly tapping her on top of her head as he went by. "And don't forget to throw some pine needles over that fresh dirt you're playing in. We don't want to leave any sign of our passing through here."

She looked up, smiled, and then playfully threw the stick at him.

Chapter 22

Patrick and his fighters had been waiting by the road only fifteen minutes when a Dissident Control pickup came screeching to a halt.

Patrick stepped out of the woods.

The driver hit the gas and drove the last hundred and fifty yards and then slammed on the brakes once again. He yelled out the window. "Make it fast. Soldiers broke through our roadblock twelve miles north a few minutes ago."

"Have any idea how many enemy are coming at us?" Patrick asked.

"It's a large force. Dissident Control and soldiers together. They're not coordinating worth a damn though." He smiled. "I hear they've had some friendly fire losses already. Still, they're hitting back hard all over District 13."

Violet was carried out of the woods, transferred to an ambulance-type stretcher, and strapped in.

Patrick yelled, "I want someone who knows her to go with her. Any volunteers? Sharon?"

She gave him a cold stare.

Patrick's chest rose and fell. He said nothing.

A girl in her early twenties, who actually did know Violet, recognized her chance and took it. She ran to the truck and jumped in beside Violet in a style that would put circus acrobats to shame.

Patrick and Sharon wished Violet well. Violet grabbed Patrick's hand and held tight, lifting her head, concern on her face, gray-white from blood loss. "Promise me you won't risk anyone for me!"

"You're just going for a ride now," Patrick said. "They're going to take you to a real doctor."

She shook her head. "They're coming. I heard about them breaking through. And you're going to stop them for me. Or die trying. Don't do it. I'm not worth it. I have only one hand. I can't fight anymore. I don't want anyone to die for me."

Patrick swallowed. "These roads must be kept clear anyway. A lot of other wounded will die without them. And we need them for supplies."

As they talked, explosives were being readied on the nearside of a hill seven hundred yards south.

Patrick squeezed her hand. "I don't want to hear anymore about you not being worth it. If you are not worth it who is? You have more heart than any of us do, and we need people like you even if you had no hands. Now good-bye and good luck." He slapped the side of the pickup and yelled, "Get out her of here." The driver floored the gas pedal and sped away.

Sharon gave him a quick hug. "Don't do that again. Next time I might not forgive you. It was embarrassing. I'm with you for the duration."

Sharon…"

She walked away. Patrick ran up the hill and passed her. She started running too.

When Patrick got close enough to the others, he gave orders while still running. "I want six triads ten yards apart on this side." He pointed to his right. "Do not position any closer to the road than necessary to see well enough to shoot, and everyone stay behind cover capable of stopping heavy machinegun fire. Three of you with battle rifles set up four hundred yards downhill so you can shoot at them from behind." He pointed at a man. "You with the hatchet, what is your name?"

A man in his thirties answered, "Ed."

"Ed, I need you to use that hatchet to chop a hole in the middle of both lanes and one on the centerline. Make them just large and deep enough to fit two pounds of C4 in."

Patrick saw where a recent rain had washed sand out of a hill that had been cut into when the road was put in, leaving a ten-foot-high cliff on the shoulder. "Look. Put the holes over here angling downhill as you cross the road so we can cover them with sand and make it look like rain washed it onto the road."

While the holes were being cut, two men were getting the explosives ready. Patrick saw them preparing radio-controlled blasting caps. "No! Use electric caps. We'll bury the wires under sand. They will never see them."

The man continued working. "RF controlled will be easier and faster."

"Stop arguing, and do what I said. They use multiple frequency signals to set off any radio-controlled explosives ahead of them."

The man's eyes grew large, and he yanked the electronic receiver from the blasting cap. He turned to his friend. "Jack, get the wire out. And the clackers."

Mathew ran up the hill, out of breath. "We have six Claymores set up on our side along the road. That rotted log that fell on the shoulder over there marks the near end of the kill zone."

Patrick looked down the road. "Good. I want you to be the one squeezing the clackers at the right time. I will have to leave that decision to you, because Bart, Tel, and I are going to be up there on the reverse slope of the hill."

Mathew nodded and ran back downhill.

The explosives were set in the holes. Patrick borrowed the ax to gouge out grooves in the asphalt for the wires.

"Why are you doing that?" Ed asked.

Patrick continued digging a groove with a corner of the ax blade. "If a tank runs over the wires it will cut them."

"Give me the ax," Jack said. "I'll finish it."

"A tank will probably cut the wires anyway," Ed said.

Patrick looked uphill but could not see Sharon. He wondered where she was. "It's the best we can do with the time we have."

Sand was hand-carried to cover the C4. The wires were placed in the grooves and covered with a layer of sand also.

Patrick was satisfied with the camouflage. "Okay, you two are our explosives experts, so you will set them off when an APC drives over them."

The one named Jack smiled. "We're not experts, but we're all you have."

The strain on Patrick's face melted away for a moment. "We're all doing the best we can. Listen, if the lead vehicle is a tank we'll let it go by, because we will just be wasting C4. If it's a thin-skinned vehicle, Bart, Tel, and I'll take it out with our battle rifles. Only use the C4 on an APC, otherwise you'll be wasting it."

"What if there is a main battle tank with them?" Jack asked.

"Then we'll attack everything else and get out of here, leaving the tank crew sitting in the road with nothing to protect."

"I liked the getting the hell out of here part best," Jack said.

"If there is heavy armor, we won't push our luck and stay long. Now get out of sight. They'll be here soon."

Patrick ran to the crest of the hill and five feet down the reverse slope. Bart and Tel were in the prone firing position near the tree line on the grassy shoulder and off the hot asphalt. They were ready to fire over the top of the hill and down the road. Both were well concealed in the tall weeds, and most of their body was protected by the reverse slope.

Patrick turned and ran two steps back up the slope until he was standing beside them. "Where is Sharon?"

Tel pointed to his left. "She's in the woods somewhere looking for a tree to climb so she can shoot from five hundred yards. She says that's her favorite range to shoot from."

Patrick looked down the road to check if the enemy had arrived yet. "Damn it. She must have trees on the brain. I wanted her here with us." He ran into the woods fifty yards and yelled for her. After a few minutes he ran back to the road, afraid the enemy would arrive at any moment. He had responsibilities that went beyond her.

"Don't worry. She's a smart girl, she will be all right," Bart said, without bothering to take his eyes off the road.

Patrick got down beside them. "We used all the stuff necessary to turn a treetop into a safe hide the morning we raided the depot. Even if she isn't shot, she might fall and break her neck. The worst thing is, this is a hasty ambush, and we don't have a rally point, or an emergency rally point. Everyone is to just head west after breaking contact. If this ambush is not successful we're bound to lose some people."

"There's something else, isn't there?" Bart asked.

"I think the convoy that's coming is just a small advance force," Patrick said. "All we can do is slow them and buy time for others. After we attack, we're going to have to run for it."

"I'm tired of running," Tel said. "And I'm tired of taking shit off the bastards."

"Running and hiding is a tactic the same as attacking. It's a vital part of asymmetric warfare," Patrick said. "They have a professional army. We don't. That's why they call us guerrillas, when they're not calling us more colorful names."

"I could say something about what they think of us running all the time," Tel said.

"Tel, this is no time for your smart-ass mouth," Bart said.

"All right!" Patrick said. "You guys asked me to lead you. I'm doing that to the best of my ability. I'm trying to produce the most results at the lowest possible price. We can stay here and die today, or we can continue to hit and run, living long enough to kill a hundred times more of the enemy. Besides, if we let them pass—after exacting a price—with the help of other fighting groups, we might be able to bottle them up later and cut them off from their supply lines. It won't be painless though. Their air support is going to bloody us bad. That's why we can't stay long. We've got to be gone before the bombs fall. Remember what I've been saying all along: Hit and run."

Patrick thought of something and pulled a map out of his pack. While examining the map, he spoke with urgency. "See where that creek branches off from the river?" He held his map up so Tel and Bart both could see and pointed to the spot.

Tel nodded. "Yes."

"That's our after-action rally point. If things don't go well, you two tell as many as you can where it is. Gather up the stragglers as you go along."

Patrick looked toward the woods. "Damn it. I don't know where she is. When we break contact she's going to be out there somewhere, and I will have to leave her behind to lead the rest of you. And she doesn't know any more than to head west." Patrick's eyes glanced down the road and swung to the treetops, searching.

Tel said, "Go on. Find her. We can handle this."

Bart was looking through binoculars. His eyes grew wide and he stuffed the binoculars under his jacket. "They're coming. There's a tank in the front and an APC in the rear."

Patrick blew out a chest full of air. He watched as the small images of the convoy came on. "Damn it. I screwed up. I should have had more explosives placed downhill also. I just hope they follow my orders to the letter."

Patrick took four clips out of a bandoleer hanging across his chest and put them on the ground in front of him. "This is not going to be fun, but we have to at least slow them down. I count four thin-skinned vehicles. I'll take the first, Bart you take the second, Tel the third. Ignore the tank and the APC. If you're done with those in your thin skin, go to the fourth. I expect the others will have taken care of it by then, but be ready anyway. Look, all we can do now is take out the thin-skins and bug out. If the APC is taken out by the C4 fine, if not, there is nothing we can do."

Bart watched the convoy come on. "Sounds like a plan. I just wish we had one of those anti-armor missiles that we haven't seen since we got them for the militia. There needs to be some big changes in our leadership."

"You got that right," Tel said.

Patrick was thinking. "I want you to shoot fast until I tell you to get out of here. When I yell, get down the reverse slope for protection and then into the woods, run downhill and tell the others to bug out. Don't hang around, just get out of here."

The Abrams tank started up the hill, its turbine engine whining, changing pitch as the operator increased power to compensate for the gradually increasing incline. The tank continued on unmolested through the kill zone and up the long slope, straight to those waiting at the top.

Patrick calmly waited until the thin-skinned utility vehicles were across from the Claymores. Shooting over the tank, he put a bullet through the windshield of the leading vehicle and through the driver's head.

Rapid, accurate fire emptied the eight-round clip, and he reached for a fresh one only inches from his right hand, pushing it in just as Tel and then Bart stopped firing to reload. Firing at a rate of fifty rounds per minute, he was vaguely aware of their rifles firing as fast as his, but he did not notice the tank firing its coaxial heavy machinegun up the hill at them.

Downhill, across from the kill zone, Mathew squeezed the clackers two at a time, triggering the Claymores. Thousands of steel ball bearings shredded the vehicles and men inside. M4s on full auto ripped up what was left.

Patrick's eyes searched over the kill zone. What he saw told him they had done all they could. Except for the viewing ports, antenna, and a few other places, the tank was invulnerable to their weapons. And unless the APC ran over the explosives, it too would survive the ambush. There was no reason to risk his people's lives any longer.

"Get out of here now!" Patrick reached for another clip and watched Bart and Tel roll downhill. He looked up as he pushed the fourth clip home and was shocked to see the tank only fifty yards away. It had turned onto the road shoulder and headed straight for him, the driver intending to run over him with the tank's left track. The tank was already so close the crew could no longer bring their weapons to bear, and they could no longer see him, as he was in their blind spot. But this did not stop the operator from trying to turn Patrick into a true "crunchy," tankers' pet name for infantry, both friend and foe.

Patrick crawled fast toward the woods, until he slammed hard against a tree with his right shoulder. He turned to his right and he kept kicking, pushing on, until he saw the tank coming at him. Pushing off another tree with his left hand to stand and run, he found his weak arm not strong enough to lift the weight of his upper body, and the load strapped to it. He felt the earth shake and heard trees splintering and crashing against neighboring trees. Panic surged through his nerves as he willed his arm to push his body off from the tree just before it fell behind his left shoulder. When his legs took the weight of his body he jumped to the side. The hulk of tons of steel sped by in a rumble, pinewood snapping and falling, needles and leaves shaken from their stems raining down in the woods like snow. The massive death beast churned and chewed the woodland floor with the deep-cutting cleats of its tracks. The left track slip-clutched slightly to turn the beast back to the road, leaving behind the smell of fresh pine sap and rich soil.

Heart pounding, chest heaving, Patrick ran deeper into the woods, his thoughts on Sharon and those downhill. He stopped when he heard firing starting up again down the road. Heavy machinegun fire from more than one gun, accompanied by full auto fire from M4s, roared and echoed in the woods. Something was wrong. He ran back to the road so he could see downhill.

The tank had stopped in the road farther down the reverse slope and was backing up without turning its gun turret around, which also contained the main coaxial machinegun. The turret hatch opened. A helmeted head appeared. The tanker's eyes grew wide just as Patrick pulled the trigger. His head snapped back and disappeared down the hatch. Now Patrick had a few seconds to look downhill before the tank would be a danger again.

Another convoy had entered the kill zone, with an armored personnel carrier in the lead and one protecting their rear, five utility vehicles between them. The others had not run into the woods, they instead, had engaged the new convoy.

Break contact. Get out of here.

Patrick watched as the tank rolled past him, cresting the hill, it stopped and began to turn its turret around to fire its main gun into the trees where the others were. In a panic to stop them, he ran to the front and fired into the vision port to crack it and blind the driver temporarily. The turret stopped and began to turn back to the front.

He ran to the side and lay down a few feet from the tank and began to fire at the men below. He fired four times and saw three fall. His rifle was empty. Reloading, he heard the turret turning again. If he did not stop it somehow those below would die.

Again, he ran to the front, this time the left corner, firing into the vision port, cracking the one that had just been replaced from inside while he was shooting downhill. A smaller machinegun he did not know was there fired at him, but the angle was beyond the limit of barrel swing and the operator could not bring it to bear.

Patrick jumped back to the side and got into the prone shooting position to shoot downhill again. Just before he shot, he heard a hatch opening on the top. He scrambled to get up as fast as possible and ran to the back of the tank, a grenade exploded exactly where he had been lying. He ran back to the side with his rifle shouldered and pointed at the hatch. The top of a tanker's helmet started to emerge from the opening. He fired as soon as enough head was exposed. The punch of the bullet slammed the helmeted head against the steel lip of the hatch. It disappeared back into the tank.

The tank crew's mistake had been a lucky break. Now he was certain one more of them was dead, perhaps the commander. Patrick hoped this would give him time to get away.

When he turned to look downhill again, he saw an armored personnel carrier speeding uphill at him. He fell to the asphalt and fast-crawled to the shoulder. The personnel carrier fired a thirty-caliber machinegun. Stray bullets pinged off the tank's armor. He thought, how ironic it was, now that those who were to set off the explosives were gone, the personnel carrier was driving right over one of the blocks of C4.

A bright flash burned his eyes, and he was blown off his knees and elbows onto his side by a tremendous overpressure shock wave just before his ears were filled with an eardrum-busting boom. He slid into a shallow drainage ditch and then crawled to the edge to look downhill.

The personnel carrier had been blown on its side and was in flames. Ammunition started to cook off, the popping slow at first, then gathering momentum and becoming rapid-fire. A soldier crawled out of the machinegun turret, his uniform smoking. Patrick shot him in the head.

Farther downhill, it looked like most of the occupants of the thin-skins were dead. The other two personnel carriers were firing wildly into the brush. The one in the rear of the convoy was backing down the road and appeared to be leaving.

The tank was on the move again when Patrick ran into the woods to tell the others to break contact, something they were supposed to have done a long time ago. As he ran, he heard no more firing from the woods. At the bottom of the hill, he was relieved to find they were gone.

The tank started firing blindly with its cannon. The first shell exploded harmlessly two hundred fifty yards away. After the third round, he saw a pattern. The tanker was working his way across the ambush site, direct-firing into the edge of the woods.

Patrick ran west and prayed everyone else was somewhere ahead of him. He thought of Sharon out there in the woods somewhere and hoped she was with her triad. He began to run faster. He needed to know now. Soon, his body started to remind him of that six hour run on the first day of his war. After thirty minutes, his chest was taking a pounding from inside. Blood pulsed in his head, and he heard the drums for the second time.

A feeling that when he caught up with them he would not find her nauseated him. Was she back there among the bursting shells, lying wounded, her body torn, life's blood spilling, and her face contorted in pain, screaming for someone to help her? Was he running away from her and not toward her? For a fraction of a second, his pace faltered, panic nearly overrode logic. He thought he must turn and run back to the road to find her but forced himself to stay on course and hope for the best. There were many others he was responsible for. He willed more power in his legs and stretched out his stride another two feet.

There was movement in the brush to his left. He gradually slowed to a walk, fighting an urge to throw up, gagging for breath. He turned to the movement, walking fast. He saw through the brush, Linda and Tel smiling as they walked along, watching him come on at high speed. Their eyes were lit up in recognition of him.

Linda's smile melted. Her face turned pale.

"Where is she?" Patrick and Linda asked each other in chorus.

Patrick did not take the time to stop. He pivoted in his tracks, kicking dirt and leaves as he picked up speed. "Keep going to the river," he yelled over his shoulder.

Linda shook her head. "Screw that." Her eyes darted to Tel. "I'm not leaving them."

"What makes you think I am? Let's get Bart."

Chapter 23

The tank crew stopped firing.

Patrick ran.

Patrick saw a boiling fireball erupt, rising above the trees for a quarter mile along his side of the road. A jet's afterburners kicked in. Patrick did not bother to look up. He ran faster. His heart pounded. He could smell death in the woods.

Someone cut loose with a squad automatic weapon. He dove under low branches and fast-crawled behind a log. The SAW continued to chop up the woods around him.

His mind raced.

It's a hammer and anvil maneuver. They thought they'd catch us by the road. Pen us in and dump airborne ordnance on us. It was close.

Patrick understood what happened now. He just ran up behind a line of soldiers surrounding the ambush site. His position was about to be fixed, frozen. He had seconds to fight his way out or be trapped.

Where is Sharon?

There was no more shooting, but he could hear movement in all directions but one. He crawled ten yards, got up, and ran, staying low. A roar of gunfire exploded from his left, right, and rear. He feinted to the right and then veered back to his left, picking up speed.

Patrick ran two hundred yards. The sound of pursuit was on his heels. He saw a depression in the forest floor, dove into to it and slid to the bottom, crawled back to the edge, and prepared to shoot them off him.

A soldier, no more than twenty, came plunging through the brush. Patrick shot him in the face. He collapsed, landing on Patrick.

The gunfire was deafening. It came from three sides. Staying low as bullets flew over him, Patrick took the SAW off the dead soldier and sprayed in a semicircle, one foot above ground level.

The woods became quiet.

Patrick jumped up and ran in the only direction he could.

Gunfire erupted again. He ran faster. The sound of pursuit faded. His lungs screamed for more oxygen. He slowed to hunting speed to avoid blundering into an ambush. Then slowed still more, flowing through the woods smooth and quiet.

He felt his killing instincts awaken and rise to a new height. The heat of hate flared. The brilliance of the colors and detail his eyes collected as he slipped through the woods, scanning, hunting, brought back memories of that morning of his first kills. He had learned that a man is never more alive than when he is about to die. Today he learned a man never hates more than when the one he loves is in danger.

Images of his environing emerald gloom were funneled in by his predator eyes. The buzzing of a mosquito yards away, and the breaking of brush as killers hunted him, funneled too, by his ears, funneled and focused to be recorded and added to a growing collection of data to be acted on by his calculating mind and hating heart.

There are hundreds of them. I will die today. But first, I must know one thing.

Where is Sharon?

Movement ahead.

A large group moved across his path from left to right. He froze. They stopped, changed direction. They were sweeping the brush. Coming his way.

Patrick sunk himself into the forest as an alligator sinks into the green depths of a bayou. Here, he waited for the kill.

Hot blood painted his right hand as he probed with the blade, seeking out the soldier's life, slicing into kidney, up from under the Kevlar vest. Then the blade slashed up to the neck. He held his left hand over the soldier's mouth many seconds past his unconsciousness and death. Then he lowered him to the ground, making no noise.

He had an opening now, and the deadly line swept past him. Silence was his only shield as he left them to sweep on.

Southward now, toward the hilltop and Sharon, he hoped. Or better, she was already halfway to the river and joining the others.

Patrick moved on, toward the place he last knew her to be. If she was still in the area, she was probably dead, or worse. If she was safe with the others, he was going to die for nothing. No. Not nothing. Either way, he was going to die for her.

A squad of soldiers rushed through the woods, coming at him fast. He found thick brush and immersed himself; the play of light and dark, the sun-painted freckling, danced in the gentle winds and cloaked him in obscurity. The soldiers rushed past and disappeared in the brush. Their noisy progress faded.

He went on; at the slow, smooth speed both predator and prey know well. All his senses at high intensity, taking in every minute detail of sight, sound, and smell. And one other sense he discovered he had on the morning the warrior in him was born.

He froze, then jumped to his right, rolled, and crawled to cover. A short, disciplined burst of automatic fire chopped the brush where he was standing before.

It took Patrick eight minutes to maneuver into position. He knew the soldier had not moved. He would have heard. The ground was covered with dry leaves where the soldier was.

There.

Movement behind the leaning water oak. The soldier had grown impatient. Patrick waited. He needed to be sure the soldier was alone.

Another one.

Inch by smooth-flowing inch, Patrick raised his rifle. The first one had moved. Patrick searched two yards farther to the right.

There.

He checked the other one's position.

Now!

The Garand barked twice, with a tenth of a second between the shots.

Patrick was gone. He knew they were dead. The flash-vision of bullet hitting flesh was enough.

Half a mile farther, he found dead soldiers, shot through the head, and hundreds of spent carbine cartridges, along with discarded empty magazines. Up on a hill one hundred forty yards beyond, in a mass of close-growing water oaks, he found many spent 30/06 cartridges. The water oaks were scarred and splintered from hundreds of bullets. On the other side of the hill, he found spent nine-millimeter pistol cartridges, two empty magazines, and Sharon's rifle and pistol. The pistol slide was locked back, the magazine empty.

Sharon!

A careful search of the area gave Patrick some relief.

No blood.

He tied her rifle to his pack.

Two hundred yards west of where he last saw her, Patrick found Sharon's boonie hat. There were signs of a struggle, with the ground torn up and leaves scraped aside. But still no blood.

She had reversed course and was running back toward the road. Out of ammunition and out of luck, she was running to him. But he was no longer there. In an act of denial, he stuffed her hat in a pocket.

But if they killed her, where is her body?

By force of will, Patrick retrieved primordial instincts from within, reaching deeper than he had ever before. The urgent pull of fierce blood kept him going. Sharon was probably dead. He hated them. He called for death to stop the pain. But he hated them, and for that reason alone, he would endure long enough to kill more of them before he died. And until he saw her dead, he could not give up.

A scream sliced into him with a sting.

Sharon!

In two steps, he was racing recklessly at full speed. After running several minutes, he lost his bearings and was not sure which way to go. He slowed to a walk. After a few more minutes, he slowed more, to hunting speed.

The sharp smack of an open hand striking flesh. A moan.

Patrick turned to the sound.

Voices. A man yelling. Patrick eased in closer.

He saw through the scrim of trees and brush. Not soldiers. Dissident Control.

"I don't play that shit!" Sergeant Gurney Appleton stood between four agents and Sharon. She was on her back, upper body propped up by her elbows, her face bleeding. Her fatigue jacket was gone. Her tank shirt was hanging by one shred. She kicked and pushed herself back away from the agents.

Appleton held his carbine at waist level, in the general direction of the other men. "You might get by with that when I'm not around, but not today. Next man who touches her dies."

She's safe for now.

Patrick used the time to appraise the scene. He could see no other agents or soldiers. He shot as fast as he could. One after the other, their heads ruptured as the one before fell.

Appleton fired from the waist, in an arc of automatic fire. Patrick expected it. He should have shot Appleton first. But he could not.

The pine tree took most of the bullets, Patrick's body the rest.

Sharon screamed, dove for Appleton's legs, wrapping her arms around them.

Patrick lay on his back, bleeding.

Appleton, close to tripping, was distracted by Sharon. Patrick aimed while on his back and shot Appleton in the chest.

Sharon ran to Patrick. "Oh God." She tried to examine his wounds.

He pushed her away. "Get your hands on a weapon!"

"You're bleeding."

"The woods are swarming with soldiers." Patrick held his side.

She helped him up.

Standing over Appleton, Patrick aimed at his head. He was alive.

"Don't Patrick," Sharon said. "He saved me."

"I know." Patrick spoke to Appleton. "Did your vest stop my bullet?"

"I think so," Appleton said. He was barely able to speak. His wind was knocked out of him.

"If you can, get up and run away." Patrick kept his rifle on him.

"Why didn't you shoot me first?" Appleton asked. He grimaced in pain.

"I saw what you did. Now get out of here. There's no time for chatting."

Appleton saw the blood. "You knew I would shoot you, but you did it anyway." He pointed to the southwest. "Fewer soldiers that way."

Patrick was unsteady. "Get out of here now, or I will kill you."

"You'll never make it," Appleton said. "You'll be unconscious soon."

"Don't bet on it." Patrick stopped holding his side, and his face lost all sign of pain.

"Look," Appleton said, "I've had enough. My best friend has gone over to your side. Merrick Raebyrne. I'd like to see him again."

"I can't trust you."

"Yes you can. You just don't know it."

Sharon had found her jacket and pack. "I'm out of ammo." She used Patrick's knife to cut her rifle from his pack, then reached into a side pocket and pulled a box of his cartridges out.

"For God's sake. I can help you," Appleton said. "I can get on the radio and mislead them."

"Why?" Patrick asked.

"Merrick's conscience was eating him. He did something about it. Since then, I've been wishing I had gone with him. Look. I've never raped or murdered anyone. I only kill when I have to." He looked Patrick over and glanced at Sharon. "You're Timucua, aren't you? You must be. Who else could have survived out here today? If you are, you know who Merrick is."

"I trust him," Sharon said. "He kept them off me twice."

Patrick shook his head. "There's no time for this. They're moving in on us as we stand here."

"Patrick."

The tone of her voice made the decision for him. "Let's get out of here and find some thick brush to hide in."

Ten minutes later, Patrick stopped and scanned the woods methodically. His ears detected no danger. "Get on the radio and do what you can, but make it quick."

Appleton dropped to his knees and spoke into his radio. "I just got some intel from a captured hostile. There's a large force coming in from the east."

A voice came back. "Do you trust this?"

"Yes. One thing's for sure: There's nothing but a few stragglers on this side of the road. The rest are gone. We worked on her for twenty minutes. So, yeah, the intel's good."

Orders came over the radio for three platoons to run back to the road and prepare for an attack from the east.

Patrick listened while he checked Sharon's face. Her nose and lips were bloody, the left side of her face red and swollen, but she seemed unhurt otherwise.

"Stop that. I'm okay. You're the one who's shot." Sharon pushed his hand away.

"We've got to go," Patrick said.

She pulled his shirt up. "If we wait here, they'll be back at the road. Then we can leave. There's time for me to look at those wounds."

"There's a lot more than three platoons out here." Patrick kept his eyes busy.

"You're hit twice. All the way through." She looked up at him, her eyes watering. "The bullets didn't hit anything that will kill you, but bone fragments from your ribs may have."

"If anything vital was hit I would never have gotten up."

She took her pack off.

"Put it back on, Sharon. We're leaving."

"You're bleeding too much. You won't be on your feet long if I can't slow it." She ripped a packet open and poured coagulate on the exit wounds first, then the entry wounds.

Patrick stifled a gasp.

"I've never seen someone so young so strong," Appleton said. "That stuff can save your life, but it'll make you wish it hadn't."

"I'll bet you're not feeling so good yourself." There was no hint of strain in Patrick's voice. "You just took a twenty-eight-hundred foot-pound punch."

"I think I'll live."

Sharon covered the wounds with gauze and taped it on.

Patrick handed Appleton his carbine back. "Any man who did what you did for her can't be all bad." He pointed. "Lead the way."

The woods suddenly roared with gunfire. It was in the direction Patrick had come from.

"Oh shit," Patrick said. "The others came back after us. I told them to keep going."

"Well, so much for my ruse," Appleton said. "They came in from the west. My name is mud now. That trick won't work again."

"What are we going to do?" Sharon asked.

"We're getting out of here," Patrick said. "If we can."

"Leave them?"

"I came for you, Sharon."

"And they came for us."

Patrick's eyes grew cold. He shot a look at Appleton. "Tell her how many soldiers and Dissident Control agents are out here."

"All together, about three hundred and twenty."

"But we can't," Sharon said.

"They'll back off when they see what they've run up against. Bart is no fool." Patrick pointed. "Let's go."

Five minutes of heated battle faded to sporadic pops, like popcorn on a hot stove, nearly done. Then the woods grew quiet, until the bombs fell.

Sharon kept glancing back over her shoulder at Patrick.

They continued to walk.

Patrick's eyes swept the woods with deliberate calm. He was relieved when the bombing stopped. Now he could hear again. And no one could walk up on him in these woods without his ears knowing.

They were almost out of it. Or so Patrick was beginning to believe. Then he heard them coming. He picked up a small stick and threw it at Appleton. He turned.

Patrick touched Sharon's shoulder. She stopped and looked at him, her eyes questioning.

Patrick pointed over his right shoulder with his thumb and made a walking motion with two fingers. He walked up to Appleton. Sharon followed close behind.

"Follow me and keep quiet. We've got to find a better place to make a stand." Patrick walked on.

"Why don't we run for it?" Appleton asked.

"Too dangerous," Patrick said. "That's a desperate move to be used only when there's no other choice. These woods are full of soldiers, and we'll likely run into an ambush."

They came to a meadow, studded with sparse brush and pine saplings, about seventy yards across. Patrick skirted the shadowed edge. The late afternoon sun slanted in, lighting the meadow, leaving the emerald forest around it dark. Shadow is life. Shadow is where he would wait.

On the southwest side, he found what he was looking for. A knoll, ten feet higher than the meadow, green with thick brush, and endowed with a reverse slope perfect for the prone shooting position. Patrick had Sharon lay down under shading brush and handed her a handful of loose rifle cartridges.

"They won't cross the opening. They're not that stupid. Most likely, they'll come around the same side we did because it's darker over on this side. But they might swing to the other side anyway."

Appleton was kneeling beside them. "You want me over there in case they do come that way, don't you?"

"Yes," Patrick said. "I'm going to be thirty yards farther back from the edge to her left." Sharon watched as he pointed. It was close enough they could see each other. "We can support each other to some degree. But if there's too many, they'll outflank us. If I think that's about to happen, I'm getting Sharon out of here anyway I can. I'll help you if possible. But she's why I'm here. And I'll do anything to get her out of this."

"I figured that out a long time back," Appleton said. "I don't blame you."

Appleton left them.

Patrick lay beside her. "If it gets hairy—I mean really bad—I need you to be brave for me. Not that you haven't been amazing. I need you—"

"They're not taking me alive again. I'll never be at their mercy again. Never."

Patrick swallowed, his jaw tensed. "I think you can get away…if you run when I tell you. And if there are no more soldiers to the west of us. I can keep them busy. But you have to be hard about it."

"You mean I should pretend I don't love you."

"Yes."

"And leave you behind to die alone."

"Yes."

"No."

"If it comes to pass, you must do it for me."

"I won't."

He reached out with his weak hand and touched her bruised face. "Sharon—"

"I knew you would come for me. And you know I won't leave you."

"I wish you would do what I say."

He got up and left her.

Patrick could not distinguish the source of the sounds, but they were coming. When they were close enough, his eyes caught the sun's dappling on a face, painted green and loam. They had sought out the darkest path around the meadow and were coming straight for him. He hoped to pin them down so Sharon could pick them off, one at a time.

In the congealing gloom of the dying afternoon, Patrick listened to the killers come on, catching patches of them in the slanting sunrays. His heart quickened. There was only one way they could hurt him. And she was thirty yards away.

He had been tainted, not so much by the killing, but the hate. She, he considered taintless, absent of sin, as taintless and sinless as any human could be, without dying and being cleansed by an absolving touch of God's righteous hand. Oh, she could hate. He knew that. But her hate was plebian, weak, mastered, and overpowered by her better nature. His hate loomed above, lording over his soul. He had invited the union of his shadow and the boy he used to be so that he may learn to kill. And with it came the hate. He hated them because he loved his mother and grandfather. Now his hate was fueled by love for Sharon. The closer they came to her, the more he hated them.

As he feared, it was not a recon team or a squad; it was a platoon. His gambit move was to kill three before Sharon or Appleton got off their first shot.

They reacted with a mad minute of continuous gunfire in all directions. In the shadows, the soldiers' carbine muzzles blinked like fireflies. Patrick emptied his rifle, rolled down the reverse slope of the knoll, reloaded, and ran forty yards. He eased up to the top and caught four soldiers coming around to flank him and Sharon. He shot them in the face.

Round after round, he poured into the main group. Sharon's rifle, he barely noticed in the back of his mind. Appleton was not in his world. They were moving in on Sharon, rushing from cover to cover. Three would survive the rush, and one would die. Three and one. Three and one. They were going to overrun her soon.

Patrick fired downhill into them, stopping the rush momentarily.

Appleton fired in two, three-round bursts, wasting little ammunition. The crossfire was taking its toll. However, they were coming on. Coming for Sharon, with her slow-firing bolt-action rifle.

A soldier threw a grenade. It landed three feet from Sharon and rolled down the reverse slope before exploding.

Patrick pressed a fresh clip in and the Garand's bolt slammed home. A soldier rose from prone to his knees, right hand cocked back. Patrick fired, and the grenade rolled out of his slack hand as he slumped to the ground. It went off and a soldier nearby screamed.

Another soldier tried with a grenade launcher. It flew over Sharon's head and exploded against a pine tree thirty feet high and seventy feet behind her.

Patrick feared she might have been hit by fragments.

They were close enough now the grenades would come in a rain. Desperate, Patrick yanked the quick release cord on his left shoulder strap, shed his pack, jumped up, and ran around the left end of the knoll, keeping low, with the reverse slope hiding him.

Sharon looked on, pale with shock, as Patrick came around the knoll and tore into them. He fired as he ran in at top speed, with deadly desperation, he emptied his rifle, a man falling with each shot. He swerved to his right as a soldier fired at him from ten yards. Sharon shot him through the neck.

Patrick dropped his empty rifle, pulled his pistol, and fired, without slowing a single step. Instead, his speed increased. In among them, he swung, two handed, the pistol held so tight it did not move in recoil. They wore vests. He fired into their faces.

A soldier slammed a fresh magazine in his carbine as Patrick rushed him, his eyes wide in disbelief. Patrick's eyes were wild with hate and desperation. He will stop them. One way or another, he will stop them from reaching her.

The pistol in Patrick's hand was empty, the slide locked back. There was no time to reload. Rushing in, Patrick pushed the carbine barrel aside as it belched flame and came down with his pistol, striking the soldier on the bridge of his nose with the bottom of the magazine and grip. The soldier's nose caved in. Blood streamed down his face and he fell back unconscious.

Patrick dropped his pistol and snatched up the carbine, spraying from the hip. There was only one direction he would not fire, anyone else was a target.

His boonie hat flew off. Something jerked rapidly at his jacket. His body was stinging, burning, in several new places. He kept shooting anything that moved. Screaming all the while. Running among them, firing, screaming, running.

In constant motion, from fast to faster, he shot, ran, and screamed. The carbine empty, he snatched up another and sprayed bullets into anything that moved. He heard Sharon and the soldiers shooting, but they were not in his world. His world was killing.

Still another empty carbine was silent in his hands.

He zeroed in on a soldier and rushed him. The man, solid, heavy, six foot six, parried Patrick's rush and threw him aside.

Patrick landed on his back. The soldier brought his carbine to his shoulder. His head exploded. Sharon's rifle shot cracked the still air of the sunless afternoon. The shooting had stopped.

Instantly on his feet, Patrick snatched up the dead man's carbine, but it was shot out of his hand. Patrick rolled, and dust flew as bullets tattooed the forest floor just behind him.

Silence.

Patrick jumped up and rushed the soldier. Drawing his knife, he tackled the man and sliced into his neck. The forest was silent again, but for the moaning of the wounded. Patrick went to them, screaming, slashing, and stabbing.

He heard Sharon yelling. Thinking they had gotten to her, he looked up the hill and saw her running to him.

"Get back!"

Patrick looked around him, screaming, and ready to kill anyone he saw, anyone who dared try to hurt her.

He saw his pistol, ran over, picked it up, and reloaded. His eyes scanned the scene, searching for any life that needed killing. His face wild and enraged, he did not stop screaming. He shot anything that even looked like it might be alive.

Sharon was yelling something.

Patrick did not hear.

A Dissident Control agent came running down the hill.

Patrick locked into a steady hold and aimed. Sharon yanked his arms down.

"It's the man who saved me!" She screamed in his ear. "Don't kill him!"

He jerked away, raised his arms to fire.

Appleton had jumped behind a tree.

She pulled down. This time she could not move his arms. She put her hand over his eyes. He fired a wild shot, blind.

"They're all dead! It's over!" She screamed.

He stood there, looking at her, eyes wild, his chest heaving, jacket soaked with blood and sweat. Calmer now, he checked her for blood, wounds.

"Are you hurt?" Patrick asked.

"No. But you are." Sharon put her hand on his pistol. "It's over, Patrick. They're all dead." She pointed. "He's the one who saved me. Remember?"

"I know." He looked around. "We've got to get out of here. Where's my rifle?"

Appleton picked it up. "I got it."

Sharon and Patrick walked up the hill to him.

Appleton's face was white. "Goddamn."

Patrick took his rifle and pushed a fresh clip in. "Let's go," he said.

They walked with him to his pack. He put it on. "Maybe we can join the others now," Patrick said. There was the same desperate determination in his eyes he had during his frenzied fight, but it was deeper, not so close to the surface and exposed.

Sharon did not ask him to let her check his wounds. She knew he would not allow her and just walked along behind. Her eyes were red.

When they reached the river, Patrick turned upstream. The river swamp was black under the canopy of trees. The sun had been down more than an hour. They used night vision monoculars.

Patrick heard splashing in the river. He turned to Sharon and Appleton. "Someone's crossing. Wait here while I check."

Sharon saw Patrick's face when he returned. The tension of his predator instincts was ratcheted down.

"It's them," Patrick said. He had left his pack with the others. Now, he took his load-bearing harness off and then his bloody jacket. "Better take that uniform off and put this jacket on," he said to Appleton. "I told them about you, but someone might take a shot at you anyway."

Appleton took the jacket.

With the jacket removed, Sharon could see his wounds through her night vision monocular. She stood there looking Patrick over and said nothing.

Bart had ordered a raft made for the wounded. There were many. Patrick was taken across on the raft to keep his wounds out of the muddy water.

Tel and Linda were shocked at Patrick's stone face. He paid them little attention when they greeted him.

Sharon pushed them away from him and then held them both. "He'll be okay," She said.

Even when Mathew looked up from his stretcher, his shoulder bloody, Patrick stopped only long enough to see how badly he was hurt.

"We showed them," Mathew said. "This is just the beginning, but they know they can't just slaughter us anymore."

Patrick looked at the other wounded as Mathew talked.

Everyone was across the river in less than thirty minutes. Bart took the lead.

They stopped five hours later and set up a night defense perimeter.

Sharon cleaned and dressed Patrick's wounds.

He was silent, looking at her in the moonlight.

She finished. "You're going to be okay, if we get you out of this swamp and some antibiotics in you, though I'll never know how you lived over that stunt you pulled. There were a couple times if I had missed…goddamn it."

Patrick said nothing. He could see she was crying.

"Don't ever do that again," she said. "I won't have it. You're not going to die for me. If you have to die for our people, that's one thing. But not for me."

He reached out with his weak hand and touched her chin, pulled her to him by her shoulder and held her, then gently began to kiss her bruised face. "They hurt you."

"Don't. It's nothing," She said. "Stop it. You'll start bleeding again. You should be lying down."

His body began to tremble. He held her tight. "You're safe."

"For now."

"One moment at a time. Enough moments make a day, enough days, a lifetime."

Also by John Grit

Feathers on the Wings of Love and Hate 2:

Call Me Timucua

(Volume 2 in the series)

And

Apocalypse Law

(Volume I in the series)

And

Apocalypse Law 2

(Volume 2 in the series)

Made in the USA
Lexington, KY
11 June 2012